THE NOVELS OF
**BARBARA
FREETHY**
ARE

"TANTALIZING."
—*Booklist*

"SUPERLATIVE."
—Debbie Macomber

"LIVELY [AND] ENGAGING."
—*Publishers Weekly*

"AN ABSOLUTE TREASURE."
—*New York Times* Bestselling
Author Kristin Hannah

continued . . .

BARBARA FREETHY

ALL SHE EVER WANTED

A SIGNET BOOK

SIGNET
Published by New American Library, a division of
Penguin Group (USA) Inc., 375 Hudson Street,
New York, New York 10014, USA
Penguin Group (Canada), 10 Alcorn Avenue, Toronto,
Ontario, M4V 3B2, Canada (a division of Pearson Penguin Canada Inc.)
Penguin Books Ltd., 80 Strand, London WC2R 0RL, England
Penguin Ireland, 25 St. Stephen's Green, Dublin 2,
Ireland (a division of Penguin Books Ltd.)
Penguin Group (Australia), 250 Camberwell Road, Camberwell, Victoria 3124,
Australia (a division of Pearson Australia Group Pty. Ltd.)
Penguin Books India Pvt. Ltd., 11 Community Centre, Panchsheel Park,
New Delhi - 110 017, India
Penguin Group (NZ), Cnr Airborne and Rosedale Roads, Albany,
Auckland 1310, New Zealand (a division of Pearson New Zealand Ltd.)
Penguin Books (South Africa) (Pty.) Ltd., 24 Sturdee Avenue,
Rosebank, Johannesburg 2196, South Africa

Penguin Books Ltd., Registered Offices:
80 Strand, London WC2R 0RL, England

First published by Signet, an imprint of New American Library,
a division of Penguin Group (USA) Inc.

First Printing, December 2004
10 9 8 7 6 5 4 3 2 1

*To my friends at the Peninsula Tennis Club
who love to give me new ideas, especially
Linda Benvenuto, Patty Kunse, Lani Fregosi,
Patty Rossi, and all the ladies on the 4.0 Team*

ACKNOWLEDGMENTS

Many thanks go to my writing friends Carol Grace, Candice Hern, Diana Dempsey, Kate Moore, Lynn Hanna, and Barbara McMahon, who helped with the brainstorming. I'd also like to thank my terrific agent, Andrea Cirillo, for her never-ending support and encouragement. Thanks also go to old friends and sorority sisters who reminded me of all the good times and those few special college years when deep friendships are formed and all seems possible.

Chapter 1

"Pick a card, any card."

Natalie Bishop stared at the playing cards in the old man's hands. "Mr. Jensen, I really need to listen to your heart. You said you were having some chest pain earlier?"

He ignored her question and tipped his head toward the cards. His fingers were long, his hands wrinkled and pale, weathered with age spots. His dark eyes pleaded with her to do as he asked. The emergency room of St. Timothy's Hospital in San Francisco was not the place for card tricks. But Natalie had learned in the past three years of her residency that healing wasn't always about medicine, and patient visits weren't always about being sick. Sometimes they were just about being old and lonely. So she did what he'd asked—she picked a card. It was the ace of spades. The death card. A chill ran through her.

"Don't tell me what it is, Dr. Bishop. Just hold it in your hand." Mr. Jensen closed his eyes and began to mutter something under his breath.

Natalie had a sudden urge to throw the card down on the bed, which was ridiculous. She wasn't superstitious. She didn't believe in card tricks, hocus pocus, or any other kind of magic. She didn't believe in anything that couldn't be scientifically proven. The ace of spades was just a card. If she were playing poker or blackjack, she'd be excited to have it.

Mr. Jensen's eyes flew open and he stared at her as if he'd never seen her before. "The dark ace," he said. "Spades."

She swallowed hard. "Good guess." Handing him back the card, she asked, "How did you know?"

"I felt you shiver." He met her gaze with a seriousness that made her feel even more uneasy. "You're afraid."

"No, I'm not." She didn't have time to be afraid. She was a medical resident working double shifts most days. She was overworked, overtired, and stressed to the max. She didn't have the energy to be scared. Except that she was scared. She was terrified that something would go wrong at this late date, that with only a month to go on her residency, after years of struggling against almost insurmountable odds to become a doctor, she would somehow fail. And failure wasn't an option. Her career was her life.

"Something bad is coming," the old man continued. "I can feel it in my bones. And these old bones have never been wrong."

"I don't know what you're talking about. Why don't you let me listen to your heart?" Natalie placed her stethoscope on his chest and listened to the steady beating of his heart. It sounded fine. Hers, on the other hand, was pounding against her rib cage. Too much caffeine, she told herself, nothing more than that.

"Your heart sounds good," she said, focusing her mind on the present. "Are you having any pain?"

"Not anymore."

Natalie wasn't surprised. Mr. Jensen was a regular in the ER, and by now they both knew the drill. "What did you have for lunch?" she asked.

"Pepperoni pizza."

She had suspected as much. "I think we found our culprit. Was it a burning pain right about here?" she asked, putting her hand on his chest.

He nodded. "Yes, that's it exactly."

"Sounds like the same indigestion you had last week and the week before. It's time to stop eating pizza, Mr. Jensen." She pulled out her prescription pad. "I can give you something to help with your digestion, but you really need to work on changing your diet."

"Maybe I should wait here for a while, make sure it doesn't come back."

Natalie knew she should send him on his way. There was nothing physically wrong with him, and they would no doubt need the bed in the next few hours. It was Friday after all, a perfect night for madness and mayhem. But Mr. Jensen was almost eighty years old and lived alone. He probably needed company more than medical treatment.

Don't get involved, she told herself. Emergency medicine was about fixing specific problems, not getting emotionally involved with the patients. That's why she'd chosen the specialty. She was good at the quick fix but bad at personal relationships.

"I can show you another trick," Mr. Jensen offered, fanning the cards with his hand. "I used to be a magician, you know, a good one, too. I once worked in Las Vegas."

"I've never been to Vegas."

"And you don't believe in magic," he said with a sigh.

"No, I don't."

He tilted his head, considering her with wise old eyes that made her nervous. "When did you stop believing?"

"I don't know what you mean."

"In Santa Claus and the tooth fairy and leprechauns."

"I never believed in those things."

"Never? Not even when you were a little girl?" he asked in amazement.

She opened her mouth to tell him she'd never really been a little girl, when an image of herself in a long pink nightgown came into her head. She couldn't have been more than seven. Her dad had swept her up into his arms so she could hang her stocking over the fireplace and they'd put out chocolate-chip cookies for Santa Claus. It was their last Christmas together. A wave of grief hit her hard. She'd almost forgotten. And she didn't know which was worse—that she'd almost forgotten or that she'd remembered.

Natalie looked down at the prescription pad in her hand and forced herself to finish writing. She ripped off the paper and handed it to him. "This should do the trick."

"I don't think I feel well enough to leave yet," he said slowly, putting a hand to his chest.

His lonely eyes pleaded with her to understand. And she did. She knew the old man lived on his own, and she knew how hard it was to be alone. But the attending physician was a fanatic about hospital policies, which always involved moving the patients along as quickly as possible, and he'd love having a reason to call her on the carpet. *One more month,* she told herself. She had to finish her residency. She could worry about changing hospital policies later. Still . . .

"You know," she said, the cards in his hand catching her eye, "I bet there are some kids up in pediatrics who would love to see some card tricks. Why don't I send one of the volunteers in, and if you're feeling up to it, she can take you upstairs and put you to work."

A smile lifted the corners of his mouth. "That sounds good. Thank you, Dr. Bishop."

"No problem." Natalie walked out of the room and down the hall, stopping at the nurse's station to drop off his chart and ask the nurse to find someone to take Mr. Jensen up to pediatrics.

"He worked you good," Gloria, the charge nurse, told her, a knowing glint in her experienced eyes.

Natalie shrugged. "It's a win-win situation. The kids will love his tricks, and he'll have someone to talk to. Maybe he can volunteer upstairs and we'll see less of him down here."

"You're trying to stop the dam from breaking with your little finger. There are a hundred more just like Mr. Jensen who come in here every week—are you going to send them all to pediatrics?"

"Only if they can do magic tricks. Do I have time for a break?" she asked, checking the board on the wall.

"A short one," Gloria replied.

"You know where to find me." Natalie headed down the hall to the break room. A lone medical student, Karen Gregg, was eating a sandwich in front of the small television. She put up a hand to shush Natalie when she started to say hello. Natalie glanced at the screen, wondering what was so intriguing. It appeared to be one of those book shows with a man seated at a desk in a bookstore, a hard-cover novel displayed next to him. The title of the book was *Fallen Angel* and the author was Garrett Malone, a man in his forties with a thick beard, studious eyeglasses, and a serious expression.

She was about to turn away when she heard his voice. It was oddly familiar. Or maybe it was his words that resounded in her memory . . .

"They stood at the gates of heaven, the pledges on one side of the room, the sorority sisters on the other," he read. *"They were beautiful young women in white dresses, rings of flowers on their heads. Their faces glowed in the light of the candles held in their hands. The hush of voices provided a beautiful harmony to the night's initiation ceremony.*

"One girl didn't belong. She had the urge to run away, but her friends surrounded her. They were called the Fabulous Four, united since their first day as college freshmen and later as sorority pledges. One wanted to be a doctor, another a model, a third wanted a husband and children. But this one girl wasn't sure what she wanted to be. She just knew that she wanted her friends to know the real her.

She wanted to stop pretending to be someone she wasn't. Only she couldn't find the courage to take off the mask, to show her true self. She was afraid they would judge her, and she was right to be afraid."

Garrett Malone paused and looked directly into the camera. Natalie drew in a sharp breath, suddenly reminded of Mr. Jensen and his prediction that something bad was coming.

"In a few moments they would become sisters," Malone continued. *"By the end of the night one of them would be dead."*

"Emily," Natalie whispered, shaking her head in disbelief. It was Emily's story. It was their story. They were the Fabulous Four: Madison, Laura, Emily, and herself. They'd met at college. They'd pledged together their sophomore year. But the man was reading from a novel. It was fiction, wasn't it? Of course it was. The plot line was just strangely similar. A bizarre coincidence. It couldn't be anything more than that. Could it?

"Is something wrong, Dr. Bishop?" Karen asked.

Natalie realized the woman was looking at her with alarm. "What?"

"You're as white as a sheet. Are you ill?"

"I'm fine. Just fine."

"Have you read the book yet?" Karen tipped her head toward the television set.

"I don't have time to read."

"I don't either, but murder mysteries are my guilty pleasure. This one got a great review in the *Tribune*."

The *Tribune*? The Parish family paper? They wouldn't have reviewed a book about their daughter's death, which meant the novel couldn't be about Emily. Natalie forced herself to breathe.

"I read today that it's going to be a movie, too," Karen continued. "I can see why. I just started it yesterday, and I'm hooked. I can't wait to see what happens."

"What's it about?" Natalie asked, then wished she hadn't. She didn't want to know what it was about. She didn't want to know anything more about it. But it was too late to take back her question.

"It's about a murder in a sorority house. A girl named Ellie falls to her death from the second-story roof the night of the initiation."

Natalie's stomach twisted into a painful knot. Ellie, not Emily, but the names were close.

"None of her friends or family knows what happened. At least that's what they say. I'm not sure how it's going to end, but I think one of those girls killed her."

Natalie turned away, her heart racing as the words ran through her head.

One of those girls killed her.

And she was one of those girls.

Cole Parish strode through the newsroom of the *San Francisco Tribune* early Friday evening, nodding to reporters and research assistants who would work into the night, making calls, tracking the wires, and scanning the Internet in search of the latest-breaking stories to fill the pages of the Saturday and Sunday editions. The energy in the newsroom never failed to get Cole's blood pumping, and he needed that energy now, having spent most of the afternoon in a meeting with the bean counters. As executive editor of the paper, it was his job to make sure the paper stayed profitable, a trying proposition in the current climate of instant electronic news.

Studying the profit and loss statement was his least favorite part of the job. He was a news man at heart, not a business man, but duty to family had landed him behind the big desk in the corner office instead of out on the front lines where he'd always wanted to be. Well, that ship had sailed years ago. No point in crying about it now.

His secretary looked up at his approach. Monica, an older woman with dark hair and shrewd brown eyes, was a longtime employee. She'd worked for his grandfather, his father, and his uncle, and if the truth be told she probably knew as much about running the paper as Cole did. Thankfully, she kept that information to herself.

"Any messages?" he asked.

"Your father called earlier to confirm that you'll be having dinner with the family on Wednesday evening when they get back from their trip."

Cole nodded. His parents, along with his aunt and uncle, had spent the past month touring Europe, and he suspected that his father and uncle, who served as chairman of the board and president respectively, were eager to catch up on what was going on with the paper.

"I told him everything was running smoothly," Monica said. "You also had a message from your cousin Cindy, who . . ." Monica frowned as she stared down at the message slip in her hand. "I didn't quite understand what she was talking about, but it was something about a book review in last Sunday's paper. She said she'd call back. She seemed quite upset. She muttered something about family loyalty."

"When she calls back, take a message. I've told her before that I leave the choices of books up to our book editor, and I don't want to get into another discussion about it. What else?"

"You have a visitor waiting in your office. She insisted," Monica added with a disapproving glint in her eyes. "When are you going to find a nice girl to settle down with?"

"Gisela is a very nice girl."

"She's very something. Nice isn't the word I'd use."

Nice wasn't the word he'd use, either, Cole thought as he entered his office. Hot, stunning, and sexy came to mind. Actually, his mind failed to function when Gisela brushed her well-endowed breasts against his chest and gave him a long, wet kiss.

"I missed you, baby. Where have you been?" she asked in a little-girl voice that immediately dampened his enthusiasm. Why did women think that kind of talk was sexy?

"I've been in meetings all day," he replied, stepping away from her.

"You know what they say about all work and no play. It makes a man very boring." She gave him a flirtatious smile. She really was pretty, he thought, ash blond hair, dark brown eyes, curves in all the right places. He just wished they had more in common outside of the bedroom. Not that he wanted a long-term relationship. He'd given up on that idea years ago.

"Ask me what I did today," she continued.

"What did you do today?"

"I went to a spa in the Napa Valley with Margarita. It was incredible. We had facials and mud baths, and they wrapped our bodies in seaweed . . ."

Cole sat down at his desk as Gisela rambled on about her visit to the spa with a fellow lingerie model. He turned on the panel of television monitors that lined the opposite wall and skimmed through the taglines on each news channel, catching himself up on the latest happenings in the world. Breaking news in war zones had taken on a new dimension in recent years with reporters embedded in battalions and marching into battle along with the soldiers. It was a dangerous but exciting time to be a foreign correspondent.

"Did you hear what I said?" Gisela asked impatiently.

"Sorry?" he asked, still distracted as he saw a breaking-news tag flash on the CNN screen. He couldn't quite read the words, but the raging winds and swirling waves suggested a hurricane heading toward the North Carolina coast.

"Cole, this is ridiculous. You're not listening to me." Gisela slapped the top of his desk with her hand, a small ineffectual tap that would not have dared to chip her red nail polish, but the fact that she'd hit anything at all with those newly painted fingers told him she was truly irritated—which was par for the course. Gisela was a drama queen.

Every minor annoyance in her life turned into a major problem.

"What was the matter this time—not enough caviar in the body wrap?" he asked.

"The problem is you."

Cole sighed. He'd heard that one before—not just once, either. The comment was usually followed by *You don't spend enough time with me,* or *I don't feel like we really know each other.* To which he often felt like replying, *Do we need to know each other? Can't we just have a good time together, a few laughs, a lot of sex, and leave it at that?* Not that he would ever actually say that. He knew better than to wave a red flag in front of a bull or an irritated woman.

Before Gisela could explain exactly why she was upset, there was a knock at his office door, and Josh Somerville entered the room. Josh had a typical California beach boy look: a wiry, lean physique perfect for riding a surfboard, skateboard or any other kind of board, sandy blond hair that was never combed, freckles that got worse in the summer, and a wide grin on his perpetually cheerful face. Thank God for Josh. His radar was still working. Growing up next door to each other, Cole and Josh and Josh's twin brother, Dylan, had developed a system with girls. If one was in trouble, one of the others always came to the rescue.

"Josh, you're right on time." Cole sent his friend a pointed glance.

Josh darted a quick look at Gisela's stormy face. "I see that I am. Hi, Gertie, how are you?"

Cole inwardly groaned. Gisela, once known as Gertrude Hamilstein, had changed her name to Gisela years ago, but Josh, a sports reporter for the *Trib*, had come across the info and couldn't resist goading her with her real name.

"We're having a private conversation, if you don't mind," Gisela said.

"I don't mind. Go right ahead." Josh sat down in the chair in front of Cole's desk and stretched out his legs. "What are we talking about?"

"Love," she said.

"My favorite topic."

"I said love, not sex. You wouldn't know the difference."

"Most men don't," Josh said with a laugh. "Don't you agree, Cole?"

"Dammit," Cole said, distracted once again by the scene on one of the television monitors. "They just hit the embassy in Jordan." He picked up his phone and punched in the extension for the editor of the foreign affairs desk, his younger cousin Randy. Fortunately, Randy was still at his desk. "Is Hal in Jordan?"

"He's on his way home," Randy answered. "His wife is about to go into labor."

"Who else do we have over there?"

"Anita is in Lebanon. I'm already on it."

"Good." Cole hung up the phone to find Gisela shaking her head in disgust. "What?"

"You're addicted," Gisela replied. "The news is a drug to you, and you can't get enough."

"The news is my business, and this is a newspaper. We're supposed to report what's going on in the world."

"How about what's going on in your own life? Aren't you interested in that?"

"What are you talking about?"

Josh cleared his throat. "I don't think you two need me for this. I'll come back later."

"Oh, you can stay," Gisela said with a frustrated shake of her head. "I'm done. I'm leaving."

"Okay. I'll see you later tonight," Cole said, as Gisela picked up her designer purse.

She shook her head, an expression of amazement on her face. "I don't think so. Did you hear nothing of what I just said?"

"Uh . . ." he said warily. What on earth had she been talking about?

"Oh, my God," she said in exasperation. "You really don't listen. I'm breaking up with you. I never want to see you again. Is that clear? Or do you need a ton of bricks to hit you in the head?" To make her point, she picked up the heavy stapler on his desk and threw it at him on her way out the door.

Cole ducked, but not fast enough. The stapler caught the side of his head and the next thing he saw was a burst of stars that went along with an explosion of pain in his forehead. He put his fingers to his face and they came away bloody. "What the hell?"

He was barely aware of the flurry of activity that followed. Someone gave him a towel. Josh helped him into the elevator and down to the parking garage, where he put him in his car and drove to the nearest hospital. Apparently, the emergency department of St. Timothy's wasn't as impressed by the gash in his head as his coworkers had been, because they handed him an ice pack and told him to take a seat in a waiting room that was overflowing with a mix of people, many of whom didn't appear to be speaking English.

"This could take hours," Cole muttered. "We should forget it."

"We can't forget it. You probably need stitches." Josh sat down in the chair next to him. "You really know how to piss off a woman, I'll say that for you. How's your head?"

"It hurts like hell." The throbbing pain made it difficult for him to speak.

"Next time you break up with a woman, make sure there aren't any heavy objects lying around."

"I didn't know we were breaking up."

"Apparently that was the problem," Josh said with a grin.

Cole moved his head, then groaned at the pain that shot through his temple. "Dammit. This is the last thing I needed today. I've got to get out of here. I have things to do."

"What things? It's Friday night."

"The news doesn't stop just because it's the weekend. In case you haven't noticed, the world has gone crazy in the last few months."

Josh leaned forward. "In case you haven't noticed, *your* world is going crazy."

"What does that mean?"

"It means you should start paying attention to problems closer to home, like your girlfriend. You can probably get Gisela back if you call her tonight."

"Why would I want to do that? She almost killed me."

"If you'd moved faster, she wouldn't have hit you. You've gotten slow, Parish."

"I have not gotten slow." Even though his job kept him at his desk for long hours at a time, he worked out every day. "Frankly, I think I've had enough of Gisela anyway. What is with that baby-girl voice she uses? It makes me want to rip my hair out."

"Thank God she finally got to you. She's been driving me crazy for weeks. She was hot though."

"Cole Parish?" a nurse asked, interrupting them. "Come with me."

Cole got to his feet. "You can wait here, if you want," he said to Josh.

"I'll stick with you. It's a zoo out here," Josh replied as a group of drag queens came into the waiting room.

They followed the nurse down the hall and into a room with three beds, each separated by a thin curtain. An elderly man lay in one bed. The other was empty. "A doctor will be in shortly," the nurse said. She had barely left the room when they heard a commotion in the hallway.

A flurry of people in scrubs dashed past the door, shouting out various medical terms as they pushed a gurney down the hall. Cole's reporter instincts kicked in despite the pain in his head. He craned his neck, trying to catch a glimpse of what was going on.

"I'll check it out," Josh said.

Cole frowned as his friend rushed out of the room, irritated that he was sidelined while someone else caught the action. He sat down on the bed, holding the ice pack to his head, and wished for a television set. If they were going to make people wait this long, at least they could offer an all-news channel to take their minds off their pain.

Josh walked back into the room a few minutes later. "Gunshot victim," he said. "Convenience store robbery in the Mission district. The owner shot the robber, a seventeen-year-old kid."

"Will he make it?"

"They took him to surgery."

"I should call Blake," Cole said, referring to the assistant editor who ran the city desk on Friday nights.

"I'm sure he's already heard about it."

"Where's my cell phone?"

"Who knows? Relax, dude. You might have a concussion."

"I don't have a concussion, and I don't want the *Trib* to miss the story. I've got enough trouble with the *Herald* going to a morning edition."

"We can handle the competition." Josh sat down in the chair next to the bed. "Besides, you have got a couple hundred people working for you. Let them do their jobs." Josh leaned back and toyed with a piece of tubing hanging from some sort of a machine. "What do you think this is?"

"I have no idea. Where is the damn doctor anyway? I could have bled to death by now."

" 'Death by Stapler,' " Josh said with a laugh. "There's a headline for you. Or how about 'Psycho Supermodel Snaps'?"

Cole groaned. "Not funny."

"It is kind of funny."

Josh was right. His personal life was now officially a joke. Gisela's parting shot had definitely

gotten his attention. Maybe he did need to focus
on something or someone besides the news. But
not Gisela. That was over. He'd known it for a
while. He'd just been too busy to end it. Now that
she'd done it, he felt more relieved than anything
else.

Cole looked up as a woman entered the room.

"Good evening, Mr.—" She stopped abruptly,
looking up from the chart with wide, shockingly
familiar eyes. "Cole?"

Natalie? His heart thudded against his chest. It
couldn't be Natalie. Not now, not after all these
years. Not here, not in his city.

She moved farther into the room, slow, small
steps, as if she wasn't quite sure she wanted to
come closer. Her hair, a beautiful dark red, was
pulled back in a clip, showing off the perfect oval
of her face. Her eyes were a brilliant blue, her lips
as soft and full as he remembered, but it was the
tiny freckle at the corner of her mouth that made
him suck in his breath. He'd kissed that freckle.
He'd kissed that mouth. God! *Natalie Bishop.* The
only woman he'd ever . . . No, he couldn't think
it, much less say it.

It should have been easy to see her. It had been
ten years, but it seemed like ten minutes.

She was older now, a woman—not a girl. There
were tiny lines by her eyes and around her mouth.
She'd filled out, grown up, and she'd come back.
He wasn't ready to see her again. She didn't look
ready to see him, either.

Cole suddenly became aware of the white coat
she was wearing, the stethoscope around her neck,

the chart in her hands. She was a doctor. *She was his doctor!*

"Well, isn't this quite the reunion?" Josh murmured, breaking the silence between them. "Remember me?"

Natalie looked at Josh blankly for a second; then recognition kicked in. "Of course. You're Josh. Dylan's twin brother and Cole's next-door neighbor."

"Good memory."

Natalie turned her attention back to Cole. "Did you come to see me about the book? Is it really about Emily?" Her gaze moved to his head. "Oh, you're hurt. You have a laceration. That's why you're here. Of course that's why you're here," she added with a shake of her head. "What am I thinking?"

"What book? What are you talking about?"

Her mouth opened, then closed. "Nothing. Are you in pain?"

"I've had better days. Are you really a doctor?"

"Yes, I am. What happened?" She held his chart in front of her like a protective shield.

"I got hit by a flying object," he said, preferring not to go into the details.

"His girlfriend threw a stapler at his head," Josh interjected helpfully. "She was trying to get his attention."

"Did it work?" Natalie asked briskly, her demeanor changing at the mention of a girlfriend. Or maybe she was just coming to grips with the fact that they were in the same room. Whatever the reason, she now had on her game face.

"I'm definitely switching to paper clips," Cole replied.

She stared at him for a long moment. He wondered what she was seeing, what she was thinking. Not that he cared. Why would he care what she thought of him? He knew what he thought of her. And it wasn't good.

"You may need stitches," she said.

He wondered how she knew that when she hadn't looked at the wound. In fact, she'd stopped a good three feet away and couldn't seem to make herself come any closer. "How long have you worked here?"

"A few years."

"A few years?" he echoed. She'd been in San Francisco a few years, working at a hospital a couple of blocks from the newspaper?

"St. Timothy's is an excellent hospital. They offered me a terrific opportunity, better than I could find anywhere else. That's why I came to San Francisco," she said in a defensive rush. "It had nothing to do with you. I'm going to get some sutures. I'll be back."

Josh let out a low whistle as Natalie left the room. "I didn't see that one coming."

"I didn't either," Cole murmured. It must be his night for getting blindsided by women.

"She looks good."

"I didn't notice."

"Yeah, tell that to someone who doesn't remember how crazy you were about her."

"I can't believe she's been in San Francisco for years. Why would she come here after everything that happened with Emily and with me?"

"She always did love the cable cars."

Cole's chest tightened. Natalie had loved the

cable cars and the sailboats down at the marina, the fresh crab on Fisherman's Wharf, the long walk across the Golden Gate Bridge. At one time, he'd thought she'd fallen in love with the city as much as with him. Hell, maybe it had always been the city and never him. Not that he cared anymore. She was old news. Nothing was worse than old news.

"What was that book she was talking about?" Josh asked.

"I have no idea." It occurred to him that it was the second time that day someone had mentioned something about a book.

Silence fell between them as several long minutes passed. It was too quiet. Cole didn't like it. "Do you think she's coming back?"

Chapter 2

Natalie could not go back in there. She could not stitch up Cole's head and act like there was nothing between them. Like they'd never been friends, never kissed, never made love . . .

She leaned against the wall and tried to breathe. She hadn't felt this unsettled since she'd seen her first dead body. She was a twenty-nine-year-old doctor, not a foolish nineteen-year-old girl with a mad crush on the most attractive man she had ever seen. She wasn't naive anymore. She wasn't reckless. She wasn't stupid. Was she?

No. She couldn't go back there—not to his room, not to the past. She had her life together now, and she'd worked damn hard to get it that way. Cole Parish was no longer part of that life. That's the way he'd wanted it then and the way she wanted it now.

Why was it all happening tonight? First that author on television talking about a story that sounded a lot like Emily's, and now Cole. Was there a full moon? For three years she'd lived and worked in San Francisco, and he had never crossed her path. She'd almost forgotten about him, or pretended to forget about him, which wasn't easy considering he ran the biggest newspaper in town. And today he was here in the flesh, all six foot two inches of him.

He was bigger than she remembered, a full-grown man with strong shoulders, muscular arms, and long, lean legs. But some things hadn't changed. His hair was still a rich, deep brown, and his eyes were as dark and unreadable as ever. In the past those eyes had accused her of terrible things. And his voice . . . his low baritone voice had once told her he loved her, then later told her he never wanted to see her again.

She'd loved Cole more than she'd loved anyone in her life, and he'd hurt her. Even now she could feel the deep ache in her heart that had once been a blistering, unbearable pain. She didn't think she could go through that pain again. Nor did she think she could go back into the examining room.

"Steve," she said abruptly, as a second-year resident walked by, "there's a head laceration in room two that needs stitches. Can you take it for me? I've got a phone call."

"Sure. I'll be right there."

Natalie nodded and walked quickly down the hall. She was a coward. There was no doubt about that. It was better this way. Cole could get treatment for his injury, and she could take care of people she didn't know. People who hadn't broken her heart.

Cole stared at the young man preparing to stitch him up. "Where's Natalie?"

"Dr. Bishop? She had to take a phone call. I'm Dr. Fisher. I'll take care of this for you."

The doctor might believe that Natalie had a phone call, but Cole didn't.

"Could you hold still, please?" the doctor asked.

It took all of Cole's willpower to do just that. His mind was running in a dozen different directions, and they all led back to Natalie. She was living and working in San Francisco. They could have run into each other at any time. Maybe they'd even seen each other in a crowd or almost bumped into each other at the grocery store or the movies.

Why had she come to San Francisco to work? She could have gone anywhere. St. Timothy's was a good hospital, but there were good hospitals across the state—across the country for that matter. Had she had another reason for wanting to take up residence in his city? Because there was no doubt that San Francisco was his town. His family ran the major newspaper. They were in the middle of things; they always had been. Natalie knew that. She'd spent holidays and weekends with his family. She would have had to know there was a possibility she'd run into him. Maybe that's what she'd wanted . . . to see him again.

He shoved the thought away. He didn't care what she wanted. She was no longer in his life. She hadn't been for a long time. In a few minutes he would be on his way, and with any luck they wouldn't meet again for another ten years.

Dr. Fisher finished his stitching, handed Cole a prescription for a painkiller, and discharged him.

Cole got to his feet, feeling off balance. He suspected that had more to do with Natalie than with the gash in his head. When they reached the hall, he paused, unable to stop himself from looking around. There were a number of people in scrubs and white coats rushing around, but none of them had red hair. Or blue eyes. Or a mouth he could almost still taste . . .

"Do you want to talk to her before we go?" Josh asked.

"No, I don't want to talk to her. Why would I want to talk to her? She is the last person I want to talk to," he added, finally cutting himself off. Judging by Josh's amused expression, he was making a fool of himself.

"Whatever you say," Josh replied. "I'll take you home."

Home for Natalie was a tiny attic apartment under the eaves of a three-story pink Victorian house, one of San Francisco's infamous painted ladies. But Natalie wasn't thinking about the city when she slipped into bed just after midnight. She was thinking about Cole and Emily. She hadn't been able to get either one of them out of her mind. On her dinner break, she'd run down the street to the local bookstore and picked up a copy of *Fallen Angel.* She was sure the book had nothing to do with Emily. Cole's newspaper wouldn't have reviewed it if that had been the case. And he hadn't appeared to know what she was talking about when she'd mentioned a book to him.

Still, she couldn't get the story out of her mind. She opened the first few pages and began to read. The opening scene took place in an off-campus dorm room where Ellie first met Nancy and their fellow suite mates, Linda and Maggie. Settling back against the pillows, she began to read.

Their friendship began on a sunny day in late September when Ellie and her parents arrived at Santa Cruz University, an hour and a half south of their home in San Francisco. The college spread across a bluff overlooking the Pacific Ocean and the infamous Beach Boardwalk with its aging but treasured wooden roller coaster.

Ellie was filled with excitement and joy but also a sense of trepidation. She had been worrying about her prospective roommate since she'd been assigned to room 232 at the off-campus dorm called Fontana Gardens, a three-story building a half mile from the campus. The only thing she knew about her roommate was that her name was Nancy and that she was from Los Angeles. It would be the first time in her life that Ellie had ever shared a room. Actually, it was the first time Ellie had ever shared anything. Her parents had spoiled her rotten. She knew that even if they didn't.

Ellie hoped that Nancy would like her. While Ellie had had all the material things money could buy, what she'd never really had was a girlfriend. She hoped more than anything that Nancy would be the best friend she'd always wanted.

Natalie drew in a sharp breath and closed the book, her heart racing as if she'd just finished a long-distance run. The names were changed, but the story was theirs. Fontana Gardens, the three-story dorm, was Paloma Gardens, named for the street on which it was located. Ellie was Emily.

And Nancy was her. Their suite mates Maggie and Linda were Madison and Laura. And that first day in the dorm rooms still burned brightly in her memory. She'd been just as worried about meeting Emily as Emily had been about meeting her. And she knew what was going to happen next.

She set the book the aside. She didn't have to read the next page. All she had to do was lay back and remember. She pulled the covers up to her neck, and stared up at the ceiling, suddenly afraid to close her eyes. Did she want to remember? Did she want to go back to Paloma Gardens, to Emily, to the day where it had all begun? Her eyes burned as she tried to keep them open, but the past was pulling her back. Her lids grew heavy, as she gave into the desire to see it all again.

The dorm room was smaller than she'd imagined, the walls bare, begging for posters. A cheap-looking dresser sat next to each twin bed. This was it? Natalie wondered. This was college? She'd worked so hard to get here, holding down two, sometimes three jobs, as well as maintaining a straight-A average. And she'd ended up in a bedroom that didn't look much better than the one she'd shared with her mother in a run-down apartment in Los Angeles. But the room didn't matter.

She was free. She was starting a new life, and she couldn't wait. This life would be different. No one would have to know where she came from or what she'd left behind. No one would have to meet her poor excuse for a mother, who was drunk more often than she was sober. No one would have to know that she'd taken a five-hour bus ride to get here, with no one to send her off or say good-bye.

No one would know that she owned nothing more than what was contained in the two old suitcases now sitting next to one of the beds.

She could be anything she wanted to be, and she wanted to be a doctor. She wanted to make her father proud. He'd told her that the one thing he'd always wanted was a college education. But his parents hadn't been able to afford it, so he'd taken a job as a truck driver. He'd told her it would be different for her. And it would be different, but not because of him. He'd died when she was eight years old. But his dream for her had continued to burn in her heart, despite her mother's best efforts to squelch it. That dream was beginning today. She just hoped her roommate, Emily Parish, wouldn't be a total freak or a big party girl. Natalie might have made it to college, but this was just the first step in her ten-year plan to become a doctor, and she would need somewhere to study.

The door burst open and a girl came flying into the room with so much energy and sparkle that Natalie took an instinctive step backward. Wavy, long brown hair, laughing brown eyes, and an incredible smile. Emily Parish quite simply lit up the room.

"Natalie Bishop?" Emily asked. "Are you my roommate?"

Natalie nodded and said, "Yes" as Emily enveloped her in a big bear hug.

"Wow. Can you believe we're here?" Emily asked when she finally let go.

"Not really."

"We are going to have the best time. I've been waiting for this day for so long. I can't even tell you."

"Me, too," Natalie muttered, as Emily's parents entered the room. Richard and Janet Parish were the picture of rich sophistication in fancy clothes and expensive jewelry. They were polite to Natalie, but she could see from their expressions that they were more than a little worried about leaving their daughter in the dorm. With the help of a few strong guys down the hall, Emily's belongings were unloaded. By the time they were done, there was barely room to turn around.

"Don't worry," Emily whispered. "As soon as they leave, we'll have a garage sale."

"You can't sell your stuff."

"I didn't want to bring it all. They insisted. They're a little overprotective."

Overprotective was right. Both Emily and Natalie received endless instructions about staying safe. Mrs. Parish pulled Natalie aside at the last minute and said, "Watch out for our Emily. She's an innocent. She doesn't know what she doesn't know."

Natalie promised she would, because there was no way she couldn't promise. Besides, she was used to watching out for her mother, and Emily couldn't possibly be as difficult as that.

When the door closed behind the Parishes, Emily cranked up the newly connected stereo, jumped on her bed and began to dance, her long hair flying out behind her. "Come on," she said.

"Are you kidding?" Natalie asked doubtfully. "We might break the beds."

"So what? I don't know about you, but this is the first time in my life that I can do whatever I want to do. I have been waiting for this moment forever!"

A moment later, Natalie found herself attempting

some sort of a dance on her own bed. She couldn't remember ever doing anything so silly or so girlish. And that was the way Laura and Madison had found them when they'd walked through the connecting bathroom to meet their suite mates.

Laura, a short and slightly overweight girl with dirty blond hair, offered them chocolate-chip cookies. Madison, a tall and thin blonde with a model's face and body, offered them some beer her boyfriend had stashed in her suitcase. Within minutes Emily had dubbed the four strangers the Fabulous Four. It was the beginning of a friendship meant to last a lifetime.

It had only lasted a year and a half.

Natalie's eyes flew open. She ran a hand across her wet cheeks, realizing she'd been crying. She'd closed off those memories for ten years, and now they were back. She didn't know whether to be furious or happy. With a sigh, she stared down at the book, flipping it over to gaze at the author's face. Garrett Malone. Who was he and how did he know so much about them?

Emily couldn't have told him. Had someone else in the Parish family talked to him? It didn't make sense that they would. They were devastated by Emily's death. They wouldn't have wanted a book to be published about their daughter, especially not a piece of fiction, especially not a book about . . . murder.

Natalie's stomach turned over at the thought. Emily's death had been a tragic accident. She'd fallen off the rooftop deck during a party at the sorority house. Everyone knew that. If it had been anything else, Cole and his family would have made sure someone was punished. She needed to keep reading, to find out where the story was going. If the author was right about some of the stuff, was he right about Emily's death? Was there more to it than any of them had suspected? She opened the book and began to read.

Natalie woke up hours later to a persistent knocking on her door. She pulled a robe over her sweats and thin T-shirt and stumbled to the door, dimly aware that it was obviously morning and she'd managed only a couple hours of sleep. She expected to find Mrs. Bailey, her downstairs neighbor, who often dropped by with bagels on Saturday morning. Instead she found Cole.

"Why did you walk out on me?" he demanded.

"What?"

"You heard me." He marched into her apartment with a determined look on his face.

Wearing a pair of blue jeans and a long-sleeve black knit sweater that emphasized his broad chest and muscular build, Cole was even more impressive than he'd been the night before in his suit and tie. Or maybe in casual clothes he just looked more like the guy she remembered, the man she'd fallen in love with.

Shutting the door behind him, Natalie drew in a deep breath, telling herself to stay calm. Unfortunately, her racing heart and sweaty palms didn't seem to be paying attention. It had always been like this with Cole, an incredible physical attraction that made her feel like she was going up in smoke every time he looked at her. The chemistry between them should have disappeared by now.

They'd certainly done their best to bury it. But it wasn't gone, and she had to keep her cool. "What are you doing here?" she asked finally.

"I want to know why you bailed on me last night."

"You were in good hands, and I had another case."

"That's a lie."

"Fine. I didn't want to see you, and I certainly didn't think you wanted me to be your doctor. Was I wrong?"

Emotion flickered in his dark eyes, but she couldn't tell what it was. Had he thought about her over the years? Had he wondered where she was, what she was doing, who she was doing it with? Or had he been able to forget her as he'd said he intended to do?

Natalie ran her hands down the sides of her sweats, wishing she had on something more professional. Her feet were bare, and her toenails weren't even polished. She could definitely use a pair of shoes about now. She always felt taller and more in control when she had her shoes on.

"You shouldn't have walked out on me," Cole said abruptly.

"Why not? Did you want to walk out on me?" She saw the flash of annoyance cross his face and knew she was right. "How did you find me anyway?"

"I run a newspaper. I can find anyone."

He glanced around her studio apartment, probably noting the sparse furnishings, the secondhand couch, the wooden crate that held her TV and the matching crates that served as a coffee table. Her unmade bed was barely hidden behind the Oriental screen she'd picked up at a flea market. The only remotely inspiring pieces in her apartment were the movie posters on her walls. A longtime insomniac, she'd always found escape from the lonely hours of the night in old movies.

She wouldn't apologize for her place. It had taken every cent she had to get herself through medical school and residency. She still had loans the size of Mount Everest to pay off. Secondhand furniture was the least of her worries. It wasn't as though she were home that often anyway. Or even as though she would be living in this apartment come next month. She had job offers elsewhere. Since running into Cole yesterday, she was leaning toward taking a job at the southern end of the state. She sat down on the arm of her sofa, watching Cole pace.

He'd certainly grown into his looks, filling out his jeans in all the right places. His thick brown hair framed a face that was more ruggedly attractive than truly handsome. His square jaw spoke of his strength, passion, and sense of purpose. The crooked tip at the end of his nose reminded her that he had never been willing to let an errant baseball or a broken nose deter him from what he wanted when he wanted it. Cole was the kind of man who made a girl want to turn him from being a guy's guy into a girl's guy. She'd certainly tried.

She wondered if Cole was married now or single. Then she recalled Josh's comment at the hospital that Cole's girlfriend had thrown a stapler at his head. If she'd wanted to maim him for life, she'd failed. The stitches on his forehead made him look like a wounded warrior, which was even more appealing. What woman could resist that?

She could. She definitely could. And she would.

When he didn't speak, she asked, "How's your head?" It was easier to act like a doctor than an old friend—if that's even what they were.

"All right." His gaze sharpened as it met hers. "Why here, Natalie? Why San Francisco?"

"I told you—"

"There are good hospitals all over the country."

That was true. "I thought enough time had passed that it wouldn't matter. I didn't believe anyone would care where I was, least of all you."

"Well, I don't care."

"That's what I thought." She threw every bit of bravado she had into those words and wished he would look somewhere else, but she'd be damned if she'd look away first. She wouldn't give him the satisfaction. "Is that it?"

"No. That isn't it." He paused. "You said something to me last night about a book and Emily. What was that about?"

Damn. Why did he have to remember her comment? If he didn't know about the book, she didn't want to be the one to tell him. On the other hand, wasn't that the way it should happen? They'd been brought together by her friendship with Emily and ripped apart by Emily's tragic death. Their entire relationship from beginning to end was irrevocably tied to Emily. And here they were again. They'd come full circle. "I picked up a book last night after I heard the author on television. The story line sounded familiar."

"What's it about?"

"It's there if you want to take a look." She tipped her head toward her nightstand.

Cole walked across the room, opened the book, and began to read the jacket copy. She doubted it would take long for his sharp brain to compute the facts. It didn't. His shoulders stiffened, and there was anger in his eyes when he looked at her. "What the hell is this? Fabulous Four . . . sorority house . . . pledge falls from the roof . . . Ellie Parks?" His voice rose with each muttered word. "Is this about—Emily?" He looked at her as if she should know the answer, as if she were responsible somehow. He shook the book at her when she didn't immediately reply. "Is this about my sister?"

"It looks that way."

"I don't understand."

"I don't, either. I've only just started it, but the book is about four friends in college who call themselves the Fabulous Four. The characters' names are different, but they all start with the same letters as our names. The book suggests that the main character, Ellie," she said, deliberately using the character's name, "did not die in an accidental fall from the roof of her sorority house. Instead, the author believes that she was . . ." Natalie drew in a deep breath, not sure she could say it.

"That she was what?"

"Murdered." The word shot out of her mouth like a bullet.

It hit him straight in the heart. Cole put a hand to his chest. "That's impossible. The police conducted a thorough investigation. I saw the report. My father made sure every question was asked."

"I know. It was an accident, a terrible accident. The book is trying to make it into something else."

"Who did it?" he asked abruptly. "If it's a murder mystery, there must be a murderer. Who killed my sister?"

"It's fiction, Cole. It's part truth, part fantasy. It's Emily's story, but it's not. It's pieces put together in a puzzle that doesn't make sense."

"So tell me the name of the *fictitious* killer."

"I don't know yet. I haven't finished it."

"And you weren't curious enough to look ahead?"

Actually, she was terrified to look ahead, because she didn't like the way things were lining up.

"Who are the suspects?" he asked.

"Madison, Laura, and me. The author seems to think one of us killed our best friend, but he's wrong. You know that, and I know that."

"Do I? Do I know that?"

"Of course you do," she said, truly shocked at his words. "We were friends, all of us. We loved Emily, and she loved us."

A tense silence stretched between them for long, painful seconds. She knew Cole blamed her for letting Emily down, for not watching out for her the way she'd promised, but surely he couldn't believe that she would have ever intentionally hurt Emily.

Finally, Cole looked back at the book in his hands. He flipped it over to stare at the author's photo. "Who is this guy?"

"I have no idea. He must have talked to someone who knew us."

He threw the book down on the coffee table with

such force that she jumped. "I'm not going to let this happen."

"What are you going to do?"

"Find Garrett Malone for starters. I have plenty of investigators on the newspaper payroll. I'm sure we can ferret out one best-selling author."

"You won't need an investigator." She picked up the *Tribune* and leafed through the pages until she got to the entertainment section. "You might want to read your own newspaper once in a while." She handed it to him. "Apparently, there was also a review in last Sunday's paper. Don't you oversee what's printed?"

"I don't spend time reading the book reviews," he snapped, taking the paper from her hand. "Garrett Malone will be signing copies of his novel, *Fallen Angel*, at the Page One bookstore, Saturday, noon to two," he read. "He's right here in town." He looked at Natalie with a glint in his eye. "What time do you go to work?"

"Three o'clock, why?"

"We have a book signing to attend."

"I don't want to go."

"Sure you do. That's why you circled it." He handed her back the newspaper. "Don't you want to find out what's going on, Natalie?"

Of course she did. She hadn't been able to think of anything else since she'd heard about the book. She just didn't want to spend more time with Cole. It was difficult to be with him, to look at his face, to hear his voice. Everything was coming back—all the feelings, the love, the hate, the emotions she'd shut off the last ten years.

"Come with me," Cole urged.

His words took her back to a time when she would have gone anywhere with him, said *yes* to anything he asked. That time was long gone, but still she wavered . . .

"If it's about Emily, you owe it to her to find out."

"All right, I'll come," she said finally. The sooner they got to the bottom of this mystery the better. Then she could get back to her life. And Cole could get back to his.

Chapter 3

Come with me. What devil had possessed Cole to utter those words? He didn't want to spend time with Natalie. He still couldn't believe she'd been living in San Francisco the past few years. Had she come here in the hope of a reconciliation? If she had, why hadn't she tried to contact him? If she hadn't come back because of him, then she should have stayed away.

He looked into his rearview mirror and saw Natalie's car behind his. The paint on the hood of her Ford Taurus was peeling, reminding him that she was a woman who had never had much in the way of material things. She'd always struggled to keep her head above water, and it appeared she was still struggling. But she was a doctor now. She'd made it, just like she said she would, and he couldn't help feeling a grudging admiration for that success. Not that he intended to tell her that. In fact, the less personal information they shared the better.

He shouldn't have asked her to go with him to the book signing. He didn't need her. He was a trained journalist. He knew how to sniff out a story. Unfortunately, this story struck too close to home.

He was still reeling from the cover copy he'd read and what Natalie had told him about the story line.

How had this happened? How had his sister's life come to be the plot of someone's novel? This must have been the book his cousin Cindy had called about the day before. She must have seen something in the review that reminded her of Emily. How did the author know so much about his sister? He had to have had an inside source. Who?

Still pondering that question, Cole pulled into a parking space down the street from the bookstore and got out of the car. He waited on the sidewalk as Natalie put money in the parking meter. Her red hair was a bright splash of color against the gray day. She'd changed out of her sweats and put on a cream-colored sweater, a pair of dark brown slacks and shoes with two-inch heels. She'd always loved a good pair of high heels. And he'd always loved her legs in a good pair of high heels. His body tightened at the unwanted thought, and he hated his physical reaction to her. The connection between them should have died with Emily and all that had happened. But one look into those brilliant blue eyes, and he'd felt sucked back in. He couldn't let that happen. Natalie was his past. She had no place in his present or his future.

A moment later, Natalie joined him in front of the bookstore where the double doors were held open by a line of people spilling onto the sidewalk.

"Is this for the signing?" she asked in amazement.

"It looks that way." They moved around to the back of the line, not talking as conversation swirled around them. Cole's uneasiness grew as the line lengthened. He wasn't much of a reader, but he'd been in the media long enough to know that most book events were not standing-room-only attractions, especially for an author no one had ever heard about before.

"This guy must have a hell of a publicist," he grumbled. Checking his watch, he realized it was almost noon. The line would probably move quickly once the signing began. He needed to think about what he wanted to say. He could hardly confront Malone in front of all these people. He'd never expected it to be this crowded.

"Oh, no!" Natalie said.

What now? He followed her gaze to the slightly overweight woman crossing the street. Of average height, she had short dark blond hair that just touched her shoulders. She wore black pants and a matching jacket. A heavy black purse hung from one shoulder and she carried a copy of the novel in her hand. Dark glasses covered her eyes, but he had the distinct feeling he knew her.

"Laura," Natalie muttered, putting her hand on his arm. "I think that's Laura Hart. She's coming this way."

Cole didn't know if he was more unsettled by Natalie's touch or by the appearance of another member of the Fabulous Four. "It might not be her." He took a step back, putting a good foot between them.

"It is her. I'd know that walk anywhere."

Laura suddenly stopped dead in her tracks. She stared at them for a moment, then slipped off her sunglasses to reveal a pair of familiar brown eyes. "Natalie? Is that you?"

Cole waited for Natalie's reply. But she couldn't seem to say a word. She just stood there and stared at Laura as if unable to believe her eyes. Finally, she cleared her throat and said, "Yes, it's me."

"I can't believe it. It's been so long." Laura's gaze moved to Cole. Her eyes widened even further. "Cole Parish? You're here, too? You're together? I thought that ended years ago, and—"

"We're not together," Natalie said quickly. "I ran into Cole last night—by accident. He came into the emergency room at St. Timothy's. I'm a doctor there."

"You live and work right here in San Francisco? Are you kidding me?" Laura shook her head in amazement. "I live on the Peninsula, in Atherton. I had no idea we were so close." She paused. "I've thought about you so many times in the past ten years, Natalie, I can't even tell you. And here you are. You look good, too, exactly the same. I would have recognized you anywhere."

"I wouldn't go that far, but you look good, too, Laura."

"I have two kids now, daughters. Oh, and I married Drew McKinney. Can you believe it?" she asked with a proud smile.

"You always said you would. How is he?"

"He's wonderful. He's an attorney and maybe a soon-to-be politician."

Cole thought politics sounded right up McKinney's alley. He'd met the man a few times when he'd visited Emily and Natalie in Santa Cruz, and he'd pegged Drew as a slick player, the kind of man who didn't mind cutting corners. He was surprised Drew had married a girl-next-door type like

Laura. He wouldn't have put money on their relationship lasting this long.

"This line is really long," Laura said, taking a moment to look around. "I didn't imagine there would be so many people here."

"I didn't, either," Natalie muttered.

Laura's expression turned somber. "Since you're here, I assume you've both read the book?"

"I've read some of it," Natalie replied. "Cole hasn't started it yet."

"Really? It was reviewed in your paper," Laura said.

That again. At least it was nice to know people were reading the paper. "That's probably the only page I don't read," he said. "Do you think it's Emily's story?"

Laura nodded. "Yes. Reading it is like taking a bad trip down memory lane. Don't you think so, Natalie?"

"Absolutely," Natalie agreed. "Do you know anything about Garrett Malone?"

"No. That's why I came. I wanted to see him in person. Maybe talk to him about the story. I never expected to run into you two." She took a breath. "Are you married, Natalie?"

"No. I've been too busy for that."

Cole turned away from Laura's questioning eyes. He didn't feel like sharing details about his personal life. Just being with Natalie and Laura felt wrong. He'd never intended to see any of them again, yet here he was with two of them. They'd let Emily down. His sister was dead and these two women were alive. They were beautiful, energetic— one with a family and children, the other a doctor.

Emily hadn't lived to see her twentieth birthday, hadn't had a chance to fall in love, get married, or have children. His stomach churned at the injustice.

"Cole?" Natalie's questioning voice made him turn to her.

"What?"

She tipped her head toward the door, and he realized the line had moved. A few moments later they entered the bookstore and caught their first glimpse of Garrett Malone. The author sat at a large oak table, a pile of books in front of him, an assistant standing next to him, preparing each book for his signature. Malone looked exactly like the photo on the cover of his book. A brown beard covered most of his face, thick eyeglasses made him appear supremely intelligent, and neatly styled brown hair was just long enough to give him a creative, artistic look.

"Do you recognize him?" Natalie asked.

He shook his head. "Do you?"

"There's something familiar . . . I don't know what though. He's too old to have been a student with us or to have been at the party that night. He must be in his mid-forties. That would have put him in his mid-thirties back then. Anyone that age would have stood out."

"I agree. That doesn't mean he didn't have friends. Hell, maybe even a daughter," Cole said abruptly. "He could be older than you're guessing. He could be fifty with a twenty-nine-year-old kid who was nineteen and a college sophomore that night."

"I suppose. I don't remember any Malones."

"Let me see that book." He took the copy from Laura's hand and opened it to the copyright page. "That's interesting. The copyright is in the name Pen Productions."

"Sounds like a business name. Why is that interesting?"

"I don't know yet."

The line moved again, and they drew within a few feet of the table.

Garrett Malone looked up as a woman with a baby on one hip bent over her stroller to get a copy of the book. He glanced at the line and smiled, a very self-satisfied smile. Cole didn't like him. He was up to something. Something that might hurt his family.

Malone's gaze moved toward Cole. There was a split second of eye contact between them, but no clear recognition on Malone's part. If he knew so much about Emily, why didn't he recognize her brother? Cole wondered. Then he saw Malone's gaze shift, and he realized the man was looking at Natalie now, or maybe Laura. Suddenly Malone was on his feet.

"He's getting up," Natalie said. "Is he coming over here?"

"I think he saw us," Laura added.

Malone said something to his assistant, who looked surprised and worried. A moment later Malone left the table entirely, walking briskly toward the back of the store and away from the line— away from them.

"Where's he going?" Natalie asked.

Before Cole could move, the assistant stepped up to the table and raised her hand for quiet. "Mr.

Malone is feeling ill. He's very sorry, but he can no longer continue the signing." She paused, clearing her throat, obviously upset by the sudden change in events. The crowd of people began to complain. The store manager stepped up and offered those in line ten percent off their purchases.

Cole didn't wait to hear more. He headed toward the back of the store, knowing he was too late when he saw the door leading to a back parking lot.

"Is he gone?" Natalie asked, almost tripping over his heels as he stopped.

"Looks that way. Damn."

"Do you think he's really sick?" Laura asked.

"Hell, no."

"He ran away," Natalie said. "He ran away when he saw us."

"When he saw you," Cole corrected. "He looked right through me, but he knew one of you, maybe both of you."

"But we don't know him," Laura said. "Do we, Natalie?"

Natalie was still thinking about Laura's question as they walked into the Starbucks next to the bookstore. She wasn't quite sure why she'd agreed to have coffee with Laura. She had mixed feelings about renewing their friendship. Fortunately, she didn't have Cole to worry about. He'd taken off, muttering something about "getting to the bottom of this."

"I'll have a nonfat, decaf latte," Laura ordered. "I'm on a diet again. Or should I say still?" she added with a little laugh.

"I'll take a double espresso," Natalie said, stepping up to the counter. Caffeine was as much a part of her life as breathing, and far more important than food, which was probably why she didn't battle the bulge as often as Laura did.

They sat down at a small table while they waited for their drinks.

"I was thinking about you last night, Natalie," Laura began, her voice a bit wary. "The book brought everything back. It was as if the last ten years just vanished. And seeing you now, it feels like it was yesterday that we were ordering coffee at Pete's on the Boardwalk and talking about school and friends and guys that were driving us crazy. I feel like Madison and Emily are going to walk in any minute and join us." A shadow crossed her face. "But I know that can't happen. I shouldn't have even said it. I always did talk too much."

"I know what you mean," Natalie replied, letting Laura off the hook. "It does feel the same. I don't know why it does. We're not nineteen anymore. And a lot has happened since then." Their friendship had not ended naturally. They hadn't just drifted apart as college friends do. Their relationship had been shattered by Emily's death, by their behavior that night at the party and by the guilt they each felt for letting Emily down. Madison had taken off before the funeral, sent to Europe by her parents, and Natalie had transferred within the week to a college in Los Angeles. It hadn't taken more than ten days to end what had once been intense and beautiful friendships, the best Natalie had ever had, and something she doubted she would ever share again.

"Do you miss her?" Laura asked.

Natalie looked into Laura's eyes and said with utter sincerity, "Every day. She was the best part of all of us."

Laura nodded, blinking back a tear. "I always thought so, too. I've tried to tell people about Emily, but I can never find the right words to describe her. It's easy to say that she was beautiful and fun and full of life, but she was more than that. She was our spirit, our inspiration. She made us believe in ourselves." Laura shook her head. "But that's not even right, because it makes her sound like she wasn't real, like she couldn't get down and dirty, you know? Of course, you know . . . I'm rambling, aren't I? I just can't believe we're sitting here together after ten years of silence between us." She took another breath, her brown eyes softening even more. "I missed you, too, Natalie. You and Madison. I missed us, the way we were together. Actually, I missed me, the fourth girl in the Fabulous Four. I don't think I've been fabulous in a while. And I don't think I realized that until last night when I started reading the book."

"You weren't the fourth girl," Natalie said, trying to defuse the emotion in their conversation. She'd never been as comfortable with sharing personal thoughts and feelings as Laura had been. "It's not like we had numbers or anything."

"Oh, please. I was definitely fourth. Emily was number one, because she was the ringleader. You were two, because you were her roommate. Madison was three, because there's no way she could ever come in behind me, so that makes me four. It's okay. I was happy just to be in the group."

Laura slid her locket along her gold chain necklace, a nervous habit that reminded Natalie of other occasions when Laura had done exactly the same thing. With two older, beautiful, and accomplished sisters, a father who was a brilliant lawyer, and a mother who expected her daughter to be perfect, Laura had always been insecure. She'd worried endlessly about saying and doing the right thing, about people liking her, about fitting in. Her need to please and desperate desire for love had been both endearing and irritating when they were in college, and having heard the raw vulnerability in Laura's voice just now, Natalie suspected those needs had not disappeared in the last ten years.

"You haven't said anything in at least a minute." Laura's brows drew together in a frown. "Did I say something wrong?"

"I was just thinking."

"You were always good at thinking before you speak. I'd still like to learn how to do that. Drew often complains that I talk when I shouldn't, especially at law-firm cocktail parties. Did I tell you that Drew works at my father's firm?"

"That keeps it all in the family."

"A little too much all in the family. I feel like we can't get away from my parents. And the more we're all together, the more Drew acts as critical of me as they do. Sometimes I don't think any of them believe I have a brain in my head."

"Well, they're wrong," Natalie said, not just because it was expected, but because it was true. Laura might have a desperate need to please, but she wasn't dumb; she never had been.

"Thanks. That's nice of you to say. But to be fair, my brilliant conversation for most of the past eight years has been about kids, diapers, potty training, sleep deprivation, elementary school teacher selection, PTA gossip . . . It's not exactly brain surgery. Hey, do you do that? Brain surgery?"

"Absolutely not. You remember how bad I was at sewing, don't you?"

Laura grinned as they both remembered a particularly bad hem job.

Their orders were called, and Laura jumped to her feet. "I'll get those." She was back in a moment with their drinks.

Natalie took a sip of coffee, feeling immediately more relaxed. Oddly enough, she was happy to see Laura again. They'd parted under such tense circumstances that she never would have predicted they could come back together so easily. She had to admit it was nice to talk to someone who wasn't involved in her current life, someone who didn't know squat about medicine or hospital politics, someone she didn't have to impress with her intellect or medical knowledge. The last ten years had been exhausting. She'd run like a rat on a wheel, never stopping to catch her breath or look around for fear she'd fall off that wheel and never get back on. She'd never let anyone get close enough to see her true self . . . whatever that was. Not only did she not have time for relationships, she had little time for personal introspection. In fact, she hadn't done this much thinking about anything that didn't involve a disease or a medical procedure in . . . she couldn't remember how long.

"I can't believe we live so close to each other," Laura said, interrupting her thoughts. She sent Natalie a quizzical smile. "It didn't bother you that Cole—"

"No." Natalie cut off the question she knew was coming. "It's a big city. A lot of years have passed."

"Sure. You're right. I'm not completely surprised you ended up here. You always loved this city. After your first trip home with Emily, you talked endlessly about the cable cars, the narrow hills, the bridges. You were in love."

And not just with the city but with Cole.

"So what happened to Cole?" Laura asked. "I noticed the bandage on his head."

"His girlfriend threw a stapler at him."

Laura's eyes widened. "Really?"

"That's what he said in the emergency room. Josh was with him. Do you remember Josh? He was one of the twins who grew up next door to the Parish family."

"The laughing, smiling one, or the dark, brooding one?"

"Laughing, smiling. The other one was Dylan."

"Right, the magician. I wonder what happened to him."

"I have no idea."

"What did you do when you saw Cole?"

"I was startled." Which was an understatement to say the least. Natalie didn't bother to explain that she'd taken off and Cole had made it his business to find her. Instead, she said, "I told him about the book and the signing. That's why we were together today."

"So, any lingering sparks?" Laura asked, a curious gleam in her brown eyes.

"We barely spoke," Natalie prevaricated. "And it was a long time ago."

"You know what they say about first loves. You never forget 'em."

"Well, you married your first love, so you can't forget him," Natalie said, changing the subject. "Tell me about your wedding. Did you wear the white dress with the long train that you dreamed about? Did you have the evening ceremony in a small chapel lit only with candles?" Laura's mouth trembled and Natalie could see she was on the verge of crying again. "I'm sorry. Did I say something wrong?"

"I just can't believe you remember that."

"You talked about it enough," Natalie said lightly.

"I guess I did." She looked down at her coffee, then back at Natalie. "It was a morning wedding, big church, hundreds of people, many of whom I didn't know. It was wonderful."

Somehow Natalie didn't believe her, but she didn't want to get into what was obviously a touchy subject.

"My parents love Drew," Laura continued. "My dad considers him the son he never had." She paused, a somber expression on her face. "Marrying Drew was the smartest thing I ever did. That's what my mom always says. And she's right. He gave me two great girls. I live in a beautiful home. What more could a woman want? Nothing, right? My life is perfect."

"If you weren't trying so hard to convince me, I might believe you," Natalie said quietly, taking a sip of her coffee. "No one's life is perfect."

"It's just that Drew works a lot. I haven't even had a chance to tell him about the book. I know he'll be shocked." Laura leaned forward as she said, "When you read the book, Natalie, didn't you feel like one of us was talking? It's crazy. I didn't write that book, and I don't think you had anything to do with it, so who? Madison?"

Natalie hated to think that Madison would have done anything to exploit Emily's memory, but someone had to have spoken to the author. "It seems the most likely possibility."

"Maybe we should try to find her. We could look on the Internet. She might be here in the Bay Area. Her parents lived in Marin County. It would make sense for her to be somewhere around here. Although she could still be in Europe." Laura took a breath. "Do you remember that Halloween when Emily dressed up as a fortune-teller and predicted our futures? She said Madison would live in Paris, meet a sexy painter, and make love all afternoon. Maybe that came true."

"Maybe, but she also said you would marry the prince of a small foreign country and wear a tiara in your hair. And I would end up globe-trotting the world with an adventurer, braving rapids, climbing mountains, and jumping out of airplanes. That was the silliest prediction of all." It saddened her to realize that no one had ever predicted a future for Emily. Why hadn't one of them donned the fortune-teller's cape and looked into the crystal ball for Emily?

They sat for a moment just looking at each other. The air between them was thick with sadness and regret, two emotions that Natalie had spent a lot of time living with. She glanced down at her watch, relieved to see the time. She had to go to work. Work was the only place where she could forget. "I have to go," she said to Laura. "My shift starts in an hour."

"What about Malone? I think it was you he ran away from, Natalie, not me."

"Why do you say that?"

"Because if you read a little farther in the book, you'll see that . . ." Laura's voice dropped off. "Never mind. Just keep reading."

"What am I going to find out?" Natalie asked, feeling suddenly queasy.

Laura bit down on her bottom lip. "I could be wrong, but you know in the prologue how he says one of us knew what happened to Emily that night? Everything seems to be pointing to you."

"In what possible way?"

"In the book, Ellie asks Nancy to get her a drug from the health center to help her focus on her homework better, because Nancy works there and has access to the medication."

"But I didn't have access, and I told Emily that she should never take anything that wasn't pre-scribed by her doctor, that it would be dangerous."

"I know that, Natalie, but in the book it makes it sound like you and Em had a huge fight about it. And we both know she got that bottle of pills somewhere."

"But she didn't take any," Natalie said, as her heart sank to her stomach. The police had found a bottle of Adderall in Emily's dresser drawer, a medication used to treat attention deficit disorder, and one that had become the drug of choice for normal kids wanting to improve concentration in late-night cramming sessions. Which reminded her that this nightmare was getting worse. If the book became connected to her . . . if St. Timothy's found out that she was supposed to have played a role in someone's death with medication she'd stolen from a health center, her reputation could be ruined. She couldn't stand the thought of losing everything she had worked so hard to get.

"It might not have been the only bottle," Laura said. "No one knows where she got it or how much she had. But that's not all. The story line also implies that you and Emily were fighting about Cole, that Emily was against your relationship, that she thought you were using her to get to Cole."

"God," Natalie said on a sigh. It was getting worse and worse.

"And you were drunk the night of the party— so drunk you couldn't remember where you'd been or who you'd been with."

Natalie didn't need to be reminded of her behavior that night or the fact that she hadn't been able to remember where she'd been or what she'd done. It had been a defining moment in her life. After Emily's death, she'd taken a good look at herself, at who she was, what she'd become, and she hadn't liked what she saw. So she'd changed. But changing hadn't brought Emily back. And not being there for her friend, not being able to remember what she'd done in those few important hours, would haunt her for the rest of her life.

"So I'm the villain," Natalie said, feeling a surge of anger. "Who the hell does this guy think he is to accuse me of things he knows nothing about?"

"Well, he knows more than nothing, that's for sure. Maybe no one besides us will recognize the story, though," Laura added hopefully.

"I doubt that. There are too many people reading the book. And there were a lot of people at the party that night."

"What can we do? We can't pull the book off the shelves."

"The publisher can—if they believe the book has been misrepresented as fiction. I'm going to call a lawyer, find out what our options are."

"Wouldn't we have to prove that the story was true? Wouldn't that mean bringing it all out in the public? Do we want to do that, Natalie? Wouldn't that just make it worse?"

Laura was right. The last thing they needed was more publicity. "At the very least we should find out what choices we have. Then we should try to find Madison. If you didn't talk to Garrett Malone, and I didn't talk to him, then it had to be Maddie."

"Why would she tell?"

"Money," Natalie tossed out. "If there was ever a girl who knew the value of a dollar, it was Maddie."

"She wouldn't sell out Emily."

Natalie looked Laura straight in the eye. "If she didn't, then one of us is lying."

Chapter 4

Madison Covington sat at the head of the conference table. Three of her coworkers awaited her instructions. Since transferring from the New York office three months earlier, she had been promoted to senior account executive for Barney and Baines Public Relations in San Francisco. With any luck, she intended to change the name of the firm to Barney, Baines, and Covington Public Relations in the very near future. The masquerade ball they were planning, the event that had brought them all together on this Saturday afternoon, was going to blow the lid off celebrity charity events. Madison intended to raise over five hundred thousand dollars in one night for crippled children. Her future would be made. And the crippled children wouldn't be bad off, either.

"I want everyone to wear masks," she said. "No exceptions. This masquerade party will be the talk of the town." And she would be the talk of the PR world, the queen of the celebrity charity event. She so enjoyed being the queen, she thought with a small smile. But first she had to get back to business. "Lisa, how are we doing with the hotel?"

The twenty-two-year-old newly minted college grad glanced down at her checklist. "Everything is on target. The menu is set. The decorations have been ordered. The seating chart is almost complete." Lisa hesitated, then said, "We've had some last-minute cancellations, Ms. Covington. I have the names right here."

"Who?" Madison asked, suddenly worried that it would be the Parishes sending regrets. Ever since she'd seen their RSVP come in, she'd been waiting for them to figure out it was her party, giving them more than enough reason to pass. She was one of the girls who had led Emily astray, and she hadn't even had the decency to stick around for their daughter's funeral, not that that was her fault. Her parents had given her no choice.

She knew coming back to San Francisco would mean seeing the Parishes at some point, especially Richard and Cole, who ran the *Tribune*. It was her job to work the press, and they were the press. Her boss had already suggested on more than one occasion that she find an opportunity to get personally acquainted. So far, she'd managed to put that off without explaining why. "Well?" she asked impatiently as Lisa shuffled through her papers.

"Gwen Parker. She has to fly to Madrid for an early start on her movie."

That wasn't so bad. Gwen Parker wasn't that big of a star.

"And Harry Stone," added Jean, an older woman who had returned to public relations after taking ten years off to have babies. "His wife is nine months pregnant and doesn't want to attend any more parties this close to her due date."

"Who do we have to replace them?"

"Stephan Paoletti, the tenor," Jean replied. "He just had a special on HBO. And Colin Davies, the quarterback of the 49ers."

"Good. Now on to entertainment. We still need a preparty act." She turned to Robbie, a junior account executive with a lot of ambition. "What have you found?"

"An illusionist," Robbie replied. "He runs the new club south of Market that specializes in virtual reality, techno-magic. Everyone is talking about him. His name is Dylan Somerville. Have you heard of him?"

Her heart skipped a beat. Had she heard of him? She'd lost a lot of sleep over Dylan Somerville, and she was a woman who prided herself on not losing sleep over anyone. She'd figured Dylan was somewhere in San Francisco. She'd even thought about trying to hook up with him again but to date hadn't quite found the nerve to go looking for him. Now an opportunity had just landed in her lap.

"He's very good," Lisa added. "His club is sold out every weekend."

"What would he do at the event? Pull rabbits out of a hat? This is a classy party."

"He can make things disappear," Robbie replied. "Big things, like a car or a person. Right before your eyes."

"Sure he can," she said cynically.

"It's true," Lisa said. "I was in the front row last weekend and he did some amazing tricks, really cool stuff. You should go see him at the very least. I think magic would add a nice touch to the masquerade party."

They had good points. She could drop by Dylan's club and check him out. She could even personally extend the invitation to perform at her event. And maybe if Dylan didn't react to her with absolute horror, he could be a bridge to Cole; he could help her smooth things over with the Parish family. She loved it when everything clicked into place.

"All right. I'll go by the club." She glanced around the table. "If that's it, you can take off. Have a good rest of the weekend."

As her associates left, Madison sat back in her chair, wondering if the past would have come back in such vibrant technicolor if she hadn't made the decision to transfer to San Francisco. Maybe if she'd stayed in New York, she would have been able to keep it all at arm's length, the way she had for the past ten years. Oh, well, too late now. She'd made her choice, and she'd make the most of it. This was a great city with great opportunities. And she was a beautiful, successful woman. Dylan Somerville would not be able to ignore her this time around. Not to mention the fact that she didn't have Emily for competition.

What a horrible thing that was to think. Poor sweet Emily was dead. And it had never been Emily's fault that Dylan had been infatuated with her. Sometimes Madison wondered if Emily had even known about his crush. He'd certainly kept it hidden from everyone else, including his best friend, Cole. But Madison had known. At nineteen she hadn't understood that her attention to detail, to the things that made people tick, would actually become a very handy tool in the business world.

At twenty-nine, she knew quite well that the best way to get what she wanted from people was to give them something they wanted. The question was—what did she want from Dylan after all these years? A little revenge, she thought with a self-indulgent smile. Payback for those sleepless nights. Maybe it was time to show Dylan what he'd passed up all those years ago.

Standing up, she gathered her papers together, and turned on her cell phone just in time to take an incoming call. She didn't recognize the number and was startled, not to mention annoyed, to hear her mother's voice. She'd been avoiding her mother all week. "Mom, where are you?" she asked sharply.

"I'm at Alice's house," Paula Covington replied, referring to her sister. "I left you two messages at your apartment yesterday and today. Are you screening my calls?"

"I've been busy."

"Too busy to talk to me?"

Madison refused to be taken in by the hurt note in her mother's voice. Her mother only wanted to talk to her when it was convenient or when she needed something. Madison had learned that before she was out of diapers.

"We have to talk about that book. And don't pretend you don't know what I'm talking about."

Madison toyed with the idea of pretending just that, but ignorance would only elicit a long-winded explanation from her mother. "I know about it, but there's nothing to talk about."

"Of course there is. Someone is trying to create

a scandal, and we can't have that. Edward's seat in the assembly is up this year. We can't have any rumors attached to the family."

"Edward is hardly family, Mother. He's been your fourth husband for a year, and quite frankly I've lost interest in acquiring any more step-fathers."

"Madison, that's very rude. Edward has been nothing but good to you. Don't tell me you've forgotten that he took care of everything when you ran out on your wedding last year. You should show some loyalty."

Madison sighed. She did not want to get into a discussion about her botched wedding plans or family loyalty. "Look, the book isn't about me. It's about Natalie."

"Are you sure?"

"Positive. I've read every word."

"This could still spill over. I know your name isn't mentioned specifically in the book, and you certainly aren't accused of murder, but you could be connected to the story, and we can't have that. I thought this was over ten years ago when we sent you to Paris to get you away from those girls."

"Don't worry, I'm fine. I really have to go back to work. I'll talk to you soon." Madison ended the call on her mother's protest and closed her phone. She walked over to the window and stared out at the San Francisco skyline. Yes, it was all coming back. There was no escape. Not for any of them.

She couldn't help but wonder what the others were thinking, especially Laura and Natalie. Their private moments, conversations, and thoughts had been put into a book that millions could read.

They'd been stripped naked and exposed . . . It wasn't fair, but then life wasn't fair. Natalie had told them all that a million times. Natalie, with her fiery hair and intense drive to succeed, was now being called to account for the murder of her best friend.

Had Natalie read the book? Did she have any idea who was after her?

Natalie couldn't sleep. She'd been tossing and turning since she'd returned home from the hospital just after midnight. It was now almost three a.m. and her eyes felt dry, incapable of closing. She supposed she could read. The book was on her nightstand just waiting for her to pick up where she'd left off. But she was afraid.

Turning those pages would take her back to a place she didn't want to go. A place where youthful dreams had flourished, where passion had run her life, where friendship and love had been more important than anything else. She'd loved those girls, Emily, Laura, and Madison—loved them as she'd never loved anyone in her life. For fifteen months, a blink of an eye, she realized now, she'd been a part of something special, wonderful, irreplaceable.

A knot of sweet emotion made it hard to swallow. She closed her eyes, willing sleep, blessed oblivion, to come, but instead the past came rushing back to greet her.

Emily sat up in the twin bed next to hers and turned on the light. She wore her brown hair in two long braids, which made her look about twelve, especially when combined with the pink T-shirt that said GIRLS RULE, *baggy pajama bottoms, and thick socks that didn't match.*

"What's wrong?" Natalie asked, blinking against the bright light. "It's two o'clock in the morning."

"And you can't sleep. I heard you tossing and turning."

"Sorry, I'll be quiet. I just have a lot on my mind."

"You always do," Emily said with a rueful smile. "What is it this time?"

"Money, bills, loans, classes, grades, everything."

"I can always lend you money if you need it. No questions asked."

"Thanks, but I'll make it on my own."

Emily shook a finger at her. "That's just it, Nat. You don't have to do everything on your own. I'm here. I'm your friend. And I can help you. All you have to do is ask."

"I'm not very good at asking, and you should stop offering so much. People will take advantage of you."

"I wish they would," Emily confessed. "I spent so much of my childhood alone in my room, protecting myself from germs or recovering from one illness after another that I got really tired of my imaginary friends. And they got so bored, they all ran away," she added with a laugh that wasn't quite true.

Natalie stared into Emily's beautiful face and saw the lingering shadows of loneliness in her eyes. She knew that Em had suffered from acute asthma as a child. Every mild cold had turned into pneumonia or bronchitis or some other disease, often requiring a hospital stay. Her parents had done everything but put her in a bubble to keep her safe. Thankfully, as she got older her asthma and her immune system had improved and she'd managed to convince them to let her go away to college and start living her life.

Emily opened the drawer between their beds. "I have an idea," she said, as she pulled out a small cardboard box. "If we're not going to sleep, we should wax."

"What?" Natalie turned onto her side, propping herself up on one elbow. Her dad's big gold watch hung heavy on her arm. "Wax our legs? Now? You're crazy. It's the middle of the night."

"That's when the hair grows." Emily held up the box in her hands that showed a picture of two smooth legs. "I saw this on televison. You put the wax on your legs, cover it with strips of paper, leave it on for a couple of minutes, then pull. Hair gone."

"Great, we'll have bags under our eyes but perfectly hairless legs. What we really should do is study." She was surprised when Emily picked up the phone next to the bed. "Who are you calling?"

"Maddie and Laura. They'll be mad if we wax without them."

Natalie was still considering that logic when Emily started talking. "We're going to wax our legs, watch TV, and eat popcorn. Natalie can't sleep."

"I could try," Natalie protested, but her words fell on deaf ears. "They're not going to come over here for me," she added.

She was wrong. A few minutes later Maddie and Laura plopped down on their beds. Maddie had on hot red silk shorts and a matching tank top. Laura wore a long flannel nightgown. She had curlers in her hair and some kind of acne cream in thick spots on her face. Emily made popcorn in the popper her

*parents had given her while Maddie flipped through
an x-rated magazine with pictures of naked guys.
With embarrassed giggles, they voted on the best
penis, ate burned popcorn, and waxed their legs with
shrieks of pain. A late-night Three Stooges marathon kept them laughing until they finally fell asleep
an hour before their alarms went off.*

Natalie's eyes flew open as her heart filled with
a bittersweet regret that those beautiful days of
simple responsibilities and incredible friendship
were gone. She missed those moments, the long
talks in the dark of the night with her very best
friends. She missed those girls, too. And as Laura
had said earlier, she missed herself, the girl she'd
once been. But that girl was an adult now. The past
was gone, and it wasn't coming back. Unless . . .

Her gaze moved to the book by her bed. Maybe
she'd just read a few more pages.

Natalie wanted to escape. It was the only thought
driving her actions as she set down the book just
after eight o'clock the next morning and pulled on
sweats and running shoes. She'd spent the night
reading every shocking word of a horror story in
which she was the star. The plot resembled her own
life yet seemed distorted and unreal. Some of the
words were hers. Some were not. Some of the actions she'd committed, some she'd never dreamed
of. Underneath it all was the sense that someone
had been watching, listening, a secret voyeur who
knew far more about her than she knew about him.

Adrenaline surged through her body at the
thought—the instincts for fight or flight battling
with each other. She knew how to fight, but not

who, so she would go with her second option—run. Grabbing her keys, she headed out the door and down the stairs. The cold morning air blasted her face as she hit the sidewalk. This was reality, she told herself, this moment, this street, this city, not the past she'd spent the night revisiting. She had to remember that. Glancing up at the sky, she realized the morning fog was beginning to break up, patches of blue sky and sunlight shining through the tree branches. She felt better already.

That feeling faded with the screeching of tires coming around the corner. Cole's car. Damn. She turned and started running in the opposite direction, hoping he wouldn't see her. The fact that he was here could mean only one thing—he'd read the book, too. God! What he must think of her now. His already bad opinion had probably sunk even lower.

"Natalie!" Cole shouted, his car slowing as he caught up with her.

She refused to turn her head and started to run faster.

"Natalie, stop."

She threw him a quick glance. "Go away."

"Not a chance," he replied, his car keeping pace with her. "I want to talk to you."

Well, she didn't want to talk to him, not now, not while she was feeling so raw and vulnerable. She didn't want to hear his accusations again, see the anger in his eyes, hear the agony in his voice or in her own. She needed time to rebuild her defenses, gather her ammunition, find a way to fight the questions she knew were coming. Turning the corner, she dashed through the alley that ran behind the row of houses and apartment buildings and turned up the speed.

She thought she'd lost him until he yelled again, this time from behind her. He must have ditched the car. She could hear his footsteps drawing closer.

"Natalie, stop, dammit."

Her legs were beginning to burn from the sprint, but she pressed on. She was a good athlete and she was used to running. Cole was even better. She could feel him bearing down on her. As she reached the end of the alley, she paused for a split second, debating which way to turn—toward the marina or Union Street. It was a mistake. His hand came down heavy on her shoulder.

She bounced free for a moment; then he caught her arm. She stumbled forward. Cole stopped her from falling by yanking her up hard against him. She would have preferred to hit the pavement face-first, because looking into his angry, bitter, betrayed eyes was even more painful.

For a long moment they both drew in ragged, angry breaths of air.

"Don't say it," she burst out, finally finding her voice.

He shook his head. "Did you do it? Did you push Emily off the roof? Were you fighting with her? Were you both so drunk that you didn't know how close you were to the edge? Is that what happened?" He gave her shoulders a shake.

"No," she cried. "No!"

"Then why did you run just now? Why is there a guilty look in your eyes?"

"That's not guilt. That's anger. I can't believe

you of all people could even ask me those questions."

"That's not an answer. Only the guilty run away."

"I ran because I knew deep down that you would choose to believe a stranger rather than to believe me." She yanked her arm away from his grasp. "How could you, Cole? How could you think that I would hurt Emily? I loved her. She was my best friend." A stabbing pain ripped through her, and she felt her eyes fill with tears, but she blinked them away. She wouldn't cry now, not in front of him. She wouldn't give him the satisfaction.

Cole stared at her through bloodshot eyes. He looked like hell; his hair was a mess, his face covered with stubble. He must have been up all night. She steeled herself not to care that he looked wiped out, that he was probably devastated by everything he'd read. That didn't give him the right to come after her.

"Dammit, Natalie," he said finally. "There was truth in that book. You know it as well as I do."

"And lies. I know that, too."

"Which is which?" He sent her a long, searching look. "I don't know what to believe."

It hurt that he couldn't believe her. She wrapped her arms around her waist, feeling cold and utterly alone. She should be used to those feelings by now. But they were worse with Cole so near. She was reminded of that brief period in her life when love had filled her heart, when she'd begun to believe there might still be a happily ever after. That had ended with Emily's fall. Actually, it had ended before that.

"I wish you could remember where you were that night," Cole continued. "It doesn't help that you were passed out drunk in the upstairs bathroom when Emily fell and that you have no memory of anything that happened at the party."

"You think I don't know that? You think I don't wish a thousand times every day that I hadn't gotten stupidly drunk that night? You think I don't feel horrible that I wasn't there for Emily? My God, Cole. You could never blame me as much as I blame myself for putting my needs above Emily's, for not watching out for her as I'd promised, for not knowing who she was with or what she was doing. She was my best friend, and I let her down."

"You never said that before," he said slowly.

"You never gave me a chance." She held his gaze for a long moment. "I'm sorry, Cole. I'm sorry, and I'm sad. But I'm not guilty. I wouldn't have hurt Emily, not because of some pills that I never stole or some fight that I supposedly had with her over you. Can I prove it? No, I can't. But I know it in here." She put her hand on her heart. "And you should know it, too, because you knew me once. You knew me better than anyone."

Cole ran a hand through his hair. "I thought I knew what happened. I believed Emily drank too much, went on the roof to stargaze, and just slipped. But this damn book is turning that night into a murder mystery. Emily is portrayed as someone I don't know. Her thoughts about school and friends and men . . ." He shook his head in bewilderment. "Some sounded like her. Some didn't."

"Because some of the words were hers and some weren't. I felt the same way when I was reading it, like I was there but it wasn't quite the same party I remembered, and the people weren't exactly right, but some of their traits were familiar."

"You would be able to tell the truth from the fiction better than I would, because you were there all the time. I just came down on the occasional weekend. I didn't know what was going on the rest of the time." He drew in a long breath. "The worst part is knowing that I was close by that night. That I could have stopped it. I was with Josh at Dylan's apartment, less than a mile away. Emily wanted me to come to the party. She called me and begged me to come. I didn't feel like it, and I told her maybe later." There was agony in his eyes when he looked at her, and Natalie could feel his pain down to her soul. "I didn't go, Natalie. I didn't go to that party until it was too late. Em wanted me there with her, and I didn't go."

"Because of me," she murmured. "You didn't want to see me. I was getting too serious." She'd told him she loved him. It was the first and last time she'd ever said those words to a man. And he'd run for the hills.

Cole looked down at the ground. "I should have been there for my sister. I failed her."

His guilt was as tangible as her own, and the anger inside her began to dissipate. "We both could have acted differently, but we didn't, and we can't change it now. It's over. It has been for a long time."

"It's not over, not with this book making the rounds. I went back to work yesterday and ran through everything I could find on Garrett Malone. It turns out there's very little information on the guy. It's like he came out of nowhere. I've put in calls to his publicist, his agent, and his publisher, but it's the weekend. I won't hear back from any of them until tomorrow. And his Web site hasn't been updated with any appearances after the book signing yesterday."

"Where does he live?"

"His press materials say California, nothing more specific than that. I will find him, Natalie. And he will talk to me."

"And me," she said decisively. "I have a few questions of my own to ask him."

"I'll bet you do." Cole hesitated, then said, "I'm glad we cleared the air."

"Me, too." Natalie wasn't sure how she felt about Cole now or how he felt about her, but at least they'd broken the icy distance of the past ten years.

Cole cleared his throat, then said, "So where are we running?"

She didn't like the word *we*. "*I'm* running down to the marina and out to the Golden Gate Bridge."

"Sounds good. I was going to work out at the gym, but I could use some fresh air."

He was wearing running shoes and sweat pants, she realized belatedly. "I'm not going to run with you."

"Afraid you can't keep up?"

"I remember that I always beat you," she reminded him. Running in the early hours of the morning was a joy they had shared during their time together.

"I remember that I always let you."

The challenging gleam in his eyes built a fire

under her already overcharged emotions. "Fine. Let's go." She took off before he could say okay. It was a small and cheap trick, but she knew how strong Cole was, and how easily his long strides would keep pace with her shorter ones. Within a minute he was right next to her.

"Going kind of slow, aren't you?" he needled.

"I'm warming up."

"You never used to take so long to warm up."

She quickened her pace to get away from his sarcasm and from the memories his words had stirred up. They'd made this run before from Cole's parents' house in Presidio Heights, an elegant neighborhood of fancy homes that lined the Presidio. The last time she'd visited there had been the Christmas before Emily's death, which had occurred in the middle of February, just six weeks later. How much everything had changed in those weeks—especially her relationship with Cole, which had taken a serious turn that Christmas. In fact, that turn had started with a run just like this one.

Natalie crept quietly down the stairs. The Parishes were still asleep. It was just after seven a.m. on Christmas Eve. Tonight they would go to the Fairmont Hotel for an elegant dinner. Tomorrow morning they would gather around the stately ten-foot Christmas tree in the living room, open presents, and have brunch. Christmas dinner would follow a few hours later. There would be plenty of food, friends, and holiday cheer, and Natalie was lucky to be a part of it. It was the first Christmas she'd spent with a real family in a very long time, and she wanted to cherish every second. At the same time, she was feeling overwhelmed and stressed out.

The Parishes were so different from her family. They were classy, sophisticated. Their table settings would come with at least three forks and two spoons and several plates, and she'd have to remember which went with which. There would be business moguls and politicians at tonight's party, which meant witty, intelligent conversation would be flowing like wine, and she would have to make sure she didn't make a fool of herself. Maybe she should just run out the door and keep running.

Shaking her head, she told herself to stop worrying so much and just enjoy, as Emily always told her to do. Emily, who was fast asleep in a beautiful bed filled with the most expensive allergy-free pillows and comforters and surrounded by luxuries suitable for a princess. Sometimes Natalie wondered why they were friends. They were different personalities and they came from different worlds, but college had been the great equalizer.

Natalie opened the front door and shut it quietly behind her. She took a moment to stretch on the front steps, then headed toward the sidewalk. She was just about to take off down the block when she heard Cole's voice.

"Wait up," he said, as he jogged toward her. "You weren't going to leave without me, were you?"

"I didn't know you were coming," she said, already flustered by the gorgeous smile on his equally gorgeous face. Every time she saw him he took her breath away.

"I told you I was doing whatever you were doing this weekend."

"I thought you meant the parties."

"I meant everything," he said.

The intensity in his voice made her lick her lips. His glance darted to her mouth, and she knew he was remembering, too. They had come so close to making love just two weeks ago when Cole had visited Santa Cruz. They'd been interrupted by Emily. Natalie had been both relieved and disappointed. She wanted to make love with Cole. She wanted to give herself to him. It would be her first time, but she knew she was finally ready.

"Are we running or . . ."

"We're running," she said quickly. She was ready for him—but not at this very moment.

Heading down the street, they ran faster and faster until their jog turned into a race. By the time they reached the Marina Greens, they were in full sprint mode. As they approached the end of the grass, Cole changed directions.

"You're going the wrong way," Natalie gasped, but she followed him all the same down a path that led to the St. Francis Yacht Club. "Where are you going?"

"Here," he said, grabbing her hand and pulling her around the corner of the building.

"Why are we stopping?" she asked in confusion.

"Because I can't wait a second longer to kiss you."

"Wha—"

He cut off her question with a hot, passionate kiss that went on and on. They both refused to give in or give up. Finally, Natalie surrendered to a need for air. She pulled away from him, shocked by her passionate response and her complete disregard for her surroundings. Granted there were only a few other early-morning joggers around, but she'd never felt so swept away by a man, never wanted to throw all her caution and good sense to the wind. But she wanted to do just that with Cole and a lot more. She was in love with him. God, she'd just realized how much she was in love with him.

"Natalie! Come on."

Natalie blinked, realizing she'd once again been lost in the past and was lagging behind Cole. Shaking her head, she picked up the pace as they neared the object of her memories, the St. Francis Yacht Club. She saw Cole glance toward the building. For a split second, she wondered if he, too, remembered that day. No, she couldn't let herself go there. Cole didn't like her, love her, or want her anymore. He hadn't in a long time.

She didn't give the building another glance as she sprinted past Cole, leading the way to the end of the path that stopped under the Golden Gate Bridge. The bridge was actually red, not gold, but it was awesome and inspiring in its construction. The Pacific Ocean flowed under the bridge and into the bay, the gateway to the west.

The wind whipped her hair out of its ponytail as she bent over to catch her breath and stretch out her legs. Cole stopped just a few feet away from her, his own breath steaming up the morning air. She hadn't beat him, and she hadn't lost him. What was she supposed to do with him now?

She straightened up, and said, "Why are we together?" the words bursting out of her mouth before she could stop them.

His gaze was steady. "Because of the book. I need to know what happened."

"I can't tell you what happened."

"You can help me find out."

"Believe me, I want to know as much as you do, but I don't think we're ever going to find out. No one was with Emily when she fell. No one saw her fall. The police asked everyone who was there those very questions."

His gaze didn't waver. "But there was someone there. There had to be. Malone mentions a number of people talking to Emily that night, people who claimed the opposite."

Natalie had noticed that, too, but since so much of what she was accused of was false, she didn't know what to believe. "He could have made it up like the other things he made up."

"Or someone didn't tell the truth. Did Laura say anything after I left yesterday?"

"No. She seems as confused as I am."

"What about Drew?"

"Laura said she hadn't had a chance to tell him about the book yet."

"Maybe he already knows. Drew was there. He wasn't just dating Laura; he was friends with you and Emily. Think about it, Natalie. Was there anyone who knew as much about the four of you as Drew did?"

"I guess not," she said slowly. "I've never given it much thought."

"Well, think about it. Drew was at the party that night. He was privy to a lot of personal conversations and information."

"That's true. Emily and I actually met Drew first. We were all in a chemistry class together freshman year. We worked on some group projects."

"So he knew you from the beginning, when you lived in the dorm."

"Yes, but I was never that close to him. There was something fake about him. I didn't really trust him."

Cole nodded. "I thought the same thing the few times I met him. What about Emily? What did she think of him?"

"She liked him. He made her laugh. They were good friends, at least until Drew and Laura hooked up our sophomore year." Natalie paused, thinking about the equation Cole was putting together. "It doesn't make sense, though. Why would Drew help someone write a book about us and call it fiction? He's married to Laura. And she's not happy about being in the story. She also said Drew is a lawyer now with an eye on a political career. I can't see how he could possibly be involved in this."

"All good points. None of it makes sense," Cole replied. "But we have to start somewhere. I think we should pay Laura and Drew a visit today."

There was that *we* again. Natalie didn't want to spend more time with Cole, but she also didn't want him talking to Laura and Drew without her. If Drew had something to do with the book, Natalie wanted to be there to ask him about it. "All right. I'll call Laura when we get back."

"I have a better idea. Don't call. It's always better to catch your enemies off guard."

"Laura and Drew aren't my enemies."

"Well, someone is, Natalie, otherwise you wouldn't be the villain of this book."

He had a point. "True."

"Ready to head back now?"

"Let's go a different way," Natalie said, preferring to avoid any more trips down memory lane.

Cole raised an eyebrow. "What's wrong with the way we came?"

"Been there, done that," she said pointedly, leaving him to take that in whatever way he wanted.

Chapter 5

Laura opened the door to Drew's study, not surprised to see her husband sitting at his desk in front of his computer. Work was his passion, whether he was at home or in his law office, and the fact that it was Sunday made absolutely no difference. He'd obviously been working since the early morning. The shades were still drawn, the room dark save for the desk lamp illuminating a circle of light over the computer and Drew's golden blond hair.

Drew's dark blue eyes were focused on the screen. She didn't know whether to be impressed by his powers of concentration or irritated that she was so invisible to him. Walking farther into the room, she shut the door behind her with a decisive click. Drew's head snapped up, a scowl on his handsome face.

"What do you need?" he asked sharply.

"I thought you might want to take a break, have some lunch."

"I'm busy. I have a lot to do before I leave tonight."

She'd forgotten he was flying to L.A. later in the evening for a three-day business trip. He'd been in and out of town so much in the past six months, she felt as if their house was more of a pit stop than a home. "I hardly see you anymore," she murmured.

His frown deepened. "Laura, I really don't have time for this."

"Time for what? Time for me?" She hated the way her voice came out whiny and desperate, but it was too late to take back her words.

"It won't always be like this, but if I want to make partner, I have to put the time in now. Your father has very high standards. I hope you can understand that."

"I do." She especially understood the part about her father having high standards. Lord knows, she'd never been able to live up to them. No wonder Drew was so stressed all the time. Feeling guilty, she walked around the corner of the desk to give him a neck rub.

"What are you doing?" he snapped, hitting a button on the computer to shut down the screen.

"I'm going to rub your neck."

"I appreciate the thought, but I really need to concentrate."

"On what?" She stared at the now dark screen and wondered why he didn't want her to see what he was working on. "You're being awfully secretive, Drew."

"I have to protect the privacy of my clients."

"From your wife?" She slipped in front of him, leaning against the edge of the desk. "You can trust me."

"It's not about trust."

She wanted to ask him what it was about, but not

now, not here, while he was so obviously distracted. "Take a break, Drew. There's a free concert in the park. We could take a blanket, make a picnic. It would be fun."

"I don't have time. Didn't I just tell you that? And don't you have something more important to do than make a picnic and listen to some band?"

She had a million things to do to keep their lives running like a well-oiled clock, but at the moment she didn't feel like focusing on laundry, bills, the kids' homework, the latest PTA project, or cleaning the house. She wanted to talk to Drew away from the house and work. She wanted to talk to him about the book, about seeing Natalie and Cole. Before she could say so, Drew's cell phone rang.

He immediately picked up with a brisk, "Hello." His expression softened. His mouth curved into a smile. Then he laughed. Laura couldn't remember the last time she'd heard him laugh. "You're the best, Valerie. I owe you." He paused. "I'm sure you will collect. Hang on a second." He put his hand over the phone and turned to Laura. "This is going to take a while. Do you mind?"

She did mind—not because he wanted to finish a work call from one of his associates, but because Valerie Cain had put a smile on her husband's face. "We need to talk, too."

"Later. All right?"

Did she have a choice? As Laura left the study, she was tempted to eavesdrop, but she forced herself to shut the door behind her. She had to trust her husband. Trust was the basis of a good marriage. It wasn't as if Drew even had time to have an affair. He worked twelve hours a day. Of course,

Valerie was also at work. Didn't most affairs happen in the workplace?

She had to stop thinking this way. Drew wasn't being unfaithful. Just because they didn't sleep together all that much didn't mean anything. They'd been together ten years. The frequency of sex often fell off after that amount of time. Didn't it?

Had she done something wrong? She kept a nice house. She put healthy dinners on the table every night. She tried to keep Drew's home life smooth and trouble free. Had she gained too much weight? She knew she was up ten pounds from when they'd first married, but she tried to eat right and exercise, and she always dressed well. Maybe she should get liposuction or Botox. Pausing by the hall mirror, she frowned at the little lines around her eyes and mouth. Maybe she was starting to look old. She was almost thirty, not the nineteen-year-old girl Drew had fallen in love with. Or maybe it was all in her imagination. Who knew what went on in Drew's mind these days? She certainly didn't.

With a weary shake of her head, she walked up the stairs and checked on her daughters, who were supposed to be reading. Instead they were squabbling over their dollhouse. "Books, girls," she said sharply. She had a rule that the girls practice their reading every day for at least an hour. They both muttered something under their breaths, but the books came out from beneath the bed.

Laura continued down the hall to her bedroom. She'd decorated the room in pretty pastels and floral patterns that were supposed to calm and soothe, but today the flowers only made her feel tense and irritated. Her mother would tell her she had nothing to complain about. She had a husband, a house, children. Those were the things she had been trained to want her entire life, because as her parents had told her on numerous occasions, she hadn't been blessed with an enormously high IQ like her two older sisters. Her father had even joked when he'd sent her off to college that she better come back with her MRS degree. And she had done just that. Sometimes she wondered if she had been so desperate to have a man that she'd rushed Drew down the aisle. Not that she hadn't loved him—she had, and she still did.

But since she'd run into Natalie and Cole at the bookstore yesterday, she'd felt a sense of restlessness and yearning for more. Natalie was a doctor. Cole ran the *San Francisco Tribune*. Drew was working toward becoming partner. Everyone she had known in college was doing something important with their lives. Except for her. Not that being a mother wasn't important. She knew it was. She knew she was good at it, too. Her girls were well behaved, nicely dressed. She volunteered at school and in the community. But was this really all she was meant to do?

In college she hadn't just gotten an MRS degree, she'd also gotten a BA in music. Why hadn't she done anything with that? She'd once wanted to play her flute in a symphony orchestra. Now it was gathering dust somewhere in the depths of her bedroom closet. She couldn't remember the last time she'd played. She couldn't remember the last time she'd gotten excited about something that was only for her and not for her daughters or for her husband.

Seeing Natalie again had brought back memories

and old feelings. Laura had caught a glimpse of the girl she used to be. For that short time in college when she was a member of the Fabulous Four, she'd explored sides of herself she hadn't known existed. Madison, Natalie, and Emily had introduced her to new activities, challenged her, dared her, and supported her in whatever she wanted to do. She'd read books, debated politics and religion, taken art classes, and played her flute in a college orchestra. Those girls had convinced her that she wasn't as dumb as her parents had always led her to believe. Maybe she didn't get straight A's. Maybe she couldn't figure her way out of a math problem, but she could do other things. She was creative and musical. She was more than just her low IQ scores.

She'd thought marrying Drew would free her from her parents' expectations, but she'd only traded their expectations for his. And deep down inside of herself, she had a terrible feeling that she'd married a man just like her father, a person who put more value on material things and accomplishments than on emotional character, kindness, compassion, being a good person.

How had she let that happen?

She knew how. Because her parents had loved Drew from the very beginning. Her father had taken him under his wing, helped him get into the right law school, and offered him a job after graduation. Drew was the son they had always wanted, making up for their disappointing daughter. She'd finally done something right.

But somewhere inside this perfect life she'd created, she'd lost a piece of herself. She'd become a slave to daily rituals, to organized living, to bills and taxes and the same sitcom television shows every night. She'd come to accept scraps of attention from her husband, always hiding her worries and troubles from the other wives with whom she kept company.

Sitting down on the bed, she took care not to disturb the pillows she'd fluffed that morning, then realized the absurdity of it all. She couldn't even let herself be free to smash the pillows on her own bed. In a burst of anger at herself, she trashed her bed, pulling off the quilt, the blankets, the sheets, the pillows, until they were tangled in one big mess. She felt only marginally better.

Walking into the closet, she reached past her clothes and shoes and other belongings, feeling the top shelf with her hand for the familiar shape of a black musical case. She pulled it down, and a flurry of dust made her sneeze. Maybe she wasn't as good a housekeeper as she thought. But inside, the silver flute sparkled with promise. Laura felt a rush of excitement at the sight of her old friend.

She knelt down on the floor of the closet and pulled out the pieces of her flute. She lovingly put it together, taking a moment to stroke her fingers against the smooth, polished metal. Could she still play? Would she sound horrible? Did she even want to try?

Insecurity made her hesitate. Did she really want to know if she could still do this? Wouldn't it be better to just leave her head buried in the sand?

She closed her eyes for a moment and Emily's image came into her head.

"You should play in a band," Emily said, as

Laura put down her flute, the last note still lingering in the air.

"I'm not good enough. And it doesn't pay anything."

"It makes you happy. That's what's important."

"Happy is not what it's about. Success, achievement, that's what's important. Everyone knows that making a living in music is next to impossible."

"Life isn't just about making money. It's about doing something that you love. Don't sell yourself short, Laura. Don't let someone else define who you are. You and I are a lot alike. We've both spent way too much time looking out the window, watching everyone else have fun. It's our turn now. I have my health—finally. And you're away from your parents and all the people who have you convinced that every moment should be spent in the pursuit of future happiness. I say we concentrate on being happy right now and let the future take care of itself. After all, everyone says this is the best time of our lives. Let's make that the truth."

It *had* been the best time of her life, Laura thought, as she opened her eyes and stared at the flute. Maybe she should take Emily's advice and stop worrying so much about the future and concentrate on the now. So what would Emily do? The answer suddenly seemed very clear. She pressed her lips against the mouthpiece and blew. The squeaking sound was terrible in terms of music, but incredibly rewarding. She relaxed and began to play. The notes came out of her head, her heart, her soul. She didn't know how long she'd been playing until she saw two small, very astonished faces peering around the closet door.

"What are you doing, Mommy?" six-year-old
Jennifer asked.

"Can I play?" seven-year-old Suzanne added. "It
sounds so pretty."

"You're really good," Jennifer continued.

Her heart swelled. Her daughters thought her
music sounded pretty and that she was good. She
blinked back a silly tear and laughed. "I think it's
time you two learned how to play."

"Today?" they echoed with excitement.

"Yes, today, but later," she said, making a sudden decision. "First I want you to hear what really
good music sounds like. Go get your shoes and
sweaters. We're going to the park."

"No one is home," Natalie said, as the door to
Laura's house remained closed. "So much for your
surprise-attack strategy." She took a step back to
gaze at the two-story salmon-colored Mediterra-
nean villa, which fit in perfectly with the other well-
built, well-designed homes in this upscale neighborhood thirty minutes south of San Francisco. "Laura
and Drew have certainly done well for themselves."

"It's not bad for a house in the suburbs," Cole
replied. "I prefer the city."

Natalie did, too. Or maybe she was just more
used to an urban environment. The last time she'd
lived in a house like this, actually a more modest
version of a house like this, had been when her
father was alive. After his death, she and her
mother had moved into a series of apartments,
sometimes sharing one with her aunt or some guy
her mother hooked up with.

"Maybe they didn't hear the bell. It's a big

place." Cole pressed down on the bell three times in succession. It was so loud Natalie thought the neighbors could probably hear it.

The door suddenly flew open. She jumped back as Drew appeared in the doorway, looking none too pleased to see them. Dressed in tan slacks and a long-sleeved button-down white shirt, he appeared conservative and businesslike, a far cry from the laughing, flirtatious playboy who'd worn faded blue jeans, tank tops and flip-flops. Aside from the blond hair and the golden tan, that guy had completely disappeared.

"What the hell are you two doing here?" Drew muttered, staring at them for a long moment.

Natalie wasn't sure how to respond. She couldn't really blame Drew for being angry. It had been ten years since they'd seen each other, and now they'd shown up out of the blue. It was no wonder he was taken aback.

"Can we come in?" Cole asked.

Drew stepped back and motioned for them to enter. The inside of the house was just as beautiful as the outside, Natalie thought, noting the polished hardwood floor in the entry, the fine detail work on the staircase banister, the arched doorways leading into the living room and dining room. Drew waved them toward the living room where a grand piano took up one corner. The rest of the room was decorated with antique furniture and carefully chosen vases, lamps, and side tables. Everything matched, right down to the strip of wallpaper that ran along the crown molding and the floral curtains that covered the windows.

"This is beautiful," Natalie murmured. "Is Laura here?"

"She must be here somewhere, although I don't know why she didn't get the damn door." Drew moved toward the entry and yelled up the stairs for Laura, but there was no answer. "I'll be right back."

Natalie sat down on the couch while Cole perused the photographs on the mantel. They could hear Drew yelling for Laura, but she wasn't yelling back. A moment later he reappeared, an irritated look on his face. "I guess she went out with the girls. So, what can I do for you?"

"I ran into Laura yesterday. She didn't tell you?" Natalie asked.

"No, but we've both been moving in opposite directions this weekend. In fact, I have to take off on a business trip shortly." He made a point of checking his watch.

Natalie glanced at Cole, wondering why he wasn't leading the conversation. Hadn't it been his idea to talk to Drew? When the silence between them lengthened, she said, "That's too bad. We thought we could talk about old times. Catch up."

"I usually save those conversations for reunions." Drew frowned. "What are you doing here, Natalie? You took off without saying good-bye to anyone years ago. Why come back now? What do you want?"

"I said good-bye." She was surprised by the animosity in his voice.

"You deserted Laura. She cried for days after you left," Drew continued, a harsh note in his voice. "She doesn't need you in her life now. Maybe she was too polite to tell you that, but—"

"You're not," Cole interjected.

"No, I'm not. Look, Parish, I don't have anything

against you, but I'm busy and I don't have time to rehash the past."

Natalie stared at him for a long minute, trying to read between the lines, but Drew wasn't giving anything away. "I'm sorry we bothered you," she said as she got to her feet.

"Hang on a second, Natalie," Cole said. "I have a couple of questions for you, McKinney."

"About what?"

"My sister's death. It has been brought to my attention recently that Emily's death might not have been an accident."

"Who would suggest that?"

"The author of a best-selling novel. Maybe you've heard of it."

"I've heard of it," Drew admitted with a tightening of his lips.

"Do you remember seeing Emily the night she died?" Cole asked. "Did you talk to her? Share a drink with her?"

"I didn't get her drunk, if that's what you're implying." Drew put his hands on his hips in a stance that was pure aggression.

Cole didn't back down. "Did you talk to her?"

"No, I didn't. It was crowded at the party. There were over a hundred people there. I told the police that when they questioned me along with everyone else who was present that night."

"So you weren't upstairs that night? You didn't hear Emily arguing with Natalie?"

"I didn't hear a thing. I told you—I wasn't upstairs."

"The author thinks Natalie pushed Emily off the roof. Do you?"

Drew shot Natalie a quick look. "Of course not. Emily fell. That's what happened. Although . . . everyone knew Emily and Natalie were fighting over you. There were lots of rumors after you all left town."

"Where were you when she fell?" Cole asked. "If you don't mind."

"I do mind. I answered that question ten years ago. If you don't remember my answer, I'm sure you can put your hands on a police report. Now, if *you* don't mind . . ." Drew walked into the entryway and opened the front door, leaving them no choice but to follow.

"If I find out you're responsible for this book, you will be sorry." Cole paused by the door. "No one messes with my family."

"No one messes with mine, either," Drew snapped back.

Natalie followed Cole onto the porch, wincing as the door slammed behind them. "That went well."

"I think we can add Drew to your growing fan club," Cole said as they walked out to the car.

"I don't remember him disliking me so much."

Cole unlocked the car door and held it open for her. "I found that interesting, too."

Natalie didn't like the sound of that. "Drew made you doubt me again, didn't he? Are you so easily swayed, Cole?"

"I make up my own mind after I look at all the facts."

"Of which there are few," she said, as she slid into the passenger seat. "Maybe we should talk to some of your friends. Emily spent time with Dylan

Somerville. He might know something about what went on that night. And what about Josh?"

Cole didn't answer until he got into the car and closed the door. "I told you before that Josh and I were at Dylan's apartment that night."

"But Dylan wasn't with you." A brief image of Dylan walking down the hall at the sorority house flashed through her mind.

"What are you talking about?"

"I saw Dylan at the house. I just remembered that." She saw the skepticism in his eyes. "I did," she added defensively.

"That's convenient."

"It's probably because we've been spending so much time talking about the past. Things are starting to come back."

"Maybe some other things will come back, like where you were when Emily fell."

"Cole, you already said you didn't think—"

"I don't. Look, Natalie, Dylan and Josh were like brothers to Emily. There is no way in this world they would have hurt her. But I agree with one thing—we should talk to them, especially Dylan, since he lived in Santa Cruz. We'll stop at his club on our way back." He turned the key in the ignition and started the car.

"His club?"

"He runs a nightclub south of Market called Club V. It's a techno-magic club and very popular. I take it you haven't been there."

"No, I haven't. And what's techno-magic?"

"Virtual reality, technological illusions, and other cutting-edge magic tricks. He opened the club last year and has a line out the door most nights."

Dylan had always been into magic, Natalie re-membered. He'd worked as a magician at a night-club in Santa Cruz while they were in college. Emily had gone there a lot; she'd even worked as his assistant on occasion. The two of them had been very close. Personally, Natalie had never warmed to Dylan. He'd always played the man of mystery, riding up to the dorm on a motorcycle, dressed in black leather and dark glasses. She didn't remem-ber him saying much of anything to anyone except Emily. That little fact had driven Madison crazy. Dylan Somerville was probably the only guy who hadn't taken one look at Madison and fallen in love. Which reminded her, they also needed to find Madison.

Madison glanced down at the paper in her hand, which listed the address for Club V. Located in a refurbished warehouse, the club was very unpreten-tious, one of those places that was known by word of mouth rather than by visible advertising. In fact, the only indication that this was in fact Club V was a small bronze sign on a solid black door. Ac-cording to the Club V Web site, the main club was open nightly for drinks, dinner, and shows of magic and illusion, with the virtual reality room also open on weekends beginning at one o'clock. She was a few minutes early, but maybe that would work in her favor. She could catch Dylan before the crowds came.

She put her hand on the door and hesitated, al-ready having second thoughts. Dylan Somerville was one of the few people in her life she had not been able to figure out or control. It was doubtful he'd be receptive to her invitation to perform at the masquerade party and even more doubtful that he'd want to renew their old acquaintance. In fact, it was highly likely he'd blow her off as he'd done before, and she wasn't really in the mood for that.

The sudden wave of insecurity annoyed her. It reminded her of the early days of her childhood, before she'd gotten pretty and grown breasts. In those days, she'd been filled with doubts about herself, a lack of confidence borne from being the illegitimate daughter of an actor who refused to recognize her as his child. One of the many shrinks she had been to, at her mother's insistence, had told her that it was that failed relationship between child and biological father that fueled her need to succeed, to make everyone see that she was someone special, beautiful, and important. When she achieved that goal with a person or a job, she moved on, which was probably why she'd run out on two fiancés, the last one only days before the wedding.

Frowning, she realized that's exactly what she was doing now, trying to impress Dylan Somerville, because, dammit, he'd never seen how great she was. She hated when the shrinks were right. But so what? This wasn't a big deal. There wasn't a woman alive who hadn't at one time felt the need to find the "guy who got away" and show him what he'd missed. And Dylan had missed a lot. She was even better now than she'd been at nineteen. She'd acquired sophistication over the past ten years, not to mention a better understanding of what men wanted. She could get Dylan—if she wanted to. That was still to be determined. He might have grown ugly in the last decade, gained weight, gone bald, sprouted a hairy mole on his face. Any number of things could have happened to him. She wouldn't know what unless she opened the damned door and walked inside.

Squaring her shoulders, she did just that, letting the heavy door swing silently shut behind her. The lobby was small, round, and dimly lit with dark wood paneling, thick black carpet on the floor, red leather benches that wound around the room, and a series of monitors along one wall that flashed with animations. A reception desk sat between two doors but was currently empty. Stepping farther into the room, Madison noted a wall full of newspaper and magazine clippings. Taking a closer look, she saw that Club V had been written up in a number of publications, including several articles in the Parish family newspaper. Trust Cole to take care of his good friend Dylan. She would have expected no less. The men had always been as close as brothers, although Madison had sometimes wondered if Cole had any idea that his best friend had a raging crush on his sister, Emily.

A door opened, and Madison caught her breath, not letting it out until she realized it wasn't Dylan, but a young woman approaching her. Wearing low-rise blue jeans and a clingy tank top, she came across as young and very hip, probably not more than twenty-one years old.

She offered Madison a smile and said, "I didn't realize anyone was out here yet. We don't officially open for a few more minutes, but I can get you set up. What are you looking for today? A trip down Niagara Falls, a walk across a tightwire under the big top, or a lap at the Indy 500? We offer virtual experiences for every fantasy."

"Really?" Madison wondered if she could purchase a fantasy that involved Dylan. She'd certainly had a few ideas over the years.

"Absolutely. What's your pleasure?"

"That's a loaded question."

The woman laughed. "I'm afraid all of our virtual adventures are rated PG-13."

"Actually I just want to speak to Dylan Somerville. Is he here?"

"I'm always here," a man said from behind her.

Madison whirled around, caught off guard by Dylan's unexpected appearance. She'd hoped to see him first, catch him by surprise, instead of the other way around. She should have known it wouldn't be that easy. Well, she wouldn't make it easy for him, either. She flashed him the smile that had won her legions of admirers and deliberately ran her gaze up and down his body.

Dressed in black leather pants and a black turtleneck sweater, Dylan was all male. He was only of average height, but he was well built, broad shoulders, flat stomach, narrow hips, tight ass. And his face, all angles and planes, thick eyebrows and dark eyes, a long nose, full lips, and a sexy stubble darkening his jaw. All that marred his face was his expression, which was exactly the way she remembered it, irritated and grumpy. His mouth had always been set in a perpetual frown, at least when she'd tried to talk to him. The only person who had ever made him smile was Emily.

"What can I do for you?" Dylan asked.

Her jaw dropped at the casual question. He was

acting like he didn't remember her. What the hell was wrong with him? No one forgot her. Ever.

"The question is—what can I do for you?" she replied, gathering herself together. "I've come to offer you a very special opportunity."

"I don't think I'm interested in whatever you're selling," he said briskly.

"You haven't heard what I'm selling."

"I have a pretty good idea." This time he was the one to run his gaze up and down her body. "You haven't changed a bit, Madison."

So he did remember her. She felt a foolish wave of relief, not that she intended to show it. "You haven't, either. You're still in a bad mood."

"So what's this opportunity you're offering?"

"I'd like to hire you to perform some of your magic tricks at a masquerade party benefiting charity. It's a very big deal. Everyone who is anyone in San Francisco will be there. It would be terrific exposure for you."

"I don't need exposure."

"Everyone needs exposure. Trust me. That's what I do for a living."

"You expose people?"

Was that a tiny smile playing around the curve of his mouth? Who could tell? "I'm in public relations," she explained. "I promote people and their businesses. I'm sure your club could use some publicity."

"We do all right."

"Is all right good enough?"

He considered that for a moment, then said, "What do you really want?"

"I just told you—"

"No. You had an agenda when you were nineteen, and I suspect you have one now. There are lots of magicians in this city. Why me?"

"You're cutting-edge, not old-school card tricks. Everyone is buzzing about your club. I think it would be great to bring some of your technological magic to my party," she said, thinking quickly. "It's a benefit for crippled children. Surely, you don't have anything against helping sick kids?"

"Nice try, but I'm not buying it."

"It's the truth. I need something different to set off my event from all the others, and you've always been different—bold, daring." She paused. "I know you never liked me, but surely you can put personal prejudice aside for your business." When he didn't reply, she pressed on. "Why don't you show me around while you're thinking about my invitation? I'd love to see what's behind those doors."

He hesitated, then waved her forward. "All right. After you."

She didn't quite trust his sudden acquiescence, but she decided not to question it. More time with Dylan could only work in her favor. She had to get to know him again, figure out what he wanted, so she could get what she wanted.

"We can start here." Dylan opened one of the doors leading off the reception area and ushered her into a room that looked like something out of a futuristic science-fiction movie. There were computer screens, platforms, and several enclosed booths in the laboratory-like room. "This is our virtual-reality room. You can have any adventure you want."

She sent him a doubtful look. "I've never been big on video games."

"These aren't video games. We've created worlds for you to explore and participate in. You will feel like you're really in the event that's happening, whether it's at King Arthur's court or the White House or the Taj Mahal. We combine video with digital pictures that we've created from history books and old films."

"That sounds like a lot of work."

"I've spent the last ten years creating a digital library that is incomparable."

It sounded like he'd been doing more than pulling rabbits out of hats, she had to admit. Still . . . "I can't imagine being swept away just by looking at a screen," she said. "I could never forget where I was. It must be like watching a movie."

"You'd be surprised. The mind is very powerful, but it can be manipulated with music, images, memories, sounds, and actions."

"So if I stand on that platform, and you rock it, I'm actually going to believe I'm taking off into space?"

"Absolutely," he said with an arrogance that annoyed as well as excited her.

She did love a confident man, especially in bed, but there was a fine line between confidence and arrogance, and she doubted Dylan could walk that line.

"I can probably get you to believe just about anything is real," he added.

"You sound awfully sure of yourself."

"I'm very good."

"Now I remember why I never liked you."

"That's not the way I remember it." His eyes dared her to challenge him on that statement, but unfortunately a vivid and embarrassing memory of throwing herself at him one night still burned bright in her mind.

"I doubt you remember things the way they really were," she said. "Everyone has their own version of the truth." She looked around the room. "So what next?"

"Why don't you try one of our adventures, see if it's something you want to help me promote."

"I'm not sure virtual reality is exactly what would work for our event." She couldn't imagine these contraptions being effective at a masquerade party.

"Then we'll say good-bye." He turned toward the door.

"Wait. I'll give it a try. I'm sure it's fun." And she wasn't ready to walk out of here yet. She needed time to think of just how his technological magic could work at a high-society party. There had to be a way. Maybe she could set up a special-event area . . .

Dylan led her to one of the booths. "Have a seat there. Put on the goggles and headphones and just sit back." He paused, sending her a thoughtful look. "I have a special treat for you."

"What is it?"

"You'll see." He drew the curtain around her, leaving her in darkness. She put on the goggles and was completely blinded. The headphones cut out the noise, and she suddenly felt very isolated and unsteady, as if she couldn't quite find her balance or her bearings.

She was startled when music came blaring through the headphones. She was even more surprised to hear Gloria Gaynor singing "I Will Survive," one of their favorite songs in college. Emily had played it every time one of them had had a bad date or a boyfriend fell through. They must have played it a hundred times. Emily had been one of those girls who loved to play a favorite song over and over again until you wanted to pull your hair out. Whenever they'd complained, Emily had laughed and said she was building memories. She'd told them that someday, thirty years from now, they'd be driving along in a car, maybe with their kids, and the song would come on the radio, and they'd remember the good old days, their friendship, and they'd smile.

Madison didn't feel like smiling. She felt like crying, and she never cried. But, dammit, why hadn't Emily lived another ten or thirty years? Why hadn't she had the opportunity to hear those old songs and remember the good old days?

The screens in front of her eyes suddenly lit up. She jerked at the familiar sight of the two-story sorority house in Santa Cruz where they'd pledged and lived—and where Emily had died. Was her mind playing tricks on her? What was this?

She wanted to look away, but she couldn't.

The front door to the sorority house opened, and a group of girls came out—girls who looked a lot like Laura, Natalie, and Emily. It was them, she realized, dressed in fashions at least ten years old.

Where was she? Why wasn't she with them? Her heart stopped as Emily came forward—Emily with the laughing dark eyes, the brown hair blowing in the breeze, the infectious smile on her lips that had always made Madison want to smile, too—an Emily who was still alive, still happy, still filled with hope for their futures.

She was so close, Madison wanted to reach out and touch her, grab her hand and hold on for dear life.

Emily suddenly wagged a finger at her. "You are so bad. Stop it right now."

Madison gasped. Was Emily talking to her? God! She couldn't take it. Yanking off the headphones and goggles, she burst out of the booth to find Dylan waiting for her with a cool, calculating smile.

"What the hell was that?" she demanded, shaken to the core.

"That was Emily. Isn't that why you came here, Madison? To talk about Emily?"

Madison stared at Dylan in bewilderment. She saw anger in his eyes and a gleam of satisfaction. He'd wanted to knock her off her feet, and he'd done a damn good job of it. "Where did you get that film?"

"I took it—a long time ago."

"I don't remember you filming us."

"You weren't there that day."

That's why she hadn't been in the clip, just the other three girls. Which meant Emily had not been talking to her; she'd been talking to Dylan, telling him to stop taking her picture. That made sense. What didn't make sense was why Dylan would still have that film clip or be using it in some virtual-reality game. "You use Emily's picture, her voice, her words in your games? How can you do that? You were her friend. Are you completely sick?"

His dark eyes flared with anger. "I don't use that

clip in the games. I just have it on my computer along with every other piece of film I've ever shot. I thought you might enjoy seeing your old friends, take a trip to the past."

She didn't believe him for a second. "You didn't think that at all. You wanted to shock me. Why?"

"Because you came here acting like the spoiled brat you always were. You left, Madison. Before the funeral. And now you come back like nothing ever happened. Like we're just two people who knew each other once. I think you're the one who's sick."

So he resented her leaving before Emily's funeral. At least she had one of the answers she had come for. If Dylan felt this way, Cole probably did, too, as well as his parents. She wanted to turn and run out the door and forget this stupid idea, but something inside her decided to fight back. "That was my parents' decision, not mine. They came and got me and took me straight to the airport. I was nineteen years old. I had no money of my own. What was I supposed to do? I didn't have a choice, Dylan. You can believe it or not. I don't really give a damn."

"And you didn't come here today to talk about Emily? About the book that's been written about her?"

"You know about that?" She shot him a questioning look, although she wasn't completely surprised. Despite his bad-boy aura, the motorcycle, and the dark magic, Dylan had always been into books. Reading was something he and Emily had in common. They were always passing books back and forth to each other. Madison had never paid much attention. She'd been more interested in fashion and entertainment magazines.

"Of course I know about the book." Dylan crossed his arms, leaning back against a console. "Do you know who wrote it?"

"That's a good question," a woman said from behind her.

Madison's breath stalled in her chest at the sound of that familiar voice. *Natalie!* Was her mind playing tricks on her again, or was Natalie really here? Madison wished now that she had left when she had the chance. She'd imagined seeing Natalie a million times in her mind but not like this, never like this.

Chapter 6

Natalie held her breath, waiting for Madison's answer. The last person she'd expected to find in Dylan's club was Madison. Her mind raced with a million questions. Were Dylan and Madison together now? Was Madison the one who had given Garrett Malone the personal information used in the book?

Madison slowly turned around. She was stunning, Natalie thought. Madison's beautiful face was picture perfect, her blue eyes framed by long, dark lashes and sculpted eyebrows. Her cheeks were tinged with pink, her lips a daring cherry red.

"Well, isn't this a surprise?" Madison drawled.

"You can say that again," Cole muttered. "What the hell is going on here, Dylan? You and Madison?"

Dylan threw up his hands. "Hey, she showed up fifteen minutes ago out of the blue. And I'd like to ask you the same question. You and Natalie?"

"I was wondering about that, too," Madison said.

"We're together because of the book, as apparently the two of you are," Natalie replied, not wanting to get into any long explanations. "Do either of you know who the author is or how he got the information about us?"

"I'm surprised you'd even ask me that," Madison said. "Do you seriously think that if I had created this story, I would have made you the villain, Natalie? Please, you wouldn't have had the gumption to push a cat off that roof much less your best friend. You hated to see anyone in pain."

Natalie felt a wave of relief at her words. "Thank God someone believes that." She glanced at Dylan and saw only anger in his eyes. Apparently, he didn't feel the same way. "Do you have something to say?"

He shrugged. "She knew you better than I did."

"Yes, she did."

As Natalie finished speaking, the outer door opened and three teenagers entered. A club employee followed them, helping them to choose their virtual-reality adventures. Dylan waved his hand toward the door, muttering, "Let's take this somewhere else."

That somewhere else was his office, a small cluttered room filled with one desk, two chairs, several filing cabinets, piles of papers everywhere and assorted odd items that Natalie hoped were being used in his magic acts. Otherwise, Dylan had a very kinky side to him. Heck, maybe he did have a kinky side. He'd always been into odd, dark stuff. Natalie had certainly never known what to talk to him about. She'd yet to meet a man who'd made her feel as uncomfortable and awkward as Dylan had. But Emily and Dylan had been very close. He must have been devastated by her death.

Madison picked up a long, twelve-inch feather

and held it up. "What's this for? And can I be your assistant when you use it?"

Dylan shot Madison an irritated look, grabbed the feather from her hand, and tossed it onto a pile of hats. For a long minute the four of them simply stared at each other. Natalie didn't know where to start. No one else seemed to know, either. She barely knew Dylan. Cole barely knew Madison. There was no place to begin the conversation. Fortunately, one of the employees came looking for Dylan to solve a problem in the virtual-reality room. Dylan took off with a muttered, insincere apology, and Cole quickly followed, claiming he had something to take care of. Natalie suspected he just wanted to get away from them and talk to Dylan on his own. Which was fine with her.

Pushing a stack of computer disks to one side of Dylan's desk, Natalie leaned against it, crossing her arms as she took another long look at Madison. "So, where have you been all these years, Maddie? I thought of you in Paris, London, Madrid . . . but I have to admit I never thought of you here in San Francisco, with Dylan of all people."

Madison smiled and flipped her hair over her shoulder as she'd done a thousand times before. "I could say the same about you—and Cole. But as for me, I've been here, there, and everywhere, most recently New York. I moved here three months ago because of my job in public relations."

Natalie nodded, not surprised to find out Madison was in PR. She'd always been a good promoter, and she could spin with the best of them.

"Your turn," Madison said. "Wait." She held up a hand. "Let me guess. You're a doctor. You came to San Francisco because you fell in love with the city years ago and because Cole is here."

"Half-right. I am a doctor, but I didn't come here for Cole. And we're not together in any emotional sense of the word." Natalie sighed. "It's all about this damn book. It's been a crazy few days, Madison. Every time I turn around, I see someone I haven't seen in years. And we all want to know the same thing—who is Garrett Malone and how does he know us?"

"Maybe Laura knows."

"I've already spoken to her, and she doesn't. She married Drew McKinney, by the way. Can you believe that?"

Madison raised an eyebrow. "Laura and Drew ended up together? She must have gotten a lot better in bed."

Natalie shook her head in amazement. Madison was as outspoken as ever. "I can't believe you just said that."

"Oh, come on, Natalie. Drew was a player. And Laura was scared of sex. She had to drink three vodka tonics before she let Drew take off her top."

"That was a long time ago. We were all finding our way back then."

"True." Madison walked over to the bookcase. She picked up a photograph of Dylan, barechested, in black leather pants, holding a whip and standing next to an awesome-looking tiger. "Now, this is a man." She blew out a breath. "Too bad he hates me. I left before Em's funeral. I let her down. That's what Dylan thinks." She glanced at Natalie. "Do you feel the same way?"

Despite her light tone, Natalie had a feeling her

answer mattered to Madison. "We all did what we had to do. I transferred to another school. Laura made new friends and stuck it out in Santa Cruz. It doesn't matter now anyway. We've all moved on."

"Yet here we are together. What goes around comes around."

"Because of Emily. She's not even here anymore, and she's bringing us all together, the way she always did. I can almost feel her presence in this room. It's weird."

"Not so weird," Madison said. "Before you came I was trying out one of Dylan's virtual-reality games, and he decided to play a video for me of Emily, you, and Laura. Emily walked right up to the camera and started talking. For a moment I thought she was speaking to me. It was strange and very creepy. I'm sure Dylan played it just to shock me."

Natalie frowned at that piece of information. "Why would Dylan have a videotape of Em here at the club?"

"He said he built a video library of every piece of film he's ever shot, including photos and movies he took in Santa Cruz. He uses them in his virtual-reality games. It's obvious he's still hung up on Emily."

"Hung up on her? I thought they were just friends." She didn't like the knowing smile that crossed Madison's lips. "Weren't they just friends?"

"You spent way too much time studying, Natalie."

"Dylan and Emily? You can't be serious."

"Why not? Emily wasn't a saint. She was a normal college girl who wanted to experience life in all sorts of ways."

Natalie stared at Madison in confusion, not sure what point she was making. "Are you talking about sex?"

"Of course I'm talking about sex," she said in exasperation. "Emily really didn't tell you? That does surprise me. I thought you two were really tight."

"Tell me what? I thought she was still a virgin. Are you saying that she was having sex with Dylan?" Natalie racked her brain trying to remember if Emily had said anything about Dylan in the days before she died, but it struck her now that in those few weeks before Emily's death, they hadn't shared much. There had been a distance between them, a distance created by Natalie's relationship with Cole.

"I can't say," Madison replied.

"Can't or won't?"

"Look, Emily's secrets should have died with her."

"But they didn't. And if you know something . . ."

"The only thing I know for sure is that we all had secrets."

"We didn't. We talked all the time."

"Not always about the important things. For instance, I never knew if you slept with Cole. Did you?"

Natalie was taken aback by Madison's question. It took her a moment to realize that was the intent. "Oh, no you don't. You don't get to change the subject that easily. We're discussing Emily's sex life, not mine." Natalie watched as Madison took a cigarette out of a sleek silver container and lit it. "You're still smoking? That thing will kill you."

"I've never been able to quit."

"You should try harder."

"Why do you care?" Madison asked, a curious expression on her face.

Why did she care? She hadn't seen Madison in a decade. But old habits died hard. At one time in her life Natalie had cared very much about this woman. And despite Madison's hard edge, she'd always needed someone to care. Emily had seen that need first; she'd seen all their needs first. Emily had told Natalie that Madison took their friendship more seriously than anyone, she just couldn't admit it. Had Emily been right? Or was that just her idealistic view of their relationship?

"Oh, fine," Madison said, stubbing out her cigarette on a nearby ashtray. "It's out. Are you happy now?"

"Yes. Now about Emily," Natalie continued.

"I can't say, Natalie. Can't, not won't. I know there was someone in Emily's life, someone for whom we bought condoms one day."

"You bought condoms with Emily?"

"She was too embarrassed to do it by herself."

"And you didn't ask her why she needed them?"

"I knew why she needed them. She was going to have sex. I had my suspicions about who that someone was, but no real proof."

"I can't believe Emily wouldn't have told me she was planning to have sex. I thought we were so close."

"She knew I wouldn't judge her."

"And I would?" Natalie pressed a hand to her head, feeling the beginning of a bad headache.

"Of course you would. You were always trying to protect her."

"I did a terrible job in the end."

"Emily made her own choices."

"Not the choice to fall off the roof. That was a tragic accident."

"Probably."

Natalie didn't like the doubt in her answer. "Probably? You just said you didn't think I had anything to do with it."

"I didn't say it wasn't someone else. I always thought it was a bit odd for her to just fall like that." Madison glanced down at her watch. "Damn, I have to go. I have an appointment." She turned to leave, then paused. "You should watch your back, Natalie. Someone doesn't like you, and that some-one went to a lot of trouble to make you look bad. Who knows what else they have in mind?"

"Natalie Bishop? Are you out of your fucking mind?" Dylan asked, as he handed Cole a beer from behind the bar. After fixing the technical glitch in the virtual-reality room, Dylan and Cole had moved into the main nightclub, which was cur-rently empty.

"Probably." Cole took a sip of his beer. "How-ever, Natalie is involved in all this, and I can't let her go until I get to the bottom of it." He didn't like the knowing glint in Dylan's eyes. "What? You think I still like her?"

"She's the only woman who ever got under your skin."

"That's not true." But as Cole took another swig

of his beer, he silently admitted that he couldn't think of another woman who'd made him so crazy and so happy at the same time.

"Maybe you don't want to let go of her now that you've found her again," Dylan suggested, a speculative gleam in his eyes.

"It's just about the book. That's the only reason we're together. She knows more than I do about what went down that night."

"I thought she couldn't remember anything. Has that changed?"

"No, but she knows what happened the day before and the day before that. I have to start somewhere."

"I wouldn't trust a word she says. You should stay away from her. She's bad news."

"You think Natalie had something to do with Em's death?" He couldn't bring himself to say the word murder. "Why?"

"She used Emily to get to you, and when that didn't work, she got pissed off."

"Why would you think she was using Emily to get to me?" Cole asked, confused. "They were friends before I came along."

"Emily told me that she wished the two of you had never hooked up. She was caught in the middle, torn between the two of you."

Cole felt his stomach turn over. "You never said that before, and Emily never told me that."

"I didn't say anything because you were already beating yourself up about not getting to the party earlier. And Em probably didn't want to hurt your feelings."

Cole had never really considered Emily's thoughts about his relationship with Natalie. He realized now that they'd never talked much about it. In the three months before Emily's death, he'd been splitting time between San Francisco, where he was supposed to be working for the family paper, Washington D.C., where he'd actually been hustling a news connection that would land him a job with CNN overseas, and lastly Santa Cruz. When he was in Santa Cruz, he'd spent all his time with Natalie. Conversations with Emily had been sparse and never touched beyond the surface. She'd seemed happy enough, and he hadn't pressed for any more information than what came with her smile. Now he wished he'd done more talking. Actually, he wished he'd done more listening.

"I never meant to put Emily in the middle," he muttered.

"She wasn't mad at you," Dylan said. "She was angry with Natalie. She wanted her to let go and move on. You'd made it clear to Natalie it was over. She was the one who wouldn't take no for an answer—from either of you. She kept pushing Emily to intervene. Who knows what she would have done in desperation?"

Cole couldn't quite see the picture Dylan was painting, maybe because he knew the other side of the story. He hadn't made it clear to Natalie that it was over. He'd been vague, stalling, not sure what he wanted to happen. She'd overwhelmed him with feelings he hadn't wanted to feel. He'd had plans to travel, to work abroad. Falling in love had not been part of those plans.

"Putting aside Natalie and Emily," Cole said, trying to refocus his thoughts, "what's your take on this book?"

Dylan shrugged. "Someone wants revenge."

"At Emily's expense. It's not just Natalie's reputation that's going to take a hit. Emily's life has been put under the microscope. Words and thoughts that might not even be hers are portrayed as utter truths. I don't care how the names have been changed. We know, and soon a lot of people will know, that the character in that book is Emily. My parents are going to go crazy when they find out about this. It will destroy them."

"They're still in Europe, aren't they? When do they get back?"

"Wednesday. I have three days to come up with some hard answers. Do you have any ideas? You were in Santa Cruz with the girls. Who knew all this stuff about them? Was there someone Emily confided in outside of Natalie, Laura, and Madison? What about Drew McKinney?"

Dylan's mouth tightened at the mention of Drew's name. "That guy was a first-class asshole."

Cole didn't disagree, but he had to ask, "Was that your opinion or Emily's?"

Dylan sighed. "Emily liked everyone. She wasn't a good judge of character. She was easily taken in. I tried to look out for her, but I wasn't around twenty-four/seven."

"So she might have confided in Drew, maybe even talked to him the night of the party? Because I just saw him, and he was definitely hiding something. He also doesn't like Natalie. He was in the right place at the right time back then. He now has the means and the motive. Except that Laura's reputation is also on the line, and she's his wife, so why would he help someone write a book about a girl he knew ten years ago?"

"I wouldn't put anything past him. For that matter, I wouldn't put anything past Madison. She always had an agenda." Dylan paused. "There's something else you should think about. If Emily was pushed, then maybe this book is a way to get justice for Em. Wouldn't you want whoever killed Emily to pay?"

Cole stared into the eyes of one of his oldest friends and wondered why Dylan's words made him feel so uneasy. Did Dylan know something? But if he did, wouldn't he say? Wouldn't he have said a long time ago? He was practically a member of the Parish family. No, he didn't know anything. He was just guessing, like the rest of them. "This isn't the way to get justice," Cole said finally. "If someone had hard factual information, they could have contacted me or my parents or the police. They could have come forward in a less public, less sensationalized manner."

"Obviously, the writer didn't have hard facts."

"Emily would hate this," Cole murmured. He was surprised to see a smile play in Dylan's eyes. "You don't agree?" he asked sharply. "You don't think this would upset her, to know that someone has invaded her privacy, put words into her mouth, feelings into her heart, made her look like a victim?" His blood boiled at the unfairness of it all, and he silently dared Dylan to disagree with him. He was itching to fight someone, and right now his old friend was looking like a pretty good target.

"I agree with you," Dylan said hastily, the smile disappearing as quickly as it had come. "Relax, dude."

"I can't relax. Not until I know who's behind this."

"We'll find out," Dylan promised. "In the meantime, if you're going to hang out with Natalie, stay away from high places."

"That isn't funny," Cole snapped.

"It wasn't meant to be. Now, I've got to get back to work."

Cole sat at the bar for several minutes after Dylan left, feeling frustrated and pissed off. He'd come to Dylan for answers and had ended up with more questions. Why wasn't Dylan more upset by the book? What the hell was wrong with the guy? Was there something he wasn't telling? Dylan had always had a sarcastic and macabre sense of humor. It was what made him a good magician. Unfortunately, at the moment it didn't make him a particularly good friend.

Natalie was waiting by his car when Cole came out of the club. He wasn't sure if he was relieved or disappointed that she'd waited for him.

"I would have left, but you're my ride," she said.

"Where's Madison?"

"She had somewhere to go. What did you and Dylan talk about?"

He tipped his head to the car. "Why don't we do this over lunch? I'm starving."

Natalie hesitated, then said, "All right. Let's go somewhere with an outside patio. It's a beautiful day, and I could use the air."

"I know just the place."

Rosie's Cantina was located on Pier 24 along the Embarcadero. It was a lively Mexican restaurant with salsa dancing and fire-eating performers in the evenings. Per Natalie's request, they opted for a table on the deck overlooking the bay. Natalie ordered a soda, and Cole chose a beer. The waiter set down chips and salsa and they both dove in. It was easier to eat than to talk. For the first time since they'd reunited on Friday, they were not chasing someone or something; they were just sitting together, sharing a meal.

It reminded him of the old days when having dinner with Natalie had been the high point of his day. She'd challenged him so much with her sharp mind, her astute comments, her insight into what made him tick. In the beginning it had been incredibly attractive. In the end it had terrified him that he'd let this one woman get so deep into his heart and into his head.

"This salsa is fantastic." Natalie gave him a satisfied smile that took his breath away. He remembered that smile, that look on her face, and it hadn't come from food—it had come from him. For some reason the fact that she was now so easily pleased by salsa and chips irritated him. "You should try some," she added. "Oh, wait, I forgot, you don't like it hot and spicy, do you?"

To prove her wrong, he picked up a chip, soaked it in salsa and popped it into his mouth. It burned a fiery hole down to his stomach. He coughed and reached for his beer, draining it in one long swallow. "Damn. That's hot."

"You never could resist a dare," Natalie said with a laugh.

"Neither could you," he retorted, when he got his breath back.

"I've changed. Apparently, you haven't." She smiled as he coughed again, and her eyes sparkled with amusement, transforming her into the beautiful girl he remembered. Her cheeks had reddened, and her mouth, her hot, sexy mouth was so full, so inviting . . . He really needed to stop looking at her lips before he did something stupid.

"Tell me about your life," he said hastily. "I know you work a lot. Do you have a boyfriend? A significant other? A cat?"

"If I had a boyfriend, I wouldn't put him in the same category as a cat. However, as a matter of fact, I don't have either, but I want you to know that I have had boyfriends. You were not the only one." She waved a chip at him and said, "I got over you a long time ago. There have been dozens since you."

"Dozens, huh?" he asked with a small grin.

She tipped her head. "Maybe not literally dozens, but plenty. What about you? Why did your girlfriend throw a stapler at your head?"

"Apparently she was breaking up with me, and I wasn't paying attention. CNN was running a clip about a bombing in Lebanon."

"Oh." She nodded with understanding. "You're still a news junkie."

"It's what I do. Gisela didn't understand that. And she didn't care about the news."

"Gisela? As in Gisela the lingerie model?"

"One and the same."

"How surprising that you wouldn't have anything in common with a lingerie model," Natalie said.

"Although I don't imagine that scintillating conversation was a requirement."

Cole could hardly argue with that. He sat back in his chair, watching as Natalie scooped salsa onto another chip and popped it into her mouth. He was enjoying her company, he realized—probably too much. He itched to run his fingers through those fiery red waves, pull her face to his, plant a kiss on those sexy pink lips. His body tightened uncomfortably as his thoughts took him into dangerous territory. They weren't college kids anymore. He wasn't foolish or reckless enough to rekindle a romance with this woman. His parents hated Natalie. And he was supposed to hate her, too. He'd certainly given it a good shot, especially those first few years when he'd reminded himself that Natalie had let Emily down. She'd gotten his little sister drunk and let her pay the consequences. It was Natalie's fault that Emily was dead.

Now the words sounded hollow, and memories of his own not-so-perfect behavior flashed through his brain. Hadn't he been just as much to blame? Hadn't he ignored Emily? Hadn't he made bad choices, too?

It had been a lot easier to hate Natalie when she was a distant memory. Today he was having a hard time drumming up any dislike. He thought about all she'd accomplished in her life. She was a doctor. She'd put herself through years of school without help from anyone. He couldn't help thinking there were more things to admire about her than to hate.

Maybe he was being sucked in by her beauty, her smile, her blue-blue eyes that made him want to keep looking at her. Maybe it was the tiny freckles that dusted her nose, her soft skin, her beautiful breasts that even now brought his gaze down to her chest.

"Stop looking at me," she told him. "It makes me uncomfortable."

"It makes me uncomfortable, too." He saw by the flare in her eyes that she understood his meaning.

"Let's talk about something else," she suggested.

"Like what?" He leaned forward, resting his elbows on the table. "What's on your mind?"

"Tell me about your job. I know you run the paper with your dad. Did you ever do the foreign correspondent thing you talked so much about?"

He stiffened. "I couldn't do that after Emily died."

"Why not?"

"My mother fell apart. She had a nervous breakdown. She couldn't get out of bed for about a year. My father had to spend all his time with her. There was no question that I would go to work at the paper, try to hold it together. My uncle is a business guy, not a news guy, and my other cousins are all younger than I am. I was the only one who could keep things afloat. So I gave up my plans and devoted myself to the paper."

"I'm sorry. I had no idea." She paused. "Why didn't you go later, when your parents were feeling better?"

It was a good question. He didn't have a good answer. "It was never the right time. There was always too much to do here at home."

"Do you have regrets?"

"I don't want to talk about it."

"It's not too late—"

"It is too late. Some things aren't meant to happen."

"They can't happen if you don't try."

"I still have a duty to my family. Yes, things are better now, but I'm all they have left. I can't take off across the world, put myself in danger. My mother would go crazy worrying about me. Every time I see her she tells me how lucky she is that she still has me. She can't lose a son as well as a daughter. It would kill her. I'm stuck where I am."

"You're not stuck. You have choices."

"Look, it's different for you. You don't have anyone else to answer to."

"You're right." She leaned forward, her eyes dark with passion and purpose. "I don't have a crutch, Cole. I can't use my family as an excuse not to do what I want to do. I have only myself to blame for my failures and for my successes. There's no one else but me. I'm alone."

"I'm not using my family as an excuse or a crutch."

"I hope that's true, because Emily wouldn't have wanted you to give up your dreams because of her. She loved you too much. And she was a big believer in experiencing life to the fullest. She made me try things I never would have considered doing. She had a tremendous curiosity and joy for life. Emily made me believe that the world is a beautiful place and looking ahead is much better than looking backwards."

His gut twisted at her words. She was right. Emily would have told him to move on. She probably would have told him that years ago. She'd spent most of her life encouraging him in his adventures. And when he'd come home from those adventures, she'd always been waiting to hear every last detail. The only adventure Emily had ever embarked on was her trip to college. He wished now he'd been around to hear more of those details. He was beginning to think he hadn't known his sister as well as he'd thought, and he felt bad about that.

"It's complicated," he said, realizing Natalie was still waiting for an answer. "I don't want to get into it right now."

"Fine. Then tell me what you and Dylan discussed at the club." She paused, her expression turning more somber as her thoughts focused on the problem at hand. "He doesn't think that I—"

"He wouldn't put it past you." Cole saw the hurt in her eyes and wondered why the men in Natalie's past didn't seem to like her anymore. Maybe they never had. He hadn't paid attention back then to what anyone else thought. "How well did you ever know Dylan?"

"Not well. He came to see Emily all the time. They were very close. She used to help him in his magic act sometimes when he worked nightclubs."

"She did?" He knew the kinds of clubs Dylan had worked while in college, and they certainly wouldn't have been places he'd have taken Emily. And why hadn't Dylan ever told him? "What the hell was he thinking?" he muttered.

"Emily enjoyed it," Natalie said. "She loved magic. I couldn't talk her out of the idea that there was something mystical going on in the universe. Believe me, I tried. Actually, it was nice to live with such a positive person. Every breath she took made her happy."

He sent Natalie a long, searching look, hoping to see the truth in her eyes. "So she was happy, right up until the end?" He needed to hear her say it. He needed to believe that Emily hadn't died hating him.

Natalie hesitated a moment too long. "I'm not sure, Cole. I thought she was, but Madison said that I wasn't paying attention, that Emily had things going on in her life that I didn't know about."

"What kinds of things?"

"Apparently, she was thinking about having sex, or maybe she was having sex, but she never told me." Natalie drew in a breath as she ran her finger around an imaginary circle on the tablecloth. When she looked at Cole, there was guilt in her eyes. "I never told her what you and I did, either. I guess there were some things we didn't share with each other."

Cole's chest tightened at the memory of just what he and Natalie had done together. He was glad she hadn't told, ridiculously pleased that it was just between the two of them.

"Madison doesn't know who's behind the book," Natalie continued. "We're striking out, Cole, everywhere we turn. No one who was there claims to know anything."

"Someone is not telling the truth. It has to be Madison, Laura, or maybe Drew. There's too much information in the book for it to be some random person."

"I've been thinking about that. There were other people around, sorority girls who could have described the initiation ceremony. We also had a housemother, Connie Richmond, who knew about some of the incidents. And Diane Thomas, who was our sorority adviser, acted like a confidante for the pledges. Emily talked to her all the time. We were encouraged to go to either Connie or Diane with our problems. Then there were the guys who lived next door to us at Paloma Gardens, Eric and Anthony. They used to hang out in our room late at night. They heard us bitch about all kinds of things. Drew was around. Dylan and Emily were close. And there was Jessica Holbrook, Em's big sister in the sorority house. I'm sure Emily talked to her about things. The list goes on and on. Any good researcher could probably have put the book together just by talking to a lot of people."

"But not without talking to the most important people," he argued. "Maybe not you, because you're the target, but why wouldn't Malone have talked to me or Madison or Laura or Dylan or Josh? Why leave out the core group?"

"He must have known you wouldn't be happy about the book, about seeing Emily's life sensationalized. The others—I don't know."

"I still think we can narrow down the list to people who didn't like you, and I don't think we should discount Madison or Laura. Maybe you did something to offend one of them. This type of revenge is very female."

Natalie straightened in her chair. "I resent that for a number of reasons."

"Resent it all you want. The way I see it, we

have at least four suspects, probably more based on the list you just gave me." Cole wanted to discount Dylan out of hand, but he had to admit he'd been surprised by Dylan's animosity toward Natalie. He'd also been taken aback by Dylan's reaction to the book, actually suggesting that it wasn't such a bad thing.

"We aren't any closer to the truth than we were yesterday," Natalie said with a sigh.

"I wouldn't say that. We've talked to everyone. Now we just have to figure out who's lying."

"You make it sound like that will be easy. I guess I shouldn't be surprised. You were always good at getting what you wanted," she muttered.

"So were you."

She sent him a regretful smile. "Except you. I never got you."

Little did she know that she'd come closer than any other woman.

Chapter 7

Finding Malone didn't seem nearly as pressing after Natalie had finished off a chicken burrito. She hadn't felt so stuffed or satisfied in a long time. They'd tabled all discussions of the past when their food had arrived, turning their conversation to more neutral topics: Natalie's residency, Cole's work at the paper, movies, and politics. Cole had always been well read. He knew everything that was going on in the world, and Natalie loved hearing his opinions. She'd known smarter men in her life, brilliant doctors who could discuss the cellular structure of the human brain, but Cole knew the interesting stuff. She hadn't read much besides textbooks and medical journals the past few years. While she hadn't been lying about having had a few boyfriends, dozens was a vast overstatement for the two rather disappointing relationships she'd made her way through in the last decade. It hadn't been just work that had gotten in the way; it had been Cole, memories of how great love could be.

As she listened to him now, relating a story about a thief who got caught with his pants down, she couldn't help thinking fondly of how many times he'd made her laugh. Despite his intense drive to succeed, Cole had always had a fun side, a way of making her relax, forcing her to let go of the little worries that drove her crazy. Cole had understood her like no one else had. He'd respected her ambition to be a doctor, her need to achieve and make something of her life, because it was a need he shared, too.

Unfortunately, their ambitions had begun to collide even before Emily's death. With ten years of distance and clarity, Natalie saw now that Cole had begun to think their love was an obstacle to what he wanted. As single-minded as he was, he couldn't believe that they could make it work. At least, that's what she thought. She didn't really know for sure exactly what had gone wrong. There had been no real "break-up" conversation where accusations or complaints had been hurled, where they'd cleared the air. Instead, their relationship had soured slowly like a carton of milk sitting out too long, until Emily's tragic death had tipped that carton of milk over. Then the accusations flung had been all about Emily and not about each other.

"You're not listening," Cole said.

"Sorry," she said, wondering what she had missed. "I was daydreaming."

"About anything interesting?"

For a split second she thought about asking him why it had all gone wrong. Then the waiter brought their check and began clearing their plates, and the opportunity was lost. It was better that way. They had to solve the Emily problem before they could do anything else. Not that she wanted to do anything else, she told herself hastily. She just wished

Cole had grown some warts or gotten fat or started losing his hair instead of turning into one of the most attractive men she knew. She got some money out of her purse to pay her share of the bill, but Cole insisted on taking care of it.

After the waiter had brought Cole's change, they walked out to the front of the restaurant. She was turning toward the car when Cole's hand grabbed hers. His touch was warm, insistent, and oh so familiar. She tensed as he said, "Wait."

"What's wrong? Did you forget something?" she asked, pulling her hand away from his.

His eyes narrowed as she dug her hands into her pockets, but he didn't comment. Instead, he said, "Let's take a walk. I need to work off that burrito."

And she could use some cool air blowing in her face before she sat down next to Cole in the quiet intimacy of his car. It was ridiculous to be so affected by a casual touch, to be so aware of a man's sexuality. She'd seen hundreds of naked men in her work as a doctor and not been remotely interested, but this man got to her and he wasn't even trying. She really needed to get out more.

They strolled along the Embarcadero, which was filled with tourists and locals enjoying the unseasonably warm October weather. The scents of flowers and fresh fruit wafted through the breeze as they passed by an open air market in front of one of the docks. It would be winter soon, but now there was nothing but sun and a cool, refreshing wind coming off the water.

She did love this city. Like the song, she'd left her heart in San Francisco a long time ago. That's

why she'd come back. She'd lied when she'd told
Cole it was because of the opportunity to work at
St. Timothy's. She'd actually had better offers from
a medical point of view, but the chance to live and
work in San Francisco had been too tantalizing to
resist. Maybe she couldn't share her life with Cole,
but she could at least share his city.

They paused a few moments later to look at two
sailboats racing across the water. "That's the life,"
Cole said.

"Do you sail?"

"I've been out a few times on the bay. My uncle
has a yacht."

Of course his uncle had a yacht, another re-
minder that they never had moved and never would
move in the same circles. Not that Cole was a snob.
She couldn't put that black mark against him. Arrogant, overconfident, possessive, bossy, impatient,
yes, but a snob, no.

"What about you?" he asked. "What do you do
in your free time? I know you don't have much,
but you must have some."

"I run every day if I can, or I try to get to the
gym."

"What about the movies?" he asked with a smile.

He'd remembered her fondness for old movies
and foreign films. For some reason that really
touched her, and she couldn't help smiling back at
him. "I went to an Italian film festival last weekend,
all subtitles and very romantic. You would have
hated it."

"I'm sure I would have. Now give me a *Star Wars*
marathon, and I'm there."

"You always did prefer action and adventure."

"I always did," he muttered, as he started walking again.

They were almost to the Bay Bridge when he stopped and pointed upward. "Do you realize this is the second bridge we've stood under today?"

She looked up at the gray steel structure, which wasn't nearly as pretty as the Golden Gate. In fact, there were scaffolding and drapes along one side of it, part of an ongoing earthquake retrofit program.

"Maybe it's a sign," she murmured. "A bridge between the past and the present."

"That one just goes to Oakland."

"You know what I mean." Her hair blew across her face as the wind decided to play. So did Cole. He pulled several strands away from her mouth, which wouldn't have been so bad if he hadn't stopped to take a good long look at her lips. She swallowed at the intent in his eyes. "Cole, you don't want to do what you're thinking—"

"I don't think I can stop myself."

"You should try."

"You're not moving away." His eyes met hers. "And you probably should."

"I'm stuck."

"You have choices," he said, repeating her earlier words. "The right ones aren't so easy to make, are they?"

He didn't give her time to answer, his mouth fitting hers perfectly, his kiss insistent, determined, passionate, everything that was Cole. His hand cupped the back of her head, drawing her into the heat of his mouth. She put her hands against his chest to push him away, but instead her fingers curled into the fabric of his shirt. She could feel the muscles of his chest bunching beneath her hand. He was so solid, strong, powerful. She was losing herself in him, and she wasn't even fighting. She should be fighting. But he tasted so good, like the past, like the best days of her life, like everything she'd ever wanted. When he finally lifted his head, she felt breathless, dizzy, heady with the taste of him still lingering on her lips.

His dark eyes glittered with desire when he looked at her. *He still wanted her.*

Did she still want him? She was terribly afraid the answer was yes.

But he couldn't erase all the bad stuff with a kiss, could he? Was she that weak? "You shouldn't have done that," she said, finally taking a step back. "We were over a long time ago."

"That's what I thought, too."

And now he wasn't sure? What would she do if he wanted to start things up again?

"We should go." She turned around and walked back the way they'd come. The silence between them was no longer easy and carefree but tense and awkward. She felt confused and unsure. What did Cole want from her? Why had he kissed her? Pure sexual attraction? Chemistry? Did it just boil down to that? Or were the memories mixed in? Were the old feelings coming back for him as well as for her? She kept her gaze lowered to the ground beneath her feet, not willing or able to put a voice to any of those questions.

Finally, they reached the car, and she couldn't stand the silence a second longer. Ten years ago she wouldn't have had the guts to take him on, but she wasn't a foolish young girl anymore. "Cole—what's going on? What do you want from me?" she asked, looking him straight in the eye.

He stared at her for a long minute. "I don't know what I want anymore. Nothing is as clear as it used to be."

"I'm not sure it was ever clear, even before Emily died. We never came right out and said what we were thinking."

"You're right," he conceded. "But as you said before, it's too late now."

"And as you said before, is it?"

"You came back." Dylan looked up as Madison strode into his office just after six o'clock in the evening, looking like a million bucks. She'd changed her clothes, now wearing a black evening dress and knee-high black leather boots. Her long blond hair framed her beautiful face and lustrous brown eyes. She was a man killer, and he was in trouble. He wasn't surprised she'd come back. She'd always been a spoiled brat. When she wanted something, she thought she should have it. It didn't matter whether or not she deserved it.

Still, he had to admit he admired her stubborn persistence. Sometimes he'd wished that Emily had stood up for herself more, especially where her family was concerned. Not that he was comparing Madison to Emily; there was no comparison.

"You knew I'd come back," she replied with confidence.

"I suppose you have another proposition for me."

"I suppose I do." She cleared off a chair in front of his desk, dumping a pile of papers onto the floor.

"Hey, I need that stuff."

"So get a secretary. This place could use some organization."

"What do you want, Madison?"

She crossed her arms and legs, the latter action revealing a generous portion of thigh. She wanted him to look, and he did just that. She was hot. No doubt about it. She was also dangerous.

"I want . . ." She paused, long enough to make him tense. "I want you to do . . ."

Me? His mind filled in the blank while her smile widened and a flirtatious expression flashed through her eyes. She was definitely playing the bad girl at the moment. And he had to admit, she was very good at it. His body hardened in pure male appreciation.

"My party," she finally finished. "I want you to do my party."

"I told you I wasn't interested," he said, irritated with himself for reacting to her.

"I think I can get you interested. And I have a bargaining chip."

He didn't want to ask, but he couldn't help himself. "What's that?"

"Cole. He doesn't know about your lust for his little sister, does he?"

His chest tightened. Damn her. How did she know about that? "I don't know what you're talking about."

She leaned forward, and this time his eyes were drawn to her breasts. They were full, generous, spilling out of her top. She certainly knew how to distract a man. "I think you do know," she said. "Emily was one of my best friends."

"Some friend you were. You didn't even stay—"

"For the funeral—I know. We've been over that. But it doesn't change the fact that Emily confided in me. Especially when it came to sex."

He knew she used the word deliberately, but he wasn't sure why.

"Emily couldn't talk to Natalie; she was way too judgmental and too closely connected to Cole, your best friend. And Laura was busy trying to get Drew on the hook. But me . . ." She shrugged. "I was around. I saw things."

She'd always been around, as Dylan recalled. In fact, she'd put the moves on him a few times when Emily wasn't looking, but he'd never been interested in her. At twenty-one, he'd had eyes only for Emily, beautiful, sensitive, passionate, joyous Emily. His heart still ached at the loss of her in his life. But in many ways she was still with him. The club was a tribute to her imagination, her belief in magic, her belief in him, that he could create a world where people could be whoever they wanted to be.

"I want to make a deal with you," Madison said. "You work my party, and we keep your infatuation with Emily between us."

"I don't give in to blackmail. Tell Cole. What do I care?"

"Oh, I think you care. Or it wouldn't still be a secret. And it is a secret. It's not even in that book about Emily." She stood up and walked around to where he was sitting, sliding between him and the desk.

He cleared his throat, feeling decidedly uncomfortable. "You're going to try to seduce me now?"

Madison ran her tongue across her lip. "I'm saving that for later. She wasn't enough for you, Dylan. If you'd ever opened your eyes and really looked at Emily, you would have seen that you were not right for each other."

"Don't say a word about Emily."

"I wouldn't dream of it. Work my party, Dylan. It will be good exposure for your club. And a chance for the two of us to get better acquainted. I was never as bad as you thought I was."

He laughed at that. "I don't believe that for a second. Look at you now, a blackmailer as well as a—"

"Don't say something you'll regret," she warned, a flash of steel in her brown eyes.

"Why is my working your party so important to you?"

"I told you. I want you to get to know the real me, and I think we will both get something out of this professionally. It's a win-win proposition."

"You're a piece of work. I'll give you that."

"I'll take it." She crossed her arms, sending him a thoughtful look. "Is there a woman in your life now? Someone I should know about?"

He was both amazed and annoyed by her bluntness and implicit belief that she could control whatever was happening between them. "I don't have to tell you that."

"Which means there isn't. Or there wasn't. Because I'm here now."

"You don't take no for an answer, do you?"

She leaned forward, her mouth just an inch away from his, and said, "I haven't heard a no yet."

"Where the hell were you?" Drew demanded.

Laura paused in the doorway of their bedroom, her good mood fading at the sight of Drew's angry face and the open suitcase on the bed. "I took the girls to a concert in the park. They loved it."

"Well, while you were gone your old friend Natalie dropped by with Cole Parish."

"Really?" She was shocked to hear that. Natalie had been friendly the day before but certainly hadn't appeared overeager to take up their friendship where they'd left off. "I'm surprised."

"Not as surprised as I was to find out you spent time with them yesterday, discussing this book that's been written about Emily."

"You know about the book?"

"Your mother called me three days ago."

"My mother called you," Laura echoed, wondering when his sentences would stop hitting her like bricks on the head. "Why didn't she call me? Why didn't you tell me? I didn't find out about the book until Brenda brought it to the book club meeting Friday night."

"I didn't have time. I was busy at work. And your mother wanted my legal opinion on the situation."

"Which is what?"

"At the moment, nothing. But here's what you're going to do," he added. "You're going to screen our calls and our doorbell. I don't want you to talk to Natalie or Cole or anyone else connected to the sorority house or this book until I know more about what's going on."

She didn't like the way he was ordering her around. He'd been doing that a lot lately, treating her like she didn't have a brain in her head. "What are you afraid of?"

"What you should be afraid of—the press and the public finding out that you're the *Linda* in the story. I'm just lucky my name isn't in there."

And why isn't it? Laura couldn't help wondering how Drew had escaped attention. Everyone else was in the book. She watched as Drew pulled socks out of his drawer and stuck them in his suitcase. "Is there some sort of legal action we can take to stop the publication?"

"Nothing that wouldn't involve a public battle. Malone was clever. He covered his tracks by using fictitious names. We'd have to prove the characters were real people, and we'd also have to prove damages to those real people, providing, of course, that what happened in the book is false and not true. And I'm not sure it isn't true."

She frowned at that. "You think Natalie pushed Emily off the roof?"

"It's certainly possible."

"I don't think it is." And she was shocked he could think it was.

"You always had on blinders when it came to those girls." He zipped up his suitcase. "Just stay out of this, Laura. Do what you do best: keep the house and take care of the kids."

"That's not all I'm good for," she said defensively. "Seeing Natalie again made me remember that I once wanted other things. Like playing the flute. I was pretty good, you know."

"Okay," he said, obviously not getting her point.

"If you want to teach the girls how to play the flute, go for it."

"I don't want to teach the girls. I want to play the flute myself."

His cell phone rang, and he immediately answered it, never minding that they were in the middle of a conversation. "Val. I've just finished packing. Oh, good. You're the best."

Laura's stomach churned at the affection in her husband's voice. She knew she was becoming insanely jealous of Val, but she couldn't help it. Drew looked at Val and saw a beautiful, intelligent, exciting woman. He looked at her and saw his predictable, uninspiring wife, who was only good at taking care of the house and the children. If he wasn't having an affair yet, she had the terrible feeling he was dangerously close to taking that step.

"Drew, why don't I go on this trip with you?" she said impulsively. "I'll call my mother. She'll watch the girls for a few days. It will be fun."

"Are you nuts? This is a business trip. I have meetings all day and in the evenings, too. I can't take you along."

"A lot of men take their wives on business trips."

"Not if they want to actually conduct business."

"Is Valerie going?"

Drew picked up his suitcase. "Valerie is my business associate. If I need her in L.A., that's where she'll be. End of story. Now, I've called a cab, so I'll say good-bye to the girls and wait outside." He moved past her, stopping briefly to kiss her on the forehead.

"Drew . . ." She hesitated as she looked into his eyes. She had the strange feeling that he wanted her to ask him if he was having an affair, that he wanted her to open the door to a conversation she wasn't sure she was ready to have. Her marriage might be floundering a bit, but did she want to end it? Did she want to say something she might not be able to take back? "I hope your trip is successful."

"I'm sure it will be," he said as he walked out the door.

Laura sat on the bed for a long couple of minutes, feeling lost and confused. Her afternoon in the park had made her feel joyous and carefree. Those emotions were now gone. She wanted them back. She'd once been so happy with Drew, and he'd been happy with her. Where had the love gone? Had it disappeared completely? Had she changed? Had he? Could they get the love back?

She had so many questions bubbling inside of her, none of which had answers. She wanted to talk to someone and for a split second actually considered calling her mother. Thankfully, that thought passed as quickly as it had come. Admitting that there was even the slightest bit of trouble in her marriage would only elicit criticism and disappointment from her parents, who had already spent most of their lives disappointed in her. Her sisters would offer condescending advice and sigh that she was always messing things up. She couldn't call her other "mom" friends. Some of their husbands worked with Drew or played golf with him. And no one was divorced, separated, or admitting to problems. She didn't want to be gossiped about as the only woman who wasn't happy in her marriage.

She wished she had a girlfriend. Then it occurred to her that she did.

Could she call Natalie? Drew had ordered her not to. Well, wasn't that just enough reason to get up and do it? She didn't have to do what he said. She was a grown woman. She could make her own decisions. Jumping off the bed, she went downstairs and found the number Natalie had given her. She dialed the phone, relieved to hear Natalie's voice on the other end.

"I heard I missed you today," Laura said. "What are you doing tonight?"

Chapter 8

Natalie opened the door to Laura just after seven o'clock, still having doubts about inviting her over. But there had been something needy in Laura's voice that had matched a need of her own, the desire to connect with someone who might understand all the craziness that surrounded them.

"This is so cute," Laura said as she entered Natalie's apartment. "I love the movie posters, but I hope that doesn't mean you're still suffering from insomnia."

"Most of the time I'm so exhausted I just conk out, but on my days off, my brain likes to stay up and worry about the rest of my life. What smells so good?"

Laura held out a large brown paper bag. "I brought Chinese food, ice cream, and chocolate."

"The three most important food groups," they said together, then laughed as their gazes met in a shared memory.

"According to Emily," Natalie added softly.

"Yeah," Laura agreed, a sad note in her voice. "I wish she could be here. I wish we could all be together again."

The phone rang. "I'll get that," Natalie said. "It could be the hospital."

"I hope you won't have to go in to work."

"Me, too. Hello?" Her spine tingled as Madison's voice came over the line. It felt so strange to be looking at Laura and listening to Madison.

"Natalie, I think we should finish our conversation," Madison said. "I'm in my car. I'm just coming from a cocktail party. Do you want to grab some dinner?"

"Why don't you come here? I have Chinese food." She didn't bother to explain that Laura had brought dinner. She simply gave Madison directions, then hung up the phone. "We're going to have company. I didn't get a chance to tell you, but I ran into Madison today."

Laura's eyes widened in surprise. "You did?"

"At Dylan's club. But that's another story."

"I can't wait to hear it. Shall I open the wine?" Laura held up the other bag in her hand. "I thought I'd better cover all the bases."

"Actually, I'm sticking with nonalcoholic these days. I haven't had a drink since—since that night. It was a sobering moment for me."

Laura looked at her with compassion and understanding. They were still connected after all these years. Still able to feel each other's pain. Was that because of the depth of their friendship? Or was it because they'd suffered through a tragedy together?

"I'm sorry, I didn't know," Laura said. "I'll put it away."

"No, it's fine. You can have a glass of wine. It won't bother me."

"Are you sure? I have a hard time sticking to a diet when I'm with someone who orders a piece of chocolate cake. But then you always did have a strong will."

"About some things."

"You can still eat chow mein, can't you?" Laura asked as they unloaded the bags on the card table that also served as a dining-room table.

"Absolutely," Natalie replied.

"Should we wait for Madison?"

"She can catch up."

Catching up was all they did for the next few hours. Natalie had never thought being with Laura and Madison again could feel so perfectly right, so natural. After the initial awkwardness and polite conversation had passed, Madison declared Natalie's apartment a disgrace to the medical profession, and Laura's dirty-blond hair color a disgrace to her stylist. Natalie retaliated by asking Madison how her breasts had grown so much since college, and Laura got even with a crack about Madison's "last season" designer purse. Then they'd kicked off their shoes, flopped onto the couch and chairs, and dug into dinner with an enthusiasm that rivaled their college days.

Without ever consciously declaring an intent to avoid conversation about Emily, they'd somehow managed to do just that, sharing stories instead about their lives in the past few years. Laura talked about her big wedding, her children, life as a suburban PTA soccer mom. Madison related tales of her travels in Europe and more recently her encounters with celebrities and millionaires in the Big Apple. Natalie had skipped over the trials and tribulations of becoming a doctor to entertain them with fascinating stories from a big city emergency room. It quickly became clear that their lives had taken them in completely different directions. They had little in common now, except where they'd been.

"You've certainly lived a glamorous life," Laura commented when Madison finished sharing the details of her last trip to Paris. "But I notice you haven't mentioned any significant men in your life, and I'm sure there have been many."

A cloud passed through Maddie's eyes before she tossed her blond hair over one shoulder and said with a shrug, "There have been a few. I almost got married last year. I had the dress, the church, the hall, and had sent out the invitations."

"You didn't leave him at the altar, did you?" Laura asked, clearly horrified at the idea.

"I thought about it," Madison said candidly. "But that would have been really mean, and he was a nice guy. Too good for me, really. Now he's probably thanking his lucky stars that I ran out on him. We wouldn't have worked."

"Why not?" Natalie asked. "What went wrong?"

"He bored me. I looked at him one night and saw my life flash before my eyes. He wanted a wife, children, a dog, a house in Connecticut." She shook her head. "I realized I didn't want any of that. It was too easy, too predictable. Years from now, I'll probably realize I made a huge mistake. My mother certainly seems to think so."

"Maybe you didn't make a mistake," Laura said. "If it felt wrong to marry him, it was probably wrong. If you'd gone ahead with it, you might have found yourself in a huge mess, with kids in the middle of it all. Then you'd really be stuck."

"Are you talking about me or yourself?" Madison asked bluntly.

"You, of course."

"Liar," Madison said. "What's happening with you and Drew?"

Laura picked up a throw pillow from the couch and wrapped her arms around it. "He travels a lot for work. He's distracted all the time, especially by this woman in his office, who's beautiful and smart and not his wife."

"Is he cheating on you?"

"I'm sure he's not. I mean, I'm not exactly sure. He might be or he might just be thinking about it. I don't know what to do. I try to be the perfect wife, but I'm falling short. I don't want my marriage to fail. It's the only thing I've ever done right in my life. I'm holding on as tight as I can, but it still feels like it's slipping away from me." She paused. "And I can't believe I just said that out loud."

"Have you told Drew how you feel?" Natalie asked.

"I've tried, but he's too busy or uninterested to care. He keeps saying he's working all these hours for me, for the family, to be the provider I always wanted. He makes me feel guilty."

"Oh, honey, you were born guilty," Madison said with a laugh. "And Drew knows just which buttons to push. He always has. Why did you marry him so quickly anyway? Why not shop around a little?"

"I was afraid I'd still be shopping when I was thirty."

"Ouch," Madison said. "I think she's referring to us, Natalie."

"I wasn't," Laura said hastily. "Please, don't think that. I actually look at the two of you and feel incredibly jealous. You both have great careers. You're making something of yourselves. Your lives matter."

"So does yours," Natalie interjected. "You're raising two daughters. That's the most important job on earth. Believe me, not everyone can do it," she added, thinking of her own mother. "Don't sell yourself short."

"My girls are great," Laura said with a proud smile. "I want you to meet them someday. They're beautiful and special and smart, too. I'm determined to raise them to believe in themselves and not to take shit from anyone."

"That's great," Natalie said. "Now, can I get anyone anything?"

"Not so fast, Dr. Bishop." Madison turned to her with purpose in her eyes. "We haven't heard about your love life yet."

Natalie shook her head. "I have no love life. I spend all my time at the hospital."

"Not all your time. Some of it you spend with Cole," Madison said.

"I told you earlier today that we're just together because of the book."

"And the old feelings aren't coming back?" Laura asked. "Because he is one good-looking man, and he's still single. Maybe this is your second chance."

Natalie refused to admit that the same thought had crossed her mind. "Cole broke my heart once.

I'd be a fool to put myself out there again. I don't think I could live through it." She looked at Madison and Laura and confessed something she'd never said to another soul. "It almost killed me to lose him before, especially after losing Emily. The pain was excruciating." She paused, taking a deep breath. "And I can't believe I just said that out loud, either," she added, repeating Laura's earlier comment.

"Especially without any wine," Madison said lightly. "Speaking of which, I think I'll have another glass. All this baring of souls is making me thirsty."

Natalie kicked her feet up on the coffee table crates and rested her head on the back of her chair, wondering if she'd just lost her mind, confiding in two women she hadn't seen in a decade. Maybe she was giving one of them more fodder for a second book, the sequel to *Fallen Angel*, probably to be titled, *Natalie Bishop Loses Everything*.

"We should talk about Emily and the book," Laura said as Madison returned, her glass of red wine filled to the brim. "Although I have to tell you that Drew gave me orders not to discuss it with either of you."

"Why not?" Natalie asked.

"I'm not sure. He doesn't like to explain his orders. It was all about legal ramifications and stuff. He wants to protect me."

"And himself," Madison said.

"What do you mean?" Natalie asked.

"Yes, what do you mean?" Laura echoed. "Drew wasn't even mentioned in the book. He doesn't have anything to protect besides my reputation."

"Drew was in Emily's room that night." Madison took a sip of wine before adding, "Did he ever tell you that?"

Natalie was as shocked by Madison's words as Laura was.

"He wasn't anywhere near Emily's room," Laura replied. "He was in our room, setting up a private party for us. You know that. He said you helped him with the candles and the wine." She paused. "We were going to make love that night. It was going to be our first time."

Natalie hadn't known that. "In the sorority house? You were going to do it in your room in the sorority house?" She'd known Drew was pressuring Laura to have sex, but doing it right there in the sorority house was something Madison would have done, not Laura.

"Madison said we'd have complete privacy. It would be better and safer than Drew's apartment where there was always a party going on," Laura said defensively. "I thought she was right. I wouldn't have felt comfortable using the guys' bathroom."

"Oh, don't look so judgmental," Madison said to Natalie. "It's what Laura wanted. I wasn't talking her into anything."

"You weren't talking her out of it, either. And you were always telling her to loosen up," Natalie said. "You told us all that."

"Laura came to me and said she wanted to have sex with Drew."

"I said I wanted to make love," Laura corrected.

"Whatever."

"Okay, fine." Natalie tried to remember the point

of their conversation. "If Drew was planning Laura's seduction, why was he in Emily's room? Did she know about it, too?"

"Did she?" Laura echoed.

"No, that was about something else," Madison replied.

"What?" Natalie asked.

"I don't know. Drew said he had to speak to Emily before Laura came upstairs, and I should go downstairs and stall. So I went to find Laura."

"But you didn't find me. I didn't even see you downstairs," Laura said in confusion.

"It was crowded. I got distracted by some guys. The next thing I knew everyone was screaming and running outside . . ." Her voice drifted away as they were all taken back to a time and place where they didn't want to go.

"So you never actually saw Drew in Emily's room," Laura said finally. "You don't know if he spoke to her or not."

"He told me he wasn't upstairs at all," Natalie said. "He told Cole and me that this afternoon when we were at your house. Why did he lie?"

"Probably because he thought you would accuse him of something," Laura said. "Look, he may not be the world's best husband, but he's not a bad person, and he didn't have anything to do with Emily's death. I know that for sure. You have to trust me."

Natalie wondered how any of them could trust each other. They had a decade of distance between them, and despite the warmth of their reunion, there were lots of things they no longer knew about each other. In fact . . . Her gaze drifted over to

Madison. "There's something else I've been wondering about since this afternoon," she said. "Dylan."

Madison set down her wineglass. "What about Dylan?"

"I remember seeing him at the sorority house that night. Was he with Emily? Or was he with you?"

"He sure as hell wasn't with me," Madison replied. "He wouldn't give me the time of day back then. Actually, he's not too crazy about me right now, but I'm working on him."

"Why?" Laura asked. "Why would you want to work on him?"

Natalie knew why. Because Madison had always had a thing for Dylan, and now that they had found themselves in the same town, she was determined to change his mind about her. "Because she hates to lose when it comes to men, isn't that right, Maddie?"

"I haven't lost yet."

"What are you two talking about?" Laura asked.

"Madison wants Dylan," Natalie said, looking Madison straight in the eye. "She wanted him when we were in Santa Cruz, and apparently she still wants him now."

"That's not completely true," Madison replied with a wicked smile. "I want him to want me. Then we'll see what I want."

"You're playing a dangerous game," Natalie said. "Dylan was never an easy man. He was moody, unpredictable, rude, and from what I can see that hasn't changed. He certainly doesn't care for me. He told Cole he wouldn't be surprised if I had pushed Emily off the roof."

"He didn't like you because you were always getting in his way, encouraging Emily to study instead of going to the magic club with him," Madison pointed out. "And I only play games that are dangerous. The rest are just too boring."

Her comment struck Natalie wrong. "Is this a game for you? Are you the one who did this, Madison? Is this book one of your dangerous games? Because if it is, your life from here on out will not in any way be boring. I can promise you that."

"If I was playing a game, do you think I'd tell you?" Madison answered. "But as it happens, I'm not."

Natalie searched Madison's eyes and saw nothing but the truth. "I don't want it to be you, Maddie. Not you. Not Laura. I couldn't take it if either of you was the one sticking the knife in my back."

Her words lingered in the air long after she'd said them, and the fact that neither Madison nor Laura immediately jumped into the silence did not reassure her of their innocence. Still, if one of them had gone to so much trouble to hide themselves behind Garrett Malone, it was ludicrous to think they would suddenly come clean now.

"It wasn't one of us," Laura said finally. "How can you think that? And it's not just you who's getting hurt here. There are things in the book about me that I'd prefer no one else know, like that pot-smoking incident with Eric and Anthony next door. I don't want my daughters or my parents, for that matter, to know I smoked pot in college. And I'm sure Madison doesn't want her coworkers to know she once stripped and ran naked through the Sigma Chi house. That wasn't her finest moment."

"Hey, I looked damn good," Madison said. "But you're right. It's not an incident I would have chosen to publicize. So who else could have done this?" She picked up her wineglass again and took another sip while she considered the question. "What about Jessica Holbrook? That bitch hated us."

Jessica Holbrook was Emily's official "big sister" in the house. Jessica had loved Emily but had never been a big fan of the Fabulous Four. She'd told them on more than one occasion that the sorority was all for one, one for all, and that smaller cliques like the Fabulous Four should not exist. "I wonder what happened to her," Natalie murmured.

"I know," Laura said. "She's still in Santa Cruz. In fact, she works with Diane Thomas at the Panhellenic Office. She's the current adviser to the Gamma Delts. It was in the alumni newsletter."

"That figures," Madison said. "Jessica was the ultimate sorority girl." She paused, a mischievous smile spreading across her face. "We should call her."

Natalie immediately shook her head. "Absolutely not."

"You want to find out who has the knife in your back, don't you?" She turned to Laura. "I bet you have her phone number, don't you? Probably in that big purse of yours."

"I might have my address book in my purse," Laura admitted. "But I can't just call Jessica out of the blue. What would I say? I haven't talked to her since she graduated. And it wasn't like we were ever friends."

"You can say you're planning a reunion for everyone in the house during the four years you were there. And since she's now the adviser for the Gamma Delts, you wanted to start with her. It's perfect."

"What do I say after we get past the fake reunion thing? I don't want to bring up the book if she doesn't know about it. That would just add to the publicity."

"That's a good point," Natalie put in.

"Just wing it," Madison advised. "If Jessica knows about the book, she'll probably bring it up. If she doesn't bring it up, try to find out what happened to some of the other girls who were there that night, like Marie or Danielle."

"Drew is not going to like this," Laura muttered as she reached for her address book. "This isn't exactly staying out of it as he ordered me to do."

"You're a grown woman. You can make your own decisions, can't you?" Madison asked.

"You make it sound so easy, but Drew and I— our lives are complicated by our children, and my parents have practically adopted Drew. If we divorced, they'd probably take him in the settlement. They like him and respect him so much. They don't feel the same way about me."

"Maybe you haven't given them a reason to respect you. People treat you the way you ask to be treated," Madison said. "If you let them walk all over you, they will."

"I don't have as much confidence as you and Natalie do. You're both so smart."

"So are you, Laura," Natalie interjected. "And Madison is right. If you don't stand up for yourself, no one will stand up for you. If you want change, you have to make change."

Laura sighed, her expression clearly troubled. "I do want change."

"So start now, with us," Madison encouraged. "Call Jessica. Help us get to the bottom of this book situation. Think of it as a small step on the way to your independence."

"Fine. I'll do it. Give me the phone."

Natalie handed her the portable phone, pleased that they were taking some action. Even if calling Jessica accomplished nothing, at least they weren't just sitting back, waiting for the other shoe to drop. She pushed the button to put the phone on Speaker as a woman's voice came over the line, saying, "Hello?"

"Is Jessica Holbrook there?" Laura asked.

"This is she. Who's calling?" Jessica asked, a brisk edge to her voice.

"Hi, Jessica, it's Laura Hart. Actually, Laura Hart McKinney now. Do you remember me?"

"Of course. How nice to hear from you. What can I do for you?"

Laura licked her lips, then said, "I was calling about planning a reunion. I know you weren't in my class, but I thought you might be able to help me track some people down. I hear you're working in the Panhellenic Office with Diane Thomas."

"Yes, I am, and both Diane and I would be happy to help. But—" Jessica paused. "I hope you're not thinking of inviting your entire pledge class."

"Isn't everyone usually invited?" Laura countered.

"Not in this case. I know you were very good friends with Madison and Natalie, but you simply cannot invite them to any reunion that would be held at the sorority house. Do you still keep in touch with them?" Jessica asked.

"I lost track of them after they left," Laura said. "But I don't see what would be wrong with inviting them."

"Some people think Natalie had something to do with Emily's death."

"They do?" Laura asked. "Why?"

"Apparently someone saw Natalie up on the roof that night."

Natalie's jaw dropped at that comment. Laura and Madison also looked stunned.

"Laura, are you there?" Jessica asked when the silence lengthened.

"I'm here," Laura said hastily. "Who saw Natalie up on the roof?"

"Well, I really can't say, and I'm not sure there's any proof, but where there's smoke, there's fire. And look how fast Natalie transferred. She couldn't wait to get out of there. Maybe Madison was in on it, too. She moved out even faster. Diane and I were talking about it all just the other day. Emily was such a beautiful person. It was tragic the way she died. And so unfair. She had so much to offer the house, far more than Madison or Natalie did. You know, we really only took Natalie because of Emily, because they were best friends. I know most of the sisters feel the same way I do, Laura. Any reunion that includes Natalie or Madison would not be well attended. I'm only telling you this so you don't waste a lot of time and energy. It's nothing against you. We all love you. You know that, don't you?"

"I really don't think Natalie had anything to do with Emily's fall."

"You always were a sweetheart, Laura."

"It's not about being a sweetheart," Laura said with spunk. "I knew Natalie and Madison better than anyone. Emily, too."

"Sometimes it's easier to read people's true intentions when you're standing farther back. Now, I have to run, but call me tomorrow at my office," Jessica said. "I have the alumni directory there. I can fax you the names and addresses."

"Thanks." Laura pressed the button to disconnect the call. "Well, what do you think? Who's this witness? Garrett Malone?"

"He did say in the book that someone saw me push Emily off the roof," Natalie replied, feeling discouraged by Jessica's comments. She'd thought she was one of the sorority sisters, accepted by everyone, just as Emily was. Now it appeared that they'd only pledged her because of Emily.

"We know it wasn't you," Laura said.

"But if there was someone on the roof," Madison continued, "then Emily didn't fall by accident."

They stared at each other—for the first time forced to address the idea that Emily had been deliberately pushed off the roof.

"We know a lot of people didn't like me," Natalie said slowly. "But who didn't like Emily?"

Chapter 9

Natalie was still pondering that question as she finished her shift late Monday afternoon. It had been a hell of a day, starting with an early-morning bus crash and multiple victims, followed by a blur of cases ranging from poison oak to a heart attack and everything in between. Dropping off her last chart at the desk, Natalie headed to the lounge. There were two other doctors in the room, one stretched out on the couch, another reading the newspaper, which did not provide the privacy she was looking for. Grabbing a cup of coffee, Natalie walked outside and found an empty bench in the hospital garden. She pulled out her cell phone and called Cole.

He answered immediately, obviously reading her Caller ID as he said, "Natalie. I'm glad you called. We have an even bigger problem."

Her fingers clenched around the phone, not sure she was ready for a bigger problem. They hadn't solved the last one yet.

"I spoke to Malone's publicist," Cole continued. "She told me that he was in L.A. on a book tour and was appearing on the *Corey Hart Show* this afternoon, which I immediately turned on, just in time to hear a woman call in and ask if the book was based on a true story about a girl named Emily, who died at a sorority house in Santa Cruz. She also said she was sure that the Fabulous Four actually existed and that she knew Natalie Bishop was really the Nancy in the book."

Natalie's heart stopped. "Oh, my God! She mentioned my name specifically, first and last?"

"Yes. Unfortunately, I didn't catch her name. I called Malone's publicist back. I wanted to challenge her to respond to the claims that the book was based on a true story. I got her answering machine."

Natalie felt sick to her stomach. "What am I going to do, Cole? The *Corey Hart Show* is national. A million people probably heard my name." Her mind raced ahead. She'd been publicly identified. It wouldn't take long for someone at the hospital to make the connection, putting her reputation and her career on the line. Doctors had to be above reproach, beyond scandal, especially medical residents seeking permanent positions in the very near future.

"We're going to find Malone," Cole answered. "I've asked my investigator to put this on the front burner. He believes that Garrett Malone is a pen name, and so do I. It may take a while to get through the red tape, but we will determine who he really is. You can count on that."

She wanted to believe him, but Malone seemed to be one step ahead of them.

"I'm going to L.A. tomorrow morning," he continued. "I have Malone's itinerary, and he's making several appearances tomorrow afternoon. With any luck, I can pin him down before my parents get back from Europe on Wednesday."

Natalie had wondered about his parents, but it was one subject they hadn't touched on.

"I'll call you when I find Malone," he added.

"No," she said quickly. "I'll come with you."

"Don't you have to work?"

"Of course I do, but my whole career is at stake. I'll take a personal day off. When are you leaving?"

"Tomorrow morning. Do you want my secretary to book you a flight?"

"Yes." She paused, knowing she had to ask. "Cole, you said you didn't hear the woman's name. Did you recognize the voice? It wasn't Madison or Laura, was it?" She felt guilty even asking the question, especially after their heart-to-heart conversation the night before, but she also felt too vulnerable to risk trusting anyone.

"I don't think so, Natalie, but I couldn't say for sure."

She ended the call, wishing just once she'd get a definitive answer to a question. As she got to her feet, she saw Gloria Grayson approaching. Gloria was one of the best ER nurses she had ever had the pleasure of working with. With ten years' experience under her belt, Gloria knew the ropes better than most of the residents and usually kept a smile on her face no matter what the circumstances. At the moment that smile was missing.

"Natalie, there you are. Dr. Raymond just called in. He wants you to call him back right away on his cell phone. Here's the number." She handed Natalie a piece of paper.

"Did he say what he wanted?" Natalie asked, surprised and wary to be getting a call from the chief resident, who was currently on vacation with his family.

"No, but he wasn't happy about something. Are you in trouble?"

"I think I might be," Natalie said.

"Let me know if I can help."

"Thanks." As Natalie stared at the piece of paper in her hand, she had a feeling she was going to have to help herself this time around. She punched in the number and was not surprised to hear the first words out of Dr. Raymond's mouth.

"Natalie, your name was mentioned on television a few minutes ago. Are you the woman they're talking about that's connected to this mystery novel? Please tell me it's another Natalie Bishop."

"I wish I could."

"Is any of it true?"

"I didn't do anything wrong or illegal, if that's what you're asking."

"Can you prove that?"

"I'm working on it."

"Work fast, Natalie. The hospital doesn't like bad press. And patients don't like doctors whose names are mentioned in connection to murder."

The temperature was fifteen degrees warmer in L.A. when they got off the plane late Tuesday morning. Cole had made a rental car reservation, so they stopped there first and picked up a small silver Honda in the parking lot. They'd flown into the Burbank Airport because it was closer to Studio City, where the book signing was being held;

unfortunately, it was also close to Natalie's old neighborhood. It was bad enough having to revisit her college years; now she had to take another look at her childhood years.

She'd grown up in North Hollywood, just a few miles away. She'd walked and shopped and worked in retail outlets along these streets. She'd woken up to the sight of the smog hanging over the foothills, the valley locked in a perpetual hot haze. She'd grown up in a town where seeing a movie star at the local burger joint or grocery store was a given, where beauty, tans, and designer clothes were everything and those who had none of the above were nothing. She'd fallen into the nothing category.

Pushing those memories away, she focused on the present. "Turn right at the next light and get on the freeway."

Cole did as she suggested and within a few minutes they were taking the turnoff to Universal Studios. The bookstore Garrett Malone was signing at was part of the Universal Theme Park shopping area. His hotel was also on the hill. Natalie checked the time. It was just eleven and the book signing was scheduled for noon.

"Book signing or hotel?" she asked.

"Let's try the hotel. He might not have left yet."

They parked in the lot and walked into the hotel and directly to the elevator. Somehow Cole had come up with a room number. Natalie felt both nervous and excited as they got off at the seventeenth floor. She wanted to face Malone. She wanted to ask him why. She wanted to make him admit it was all a lie.

Cole knocked on the door of Malone's room. There was no answer.

"He's already gone," she said, disappointed yet again. "Maybe he was doing another interview before the signing."

"Anything is possible." Cole glanced around, tipping his head toward the maid's cart next door. "I have an idea. Come on."

"Where are we going?"

He didn't answer until they had walked down the hall and turned the corner. "We'll wait for the maid to open up Malone's room. Then you'll walk in like it's yours."

She frowned at that idea. "Me? Why can't you do that?"

"Because women aren't afraid of other women. You won't make her nervous. I might."

He was probably right about that, Natalie thought. Well, what the hell. She was already being set up for murder. Why not add breaking and entering to her resume?

She sighed and walked over to the window, which overlooked the studios. The gray sound stages looked like airplane hangars in the middle of carnival rides. The San Fernando Valley spread out behind the studios, each city blending into the next, with little difference in the scenery. The neighborhoods were lined with palm trees, ranch-style homes, and swimming pools in every backyard. Suburban strip malls and chain stores made up the shopping areas in this part of Los Angeles County. The expensive boutiques were in Beverly Hills and Bel Air or in the more upscale cities closer to the ocean.

"Have you ever been down there—to the studios?" Cole asked idly.

"On the tour? A long time ago, when I was a kid. What about you?"

"Emily always got sick at the wrong time. We'd make plans, then cancel them. After a while it was easier to stay home. My parents did everything they could to turn our house into Emily's personal version of Disneyland."

Natalie nodded. "The first time I saw her bedroom, I thought it belonged to a fairy princess. She didn't just have a canopy bed, she had curtains that enclosed the bed entirely. It was very cool."

"She was happy in that room. I know she was," he added somewhat defensively. "You said she left home to be free, but I never thought she was trapped there."

"Just because a cage is gold doesn't make it any less of a cage."

"It was a cage born of Emily's illnesses, not anybody's desire to keep her in a place she didn't want to be."

"I never said that it was."

"I think you did, Natalie."

"No, I meant that Emily's college experience was something she really wanted. She enjoyed every minute of it."

"Except maybe the last few minutes," he said harshly. "Don't you ever wonder if she knew what was happening to her? If there was some split second when she realized she was going to die?"

Of course she'd thought about that, agonized over it. "Those first few days, questions like that ran through my mind every second," she said. "I couldn't handle it. I had to put them away." She wondered if he'd make some nasty comment about burying her head in the sand or denying the truth, but he remained silent. "It was the only way I could go on." She drew in a breath. "Do you want to check on the maid? If we don't get into the room soon, we might miss the book signing. It's only for an hour."

"I'll check. Wait here." He reappeared a moment later, an eager light in his brown eyes. "Showtime," he said. "Be bold, Natalie. Don't let her intimidate you."

"Please, I'm a female doctor. I learned a long time ago how to stand up for myself." She'd also learned how to fake it when she was asked a question for which she did not have an answer, usually by some arrogant male doctor who wanted to show her up. If she could handle that situation, she could certainly handle this one. Squaring her shoulders, she headed around the corner.

The door to Malone's room was open, and the maid was vacuuming. Natalie paused for a second. When the maid shut off the vacuum, she walked in and tossed her purse down on the bed. "Hello," she said cheerfully. She kicked off her high-heeled shoes. "Ooh, that feels better. I have to use the bathroom. I won't get in your way."

The maid offered a shy smile. She was young and Hispanic and probably didn't speak much English. Natalie walked into the bathroom and shut the door. She turned on the sink and prayed the maid would leave without reporting a strange woman in a room that was assigned to a man. She waited a good two minutes, then shut off the water and opened the door. The room was empty. The maid was gone.

She couldn't believe how easy that had been. So much for heightened security measures. A quiet knock on the door sent her heart back into overdrive, but it was Cole's face she saw in the peephole. She let him in and shut the door quickly. "She didn't ask me anything," she told him.

"It's amazing where you can go when you look like you belong."

"Let's get busy. I won't relax until we're out of here. I can just see the headlines. Natalie Bishop arrested on burglary and possible murder charges."

"You write a good headline. We could use you at the paper."

"Thanks, but I'd prefer to keep my real job."

She glanced around as Cole riffled through the dresser drawers. Malone was neat or had brought little with him. There wasn't much more in the room than the hotel furnishings. She opened the closet door and looked at the two suits hanging there, one brown, one gray. A couple of dress shirts on hangers were the only other items. A suitcase sat on its side on the floor. She knelt down and unzipped it, and wasn't surprised to find it empty. As she closed the closet door, she heard Cole whistle. He held up a mat of hair in his hand, hair that was the same color as Garrett Malone's. "This looks like a wig or a hairpiece."

Why would the man wear a wig? Was he bald?

Natalie moved over to the dresser and saw Cole going through a black leather case. "What the hell is this shit?" Cole muttered.

"It's makeup. Malone is wearing a disguise," she

added in amazement. "A wig, cover-up, black charcoal pencil to line his brows."

"And colored contact lenses," Cole said, holding up a case.

She looked into Cole's eyes and knew he was thinking what she was thinking. "That must mean he's afraid he'll be recognized. He's someone we know, Cole. The question is—who?"

Laura knew she should not be spying on her husband. It wasn't right. But she couldn't seem to stop herself from going through the pockets of every piece of clothing Drew had in his closet. For a while she had tried to pretend that she was simply checking the pockets before taking the clothes to the laundry. It was a lie. She was looking for evidence. She'd called Drew's hotel room late last night and he hadn't answered. She'd tried him again this morning on his cell phone, but he hadn't picked up. If she truly had an emergency, how on earth was she supposed to reach him? Didn't he consider the fact that his family might need him?

Her anger grew with each passing minute. Of course he didn't consider that fact. She was in charge of the house and the kids. She was supposed to handle everything on the home front while he went off and brought home the bacon. Maybe something was wrong. Maybe something had happened to Drew. Her imagination was capable of creating all kinds of horrible scenarios. She had to focus. Most of the time her instincts were wrong. She wasn't proud of that fact, but it was the truth. And it was a good thing, because it meant that most of the horrible things she worried about never actually came true.

Drew was fine. He was just busy. She reached into the pocket of the last jacket in the closet, and her fingers closed around a piece of paper. She pulled it out. It was a travel itinerary. But there was something different about it. And then it hit her. Garrett Malone's name was on the top of the paper, followed by a list of flight numbers, hotel reservations, book signings, and radio appearances in Los Angeles. The date was for today.

Laura walked into the bedroom and sat down on the bed, still staring at the piece of paper in her hand. Why did Drew have Garrett Malone's travel itinerary? Was he planning to contact the man? But Drew was on a business trip. *A business trip in Los Angeles.* A shiver ran down her spine. Drew and Garrett Malone were both in L.A.

She couldn't believe that Drew was behind the book. That didn't make any sense at all. There was no motive, no reason, nothing to be gained. He must have gone to L.A. to meet with Malone. Or maybe he was just going to combine law business with personal business. He was probably trying to protect her. That's why he hadn't said anything. That had to be why.

But she didn't like that Drew was keeping secrets from her. They were supposed to be partners in everything. If he was keeping secrets about Malone, what else was he hiding? The lack of communication in their marriage seemed suddenly insurmountable. They should be talking about Malone and Emily and the book and everything else that was happening. They should be working on it together, instead of separately.

The phone rang, interrupting her thoughts. Hoping it was Drew, she picked it up and said, "Hello?"

"Laura McKinney?" a woman asked.

"This is she."

"Are you the same Laura Hart who married Drew McKinney?"

"Who's asking?"

"Laura? It's Kathy Allen," the woman said. "Remember me? I went to college with you."

"Of course I remember you." She searched her mind for a face to go with the name. Kathy Allen had been a freshman pledge when she'd been a senior. They'd known each other only in passing. Still, a sorority sister was a sorority sister. "How are you?"

"I'm fine. I'm a reporter now for the *Santa Cruz Sentinel*. I loved this area so much I decided to stay after graduation."

"Really?" Laura didn't like the sound of that. Why would Kathy be calling her from Santa Cruz?

"Have you heard about a book called *Fallen Angel*? It's supposed to be a fictitious murder mystery, but the buzz is that it's really the story of that girl who fell off the roof of our sorority house two years before I came to school. You were friends with her, right?"

"I'm sure this book doesn't have anything to do with Emily."

"That's not what people are saying."

"What people?"

"I've had some calls from a few of the girls who

were in the house that night. I guess they think
since I'm a reporter, I can figure out what's going
on. Have you read the book, Laura? I wasn't there,
but a lot of it sounds familiar to me just from having heard everyone talk about it. You're in it. Although the names are changed, it's pretty clear it's
you, and those two other girls you hung out with."
She paused, the sound of paper rustling in the
background. "Natalie and Madison, right?"

"It's just a novel," Laura said with a little laugh.
"I can't believe everyone is so interested in it."

"The book suggests that Emily's accident was
murder and your friend Natalie was the murderer."

"She wasn't just my friend, Kathy. She was and
still is our sorority sister. I hope people can remember that."

"You sound a little defensive," Kathy remarked.

"I stand by my friends. Don't you?"

"I didn't know Natalie. She was long gone by
the time I got there. But I'm not out to get anyone.
I'm just looking for the truth."

"Emily fell. That's the truth."

"That's the official version anyway. I spoke to
a Detective Boland at the local precinct here. He
remembers the case. And he said, off the record,
that he always thought there was something funny
about it. He also said that he would check out
this book."

Laura's heart began to race. If the police re-
opened the case, it would garner even more publicity. What could she do to stop it? What could she
tell Kathy to make her forget about it? The woman
was a reporter. She wasn't going to let this go, especially when it involved her own sorority.

"You were easy to find," Kathy added. "I got your number from the alumni directory, but I haven't been able to locate Natalie or Madison. Do you know where they are?"

"No, I don't," Laura lied.

"I'll keep looking. With the Internet, it's not easy to hide."

"I doubt they're hiding."

"I hope you're right, Laura. It would be a terrible scandal to discover that one of our sisters committed murder, especially against a fellow sister. Even worse if the other two covered up for her."

"Thanks for the call, Kathy. I have to pick up my daughters now."

"I'm sure I'll talk to you again."

Laura hung up the phone with a shaky hand. She remembered Kathy now, a ruthless bitch who'd always loved to stir the pot, mix things up, then watch the fireworks. A little like Drew, she thought idly. He'd always loved a good fight. It was that trait that made him a good lawyer. What else did it make him? She looked down at the itinerary for Garrett Malone and wondered again if Malone was the real reason Drew had gone to L.A.

She knew Natalie and Madison and even Cole had Drew on their list of possible sources for Malone's book. She'd dismissed the idea out of hand earlier. Now she couldn't help wondering. Drew had been so secretive the past few months, working late at the office and even here at home in his study downstairs. She remembered the way he'd blacked out the screen the previous day, so she couldn't see what he was working on. He'd said it was business, but was it?

It was ridiculous to think Drew was behind the book. He was obsessed with his law job, with making partner, with setting himself up for a political career. Why would he make such a huge detour to the past? He and Emily had barely been friends. And he had no ax to grind with Natalie. She couldn't think of one good reason why he'd let himself get involved in the book.

Except for money. Drew had grown up poor, and she knew money was important to him. Financial security fueled his ambition.

Getting up from the bed, she walked down to the study and opened the filing cabinet. Drew took care of all the family finances. She was embarrassed to say that in this day and age of independent, smart women, she had no real idea of their monetary worth, because Drew handled everything. Their roles were very traditional. He was the provider. She was the homemaker. It had worked perfectly . . . for a while.

But it wasn't working perfectly now. And she didn't know what was widening the gap between them. Was it another woman? Or was it the past? She pulled out the bank statements from the last year and sat down at the desk. She was going to eliminate the secrets in her life one at a time.

Chapter 10

They'd missed Malone again. Cole stared at the empty table in the front of the bookstore where the man was supposed to be sitting and felt the wind go out of his sails. After their discoveries in Malone's hotel room, he'd become convinced they were only moments away from discovering his true identity.

"The manager said he left ten minutes ago. The books went much faster than they'd anticipated, and they ran out of stock," Natalie said with an expressive sigh. "This sucks."

"It certainly does."

"I told you we should have gotten here earlier."

"If we'd rushed through Malone's room, we would have missed the wig and makeup. We'll have to try to catch him at the radio station."

"That's not until three o'clock."

"It's all I've got. Do you want to get something to eat?" He stopped, realizing Natalie had paused next to a book rack, an odd expression on her face. "What's wrong?"

"I can't believe I didn't think of this before." She pointed to the row of slim books in front of her. "Emily wrote in a journal just like that every single night we were at school, starting with the very first day in the dorms." She looked at him with a new light in her eyes. "What better place to learn the secrets of our lives than from Emily's journal? When I was reading *Fallen Angel*, I thought it sounded like Emily was talking. Malone must have gotten the information for his book from her journal. What she didn't write down, he filled in with his own imagination. It makes perfect sense. We used to joke that Emily could use that journal for blackmail." She paused, giving a confused shake of her head. "But how did Malone get her journal? You and your parents cleaned out our room after the funeral."

His jaw tightened as he remembered that terrible task. "I didn't pay attention to what we were packing."

"Where did everything end up?"

"In Emily's bedroom in my parents' house. If the journal is anywhere, it's there."

"I don't think it's there. I think it's with Malone."

"It wasn't in his hotel room."

"He probably didn't bring it with him. We can certainly ask him about it when we find him . . . if we find him."

"We will," Cole said confidently. "He can't run out of the radio show early. We'll catch up to him there. And we'll ask him about the journal. Let's get out of here."

"And go where?" she asked, as they moved toward the door.

He thought about that. They needed a distraction, something to do for a couple of hours to take their minds off Emily and his family. Since food seemed to be of little interest to either of them, he sought another idea. And suddenly he had it. "Take me home," he said abruptly.

Natalie looked at him in confusion. "Now? We have to meet Malone at three o'clock."

"Not my home. Yours."

"I don't understand."

"Yes, you do." He saw the light slowly dawn in her eyes. "Show me where you grew up, Natalie. Take me home."

"Absolutely not."

"When was the last time you saw your mother?"

"Five years ago. She was in rehab. She asked me for cash and a bottle of whiskey. I gave her the cash. She probably used it to get the whiskey as soon as she got out."

"So why give her the money?"

"I don't know. Habit, I guess. Duty, responsibility, guilt."

"What would you have to feel guilty about?"

"I don't want to talk about my mother."

"We don't have to talk. Let's just take a drive through the old neighborhood. We won't stop unless you want to."

Natalie shook her head. "Do you ever have an idea that is not stupid or dangerous?"

"Not lately," he said with a grin.

"I should have my head examined for agreeing to them all." She studied him thoughtfully. "Why the interest now, Cole? You never wanted to know anything about my past before. Are we just killing time?"

"Maybe I wasn't ready to know before," he said candidly.

"That's a perceptive statement."

"Give me some credit. I have matured a little in the past ten years."

"I think I'll reserve judgment," she said as they walked out of the bookstore and back to their rental car.

As he unlocked her door, he said, "I'll drive. You tell me where to go."

She smiled. "I've already told you where to go—a number of times. But you're still here."

"Very funny. You know, if you're not careful, you may actually develop a sense of humor in your old age."

Natalie felt every year of her age as Cole drove down the streets of her youth. In some ways it seemed like yesterday since she'd been home. In other ways, it felt as if a lifetime had passed. With each turn, they drew closer to the house where she'd spent her early childhood. She didn't know why she'd directed him to go there. Maybe because it was so far removed from her life it was easier to look at. The one-story, ranch-style home sat at the end of a cul-de-sac in a modest neighborhood in North Hollywood, the kind of street where young families settled. It was the picture of suburbia with bikes in driveways, toys on lawns, and the sound of a barking dog.

"This is where you grew up?" Cole asked with surprise. "I thought you lived in an apartment building."

"This was my first house—where we lived when my dad was alive. It's smaller than I remember."

"Most things are." Cole stopped in front of the house. "When did you move out of this place?"

"When I was eight. About six weeks after my father died. We couldn't stay here. We didn't have enough money. There was no life insurance. My dad was thirty-six years old. He hadn't anticipated dying of a heart attack, so he hadn't prepared."

"That's understandable."

"I guess." She stared at the house, imagining the rooms inside, the green tile on the kitchen floor, the recliner in the living room, the old TV where the cat liked to nap, the small bedroom where she'd had her own twin bed, her own posters, her own things. They hadn't been rich, not even when her father had been alive, but they'd had enough.

"What are you seeing?" Cole asked quietly.

"My mom and dad sitting at the dining-room table, talking, laughing." She offered him a sad, wistful smile. "They loved to sit after a meal. I'd bring my homework to the table. I liked being around them, hearing them talk, even when they would bicker with each other. I could hear the love in their voices. It was powerful."

"I didn't think you remembered anything good about your childhood."

"I didn't think I did, either," she said, surprised at herself. "For a long time I only had one image in my head, the night my father died. My mother and I were sitting on the couch in the living room, watching television. My dad came into the room and started to say something to my mom about the credit card bill. I remember being worried, because

I knew mom spent more than dad wanted her to. Mom said I needed the clothes, and I felt so guilty when she said that." She paused, remembering that moment in vivid detail. "Dad looked like he was going to argue; then his eyes got wide and scared, as if something had just jumped out of the closet at him. He put a hand to his chest, then fell to the floor. My mom screamed. She just sat there and screamed. I ran over to him and tried to shake him, but he stared back at me without blinking. His eyes were so big. They said he died instantly, but I couldn't tell, not with the way he was looking at me . . ." Her voice broke at the memory, and it took her a moment to catch her breath.

"I thought he was begging for my help," she said, lifting her gaze to meet Cole's. She saw compassion and understanding in his eyes and felt a trust that she hadn't felt in a long time. She hadn't told anyone about that night—ever. For some reason she wanted to tell Cole now. "I didn't know what to do. My mother couldn't seem to move. She just kept crying. I felt so helpless, and I was angry with her for not helping him." Natalie wiped the moisture gathering in the corners of her eyes. "I think that's when I first knew I wanted to be a doctor. I didn't want to ever feel that helpless again."

"I never realized it was your father's death that motivated you to be a doctor. Was that why you chose to work in the ER?"

"Partly. I thought about cardiology and also pediatrics. Those were my first choices, but I realized that I was better at the quick fix than the long-term doctor-patient relationship. As you know, I'm not very good at personal relationships. Emily's death, the breakup of my friendships, my family, you . . ." She shook her head helplessly. "All failures. In the ER someone comes in with a problem, I fix it and send them home. Or if I can't fix it, I send them to someone who can."

Cole's gaze never left her face. Natalie didn't like it, wishing he would look away. He was reading between the lines of their conversation, an annoying habit as she recalled.

"In and out," he said. "No messy complications."

"Exactly. They don't get to know me. I don't get to know them. Believe me, they're safer that way. Can we leave, please?"

"Where did you go after you lived here?"

"We moved in with my mom's younger sister, Gail, for a year. Then Gail fell in love with a business executive who didn't want us living with them. Gail chose the big, two-story house in Brentwood over us, not that I could blame her. Mom lost it after dad died. She couldn't hold herself together. She drank. She took sleeping pills. She worked as a waitress or a cashier but could never hold a job longer than a few weeks."

"That must have been rough on you."

"I had to become the mother. We moved in with one of my mom's boyfriends next. He was all right, I guess. He didn't pay much attention to me. At least we had a roof over our heads. That lasted about two years. Then he took off. Mom fell apart again. She hated being alone. It's sad when I think about it."

"But she also pissed you off, because she was weak. And you despise weakness in a person."

"That doesn't make me sound very nice. But yes,

I did resent her. I was a kid. I should have been protected, provided for."

"Every kid deserves that," he agreed. "How did you ever get enough money to go to college? I know you worked a couple of jobs, but they couldn't have paid all the bills."

"My grandfather died, and shock of all shocks, he left me fifteen thousand dollars in his will. He'd wanted nothing to do with us before that. I guess he and my mom had some fight over something, and he wrote her off, but apparently he wanted to do something for me after he was gone. If he hadn't left me the money, I probably wouldn't have been able to get through school, even with all the other jobs I was working. I got some scholarships, too, and I still have a lot of loans to pay back, but someday I will, every last one of them." She'd make sure of that. She wouldn't be indebted to anyone. Someday she would be completely free of every tie, every obligation. "Anyway, we can go now. I've seen enough. And you must be bored out of your mind."

He grinned at that. "Natalie, you've been a lot of things to me, but boring isn't one of them. It's interesting to see where you come from. It helps me understand you."

That made her more uneasy. She didn't particularly want to be Cole's focus. Not that she was deluding herself. They were just killing time until Cole could connect with Malone. After that, he would forget all about this little trip down memory lane. Unfortunately, it would probably last a lot longer in her mind.

"Your mother must be proud that you became

a doctor," he continued. "You're quite a success story."

Was that admiration she heard in his voice? "I don't know if she's proud, but she believes I'll be able to take care of her. That's really all that matters."

"Does she live alone now?"

"She has a boyfriend who lives with her. I've never met him, but he's answered the phone when I've called."

"You've called?"

"Yes, you're not the only one with a sense of family duty. Despite everything, I can't forget that we're related and that she's my mother. I won't let her starve or get thrown out on the streets. As for a deeper relationship, it's not going to happen." She shook her finger at him. "And don't try to make me think about changing the way things are. A five-minute discussion doesn't make you an expert on my life or my psyche. Besides that, it's none of your business."

"Are you done?"

"That depends on what you're going to say next. I warn you, Cole. You need to back off. You're not my boyfriend, or even my friend for that matter. My personal life is my personal business."

"It doesn't sound like you have a personal life. I'm beginning to understand why. You don't let anyone get close to you. You've built a wall around your feelings. No one will hurt you ever again."

"So what? It's my life. I like it that way."

"It's not healthy."

"And you're the expert on healthy relationships?" she asked in amazement. "Do I need to remind you about the girlfriend who threw the stapler at your head?"

"We're not talking about me. We're talking about you dealing with your past."

"Oh, just shut up," she said in exasperation. "If I've built a wall around my feelings, it's not because of my mother, it's because of you." The words flew out of her mouth and once spoken, they couldn't be taken back. Nor could she seem to stop herself from continuing. He'd pushed her too far, and now he would have to bear the consequences.

"Do you know that you're the first and only man to whom I said the words *I love you*?" she asked, looking him straight in the eye. "Do you know what it cost me to bare my heart and soul to say those words? And what did you do? You said, *That's great, Nat.* The next thing I knew you were blowing me off, not returning my calls, avoiding me. I was the stupid girl who'd taken sex far too seriously, wasn't I?" She didn't wait for an answer. "You hurt me, Cole. And I should have told you that a long time ago. If anyone made me cold and hard, it was you."

He stared at her with a grim look on his face. "I'm sorry."

"No, you're not."

"I am sorry," he reiterated. "I am." He gazed into her eyes. "When you said you loved me, you scared the shit out of me. I didn't know how to handle it. I was young and stupid. I didn't know what you wanted from me. I didn't know how to say no to what you wanted, because part of me wanted it, too."

There was truth in his words, a truth she'd never

heard before but had known all along. "It doesn't matter. Forget it. None of this has any purpose. It's over and done with."

"It's not though."

"The book and Emily's death have nothing to do with us. We both know we were broken up before she died. We just hadn't formalized it."

"Natalie—" He stopped as his cell phone interrupted their conversation. Checking the number, he swore. "This is not what I need right now."

"Who is it?"

"My father." He shook his head. "I have to answer it. Hello, Dad."

Natalie could hear Cole's father yelling into the phone. He was definitely upset about something.

"I know. I was going to tell you tomorrow night when you got home, but I wanted to get more information," Cole said. "I'm looking into it right now." He listened for a moment. "If you do that, we're going to get more publicity. Let me investigate this on my own. Yes, I know. She didn't do it. I understand, but I still don't think you—" Cole paused. "Dad?" He glared at the phone. "Dammit, he hung up on me."

"What was that about?" Natalie asked. "Or shouldn't I ask?"

Cole slipped the phone back into his pocket. "My father heard about the book. He's still in Europe, but he'll be home tomorrow. In the meantime, he wants me to call the Santa Cruz Police Department and ask them to reopen the case."

That was the last thing she wanted to hear. "Why?"

"He wants them to find Emily's murderer. He wants them to find you."

"Why didn't you tell him you'd already found me?" Natalie asked.

Cole hesitated, then shook his head. "I didn't want to get into it over the phone."

"Do you think the police will reopen the case based on a piece of fiction? Don't they need more evidence than speculation and innuendo?"

"My family has a lot of connections," Cole replied tersely. "I'm sure my father can lean on someone to get something done."

"Great. That's just great. Maybe that's what Malone wanted all along, to get the police reinvolved. He couldn't pin the crime on me himself, but he could get everyone talking about it. Let's go to the radio station, Cole. I want to be waiting for him when he comes in. I want to rip that wig off his head and scrape that makeup off his face. I want to know who he is, and I want to know now."

"Just when I think you're down, you get up swinging," Cole murmured, admiration in his voice. "You're amazing, Natalie."

"I'm pissed off."

"True. And I don't think we should let all that passion go to waste."

Before she could ask him what he meant, his mouth was on hers, hot, demanding, insisting on a response, and her body gave it willingly. Anger mixed with desire, and all the emotions she'd been trying to control exploded in one colossal, spectacular kiss that completely swept her away. She gave herself up to the moment, to the need that told her she'd always wanted this man, and she probably always would.

Wrapping her arms around his neck, she pulled him even closer, and when his hands cupped her breasts, she moaned into his mouth. She wanted his hands on her. She wanted to take off her clothes, and then take off his. She wanted nothing between them . . . not even a memory. Her mind started to drift, and she yanked it back, thrusting her tongue into Cole's mouth, taking him by surprise this time. His tongue danced with hers as they battled for the lead. He wouldn't give it up willingly. Neither would she. She wanted him, but she couldn't lose herself in him. That would be disastrous.

"Damn, you can kiss," he muttered against her mouth a moment later, as they both took a badly needed breath.

"Don't stop," she murmured, the words bursting from her mouth.

"I sure as hell don't want to. There must be something about you and me and cars. I can't seem to keep my hands off of you."

Those hands ran through her hair now. He held her head in place as he pulled back to look at her. His eyes were dark with desire, his mouth full, tinged with the shade of her lipstick. She loved that small mark of possession. Maybe this man would never be hers entirely, but for a few seconds she'd had him right where she wanted him.

"You don't know how much I want to climb into the backseat with you. Just like we did before," he said.

She felt a wave of heat flood her cheeks, and she

closed her eyes. But it didn't matter. She still saw him in her mind. He'd been wearing a tuxedo that night. She'd had on a short red cocktail dress that had cost her a fortune. They'd started kissing on the way to the family Christmas party at the Fairmont Hotel. They'd made out at every stoplight, stolen kisses at every stop sign. And when they'd pulled into a parking space a block away from the hotel, they'd scrambled over the backseat like two teenagers at a drive-in movie.

It had been awkward and clumsy. They'd laughed until they'd kissed and then the sparks between them had burst into passion. It had been unbelievably intense. But that was Cole. His energy, his fire had always made her want to break the rules, throw off the restraints of her life, be someone wild and free, so different from the usually careful and cautious person that she was. She, Natalie Bishop, had given it up in the backseat of Cole's father's Mercedes. And she didn't care. Being with Cole had felt perfectly right. She'd been waiting for him her whole life, and that night she hadn't wanted to wait one second more.

Her breath stuck in her chest as she tried to breathe through the idea that she could have it all again, that passion, that intensity, that fire. She could be that young, reckless girl again.

"Look at me," Cole said.

She didn't want to look, didn't want to be dragged back to reality, but finally she opened her eyes and saw that he, too, remembered.

"It was good," he murmured.

"It was spectacular."

"We finally agree on something. That's a start."

"A start to what?"

Cole hesitated a second too long, a second that revealed more than he could ever say.

"Forget it," she said quickly, anticipating another rejection. "This is a pointless conversation. We can't go back and we can't start over. We're different people now. And what we had is gone."

"It didn't feel gone a moment ago," he muttered.

She pulled away from him, smoothing down her wrinkled blouse, as if she could erase the memory of his hands on her breasts. But in truth they were still tingling, just as her lips were still burning and her stomach still churning with desire and need. Not that she'd tell him that.

Cole sat back in his seat, his hands resting now on the steering wheel, but he made no attempt to start the car. "It meant a lot to me, Natalie, that night in the car, that Christmas, and the other times, too. It was never just sex with you. I want you to know that."

She drew in a sharp breath, feeling dangerously close to losing it. "We should go, right now, and you should stop talking before you say something you regret."

He turned his head to look at her. "I wasn't honest with you before, Natalie."

"Cole, I don't want to get into it now."

"We have to. Dylan said something to me yesterday at the club, about how I'd made it clear to you that it was over between us and how you wouldn't let go. That wasn't the way it was." He paused. "I know now that I was sending you mixed signals back then. I had too many balls up in the air. I was lying to my father about my career plans, trying to set up that job overseas so I could present it to him as a done deal. I was lying to my mother about getting an apartment in San Francisco, and I was avoiding Em, so she wouldn't see how much lying I was doing. Worse, I was lying to myself, pretending that you and I were just a casual thing, because if I let myself believe it was more, maybe I wouldn't want to go on with my plans. Maybe you'd somehow suck me into a life I didn't want."

"I guess my telling you I loved you didn't help," she said, suddenly understanding so much more.

"Love has so many strings, Natalie. I was afraid I'd get tangled up in those strings and never find my way out."

"So you cut them."

"I wish I had cut them, but we both know I just kept giving you more and more slack, confusing you with my intentions."

"Hoping I'd eventually let go. But I can be as persistent as you when I want something, and I wanted you," she said. "I couldn't see past that. I wish you'd told me this before. I thought I was doing something wrong." And she'd driven herself crazy trying to second guess Cole, trying to figure out how she'd screwed up the best thing in her life.

"You weren't doing anything wrong. I was a stupid kid back then. I didn't know how to break up with a woman. I didn't know how to call a halt, slow things down, so I just avoided it."

She thought about that for a moment and had to ask. "Have you really changed, Cole? It occurs to me that your last girlfriend threw a stapler at your head when you didn't realize she was breaking up with you. For a newsman, you're remarkably unskilled in the art of communication."

He gave her a self-condemning smile as he nodded his head in agreement. "You're right. You're absolutely right. I still don't like to make the breakup speech. It's awkward and uncomfortable."

"And it's not awkward to stay with someone you don't care about?"

"I keep busy," he said with a shrug. "Something else you and I have in common, Natalie. And I don't recall you making the big breakup speech with me, either. What happened to equal rights?"

"I didn't want to break up with you, you stupid man," she said in exasperation. "I was madly in love with you, although God knows why. You were impatient, short-tempered, and annoying."

"Come on, tell me what you really think," he said with a laugh that was irresistibly contagious. After a long, pointed glare, Natalie found herself smiling, then chuckling, finally laughing right along with him. It was a welcome release to the emotional tension of the day, and something they both needed.

"I'm glad we cleared the air," he said as he started the car. "I guess it's time to move on."

"I guess it is." She took one last look at her childhood house and knew she would never come back. One ghost had been laid to rest. It was time to get rid of the rest of them.

Chapter 11

Malone was not at the radio station. Upon their arrival, they discovered that he'd canceled his appearance due to illness. Natalie didn't believe it for a second. Neither did Cole.

"This is so damn frustrating," Natalie said as they walked back out to the car. "He's always one step ahead of us."

"I think he's running now. I doubt he'll be appearing anywhere in public anytime soon."

"Then how will we find him?"

"I'm sure my investigators will be able to track him down."

"They haven't so far," she said, feeling grumpy. "Give me your cell phone."

"Why?" he asked, handing her the phone.

"I want to call Malone's publicist. You have her number on the phone, don't you?"

"Under Malone," he said. "What are you going to say?"

"What I should have said as soon as I heard about this book," she replied. The phone rang twice before a woman answered.

"Burke Promotions," she said. "This is Tracey."

"Hi, Tracey. This is Natalie Bishop."

There was a brief, telling silence on the other end of the phone; then Tracey said, "I'm sorry, should I know who you are?"

"You absolutely should, but since you claim that you don't, I'll tell you. I'm the woman known as Nancy in Garrett Malone's book."

"Mr. Malone's book is purely fiction."

"Yeah, you can keep telling yourself that, but that's not going to make it true. Where is he, Miss Burke? We're here at the radio station in Los Angeles, and Malone is nowhere to be found."

"He's ill," Tracey said quickly. "He had to cancel."

"I'll bet he's ill. Well, you can give Mr. Malone a message from me. I'm going to sue his sorry ass for libel, and he's going to wish he never heard of me, much less decided to call me a murderer." She heard the publicist gasp. "Got that? And if I were you, I'd start looking for another job. When I get done with Mr. Malone there won't be anything left of him to publicize." She ended the call on that satisfying note.

"Feel better?" Cole asked as she handed him back the phone.

"As a matter of fact, I do. I know we wanted to take him by surprise, but as you said earlier, he's probably running now anyway, avoiding any chance of a confrontation." She paused, a sudden thought occurring to her. "You know, I can understand why he wants to avoid me, but I don't get why he's avoiding you. His book is about avenging Emily's death. And you're her brother. You want the same thing. You should be on the same side."

"That's true, but I wouldn't have gone this route. He could have called me and told me his suspicions anytime in the last ten years." Cole shook his head. "If this was really about avenging Emily's death, punishing her murderer, he would have done that. There has to be something else going on."

"Something more subtle," she agreed.

"You call this novel subtle?"

"In a way. I don't think Malone could have necessarily predicted the public reaction to the book. It was more like he decided to write a book about Emily in such a way that only a few people would know it was really her."

"It's turning out to be more than a few."

"Yes, it is." She put voice to another thought going through her head. "Instead of focusing on someone who doesn't care for me, I think we should consider the possibility that Malone is someone who really liked Emily, someone she was involved with."

"He's in his forties, Natalie."

"He wants us to think he's in his forties. Don't forget the makeup and the wig." She paused. "What we really need to figure out is who Emily was seeing in the weeks before her death. Madison said she was thinking of having sex with someone. We better find out who that someone was."

"How do you suggest we do that?"

"I sure would love to find Emily's journal."

Cole nodded. "My parents get home tomorrow. Tonight would be the perfect time to take a look through Emily's room. I have to warn you, Natalie, it's a little disturbing."

*   *   *

Emily's room was more than a little disturbing, it was shocking. After flying back from L.A., they'd come directly to the Parish house. Now, as Natalie stood on the threshold, she felt like she was stepping into a time warp. Everything was exactly the way she remembered it—the canopy bed with the sheer curtains tied back in satin ribbons and the variety of stuffed tigers strewn across the pillows. The carpet was a thick, luscious white. An overstuffed chair with an ottoman and soft throw pillows sat near the window, next to the floor-to-ceiling bookshelves full of books and across from the television set, the stereo, and the ten-year-old computer on the desk. Pictures of friends and poster pullouts from teen magazines were still posted to the corkboard that spread halfway across one wall. And there wasn't a speck of dust anywhere.

Natalie swallowed hard, suddenly overwhelmed with sadness. Emily was never going to set foot in this room again. She wasn't going to come bouncing in, her brown eyes sparkling, her cheeks flushed with the excitement of some grand new idea. She wasn't going to sleep in the bed, read the books, hold the stuffed animals in her arms. She was gone, and she wasn't coming back, even though this room looked like it was waiting for her to do just that.

She turned and walked straight into Cole's arms. He held her tight, pressing her head against his chest.

"I know," he murmured. "I feel the same way."

She closed her eyes against the tears that threatened to fall and tried to let the steady beat of Cole's heart calm her shattered nerves. In the past ten years she'd seen some people die right in front of her. She'd watched families embrace and comfort each other. She'd seen immeasurable tragedy, but she'd never felt so sad as she did right now. "I loved her," she said. "I loved her so much. She was more than a friend. She was a sister. And I don't mean a sorority sister. I mean someone who could hear what was in my heart." She lifted her head and gazed into his eyes. "I'm so sorry, Cole. I'm so sorry she's gone. You must miss her so much."

"I do," he said huskily, his eyes suspiciously moist. "That's why I never come in here."

"Who does? Who keeps it this way? Your mom?"

He nodded. "She used to sit in here every night. Sometimes she'd lay on Em's bed, holding those tigers and crying. I could hear her sobbing in my room down the hall. It was . . . horrible." He tightened his arms around Natalie.

"You couldn't let them see how sad you were, could you?" she asked. "You had to be the strong one."

"Someone had to be. I just couldn't understand how it had happened. One minute Emily was there, and the next she was gone. She had so much to offer the world. She had so much life to live. She never got to get married or have children. She never got to build a career for herself, have her own apartment, travel to Europe. She died too young. It wasn't right. If anyone in our family was supposed to die, it should have been me. I'd already seen twice as much as Em."

Natalie could hear his heart breaking in every word he spoke. Life wasn't fair. People died too young every day. But knowing that didn't make it any easier. She reached up and pressed her lips against his mouth in a tender kiss. Cole grabbed on to the kiss as if it were a life preserver and he was a drowning man. She took pleasure in giving him what comfort she could, because she needed it too, this connection to Cole, to love, to life.

When Cole lifted his head, his expression was somber but grateful. "Thanks."

"You're welcome. We better look for the journal. Unless you'd rather not. I don't want to mess up anything in here."

"We'll be careful. We owe it to Emily to find out the truth."

Natalie stepped away from him, drawing in a deep breath as she did so. "Where should we start?"

"The closet. I think my mother put Em's college things in boxes in there."

Natalie was relieved to hear that. Emily's walk-in closet did not hold nearly as many memories as the rest of the room. She opened the door and found four boxes on the floor of the closet, which was still lined with Emily's clothes from a decade ago. "I can't believe your mom hasn't given away these clothes."

"She says it's all she has left of Emily. I know it's kind of sick. She's been better in the last few years though. Dad takes her on a lot of trips, and she keeps busy with charity work. But she can't seem to bring herself to do anything about this room. I can't really blame her, can I?"

Natalie put her hand on his arm in reassurance. "Of course you can't blame her. She's your mother, and she's dealing with her grief the only way she knows how. It's not like this room is hurting anyone. You don't still live here, do you?" she asked, suddenly realizing she had no idea if he did or not.

"God, no! I moved into my own apartment years ago."

"That's good." Natalie kneeled down and opened the first box. Cole moved in beside her and opened the second one. For several minutes they dug through the remnants of Emily's college life. Natalie remembered so many of the items. She could picture them in her dorm room and later in the room they'd shared at the sorority house.

"Here's something," Cole said suddenly, pulling out a stack of three books held together by string.

Natalie felt a rush of excitement at the possibility of finally finding some answers. But that excitement quickly faded as she saw the dates on the books. "Those are all before college," she said with disappointment. "I remember Emily said she'd brought them with her because she didn't want your mom to find them. I guess she wrote some things in there that were private."

"Let's keep looking then."

They dug through the rest of the boxes but came up empty. The journal Emily had written in at school was nowhere to be found. "He must have it," Natalie said.

Cole stretched out on the floor of the closet, his back against the wall. "Malone?"

"Who else?"

"Madison or Laura?"

"I don't think so." She paused, thinking back to

all they had learned. "What about Drew? Madison said Drew went to Emily's room that night to talk to her. Maybe he took the journal."

"When did she say that?" he asked sharply.

"Oh, didn't I tell you? We had dinner last night, the three of us."

"No, you didn't tell me," he said with annoyance.

"Relax. Nothing earth-shattering came out of it. Except that little bit about Drew. But why he'd take Emily's journal is beyond me."

"Unless she wrote something in it about him, something he didn't want anyone else to know. You said before that everyone knew she wrote in it, that you all joked about her using it for blackmail someday."

Natalie thought about that. "True."

"If Em's journal is floating around somewhere, we can't overlook Laura's house."

"I'll call her when I get home," Natalie agreed. "I'll ask her to look for the journal. It might be the perfect time. Didn't Drew say he was going out of town?"

"He did," Cole muttered, a gleam coming into his eyes. "While you're talking to Laura, I'll ask my investigator to check on Drew. It might be interesting to find out where he went on his business trip."

"Dylan is out of town?" Madison asked in dismay. She sat down on a bar stool, feeling decidedly put out. She'd come to Dylan's club right after work, deciding she'd already given him a twenty-four-hour breather and it was time to make her next move. Dylan being out of town was not part of the plan.

"Will I do?" a man asked. He slid onto the stool next to her with a wide grin. "I couldn't help overhearing. I'm not Dylan, but I'm the next best thing."

She knew exactly who he was: Josh Somerville, Dylan's twin brother. As before, it still amazed her that two men could be complete opposites in looks and personalities and still share the same genes. Josh was all sunshine and sparkle, golden blond hair, flashing blue eyes, pearly white teeth, and a smile that said, "Come on in, the water's fine." There was no hint of Dylan's dark, dangerous, "don't mess with me" look. But for some reason she just wasn't turned on by the "golden boy," which was really a pity. She hadn't been with anyone in far too long. Some people would be surprised by that, but she was a lot more discriminating these days.

"Hello, Josh," she said. "Long time no see."

"You're looking good, Madison. What brings you to Club V?"

"I was hoping to catch a magic act."

"Really? I thought you were looking for my brother." He signaled to the bartender to bring him a beer. "Can I buy you a drink?"

"I'd like a martini, thanks."

"That's a sophisticated drink."

"I'm a sophisticated girl. I don't suppose you know where Dylan is."

"I think he's in L.A. I'm not really sure. He travels around a lot these days."

"Doing what? I would think he'd keep busy running this club."

Josh shrugged. "I have no idea. He doesn't tell me much. And that ESP thing that's supposed to exist between twins—not between us."

"That might be a blessing. I can't imagine what the inside of Dylan's brain looks like." She paused as the bartender set down their drinks. "He doesn't like me much, never has. But I'm thinking about changing that."

"He's stubborn once he makes up his mind about someone. It makes him a loyal friend and a bad enemy."

She popped the olive in her mouth, considering that. "What was he to Emily?" she asked, wondering how much Josh knew.

Josh's smile dimmed a bit at that question. "They were good friends."

"Were they more than friends?" Her question made him glance away, and she had a feeling she had her answer. "Were they, Josh? Do you know what I know?"

"What do you know?" he asked sharply, turning back to her.

"I know that Dylan had a raging crush on her. He was mad about her. They spent a lot of time together, a lot of time alone together."

"Emily wasn't that kind of girl."

Madison shook her head, amazed by his naïveté. "What kind of girl is that? A girl who wants love and sex and passion? Because Emily was just like every other girl in that regard. She wasn't a saint. She was a woman."

"She was the girl next door, our friend," Josh

said, a raw edge to his voice. "Dylan and Emily had a special relationship from way back."

"Why was it so special?" Madison asked, feeling an unexpected twinge of jealousy.

"Emily was sick a lot as a kid, so she was always stuck in her room. The Parishes wouldn't even let her have friends over for fear they'd bring germs. But that didn't stop Dylan. He used to climb up the tree next to her bedroom and go through the window to see her. He'd perform tricks for her. She was his best audience, believe me. The rest of us got tired of him pretty fast. But not Emily. She always wanted to see another trick. And he was always happy to give her one." Josh shook his head, then took a swig of his beer. "Cole and I preferred sports, but Dylan was into reading and books. He even used to write poems and stories for her, if you can believe that. Anything to entertain Emily. She was the princess in the tower, and he was determined to rescue her from a life of boredom. It became his mission in life to keep her amused. At least until she got healthier and started leaving the house. Then they drifted apart. Dylan went down to Santa Cruz, and I guess they renewed their friendship when Emily went there two years later."

Madison couldn't quite picture the motorcycle-riding, bad-boy Dylan writing poetry, but then nothing about Dylan added up right. There was something else about Josh's words that struck her funny. It took her a moment to realize what that was. "Did you say Dylan used to write stories?"

"Yeah, mostly stuff about magic worlds, knights of the round table, that kind of thing. He uses those stories in his virtual-reality games now. Have you ever tried one of them?"

"As a matter of fact, I have," she said, not bothering to explain just what virtual world Dylan had taken her to. She was more interested in pursuing her current train of thought. "So you would say that Dylan feels comfortable writing a story?"

Josh raised an eyebrow at that. "What are you getting at?"

"It's just a simple question."

"Nothing is simple about you, Madison. I know Dylan always thought you had a hidden agenda. Why don't you just tell me what's on your mind instead of beating around the bush?"

"All right. Do you think Dylan wrote *Fallen Angel*, the story of Emily and us?"

Josh's jaw dropped open. Either the thought had never occurred to him, or he was an excellent actor. "Are you out of your mind?"

"I don't think I am, Josh. Obviously you've heard about the book."

"I spoke to Cole about it earlier. But you're crazy, Madison. Dylan didn't have anything to do with that book. He loved Emily. He wouldn't have done this to her."

"To her or for her? Think about it, Josh. Who better to avenge the death of the princess in the tower than her white knight?"

Laura leaned back in the desk chair, staring at the bank statement in her hand. It was dated eight months earlier, and there was an unusually large deposit in the sum of fifteen thousand dollars. Where on earth had Drew come up with fifteen thousand extra dollars? And why had he never mentioned it? More important, what had he done with the money, for there was a matching withdrawal in the same amount just one day later.

She threw the paper down on the desk and stared at the photograph of herself and Drew on their wedding day. They looked so young, so in love, so trusting of each other. Now that trust was in serious question, as was the love. Could you have one without the other? She felt like crying, but she couldn't. Her daughters were upstairs, and she didn't want them to know she was upset about anything. She wouldn't make her pain their pain. She'd never liked it when her mother had complained about her father or their marriage. It had always made her feel uncomfortable and somehow disloyal to her father. She wouldn't put her girls in the same position. But she really needed to talk to someone.

As if on cue, the phone rang. She hesitated for a second, wondering if it was finally Drew calling her back. She wanted to talk to him. She needed to talk to him, but she was suddenly afraid of asking a question for which she didn't particularly want an answer. The phone rang again, and she picked it up, still not sure what she would say if it was Drew.

It was Natalie. Laura let out a sigh of relief.

"I need you to look for something," Natalie said. "Emily's journal. You remember the book she used to write in with the purple cover on it, don't you?"

"Of course I do," Laura said in confusion. "Why would I want to look for it? I don't have it."

"Do you know that for sure? Hear me out for a second. Cole and I just got back from L.A. We found a disguise in Malone's hotel room. He's someone we know, Laura. Someone who is hiding from us."

"You didn't find him, though?"

"No, we missed him again, but while we were in the bookstore, I saw a stack of blank journals, and it reminded me of the one Emily used to write in every night."

As Natalie finished explaining her theory that the journal was the basis for the novel, Laura realized where the conversation was heading. "You think it's Drew, don't you?" She couldn't believe she'd said the words aloud. "How could you think it's Drew? That's impossible. I know my husband." But did she? Did she really?

"Madison told us the other night that Drew went to Emily's room that night. Maybe while he was there, he picked up her journal."

"Why? Why would he do that?"

"We used to joke about Emily using that book to blackmail one of us one day, remember?" Natalie paused. "Maybe Drew had something to hide, something he thought Emily might have written about. I just want you to look around, see if it's stuck away anywhere in your house."

"You're asking me to spy on my husband."

"I know I am," Natalie said. "But he's not home, is he?"

"He's in L.A. on a business trip."

"L.A.?" Natalie echoed sharply. "He's in Los Angeles? That's where Malone is."

"It's a big city. A lot of people go there from San Francisco every day," Laura said desperately. "Drew is not Malone. He did not write this book. He's a lawyer. He's my husband. He's the father of my children. I trust him."

There was a long silence on the other end of the

phone. "I understand, Laura. I'm sorry I asked. You're right. It can't be Drew."

Maybe because Natalie backed off, because she acted like a loyal friend, putting Laura's feelings before her own . . . whatever the reason, Laura found herself saying, "Wait." She took a deep breath, hoping she wasn't about to do something she'd regret. "I'll look for the journal."

"But you just said—"

"I know what I said. I'll do it anyway." Laura hung up the phone and stared again at the bank statement. She'd already found fifteen thousand unexplained dollars in Drew's possession. She couldn't possibly count out one old purple journal with secrets that might have incriminated him. Because the one thing Natalie had said that was unarguably true was that Drew would do anything to protect himself.

Chapter 12

Natalie was right on time for the start of her eleven o'clock shift on Wednesday morning. After the emotional turmoil of yesterday's search for the truth, she was relieved to be able to escape to work for a while. She much preferred concentrating on other people's problems rather than her own.

As she approached the entrance to the emergency room, she saw a flurry of press activity and wondered if someone important had been brought in. Usually the press gathered at the main entrance or in one of the conference rooms used by the hospital spokesperson. She was almost at the double doors when she heard one of the reporters call her name.

"Natalie Bishop?" the man repeated.

She whirled around in surprise. "Yes?"

"Are you the Nancy Butler in the novel *Fallen Angel*?"

"What?" she asked, stunned by the question.

"Did you go to school with Emily Parish? Is the novel about the two of you?" another reporter asked.

"I—I—"

"What do you intend to do about the allegations that you killed your friend?"

"I—I have to go," she stammered, pushing past the reporters into the building. They followed her into the waiting room, but she dashed behind another pair of doors and ran straight into the attending physician.

"Natalie, I'm glad you're here," Rita Mills said, taking her arm. "Come with me." She led Natalie past several wide-eyed and curious nurses into an empty examining room. "The reporters arrived about an hour ago. The patients are asking questions about you and some seem concerned as to whether or not they're going to get you as their doctor. I don't understand why you're of so much interest to the press. Apparently it has to do with some novel that's out? I hope you can explain."

Natalie didn't know where to begin, but it was clear from the somber expression on Rita's face that she was not happy with the situation. Rita ran the ER like a tight ship. She didn't tolerate mistakes, sloppy work, or doctors who did stupid things in their time off. Until now Natalie had managed to escape her wrath.

"I'm waiting," Rita prodded, crossing her arms in front of her chest.

"There's a story in a book that resembles an event that happened while I was in college," Natalie said. "It's fiction. It's not true."

"But it involves the local newspaper family, the Parishes?"

"Yes. I went to college with their daughter, Emily. She died while we were at school. It was an accident."

"One of the nurses told me that the book suggests you had something to do with her death."

"I didn't hurt Emily Parish. That's where the book veers from the truth."

"What about dispensing medication without a license?"

Natalie sucked in a gasp of air. The hospital gossips had done a good job. "I didn't do that, either."

"You worked at the university health center, did you not?"

"Yes, but I didn't steal or dispense any drugs improperly."

"Can you prove that?"

"I don't have to prove it. The accusations are in a novel, a book that's supposed to be fictional entertainment."

Rita stared at her for a long moment. "You're an excellent doctor, Natalie. I don't want to lose you, but I think you need a break, a few days off to sort through this. You can start that break now."

"You're right, I am an excellent doctor," Natalie said fiercely. "And this book is nothing but bullshit. The police investigated Emily's death when it happened. It was ruled accidental. The case was closed. There were never any charges or even a hint of suspicion about my job performance at the health center." A rush of anger filled her as Rita remained unmoved. "I can't believe you're allowing a novel to sway your opinion of me. We've worked beside each other for three years. You know me, Rita. You know what kind of person I am, and even more what kind of doctor I am."

"And you know me, Natalie. I do what it takes to keep this department running smoothly, and right now you are causing a huge commotion. I also got a call from Bennett half an hour ago. He wants me to make this go away."

That was typical of the hospital administrator. "I didn't do anything wrong."

"I'm sure you didn't, but you need to find a way to resolve this issue and repair your professional reputation. I don't have to remind you that a physician must be above all scandal. Especially a female doctor. Fix this."

"Dammit," Natalie swore as Rita left her alone in the examining room. She couldn't believe the impact the book was having on her life. As she gazed around the room, noting the familiar machines and instruments, she felt a terrible fear that she might lose it all. The hospital was her home. The doctors and nurses were her family. Her career was everything. She told herself that it couldn't happen, wouldn't happen. She was guilty of nothing. But apparently she was going to have to find a way to prove that. She had to do what Rita said and fix it.

Cole stared at the copy on his desk. He'd already read it twice and it still didn't make sense. His cousin Marty sat in the chair in front of him. A thin, wiry, nervous type in his early twenties, Marty didn't usually deliver copy personally to Cole's desk, yet here he was today, clearing his throat every thirty seconds and running a hand through his hair, obviously worried about Cole's reaction. He had good reason to be.

"What is this?" Cole asked in a quiet voice that barely contained his anger. He looked at Marty, having the sudden urge to hit him. He was tired. He hadn't slept all night, trying to figure out the puzzle of Malone, the novel, Emily's death, and Natalie's involvement.

"We have to cover the story," Marty said in a tight voice. "It's news."

"It's old news. Emily died ten years ago."

"I know that, but the book is happening now. I wish you'd given me the heads-up on this. I was completely broadsided when a source told me that *Entertainment Tonight* is running a preview of tonight's lead story with the tagline *What really happened to Emily Parish, daughter of the Parish publishing dynasty?*"

"Shit!" After his conversation with his father the day before, Cole had known the story was about to blow up. He'd just hoped to have a few days before it exploded, enough time to locate Malone. Apparently, that wasn't going to happen. Who the hell had called *ET*? Where was the buzz coming from? He knew it wasn't coming from Natalie or himself.

"This brief article gives just enough detail to keep us in the game," Marty said.

Cole ignored that as he leaned back in his chair. "I want to stick with no comment for the moment."

"We can't do that. The integrity of the paper is at stake. We can't let every other news organization cover the story of one of our own." He paused, uttering a nervous cough. "You know we've been slipping the past year. Every day our circulation numbers go down a little bit more. We have reporters all over the world, but hardly anyone covering our own city. And now this. If we refuse to print information about this book, it might put us over the edge."

Cole heard every word Marty said. But this was Emily they were talking about.

"This is the best way to tell our side of the story, to let the world know we're conducting our own investigation," Marty argued.

He knew Marty was right. They had to put out some sort of statement and this was the best compromise. "Fine, run it. But we'll have no further comment until we speak to the author of the book."

As Marty left the room, Jack Hinkley walked in. Jack was a fifty-year-old private investigator who worked for the paper on occasion and most recently on finding Malone. He shut the door behind him and sat down in the chair across from Cole's desk.

"Malone has disappeared off the radar," Jack said bluntly. "He has canceled all scheduled appearances. His publicist claims she resigned yesterday afternoon when it became clear to her that Malone may have misrepresented himself and his book. She says she doesn't know where he is or even where he came from. Apparently, their entire contact was by phone or e-mail."

"His publisher must know who he is. His agent?"

"All of his business correspondence was sent to a post office box. His phone is being picked up by an answering machine. The copyright for the book is held in the name of a corporation with a tax ID number. I'm unraveling that trail as we speak, but it's clear that this guy set out to hide his true identity. There's no question about that."

Of course he had. Malone had plotted this scenario out carefully, even going so far as to disguise himself. As much as Cole wanted to forget Natalie's suggestion that Dylan was involved, Cole had to admit that the whole thing had a Dylan flair to it. Not that he could imagine any reason why Dylan would write such a book. Unless Dylan held Natalie responsible for Emily's death. Had he written the book to punish her for a crime he felt she'd gotten away with?

"Malone is a slippery bastard, but I'll find him," Jack continued, drawing Cole's attention back to the problem at hand. "In the meantime, I did some checking on that other name you gave me last night." He referred to his notes. "Drew McKinney." He paused and looked at Cole. "He's come a long way from his trailer park roots in Modesto. His father has a history of gambling. His mother is a hairdresser. They don't live well, but McKinney does. He's a successful, ambitious lawyer who married into a good family."

"I know all that. What I don't know is what he's been doing for the last year."

"Traveling a great deal. He's in Los Angeles now."

"Where Malone supposedly is," Cole said with a nod, remembering Natalie's conversation with Laura the evening before. "Try to find out if any of his other business trips coincided with Malone appearances."

"Already on it. I'll be in touch when I have more answers. Anyone else you want me to look into?"

Cole hesitated, wondering if he should mention Dylan; then he shook his head. Dylan was his best friend. If there was any investigating to be done, he would do it himself.

"Okay, then." Jack got to his feet. "You know, Emily was a great kid. I remember her sitting at your father's desk drawing pictures. It's a tragedy what happened to her. I'll do anything to help make this right for your family."

"Thanks, I appreciate that." As Jack left the room, Cole's cell phone rang. A chill ran through him as he saw the number. He did not want to take this call, but he knew he'd only be postponing the inevitable. "Hello, Dad? Are you home?"

"No, I'm at the hospital," his father said. "We were mobbed by reporters at the house. Your mother collapsed when they asked her about Emily's . . . *murder.*" Richard Parish's voice shook with grief and rage. "I thought I told you to take care of this before we got back."

"I'm trying," Cole said, but he knew the answer wasn't good enough for either of them.

"Try harder." His father hung up on him before he could ask which hospital.

Cole hoped to God it wasn't St. Timothy's.

Natalie sat in her car in the hospital parking lot for a good five minutes. Part of her wanted to return to the ER and persuade Rita to let her work out her shift. Being a doctor was what she did best. The hospital was her refuge, her safe haven—a haven that had just been invaded by the press. Where on earth had they all come from? What had happened between last night and this morning to alert the media? Maybe Cole had some idea. He *was* the media. Which made her wonder—had any of those reporters been from the *Tribune*? Surely Cole wouldn't cover the story, would he?

But wouldn't he have to? He was a news man, running the biggest newspaper in town. More than anyone, she knew he took his duty to family and the family business seriously. If it came to a choice between the family and her, there was no doubt in her mind which way he'd go.

Starting her car, she pulled out of the parking lot. She wasn't accomplishing anything by sitting, and she hated to be idle, which made going back to her apartment a very unappealing idea. It would be quiet there, too quiet. And it wouldn't serve any purpose. She needed to make a move. Take action. Fix things, as her boss had suggested.

But first . . . she needed a friend. It had been a long time since she'd expressed that need to herself. Over the years she'd told herself that relying on anyone was just plain stupidity. Her mother had let her down numerous times, not to mention the other relatives who had passed in and out of her life as quickly as they could. She had to remember that she was fine on her own. She got into trouble only when she let herself care, when she opened herself up—the way she'd done with Emily, Laura, and Madison, and especially with Cole. He'd knocked down her guard wall as if it were made of marshmallows. She'd let him all the way into her life and her heart, and she'd paid a dear price for those few months of love. It had taken her a while to build the wall back up and she'd thought it was strong and impenetrable. Now it was shaking again.

She'd caught a glimpse of the life she used to have with her girlfriends and with Cole, and she was hungering for that life like a woman who'd been on a diet for too long and had suddenly seen a luscious piece of chocolate cake. Just one bite, she told herself, one more conversation or two, that's all she needed. She wasn't going to see Laura just because of friendship; she needed to talk to her about the journal.

Her rationalizations continued all the way down the highway to Laura's house. Natalie considered turning around more than once, but here she was driving through the quiet tree-lined suburban neighborhood of Atherton. She parked in front of Laura's beautiful home, got out of the car, and walked up to the front door. As she raised her hand to the doorbell, she paused, hearing the sound of music coming from inside. It was so sweet, so familiar. Laura was playing the flute.

Natalie had always loved to hear Laura play. It was as if she blew out all her insecurities and doubts and was left with nothing but serenity, peace. And everyone who was listening got caught up in that peace. The music stopped and Natalie rang the bell. The door opened a moment later.

"Natalie," Laura said with a smile. "What a nice surprise."

"I know I should have called first, but there were reporters at the hospital and I had to get away."

"There were reporters where you work? That doesn't sound good. Come on in." She motioned Natalie into the house, shutting the door behind her.

"I heard you playing just now," Natalie said, catching sight of Laura's flute on the coffee table in the living room. She walked into the room and picked it up. "This is the one you had in college, isn't it?"

"Yes, I just started playing again a couple of days ago. I'm definitely rusty."

"You sounded great."

"Really?" Laura asked, an insecure note in her voice. "You're not just saying that? Because you don't have to say that. I haven't played in ten years. I'm sure it wasn't great."

"You were always a natural with the flute. The only classical concerts I ever sat through were ones in college that you insisted we attend."

Laura grinned. "I was trying to get you a little culture."

"I needed it. So why haven't you played all these years?"

Laura took the flute out of Natalie's hand and set it back in its case. "There wasn't time or room in my life for music after Drew and I got together. First there was the wedding. That took most of my senior year to plan. Then we wanted to have kids right away, and Drew was going to law school, and life was crazy. I let it go. It wasn't like I was ever going to have a music career."

"You were good enough to have a career."

"I probably wasn't good enough. But even if I had the talent, I never had the drive. Back then I had it in my head that finding a husband, getting married, and starting a family were what I needed to do."

Natalie nodded, remembering many long discussions on that very subject. They'd tried to slow Laura down, tell her to take her time. She didn't have to do it all right away. She had time to be young and foolish. But while Laura had had her friends' voices in one ear, she'd had her mother's voice in the other, telling her she needed to find a good man, because she wasn't smart enough to make it on her own. Natalie had never cared much for Laura's parents on the few occasions that they'd met, mainly because they were always tearing Laura down, making her the butt of jokes. "You let your family influence you too much," she said now. "You were always smarter than your parents gave you credit for."

"Maybe I wasn't. Look where I am now, in this perfect house, with my perfect family, and I'm not happy." She blinked rapidly, her mouth starting to tremble.

"Laura, what's wrong?"

"Everything's wrong. It's supposed to be right, but it's not. And I don't know what to do."

Natalie took Laura's hand and pulled her toward the couch. "Let's sit down, and you can tell me what your choices are."

"I don't know what my choices are," Laura complained. "That's the problem. I feel like I'm trapped, and I did it all to myself." She paused. "I looked for Emily's journal like you asked, Natalie. I didn't find it, but I did find some other stuff." Laura drew in a deep breath and continued. "There are weird deposits and withdrawals in my bank account. You have to understand that I don't do the banking. Drew does. He pays the bills, too. He's always been big on being the provider. I have so much else to do that I never fought him on it. But

I started going through our statements, and I don't know where this money is coming from or where it's going."

Natalie didn't like the sound of that, but she was trying to be a friend. "It could be legitimate, bonuses at work."

"Yes, you're right. I know he gets bonuses on big cases, so it could very well be that. I just don't like the fact that he never mentioned any bonuses or big withdrawals. Fifteen thousand dollars goes in, then it goes out. What did he pay for? I can't follow a trail."

"Maybe you should just ask him."

"He won't be back until tomorrow. I don't want to do it on the phone. Frankly, there are a lot of things we need to talk about, but Drew is so touchy lately. I can't say anything right. I think it's possible he's having an affair."

"I hope that's not true."

"It's my fault. I try to keep myself in shape, but I eat too much, and—"

"Stop," Natalie said, cutting her off deliberately. "If Drew is cheating, it has nothing to do with you, and everything to do with him. I don't care if you've gained five pounds or fifty pounds. You can't blame yourself for your husband's actions."

"You always see everything in black and white, but it's complicated," Laura said, a bit of a familiar whine in her voice.

"You make it complicated, Laura."

"That's probably true." Laura hesitated, giving Natalie a searching look. "Do you think people can fall out of love? Or do you think real love lasts forever?"

Natalie didn't know how to answer that question. "I'm not an expert on love, Laura, but I think it takes a lot of work to keep a relationship going. There are going to be good times and bad times through the years."

"I was listening to some talk show," Laura said, "and they had on this woman who'd been married for forty years, and they asked her what her secret was, and she said, 'We never fell out of love at the same time. There was always one of us trying to hang on.' I think I'm the only one right now trying to hang on. In fact, sometimes I think Drew wants me to ask him something or push him in some direction. He wants an excuse to get mad or have an affair or walk out on us, because he can't do it for some selfish reason. My parents love him to death, but they wouldn't like it if he abandoned me. On the other hand, if they thought I'd been the one to screw up, they'd probably take his side." Laura sighed. "I'm sorry. You don't want to hear about my marital problems."

"I don't mind. I wish I could give you some brilliant advice, but I don't know anything about what it takes to make a marriage work. The one thing I do know is that you have to make yourself happy, Laura. You can't rely on someone else to do it for you. You can't keep looking for support or reinforcement from people who don't want to give it to you. You have to give it to yourself."

Laura stared at her through serious eyes. "You are so smart."

"No, I've just had more experience with nonsupportive people in my life. It seems to me that you're so busy worrying about taking care of everyone else that you've forgotten to take care of yourself. Maybe you should do something just for you."

"It's funny you should say that. I saw an ad for auditions for the local community orchestra. It's a small-town thing. The orchestra plays at the recreation center on weekends and during the holidays."

"Are you going to try out?"

"I shouldn't."

"I think it's a great idea."

"My daughters will think I've lost my mind."

Natalie shook her head. "I imagine they'll be really proud of their mother. Kids want to be proud of their parents. I know I always wished my mom would make a life for herself instead of depending on some guy to make it for her."

"You'll never make that mistake," Laura said with a smile. "You'll never live your life for some guy."

"I'll probably die alone, too."

"I don't think so." She paused. "Well, I'll consider it. The tryouts aren't until next week, and I need to practice anyway. Hey, do you want some coffee?"

"I would love some." Natalie followed Laura down the hall and into her large, bright kitchen. She took a seat on a stool at the island counter. "This is a beautiful room."

"Thanks. We remodeled a couple of years ago."

Laura started the coffeemaker while Natalie looked around. The photos on the refrigerator were held in place by magnets and colorful alphabet letters. Everywhere she looked there were signs of a family. Even though there were obvious problems in Laura's marriage, she still had a pretty nice life going.

Natalie's heart twisted at the thought that she might never have this kind of normal life. And it suddenly hit her that she wanted it. For the past ten years she'd thought of nothing but her career. Now, after one moment in Laura's family kitchen, Natalie suddenly wanted to have more, specifically a husband, children, and a home of her own. She shook her head, trying to dislodge the image from her brain, because the man in the picture looked a lot like Cole, and that really was a crazy idea.

"What's wrong?" Laura asked.

"Nothing."

"While we're waiting for the coffee, let's go downstairs. I have some things in the basement I bet you haven't seen in a while."

Laura led Natalie down a flight of stairs just off the kitchen. The basement was a semifinished room, one half of the room devoted to arts and crafts, the other holding numerous boxes, suitcases, and trunks. On a table in the middle of the room was a stack of books. Natalie's heart quickened at the sight of those familiar books. Laura had always been the scrapbook queen, and she'd chronicled just about every second of their days in Santa Cruz.

Natalie picked up a book and opened it. The first few pages were filled with photos from their freshman year in the dorms. "Oh, my God, look at my hair," she muttered. "It's huge."

Laura laughed. "You have always had great hair, thick and curly. People pay a lot of money to get what you try to straighten."

Natalie turned the page to see the first photo of the four of them together taken out in the hallway in front of their dorm room. They'd done a typical girl pose, arms around each other, each one pulling up the edge of her shorts to reveal more leg. They were totally different from each other—tall to short, blond to brunette to a redhead, but on their faces were matching smiles and grins. What a look of innocence, Natalie thought, feeling a rush of emotion. They had no idea where they were heading, what they would go through, how long they would actually have each other. Her gaze zeroed in on Emily's bright smile full of promise and joy. She bit down on her lip. It was so hard to look at Emily now, to know that her promise would never be fulfilled.

"Em looks happy," Laura commented. "But then, she always did. I still can't quite believe that anyone deliberately pushed her off the roof. Everyone loved her so much. How did her tragic death turn into a murder mystery? And how did you become the prime suspect?"

Natalie had been thinking about that a lot. "Emily must have said something about me in her journal, something that led Malone to believe we were fighting that night."

"Or he just made it up. That's why he called it fiction instead of nonfiction."

"Actually, I think he just did that to make it more difficult for me to sue him." She paused, hesitant to broach the subject of Drew again, but she couldn't leave any stone unturned. "Don't you find it odd that Drew is not mentioned in the novel?

How did he escape Malone's notice? He was with us a lot. And Drew doesn't like me. When Cole and I dropped by the other day, he told me I'd let you all down, that he had no time for me. I didn't quite get it, Laura, because I don't remember Drew and I having some big blowout or anything. We were never that close, but we weren't enemies back then. Yet we seem to be now. Unless he said things to you that I didn't know about."

Laura glanced down at the scrapbook, obviously debating an answer. Natalie felt her pulse quicken. Laura knew something, but what?

"He didn't dislike you back then, Natalie, but I think you reminded him of things he didn't want to think about," she said finally.

"Okay, now I'm totally confused. What are you talking about?"

"Drew grew up in a trailer park. He came from nothing, Natalie, just like you. He was ashamed of his background, his parents. When he got to college he wanted to be someone else, someone important. I think he was afraid to get close to you, afraid you'd expose him in some way. He always used to tell me how smart he thought you were."

Natalie sat down on the chair by the table, floored by Laura's latest statement. "Why would I have wanted to expose Drew? I didn't even know about his past. Nor did I care."

"I know that. I've been with him for more than ten years. I've learned the way his mind works, and he likes to be with rich people. He likes to pretend that he's always been someone with money and the luxuries of life. We've seen his parents probably five times in the last ten years. We've never been back to Modesto, where he grew up. It's as if he wants to erase that part of his life."

"I can relate to that," Natalie said with a better understanding now of the complexities of Drew McKinney. "He had me fooled. I thought he was just an upper-middle-class beach boy who was going to party his way through college."

"That's what he wanted everyone to think."

"He did a good job reinventing himself," Natalie said.

Laura frowned at her words and gazed into her eyes with a troubled expression. "I walked right into that one, didn't I? I just don't think it's him, Natalie. I don't think Drew is Malone."

"Well, you know him the best," Natalie said carefully.

"Yes, I know him the best," Laura echoed with conviction. "I think our coffee is ready now. Do you want to bring the scrapbooks upstairs?"

Natalie glanced down at the photo of the Fabulous Four and shook her head. "I've seen enough."

"Are you sure? There are photos of you and Cole in there."

The last thing she wanted to see was a photo of her and Cole. A vivid snapshot of their young, passionate love was only going to make it that much harder to keep him at arm's length now.

Chapter 13

Cole's mother was being discharged when he drove up to the ER entrance at Good Samaritan Hospital, located across town from St. Timothy's. He thanked God for that small favor. The last thing his mother needed today was to run into Natalie. Getting out of his car, he jogged over to where his dad was helping his mom get into their car. She was obviously upset, her cheeks red from crying, her brown hair matted from sweat. When she saw him, she practically fell into his arms.

"Oh, Cole. I'm so happy to see you," she said tearfully.

"I'm happy to see you, too," he muttered. His mother had always been small and slender, but today she felt frail in his arms, as if she could be easily broken. It occurred to him that he'd spent the first part of his life worrying about his little sister and the last decade worrying about his mother. At least his father was strong, except when it came to his wife. She was his Achilles' heel. As he looked over his mother's shoulder, Cole could see the worry in his father's eyes.

"We should get you into the car, Janet," Richard

said. "It's breezy out here. The last thing we need is for you to catch a cold."

Janet pulled back and put her hand against Cole's cheek, a sorrowful look in her brown eyes. "You look tired, Cole. Are you all right?"

"Hey, I'm the one who should be asking you that question. Dad said you collapsed."

Richard gave Cole a warning shake of his head, but it was too late to pull back the question.

"I couldn't believe what those reporters at the house were saying about Emily," Janet replied. Her expression pleaded with him to tell her it wasn't true, that it was all a horrible nightmare, and he wanted to do just that, but he couldn't.

"We're going to fix it," he said instead. "Don't worry about anything. Just take care of yourself and feel better."

Her eyes blurred with tears. "I thought it was over, Cole. It should be over. Why isn't it?"

"It will be," Richard Parish said with authority. "We'll find out everything we need to know, Janet. But you need to go home and sleep now. That's what the doctor said. Lots and lots of rest."

"Will you come to the house with us, Cole?" she asked. "We can still have dinner as we planned."

"Don't worry about dinner. Rest tonight and we'll talk tomorrow."

"All right. Don't work too hard." She got into the car and Cole shut the door behind her.

"Is she really okay?" Cole asked his father.

"She's never okay, not when it comes to Emily," Richard said with a heavy sigh. "We were having such a good trip, too. She was happy in Italy. She loved Venice. I couldn't get her out of those gondolas. But she got a little stomach bug the last few days. Combine that with the long flight and the reporters waiting for us at the house—it was just too much for her. When she heard those words about Emily being . . ."

His father's face turned pale, and he shook his head, obviously unable to finish the sentence. Cole didn't blame him. He'd had a little longer to deal with the situation, and he still flinched every time he thought about Emily being pushed off that roof.

"The doctor prescribed a sedative," his father continued a moment later. "I want to get her home and into bed, so she can sleep for the next twelve hours."

Cole nodded. "That sounds like a plan."

"What's happening with the case? Have you found out anything yet? Have you spoken to the police?"

"Not yet."

"Why the hell not?"

"Because we need to find Malone first."

"And you don't think the police can help with that?"

"I've got Hinkley working on it," Cole replied. "You've said yourself he's the best. I was trying to avoid publicity."

"Obviously you weren't successful. There were reporters from all the networks at the house. We're the biggest news story in town. Speaking of which, are we covering ourselves?"

"Marty wrote up a neutral piece stressing the process of investigating the situation. It will be in tomorrow's paper."

"What about Natalie Bishop? I can't believe I

didn't see this possibility sooner. I thought she and Emily were friends."

"They were friends."

"Maybe they weren't. You broke up with her. Maybe Emily had a problem with her, too."

"It was different between us," Cole started to explain, but his father interrupted.

"I don't give a shit about your relationship with her. I want to know what was going on with Natalie and Emily. When I get home, I'm calling Detective Boland. With any luck he's still working for the Santa Cruz Police Department."

Cole was relieved when his mother opened the door to ask if there was a problem. "No problem," he lied. "We're just talking business."

"I'll be right there," Richard said, closing her door again. "Is there anything else I should know?"

"Do you know anything about a journal that Emily might have kept at school?" Cole asked.

"I don't, but your mother might. Is it important?"

"It could be."

"I'll talk to her about it when she's feeling more calm." His sharp eyes narrowed. "Is the journal where Malone got his information?"

"It's possible. I went through Emily's closet yesterday to see if I could find it in the boxes of her things that we brought back from Santa Cruz, but there was nothing there." He paused, seeing his mother once again look at them with concern. "You better go. Take care of Mom. I'll handle this problem."

"Don't let me down, Cole. More important, don't let your sister down."

As Cole watched his parents drive off, he knew that he'd already let his sister down once, and he wouldn't do it again. He'd find out the truth about Emily's death once and for all. And he wouldn't stop until he did. But first he had to warn Natalie that his parents were home, and his father wanted someone's head on a platter, preferably hers.

When Natalie returned to her apartment just before two o'clock, she saw several reporters and cameras in front of her building. She parked down the street and walked tentatively toward her home, wondering with each step if it wouldn't be better to retreat. But she couldn't stay away forever. She'd have to go past them sometime.

A woman saw her, called out her name, and suddenly the group swarmed toward her, firing questions like bullets from a gun. There was a camera this time and a man holding a microphone. Good Lord! Was this going on television?

Her head spun. She couldn't hear the questions. They were one big blur of glaring, accusatory noise. Words jumped out at her—murderer, crime, victim, tragedy, Emily, best friends, Fabulous Four, followed by why, why, and why.

"Natalie." His voice rang through the air loud and clear like a foghorn leading a floundering ship home. She searched the crowd for him. And there he was.

Cole barreled his way through the reporters, grabbed her hand, and pulled her down the sidewalk. They sprinted toward his car, the reporters following close behind. Thankfully, Cole managed to pull away from the curb without hitting anyone,

which Natalie considered a minor·miracle. For long
moments they didn't say a word. She felt like she'd
just run a marathon. She couldn't catch her breath.
Her heart pounded against her chest.

"Okay?" Cole asked.

She shook her head. He put a hand on her knee.
"It's going to be okay."

She shook her head again. It wasn't going to be
okay. Everyone thought she was a murderer—a
criminal—a horrible, horrible person. The worst
thing was that she couldn't even deny the crime
with one hundred percent certainty. She had no
facts, only a belief in herself.

"Trust me," he said.

God, she wanted to. She wanted to trust him
more than anything. "Why were you at my
apartment?"

"I thought you might run into trouble with the
press."

"It's like feeding time at the zoo. How long is
this going to last?"

"Hopefully no more than fifteen minutes."

"It's already been longer than that." She
frowned, realizing that this type of event was part
of Cole's daily life. "Did one of those reporters
belong to your paper?"

He sent her an apologetic glance. "Yes."

"You're covering this story in the *Tribune?* How
can you do that, Cole?"

"I don't have a choice."

"I see." She stared straight ahead for a long moment, computing the facts. "What are you saying
about me?"

"The article is about Emily, my family, and the book. It's short and to the point."

It was a nice explanation, but she wasn't buying it. She turned back to look at him and saw him avoid her gaze. "Come on, Cole. I'm the most interesting part of the story, the beloved sorority sister turned killer. That's why the reporters are hounding me. The fact that I'm now a doctor makes it even better. You know, I was asked to take a leave of absence today. My boss told me to fix this quick. Please tell me you have some good news."

Cole pulled over to the side of the road on a quiet neighborhood street and turned off the engine. "I wish I did," he said, turning in his seat. "My parents arrived home to the same feeding frenzy you just faced. My mother collapsed with chest pain and was rushed to the hospital. She's okay," he said quickly. "Just very stressed out. My father is crazed. I can't think of a better word than that. He's going to call the Santa Cruz Police, and he wants me to find you."

"You didn't tell him you already had?"

"It wasn't the right time."

She nodded. "They hate me. Your parents hate me."

"They don't understand what's going on."

"So what do we do next? Any brilliant ideas?"

"I think we need a break. I don't know about you, but I need to get off this treadmill and catch my breath. I can't tell you how I felt when my father called and said my mother had collapsed. A picture flashed into my mind of my mother lying on the ground just like Emily." He leaned his head back against the headrest and closed his eyes. "I can still see her." He paused for a long moment. "When Josh and I arrived at the house, we heard music and then what sounded like a scream. I didn't know what it was until I saw everyone running into the side yard when we got there. Emily was on her back. She looked like she was sleeping, but there was blood running out of the corner of her mouth. I leaned down to wipe it away with my sleeve, but it kept coming." His voice caught in his throat.

"Don't go there, Cole." Natalie put her hand on his arm, knowing she had to stop him right there. "Don't do this to yourself."

His eyes opened and he gave her a long, searching gaze. "Did you see her that night? Did you see her before they covered her up?"

Natalie tried to swallow, but there was a huge lump in her throat as she remembered the crowd of people gathered in the yard, everyone screaming and crying. Madison had her by the hand. She'd pulled her out of the bathroom and down the stairs saying they had to get to Emily. But no one would let them through. Finally, they got to the front. Natalie saw Cole kneeling beside his sister. Dylan and Josh hovered on the other side, watching the paramedics try to save her life, but it was too late. She had died on impact.

"The only thing I could see," she said haltingly, "was Em's beautiful brown hair spread across the white cement the way it used to spread across her pillow when she slept." She tightened her grip on his arm, feeling the need to hang on to him. "I couldn't get closer to her than that. I couldn't even believe it was happening. It seemed like a nightmare. For weeks I kept trying to wake up."

"Me, too," he said huskily, putting his hand behind her head and pulling her close. He rested his forehead against hers. "I still want to wake up, but I can't. I'm stuck there. I think I've moved on and then something yanks me right back. How do I let go?"

"I don't know." They'd tried to run, but the past had hunted them down with a vengeance.

"I can't go through it again," he murmured. "I can't lose my mother, too." He pulled away so she could see his face. "That year after Emily died, I was afraid every second that my mother would hurt herself or just give up on living. I felt helpless to make it better. What if the same thing happens now? What if she can't get past this?"

Natalie felt her heart opening up to Cole. His honesty, his trust to confide in her touched her deeply. She knew these were words he couldn't say to anyone else, and she was honored that he'd said them to her. She just wished she could make him feel better. "Your mom made it then, and she'll make it now," she said with conviction. "People are stronger than you think, especially mothers. And she still has you."

"Small consolation. Emily was the light of her life. I always knew that. I wasn't jealous. Emily was special. I understood that."

"Emily was special, but so are you, and I know that you have a big piece of your mother's heart. She used to tell me how smart you were, how proud she was of you."

"No, she didn't," he said skeptically.

"She did. That Christmas I spent at your house, we went through the home movies one night. You'd gone out with your dad somewhere, but your mom, Emily, and I watched the movies and talked about you. They both knew I was falling madly in love with you, and they wanted me to know you were an incredible guy. But they didn't have to convince me. I already knew that."

His mouth curved into a reluctant smile. "Now you're shoveling it on. I'm sure your opinion of me changed in the weeks after that Christmas when I treated you like shit."

"Of course it did. You really pissed me off," she said candidly. "But we've both had a few years to gain some clarity." And those years of clarity made her let go of Cole's arm and sit back in her seat.

"You must be a great doctor," Cole commented. "You have a hell of a bedside manner. I feel better."

"Good. Since I'm now acting as your doctor, I have a prescription for you."

"So we're playing doctor now?" he asked, lightening the mood with his teasing question.

"Very funny. No, I think you were right when you said you needed a break."

"I know I said that, but it isn't a good idea. There's so much to do. My father is probably on the phone right now to the police department. I need to check in again with my investigator. I need to track down Dylan, and—"

"You can do all that later. You should go home, take a nap, watch a sporting event on TV, or since it's you, turn on one of the news channels and let your mind go."

"What about you? What are you going to do?"

"I don't know," she said. "Do you think the reporters will have left?"

"Doubtful. They'll wait a while to make sure we don't circle back."

"Great."

They sat silently for a few minutes; then Cole said, "I have an idea. Do you feel like being anonymous for a while?"

"More than I want to take my next breath."

Cole glanced over at her and smiled. "We could play tourist in San Francisco, do all the things locals never do. I bet you've spent most of the past few years inside the hospital walls. Am I right?"

"You might be."

He nodded. "I knew it. Let's go." Cole started the car.

"Go where?"

"Well, first we need to get a disguise."

His words made her think of the disguise they'd found in Malone's room, and she felt guilty at the thought of taking some time off from the problem at hand. But the last few days, and especially the last few minutes, had been emotionally draining. She needed some fresh air, some wind in her face. Maybe she'd be able to think more clearly after a time-out.

A San Francisco Giants baseball cap covered her glorious red hair, a pair of dark sunglasses concealed her eyes, and a large gray sweatshirt made her look ten pounds heavier, but Cole still thought Natalie was the prettiest woman he'd ever seen. Actually, that wasn't completely true. While he was no doubt attracted to her body, he was also fascinated by the rest of her: the sharpness of her mind, the generosity of her spirit, the tenderness of her smile. She was a complicated woman—driven, ambitious, an achiever, tough when she had to be, and yet sometimes he saw the lingering remnants of a lonely girl who just wanted someone to love her the way she deserved to be loved. He'd once been that man. He'd blown it big-time, and he'd hurt her. She didn't have to tell him that. He knew. He'd known it a long time ago.

Natalie leaned over the railing to look at the water below. They were taking the Blue and Gold Ferry to Alcatraz. It was a chilly October day, especially here on the water, but Natalie seemed to be enjoying the fresh air. She looked more relaxed now than he'd seen her in a long time.

On impulse, he put his arm around her. She looked up, giving him a questioning glance, but she didn't move away. If he was going to take an inch, he might as well take a yard, he decided, drawing her closer to his body. "This is better," he said with a grin. "I was getting cold."

"That's the best line you've got? Ten years as San Francisco's most eligible bachelor, and you're using the 'I'm cold' line. Not very impressive, Cole."

Trust Natalie to call him on it. She'd never been an easy woman. Although she'd been easier at nineteen than she was now. It was funny. He almost liked her better now, because of her toughness, her confidence in herself, her unwillingness to be led. A strange tightness took over his chest, and he was struck by the ridiculous thought that he might be falling in love with her again. No, he told himself, it was just the challenge of being with a woman who didn't suck up to him all the time. That was what he was enjoying. It wasn't love.

God! He didn't even think the word *love* was in his vocabulary. Where had that come from? He didn't intend to love anyone in any kind of permanent way. Sex, friendship, that was all he needed, all he wanted. And Natalie would never be content with that. Would she?

Maybe she would. Maybe sex and friendship would fit right into her busy lifestyle. Maybe that's exactly what she would want.

"Cole," Natalie said, interrupting his thoughts, which was probably a good thing, "you haven't said a word in about five minutes. It was a joke, you know, about the 'I'm cold' line."

"I know." He slid her in front of him, wrapped his arms around her waist, and rested his chin on the top of her head as they stared at the island of Alcatraz growing bigger with each passing minute. "Have you ever been on the island?" he asked.

"Never."

"It must have been hell on earth for the inmates who lived there, but it's actually one of the prettiest spots around. There are incredible views from the prisoners' yard."

"So they were doubly tortured," Natalie said. "They could see exactly what they couldn't have. That must have driven them crazy."

Cole was beginning to feel the same way. Being

with Natalie, holding her in his arms, breathing in the scent of her skin was making him want her with an almost overwhelming need. He couldn't have her, not just because of their history, but because of their present. His family held her responsible for Emily's death. They would never accept her as his girlfriend, his lover, his . . . anything. And he couldn't choose her over them, even if he had the choice, which he didn't. Natalie didn't want him anymore. Sure, there were a few lingering sparks, but that was probably true for any two people who'd once been lovers, especially when that love had been a first love, a powerful love. What the hell was wrong with him? That was three loves in one thought. He was definitely losing it.

"My mother almost went to prison once," Natalie said, surprising him with that abrupt turn in the conversation.

"For what?"

"One of her boyfriends robbed a liquor store. She was in the car, passed out. Fortunately, being that drunk got her off from being an accessory to the crime."

"Where were you at the time?" he asked, feeling a decided dislike for Natalie's mother.

"I was studying in the library after school. I spent hours there. It was a safe place, you know. I knew who I was at school, a good student, someone who could succeed, and I loved the structure. The bells rang every hour. I knew where I had to be, and what I had to do. When I went home, life was a lot more unpredictable."

He planted a tender kiss on the nape of her neck. "I'm sorry," he murmured.

"It's not your fault. I don't even know why I told you that." She paused. "My mother wasn't a bad person. She was just weak and sick. Drinking made everything worse. I don't know why I ever took a drink, Cole. I knew it was wrong. I knew it would ruin me and the people around me. I had firsthand experience." She twisted around in his arms so that she was facing him now. "I thought I could handle it. I could be different. I was stronger than my mother." She shook her head. "But in those moments, I was just as weak. I'll never be that way again."

"I believe you. Everyone makes mistakes."

"That's not what you said before," she reminded him with a sad smile.

"I thought I knew everything back then. I was wrong, too." He pushed a piece of her hair behind her ear and smiled. "Now I know how you got so smart. All that time in the school library."

"I love learning new things, but I'm almost completely done with my education, my on-the-job-training. It's a little hard to believe that I almost have everything I ever wanted." A cloud passed through her eyes. "Unless . . ."

She didn't have to finish her thought. He knew what she was thinking—unless this book destroyed her career, the life she had built for herself.

"I'm a little surprised you chose to work in the emergency room," he said, trying to distract her. "It doesn't sound very structured or organized, the kind of environment you said you prefer. Why didn't you pick something less stressful?"

"It is organized in a weird way. It's like chaos contained. You never know what's going to come through those double doors when the ambulances pull up, sirens screaming, people crying. But the madness stays there. Or at least that's where I leave it. When I go home, I'm done with it. I realized a long time ago that I'm bad at relationships."

"That's not true—"

She put her hands on his chest, stopping him with a smile. "It is true. After Emily died, after the group split up, I shied away from making new friends. I didn't want to get close to anyone else. When I had to choose a specialty, I realized that if I were a pediatrician, I'd have to get to know families. They'd come to count on me. They'd share their lives with me. I'd watch their kids grow up. I'd become attached. What if I messed up then? What if I let them down? In the ER I don't have to deal with the person, only with their physical problems. I can think of my patients as the broken arm, the head laceration, the burned right hand. I don't even have to know their names or where they live or what their background is. It's safer that way."

"You changed your specialty because of what happened to Emily?" he asked with surprise.

"It had something to do with it, I guess. It was definitely a turning point in my life."

"Mine, too." The boat suddenly rocked against the dock and Cole realized they'd landed at the island. "Ready for some exploring?" he asked.

"Absolutely."

They got off the boat and began the trek up to the top of the island where the jail was located. It was a long, uphill walk that they took at a fast pace. They started out strolling; then Cole walked faster, just to see if Natalie would try to keep up, and of course she did. By the time they reached the very top, they were running and short of breath.

"You have to make everything a race," she said to him with a laugh.

"It takes two to race," he said, appreciating the sparkle in her eyes.

"Thank God you made me buy running shoes. I'd never have made it up here in my high heels." She looked around and waved her hand at the scene. "You were right. This is an incredible view."

He had to agree. The breeze had blown away all the clouds and San Francisco spread out before them like a picture postcard. He could see the Transamerica Pyramid with its steep point towering above the other buildings; Coit Tower, a building in the shape of a fireman's hose that sat on the rolling hills above North Beach; and the colorful boats and piers that dotted the waterfront. He'd spent so much time thinking about getting out of this city that it surprised him now to feel such a strong connection to it. This was his city. His family had lived here for four generations. His roots were here. Hell, he was here. And it didn't look like he was leaving anytime soon. He waited for the yearning to twist his gut into a familiar knot, but it didn't come. Why hadn't it come? It always came.

"Shall we take the tour?" Natalie asked, interrupting his thoughts.

"We could just walk around."

"Then we won't learn anything about the prison or the island, unless you know it all."

He made a face at her. "I don't, but that sounds a lot like school to me."

"It does, doesn't it?" she said with an eagerness that made him laugh.

"Fine, we'll buy the tour. I think we can pick up the headphones over there."

An hour later Cole was glad they'd purchased the guided tour. He'd found the story of the prison and its inmates fascinating and it had been interesting to see which of the small cells had belonged to which prisoners. The prison was certainly a bleak, horrible place to spend a lifetime. He couldn't imagine what those men had gone through, being trapped on the island. And he couldn't help wondering if the escapees who had never been found had actually made it to freedom or had been drowned by the swirling currents around the island, as the tour guide suggested.

"We should do a feature on the island," he said as they walked back out into the sunlight, an hour later. "Maybe do some investigation into those escapees. I wonder if any of their families are still alive." He realized that Natalie was staring at him with a knowing smile. "What?"

"You're supposed to be taking a break, and you're working up a news story in your head."

"Hardly news, and I'm afraid it's just ingrained in me."

"You always had a curious mind. I loved that about you," Natalie said.

"Loved? As in past tense?"

"Okay, I like it about you now," she amended.

"Like is not the same as love."

"I don't think we want to talk about love, Cole. Hey, I think there's a boat about to leave. Shall we head back now?"

He hesitated, then nodded. She was right. Love was not a subject he wanted to get into with Natalie. "Sure. What do you want to do next?" he asked as they walked back to the ferry.

"I want to eat fresh crab on the wharf, or maybe order some clam chowder in one of those French bread bowls. I want to get ice cream in a waffle cone, watch the seals by Pier 39, and take a cable car ride up the steepest hills in San Francisco."

"Are you done?"

There was pure joy in the sound of her laugh. "Sorry, but you asked, and I think you created a monster when you suggested we play tourist."

"I like you like this," he said approvingly.

"I like me like this, too," she replied. "You always brought out this side in me. I'd almost forgotten what it feels like to relax and have fun. Thanks."

He leaned over and kissed her on the mouth, tasting the salt of the nearby sea on her lips. "Don't thank me yet. We've got a lot to do, and if you think this was fun, you ain't seen nothing yet."

Chapter 14

Natalie dug her bare toes into the cool, moist sand on Ocean Beach and sighed with pure satisfaction. After riding the cable cars and stuffing themselves on an assortment of foods, they'd driven out to the beach and had taken up residence against the base of a cliff that ran along the Great Highway to watch the sun go down. "I love this time of the day," she said to Cole. "It's an in-between time. It reminds me of a story Emily used to tell us." She stopped abruptly, realizing she'd just brought up Emily's name. "Sorry."

"Don't stop."

"We agreed we wouldn't talk about the book."

"We're not. We're talking about Emily. Tell me the story." Cole stretched out on his side. He played with the sand, scooping it up, then letting it sift through his fingers.

"It was about fairies and gremlins that lived in the in-between places like doorways and windows, and they all came out to play at the in-between times—the moments between day and dusk, and the biggest in-between time of all: midnight. Emily

said if we looked really close we might see them."
Natalie laughed, feeling a bit silly for even relating
the story to Cole. "Not that I ever believed it, but
it was a good story. Emily used to tell it at night.
She'd light a candle, and we'd sit in the dark and
tell stories or share secrets. It was easier to see
shadows dancing in the doorframes in the candle-
light. I'm sure that sounds pretty wild to a prag-
matic man like yourself."

"I don't know about that. I can believe there are
things in this world that are unexplainable."

"Really?" She was surprised at that. "I thought
you were the hard-core realist."

"No, that's you." He softened his statement with
a smile. "I grew up next door to a magician, and I
had a sister who sat in the window seat of her
bedroom every night and made up stories about
the stars. While she didn't share the in-between
story with me, I heard a few others over the years."
He sat up and wrapped his arms around his knees
as they both watched the sun touch the edge of the
ocean. "I guess I shouldn't have been surprised that
Emily was up on the roof that night."

"She loved to stargaze," Natalie agreed. "She
liked this view, too, the ocean, the sky. We used
to walk on the beach at sunset, and Emily would
say, 'Can you believe that right now we're standing
on the edge of the country, the very edge? Out
there, across all that water, is another continent, a
different way of life.' I guess Emily had a little of
that Parish wanderlust in her blood."

"But she didn't get to go anywhere," Cole said
heavily.

"Actually, wanderlust wasn't the right word. Emily was more of an armchair traveler. She was a watcher more than a doer."

"You're trying to make me feel better again."

"Maybe a little." She paused, watching his hard profile for a long moment. She could look at his face for a hundred years and never get tired of it. He was so attractive to her. His strong jaw, the hard planes of his face, his tan skin, the dark stubble along his cheeks. He must have to shave every day, she thought. His nose was long, his eyebrows thick, and his long dark lashes framed a pair of intense, curious, interesting eyes.

She forced herself to look away, to take a long, slow breath, to focus on something else besides the knot of desire growing in her gut, and the feeling of recklessness that was begging to be unleashed. She was sitting on the beach watching the sunset with the man of her dreams. Only, he wasn't her man, and this wasn't supposed to be romantic. She needed to start talking again, find a way to distract her traitorous body that was telling her brain to stop thinking and just let go.

"Something wrong?" Cole asked. "You're awfully quiet."

"Just thinking," she said desperately. "What—what are your future plans?"

He raised an eyebrow. "How far in the future are we talking about?"

"A year or two, maybe three. Do you foresee any changes in your career? Do you think you might still want to try being a foreign correspondent?"

"It's too late for me to make changes."

"It's not too late. You're thirty-two years old, not eighty. However, you're not getting any younger, so I'd do something soon."

"Thanks for reminding me."

"Seriously, Cole, if you want that old dream of yours, why don't you go for it?"

"I told you before. I have too many ties, responsibilities, commitments," he said, waving a frustrated hand in the air. "I'm trapped."

"In your head. Nowhere else."

"That's not true."

"It is true, Cole. You have choices. You just don't want to choose."

"You don't know what you're talking about. There are a lot of people who depend on me to put the paper out every day."

"Yet you've managed to take time off yesterday and today without the paper falling apart."

"The last few days are the only time off I've taken in the past ten years. My father and uncle spend more time on the golf course than they do at the office. I'm not complaining about them, because they deserve a break. They all worked hard for a long time, but I carry the burden now. I'm the oldest of the cousins that are involved. No one else is ready to take over and there has always been a Parish at the helm. Right now that's me." He paused. "Marty is coming along though. He's not bad. But he's only twenty-six."

She laughed. "And you were how old when you took over?"

"That was different. We were in a crisis. It's

really only been in the last five years . . ." His voice drifted away. "Okay, you've made your point. I guess I was about Marty's age when I took over."

"Here's what I think, Cole. You're never going to be satisfied with your life until you get on a plane and go somewhere far away and send back a news story about something. Otherwise, you'll always wonder what if. You used to be a man of action. Take some action."

"You want me to take some action?"

"Yes, I do," she said, meeting his gaze head-on.

"You're sure about that?"

She saw too late the wicked gleam in his eye. Before she could answer, she found herself flat on her back with Cole sprawled on top of her. Her heart almost jumped out of her chest at the intent look in his eyes. She wanted to tell him to stop, but there was no way she could get the word out. Instead she licked her lips and watched the fire light in his eyes as he concentrated on her mouth. A long, tense second passed, then another, but he didn't move. Her nerves screamed with anticipation.

"Just do it already," she told him.

And he did—a long, slow, thorough kiss that completely swept her away. His mouth tasted, explored, teased, caressed, and she kept up with him every step of the way, until they lost themselves in each other. Nothing else seemed to matter. The roar of the ocean blended with the pounding of her heart. His legs pushed between hers. His hard body pressed against her soft curves. His fingers ran through her hair, his hands holding her head firmly in place so he could take what he wanted. And she let him. She didn't want to fight him. She wanted to make love to him, right here on this strip of sand where the sun and the sea met, where the past and the present and the future were colliding. She wanted everything to be right with her world again, a world that had never been complete since he'd walked out of her life. Now he was back. For how long, she didn't know. But she could have him now. She could have it all.

But what was all? What was she doing?

He'd hurt her once. He'd hurt her again.

Natalie pushed Cole away. It took every bit of willpower, but she did it.

He rolled onto his side, breathing heavily as their eyes met. "I guess that's a no."

"I guess it is," she murmured. "For now." She could have kicked herself for adding those last two words. She saw his eyes flare at the promise, the challenge, the possibility.

"For now," he agreed.

"I shouldn't have said that."

"Too late. It's already said."

She shook her head. "I don't know what you want from me now."

"I don't, either, Natalie. But I know I want something. And I think you want something, too. Do you want to tell me what that is?"

She thought about his question for a long moment. She knew the answer, but if she said it, he'd run. Maybe that was a good thing. Maybe she wanted him to put an end to this now, because she didn't think she could do it herself. "I think I want you to love me again," she said, staring straight out at the sea, because she couldn't bear to look at him. "What do you want?"

Silence followed her words. A silence that stretched her nerves to the snapping point. Natalie couldn't stand it, so she got up and did what she'd expected him to do. She ran.

Madison felt a momentary twinge of guilt as she ran up the stairs to Dylan's apartment, located conveniently above Club V. She felt a bigger twinge of guilt knowing that she'd taken the extra keys to his apartment out of his office after telling the receptionist she'd left her sweater there a few days earlier. She was bad. But Dylan might be even worse. He might be Garrett Malone. Her conversation with Josh the night before had refused to leave her head. Pictures of Dylan climbing up to Emily's second-story bedroom like a Romeo seducing Juliet made her want to throw up, but it also told her that the relationship between Dylan and Emily had been much closer than probably anyone knew. She suspected that Dylan's crush had turned into something a lot more personal once the two had found themselves alone in Santa Cruz.

She slipped the key into the lock and the door opened easily. Madison felt a little like Alice in Wonderland as she entered the loft, which was obviously the upper floor of what had once been a warehouse. As she moved farther into the apartment, she saw a corner area where three computers, a large television monitor, stereo system, and some kind of video camera were set up. Another area held microphones, black boxes of assorted shapes and sizes, and other types of magic paraphernalia. The king-size bed in the middle of the room was unmade, the pillows and covers tossed in abandon. She couldn't help wondering if Dylan had spent the last night he'd been here alone or with a woman.

Well, she wasn't here to figure out his love life. She was here to see if she could find any evidence that Dylan was Garrett Malone. If he'd written a book, it would probably be on one of the computers, she decided, heading over to turn them on. While they were booting up, she took a look through Dylan's clothes, which hung on two movable clothing racks. He certainly had a love affair going with the color black. And leather was obviously his favorite material. Her palms grew a little sweaty at the thought of slipping her hands down his black leather pants.

Clearing her throat, she turned a corner of the loft and saw a closed door. It was the only door in the room, and it was locked. That might have stopped someone else, but Madison had never met a locked door she didn't want to open. There was no way she wouldn't try to get in. There were five keys on Dylan's key chain, and the last one slipped in easily. The door opened. It was dark inside the small room, and it took Madison a moment to find a chain that pulled on a single lightbulb hanging in the closet. She jumped back as Emily's face appeared to her. Blinking rapidly, it took her a moment to realize that photographs of Emily covered every inch of the closet. They started from childhood and went up to college. In fact, the one right next to her was a photo of all four of them at Emily's nineteenth birthday party. They'd gone to a local restaurant to celebrate. And Dylan had taken a picture of them. She remembered that now, remembered all the times he'd been around with one of his cameras.

"Did you find what you were looking for?"

His voice made her jump. Whirling around, she looked into Dylan's furious eyes. A reason for being inside his locked apartment and inside his locked closet escaped her. She was busted. There was no way to defend her actions, so she decided to attack. "You're obsessed with Emily, aren't you? Even after all these years. Does Cole know about this?"

Dylan crossed his arms in front of his chest, his face as stony as a statue. A really pissed-off statue.

"I could have you arrested," he said.

"But you won't," she said with as much bravado as she could muster. "You don't want anyone to know about this."

Dylan suddenly grabbed her by the hand and yanked her out of the closet, slamming the door behind her. She rubbed her arm. "That hurt."

"You think I give a shit? What the hell are you doing here?"

"I wanted to talk to you."

"So you broke into my apartment? Have you heard of a phone?"

"Are you Garrett Malone?"

"No," he said shortly. "Are you?"

"Last time I looked, I was still a woman." Her words sent his gaze up and down her body, and she shivered at the look in his eyes.

"You are that," he muttered. "Get out."

"That's it? You're just going to throw me out?"

"Yes."

She stared at him, not sure how to react. She

supposed she should be grateful he wanted to just let her go. But now that she had that option, she didn't feel like taking it. "I think we should talk," she said instead.

"You didn't come here to talk, did you, Maddie?"

Dylan took a step closer, and she was suddenly very aware of the fact that they were alone in his apartment, and there was a very good possibility he was insane. She glanced toward the front door. It was a long way away.

"Nervous?" he asked, a small smile now playing around his lips. "You like to be in charge, don't you?"

"I better go."

"Lost your chance."

Suddenly his hands were on her waist and he was walking her backwards, so fast she stumbled and fell flat on her back in the middle of his bed. He pulled her hands over her head as he straddled her body, his black leather pants rubbing against her bare legs.

She felt both terrified and aroused by the intense look in his eyes.

"This is what you wanted, isn't it?" Dylan asked.

Madison licked her lips, trying not to show any fear. She could handle Dylan. He was just paying her back for breaking into his apartment. He was trying to scare her. Wasn't he? "Is this how you treated Emily?" she asked.

Fury flared in his eyes. Oh, God! She'd just thrown a stick of dynamite into the fire. When was she going to learn to think before she spoke?

"Don't talk to me about Emily," he said harshly. "You could never be as good as her."

"I never wanted to be," she replied. "But you didn't treat Emily like this. She wasn't a real woman to you. She was a saint. That's why you've set up a shrine to her in your closet. You never had her beneath you like this."

"Shut up."

"Did she love you?" Madison asked, unable to stop herself from talking, even though her brain was telling her to be quiet.

Dylan didn't say anything for a long moment; then he got up and ran a hand through his hair. "Get the hell out of here, Madison."

She sat up slowly. "You loved her, but she didn't love you, did she?"

"Do you have a death wish or something?"

"That's not an answer."

Dylan strode from the apartment. It took Madison a moment to realize he'd actually left in the middle of their conversation, if that's what you could call it. She got up and ran to the door and down the stairs to the street. Dylan was getting on a motorcycle.

"Wait," she shouted. "You have to talk to me about her."

He shook his head and put on his helmet.

"Dylan, you need to talk to someone, and who else are you going to talk to? You can't go to Cole. You probably can't even go to your own brother."

He hesitated, then reached over and pulled out a second helmet from a storage compartment. "Get on."

"On this? I was thinking we could go into your club and get a drink." She paused, realizing she had only one choice. "Okay, I'm getting on. Give me the helmet."

She put it on and swung her leg over the bike. She'd done a lot of reckless things in her life, but this was probably the worst. Wrapping her arms around Dylan's waist, she held on for dear life as the engine roared, and they sped down the street.

Cole caught up to Natalie at the farthest end of the beach where a rocky cliff had cut off any hope of escape. The sky was a deep, dark purple now, the sun having passed over the horizon, the moon coming up slowly behind them. The waves crashed on the rocks beside her with a foamy white fury that matched her churning emotions. It was the only sound on earth. There were no homes nearby, no city noise, just the ocean and her pounding heart.

Natalie glanced back the way she had come, realizing they were now the only two people left on the beach. There was no one to save her from Cole or from herself, and at the moment she was in the most danger from her own damned heart. Why couldn't she let go of him?

"Natalie." He came up behind her, his deep, husky voice sending another shiver down her spine.

She wanted to hear him say her name again—in passion, while he slid into her body, while he made her feel whole again. She bit down on her lip to stop herself from inviting him to do just that.

"Why did you run?" he asked.

"I wanted to be the one to leave first this time. You weren't supposed to come after me."

"Yes, I was." His hands moved to her waist, as he turned her to face him. She could barely see him in the dark shadows. Maybe it was better that way. "You never gave me a chance to answer your question," he said.

"I gave you a chance. Your silence told me the truth."

"The truth is I don't know what I want from you. I just know that I can't let you go."

"Not yet maybe, but you will." She felt that conviction deep in her aching heart. "I'd be a fool to think otherwise. And I do not want to be a fool around you again."

"Don't put words in my mouth, Natalie. I can speak for myself."

"This is pointless. We're going around in circles. Let me go."

"I told you—I can't." And he hauled her up against his chest, crushing her mouth beneath his.

She wanted to fight him, to fight herself, but she was overwhelmed by the pleasure of his tongue sweeping through her mouth, his hands sliding up her sides to cup her breasts. This was what she wanted, what she needed. She wrapped her arms around his neck and gave herself up to the kiss. They didn't have a past or a future anymore, just this moment, this one perfect moment.

"Natalie," he groaned against her mouth. "I want to make love to you. Let me take you home."

She shook her head. "Here," she whispered, pulling him down to the sand, until they were on their knees facing each other. "Make love to me here before I can change my mind or you can change yours, before reality makes us see how crazy and wrong this is."

"Not wrong, maybe crazy," he muttered, as he pulled her toward him for another kiss. "Are you sure?"

"Yes," she said, feeling reckless. The dark corner of the beach made her feel as if they were the only two people on the face of the earth. Why shouldn't they have each other? It was what they both wanted.

"Damn. I don't have anything with me. We can't—"

She put her finger against his mouth. "I've got it covered. I'm on the pill. Health reasons," she added at his inquiring look.

"And I've been tested," he muttered. "But—"

"It's okay. Trust me, Cole."

"I do. I do trust you," he replied, pushing her back against the sand. "I want you so much."

"Then have me," she said simply.

She ran her fingers through his thick dark hair as they kissed and caressed and explored each other with a passion that far surpassed the reckless fumbling of their youth. Natalie hadn't really known what she wanted back then, but she knew now. Her fingers moved with a purpose as she undid the buttons on Cole's shirt, as she pulled it aside to run her hands up and down his bare chest. And when Cole stumbled, trying to rid her of her sweatshirt, her blouse, and her bra, she sat up and helped, feeling more free than she ever had in her life. Stripped naked, they lay together on the cool sand, the heat from their bodies making the spray from the ocean rise like steam around them.

With no barriers between them, the last semblance of rational thought completely faded. Natalie pulled Cole into the cradle of her body, wrapping her legs around his.

"We've got to slow down," he muttered, but he was as hard as a rock, and the last thing she wanted was to go slow. "I don't want to hurt you."

"I'm ready. I have been for a long time." She caught his face with her hand and looked him straight in the eye. "Don't make me wait."

Her words were all he needed to let go, plunging into her body with a force that took her breath away. She gave a glad cry, reveling in the wild, unrestrained passion between them, urging him on. She didn't care that it was hard and rough, that the sand was scraping her back, her buttocks, her legs. All she cared about was that Cole was inside her, surrounding her, enveloping her in everything that was him. She'd wanted to lose herself, and she did. When Cole collapsed against her, she wrapped her arms around him, wanting to keep him there for the rest of eternity.

Eternity lasted about five minutes.

"I'm crushing you," Cole said.

He was, but she was reveling in it and was disappointed when he pulled out of her body and lay next to her. He took her into the curve of his arms and kissed her on the cheek. "That was . . ."

"Yeah, it was," she murmured with a smile. Then she shivered as she became aware of the cold breeze coming off the ocean. They were in San Francisco after all, not the Caribbean, which brought to mind a long-ago conversation when Cole had told her that one day they'd travel, sleep on the beach under the moonlight, the warm breezes caressing their skin.

"You must be cold," Cole said as she shivered again.

"I guess."

He sat up and started handing her pieces of clothing. They dressed quickly. Natalie felt self-conscious now, embarrassed at the way she'd demanded that he make love to her. What must he think of her? She'd always prided herself on acting responsibly, but the last few hours—make that the last week—she'd been anything but responsible.

"Don't think so much," Cole said with a knowing smile. "We didn't break any laws."

"Are you sure about that? God, I hope no one saw us." She glanced around, but the beach was so dark she couldn't see more than ten feet away. At least there was no one nearby. "I lose my mind when I'm around you."

"So do I." Cole caught her arm as she turned to leave. "I don't regret that, Natalie. Do you?"

"No, I don't regret it," she said with absolute certainty. "I wanted to make love to you. And it was perfect."

He nodded. "I want to do it again in a bed this time, really, really slowly. I want to taste every inch of you, Natalie. I want to see you in the light. I want to look into your beautiful blue eyes when we come together. I want to watch your face, feel your skin." He ran his finger down her cheek, and she trembled. "You're beautiful, Natalie, inside and out."

A rush of emotion blurred her eyes with tears. "I thought you hated me."

"I tried."

"This—us—it can't work. You know that. I know—"

He cut her off with a kiss. "I told you to stop thinking—at least for tonight. Can you do that? Can you give us one night?"

The plea in his eyes matched the need in her heart. "I can do that. Let's go home."

Chapter 15

"Oh, my God! That was better than sex," Madison declared when Dylan finally brought the motorcycle to a stop. They'd flown through the streets of San Francisco, up one hill and down the next, with absolutely no regard for the speed limit. She'd been terrified more than once, and she was sure Dylan had intended her to feel that way, but she'd hung on, and she was still alive. Where she was still alive, she wasn't quite sure. They'd crossed over the Golden Gate Bridge to the north and they were now on some remote hillside in Sausalito with an incredible view of San Francisco at night.

Dylan got off the bike and walked to the edge of the hillside. She decided to follow him, hoping he hadn't brought her here to push her off. The flippant thought suddenly took on new meaning as she drew closer to Dylan and to the edge of the cliff. Maybe he *had* brought her here for that reason. Maybe he was the one up on the roof that night with Emily.

He loved Emily. He wouldn't have hurt her.

But he *would* punish the person he thought had hurt Emily. Did he think she was the one?

Madison stopped a few feet away from him and ran her fingers through her wind-tangled hair. "What are we doing here?"

Dylan didn't answer right away, his gaze focused on the city before them. "This was one of Emily's favorite places."

She could see why. The lights of San Francisco were stunning, the tall buildings outlined against the dark sky, the bridges on both sides of the city adding the perfect frame. "It's beautiful," she said.

"Emily always loved the view from high places." Her voice faltered as she realized how dangerously close they were coming to discussing Emily's last journey up to the sorority house roof. She decided to change the subject. "Did you bring her here on your motorcycle? Maybe with a blanket and a bottle of wine?"

He laughed at that, a sound that warmed his cold, dark personality. "Do you think the Parishes would have allowed that? I brought her here in my parents' car when they thought we were going to the movies."

"It's hard to think of you with parents. Although your brother is nice. We had an interesting conversation about you and your many trips up the tree next to Emily's bedroom window."

"Josh talks too much."

"Why did you bring me here?"

Dylan shrugged.

"Okay, let's move on, then." She paused, took a deep breath, and asked, "Do you still love Emily?"

"Do you?" He shot the question right back at her, along with a razor-sharp look of inquiry. "Did you ever? Or was it all just convenient back then? You lived in the dorms. You pledged a sorority together. Did her friendship mean anything to you? Or are you as cold and shallow as I always thought you were?"

Hearing the anger in his voice, Madison instinctively took a step back. She had always believed she had a thick skin, but Dylan's words had struck home. It took her a minute to catch her breath; then she said, "You thought I was cold and shallow? Did you get that from Emily?" She hoped that wasn't the case. She could handle his dislike, but not Emily's.

"I made my own judgment. You were a party girl, a flirt. You even tried to make out with me one night."

"Most men would have considered that an honor, and you didn't exactly say no all that fast." She watched as he picked up a rock and flung it over the hillside. "That bothered you, didn't it? That you didn't say no. Because you were supposed to want only Emily. And yet for a moment, you wanted me."

"That was different, and you always did have a high opinion of yourself."

"I know my strengths. Sex is one of them. I'm very good at it," she said candidly. "You don't know what you're missing. Although it might not be too late, if you play your cards right. I always did like a man who works with his hands, and I bet you can do amazing things with those magician hands of yours."

Dylan stared at her for a long moment, then

shook his head. "You're a piece of work, Madison. You must have shocked the hell out of Emily—the way you talk."

"She liked that I was honest, that I didn't tell her what she was supposed to hear. I treated her like a friend, not a child."

"I never treated her like a child, but she was innocent. She needed to be protected."

Madison shook her head, truly confused by how many people had believed Emily needed to be protected. "What was it about her that made everyone want to take care of her?" she asked aloud. She thought about how few men in her life had ever even considered such a thing, and she came up with zero. "I can't imagine a guy doing that for me," she murmured. "I've been looking out for myself my whole life."

Dylan dug his hands into his pockets as he said, "What about your father? He must have protected you."

"Actually, he didn't bother to stick around past my conception. He was a big movie star and apparently a kid would have cramped his style. The rest of the men in my mother's life were more interested in getting her into bed and out of her clothes than they were in protecting her daughter. My latest stepfather isn't too bad though. He bailed me out of my almost wedding last year. But that was probably because my mother swore she wouldn't sleep with him again if he didn't."

"So the Covington women know how to get their way with sex."

"I learned at my mother's knee." Madison sat down on the ground and patted the patch of earth beside her. "Sit down. Tell me about Emily, how you became friends."

"Why would I want to tell you anything?"

"Because you're dying to talk to someone about Emily, and I'm the only one you've got. Come on, you know you want to."

He hesitated, then sat down, stretching his legs out in front of him. He didn't say anything for several long minutes. Finally, he said, "Emily was my inspiration. She believed in me even when we were kids. My tricks would fall apart, and Cole and Josh would laugh themselves sick, but Emily just told me to try again. When I did, she'd look at me with those big brown eyes of hers and clap as if I'd pulled off the biggest miracle in the world. I would have done anything for her."

Madison heard the love in his voice, and it was so strong, so powerful, it took her breath away. She'd never had anyone love her like that. It was something out of this world. Maybe that was appropriate since Dylan and Emily had dreamed of other worlds since they were young. Silence fell between them again. Madison didn't know what to say. Not one flippant response came to her mind. His last words stuck in her head, repeating themselves over and over again. *I would have done anything for her.*

"She probably would have done anything for you, too," Madison offered a moment later. "She said you were one of her best friends in the world. I couldn't quite figure it out, because you seemed so different. You'd come riding up to the dorm on your motorcycle, revving your engine, wearing your black leather, smoking a cigarette, acting all cocky, and you were there to pick up Emily, probably the

most naive girl I had ever met in my life. Even
Laura was more worldly than Em. I couldn't understand what you and Em would talk about."

"Anything and everything. No matter what the
subject, she was always interested in discussing it."
He laughed at some memory that he didn't bother
to share with Madison.

"Did she love you, Dylan? As more than a
friend? Were you two sleeping together?"

"That's none of your damn business," he said
sharply.

"What would it hurt to tell me?" She paused
waiting for his answer. When it didn't come, she
said, "I think Emily loved you as a friend, a very
dear, close friend—a brother. She never knew you
wanted more, did she? Am I right?"

Dylan didn't reply for a long moment, then said,
"She never knew. I didn't want to ruin anything
between us. I didn't want her to feel like she had
to say something or do something."

"So you weren't the one we bought the condoms
for," she muttered to herself. For some reason it
made her feel better to know that Emily had never
felt a passionate love for Dylan. It meant she didn't
have to feel so guilty about her own insane attraction to the man.

"What are you talking about?" Dylan asked
abruptly, turning to look at her. "What condoms?"

"Did I say that out loud?"

"Yes, you did. Explain."

"I don't know if she was going to use them. She
just said she wanted to be prepared, in case."

"So you helped her buy condoms instead of trying to talk her out of having sex?" he asked furiously.

"Of course I did. I wanted her to be able to protect herself in case the guy was an ass. I know you and Cole and Josh think Emily was some Virgin Mary, but she was a normal girl with desires and curiosities."

"Who were they for? Who were the condoms for?" he demanded.

"I don't know." Madison thought back to the conversations she'd had with Emily in the weeks before her death. "I remember her saying he was someone she wasn't supposed to have. I think she used the word *unattainable*. But who couldn't she have? He must have been someone who was going out with someone else. That's all I can think of." There was only one man who came to mind, and his name made her sit up straight. *Drew McKinney*. Why hadn't that occurred to her before? Was it possible that both Emily and Laura had been in love with Drew?

"What are you thinking?" Dylan asked, his sharp gaze on her face.

"Nothing," she lied. "I don't know what I'm thinking."

"Yes, you do. You thought of someone. I want to know who it was."

"Why? Are you going to beat him up? It's been ten years, you know."

"I might want to ask him a few questions—like where he was the night she died."

"Why would that matter? It's not like he would have pushed her off the roof." Her heart stopped at the look in Dylan's eyes. "Oh, my God. You think someone pushed Emily off the roof that night, don't you? Why? Why do you think that? Were you there?"

Dylan stared back at her, not answering.

"You *were* there," she said. "Natalie thought she saw you in the house."

"And I saw Natalie arguing with Emily. That's why I didn't go into Em's room. They were in the middle of something, so I went downstairs. I should have stayed. If I had, maybe Emily would still be alive."

"So now you're saying it was Natalie who did it?" She didn't like the way he turned away from her. "You think Emily and Natalie went out onto the roof, argued, and Natalie pushed her off—just like it was described in the book." Had Dylan lied to her before about not being Garrett Malone? They certainly seemed to share the same opinions.

"It's a possibility," Dylan replied.

"I don't believe that, and Natalie wasn't the only one who spoke to Emily that night. There were other people who went into her room."

"Like who?"

"Like Drew."

"McKinney?" he asked sharply.

"That's right. Someone who was going out with one of Emily's best friends," she added pointedly.

She knew he was smart enough to add it up quickly, and he did. His frown said it all. "She wouldn't have liked McKinney."

"He could be very charming when he wanted to be."

Dylan shook his head and got to his feet. "We're done."

"Wait a second, we're not done." She scrambled after him as he headed toward the bike. "Are you ever going to let her go, Dylan? Are you going to be able to move on from Emily?" She wanted to ask him if he'd ever give her a chance, but even her nerve wouldn't take her that far. "She wouldn't want you to waste your life pining after her," she added.

Dylan stopped and stared at her. "Don't tell me what she'd want."

"Why? Because you know I'm right? Emily would have wanted you to be happy."

"And you think I'd be happy with you? Like I said, you always did think highly of yourself."

"I think you'd be happier than you are right now."

"You don't know anything about my life, Madison. Now, either get on the bike or stay here. I don't much care either way."

"Why are you in such a hurry to leave?"

"I have something to do."

She saw something flash through his eyes and her instincts told her what it was. "You know, don't you? You figured it out while we were talking. You know who Emily was in love with. Tell me, Dylan."

"I don't know anything," he denied.

"You're lying."

He shrugged. "Are you coming or not?"

Madison watched Dylan put on his helmet and knew that he wouldn't think twice about leaving her on this remote hillside. "Fine," she said, strapping on her own helmet. She'd make him tell her what he'd remembered, or she'd figure it out herself. In the meantime, she had a lot to think about. She couldn't wait to tell Natalie what she'd learned.

"You're torturing me," Natalie said, as Cole's fingers played with the front clasp of her bra. They'd made it to his bedroom in record time, but after stripping off her shirt, Cole had slowed things down considerably.

He smiled wickedly as he pressed a teasing kiss against the corner of her mouth. "You really need to learn some patience, Natalie."

She didn't care about patience. She wanted his fingers on her bare skin. Then she wanted his mouth to follow suit. But Cole seemed more interested in tracing a line along the edge of her bra, one fingertip grazing her skin like a branding iron. She knew there was only one way to get him to hurry. Her hand dropped to the snap on his jeans. Unlike him, she got it open right away, along with the zipper. She heard him suck in a breath of air as her fingers dipped lower, teasing him as he was teasing her.

"You're not playing fair," he muttered.

"Who cares about fair? I want what I want. So do it already."

"I love it when you talk sexy." He unhooked her bra and pulled the edges apart, freeing her breasts to his gaze, his touch. His thumb circled one nipple, then the other. She closed her eyes as his mouth moved down the side of her neck, the valley of her breasts, finally closing over her nipple. Her breast swelled as he sucked and licked, igniting the sparks that had barely died down from their last encounter. He reached for the button of her slacks and pulled it open, his hands pushing her pants down until she was left standing in only her skimpy bikinis. Breathing hard, she pushed him away and said, "Your turn."

Cole didn't hesitate, taking off his jeans and his boxers in one fell swoop. A pile of sand from their beach adventure followed suit, and they both laughed. But the tension returned as Natalie let herself look at him. Her breath quickened, and her heart began to thud against her chest. He really was a beautifully made man.

"Your turn, Natalie." He put a thumb through the band of her panties and pushed them down her legs. She kicked them off, then tried to cover herself, feeling self-conscious.

He pulled her hands away, his fingers intertwining with hers. "Let me look at you in the light." He shook his head, something like awe flashing in his eyes. "Beautiful."

She blushed from the tips of her toes to the top of her head. She could feel the warmth sweeping across her body as his gaze made the same journey. "Let's lie down," she said, pulling him toward the bed.

"I thought you'd never ask."

Natalie laid down on her back, wishing this was all happening a lot faster. It was easier not to think, not to worry when he was touching her, kissing her, making her forget her own name.

Cole turned on his side, letting his hand move lazily up and down her leg while he studied her mouth and her breasts.

"Could we get on with it?" she said.

He smiled. "More sexy talk. Wherever did you learn it, Natalie?"

"I don't do this very often. I don't know the protocol."

He leaned over and kissed her on the mouth, a long, wet kiss that ended with him tracing her lips with the tip of his tongue. Her body was tingling by the time he was done. "Better?" he asked.

"Not if that was it," she complained.

"We're just getting started." His hand moved to her inner thigh, promising, teasing . . . "You're so warm," he purred, his mouth moving over to her ear as his fingers slid between her legs. "Even hotter down here." She swallowed hard, every nerve ending in her body on fire. It was too much.

She turned over on her side, letting her fingers run through the fine dark hair of his chest. "My turn," she said, cupping him with one hand. He was hard, ready, and as his breathing quickened, she sensed the game had just moved ahead a little. And she was happy about that.

"Uh, Natalie, if you want to go slow—"

"Who said I did?" she asked against his mouth. "I want you now, Cole. I'm taking charge. Do you have a problem with that?"

"No problem," he muttered as she pushed him back against the mattress.

She put one leg over him, then straddled his body, moving as slowly as she could up and down his body, teasing him with her breasts, her mouth . . .

"Enough," he said, putting his strong hands on her waist. "I need you."

"I need you," she whispered, as she took him into her body with a satisfied gasp of pleasure. And for a while all was right with the world.

Laura sat at her kitchen table late Wednesday night staring at the two place settings that had yet to be used. The steaks she'd broiled two hours earlier had long gone cold. The baked potatoes were wrinkled and soft. The lettuce in the salad had turned brown. It was after eight thirty and Drew had not yet arrived home, nor called. She'd checked the airport an hour earlier to learn that his plane had landed on time at five forty-two. Where the hell was he?

She'd become her mother, Laura thought with a sad sigh. Closing her eyes, she could see her mom sitting at the empty dining-room table in her expensive Atherton home, her beautiful china filled with the homemade dinner she'd lovingly prepared for a man who hadn't bothered to call and say he'd be late—again. Her mother would wait and wait, finally turning off the lights and going up to bed, where she would cry into the night.

Laura had married Drew determined to have a different life for herself. She'd thought he would be her lover, her husband, her best friend, the father of her children, the man of her dreams, and most of all, her companion. She'd known he was ambitious and determined, but she'd never believed that he would put everything before her—or that he would cheat on her with another woman.

Was he cheating? Or were his frequent absences, his secrets about something else entirely? Like maybe a best-selling novel?

The clock ticked relentlessly loud, each beat making her feel increasingly more frustrated. Getting up, she walked over to the phone and picked it up, debating her options. She could call Drew for the fifteenth time or leave it be.

Before she could decide, the phone rang in her hands, making her jump. "Hello?"

"Laura, it's Drew."

She let out a breath of relief. "Thank God. I've been so worried. Where are you?"

"I'm still in L.A."

"I thought you were coming back tonight."

"Something came up. I won't be home for a few days."

The uneasy knot in her stomach grew bigger. "Why not?"

"I can't go into it right now, but I need you to give me some time and some space. Can you do that?"

She hesitated. "I don't think I can, Drew. Why are you being so secretive?"

"I'm working on a very private matter. I can't go into it, not even with you. You have to trust me."

Laura wanted to trust him, but how could she? There were too many unanswered questions. And it was about time she started asking some of them. Taking a deep breath, she said, "Drew, I found an itinerary for Garrett Malone in your pocket. Did you speak to him?"

Silence met her question. She knew he was angry. She could feel it.

"I can't get into that right now," he said tersely. "I have people coming in for a meeting. We'll discuss it later."

"I'm not sure it can wait. I got a call from a reporter in Santa Cruz. She knows I was one of the Fabulous Four. She said she has been talking to the Santa Cruz Police Department, and they're considering reopening the investigation."

"They don't have any evidence to do that."

"Are you sure?"

"I'm a lawyer, aren't I? Look, Laura—you don't have to worry about the book. Natalie is the one who should be concerned, not you. You didn't do anything to Emily. Your hands are clean. However, it might be a good idea for you and the girls to get out of town for a while. Why don't you go up to Tahoe, stay in your parents' cabin for a week? You can come back when this all settles down."

"The girls have school, and I have appointments," she said, surprised by his suggestion.

"They can miss school, and you can reschedule. I don't want you or the girls hounded by the press. And I don't want you to say the wrong thing."

Which was probably his main concern, Laura thought cynically. "I can't go out of town. I have an audition on Monday for the Community Orchestra. What do you think about that?"

"What are you talking about?"

"I want to play the flute in the Community Orchestra."

"You're not good enough to do that, are you? You haven't played in years, and don't you have enough to do taking care of our children and our home?"

His words made her feel immediately guilty. Madison was right. Drew had always known exactly which buttons to push. But she had Madison in her

head now, too. And Natalie. Even Emily's voice
could be heard, telling her it wasn't a crime to want
something for herself. Before she could tell him
she'd do what she wanted, he was speaking again.

"I've got to run," Drew said. "We'll talk about
this when I get back."

"I love you," she said quickly, automatically, out
of habit—but he had already hung up. He hadn't
told her he loved her. Maybe he didn't. Maybe she
didn't. Right now even her own words of love had
a hollow echo to them. They needed to talk, share,
trust each other again. But that wouldn't happen
until he came home, until this secret case he was
working on was over. She just hoped the secret
case had nothing to do with Malone's book, because there were a lot of things she could forgive,
but that might not be one of them.

Chapter 16

Natalie awoke to sun streaming through the blinds in Cole's bedroom early Thursday morning. A glance at the clock told her it wasn't that early—almost eight. She rolled onto her back with a sigh of delicious satisfaction; she hadn't slept so well in years. She was just sorry that tomorrow had finally come. They would have to talk about the past, the present, and maybe even the future. It wouldn't be just the two of them anymore. The rest of the world would have its say. And she wasn't quite ready to give Cole back to the rest of the world.

Maybe she never had been.

She'd told him before that she'd never asked him for anything, no promises, no ring, no happily ever after. That had been true. She'd never said the words out loud, but in her heart she'd wanted all of that. Maybe he'd run from what he'd seen in her eyes, not what he'd heard in her voice. Maybe the same thing would happen again. Because she was falling in love with him for a second time. Her heart wanted to believe that there could be a different outcome this time around, but her brain knew it was a long shot.

The bathroom door opened and Cole appeared, his hair and chest damp from a shower. She swallowed hard at the sight of him wearing only a pair of skimpy blue boxers. She would have liked to just stare at him for a while, but after giving her a sexy smile that completely undid her, he jumped into bed, pinned her beneath his body, and proceeded to kiss her like he was never going to let her go.

As soon as one kiss ended, another began. He gave her no chance to protest or even to tell him to keep doing exactly what he was doing. Which was really all she wanted to say. He pressed his lips to her neck, her shoulder, her collarbone . . . and she sighed with pure pleasure. She didn't want him to stop. She didn't want to think anymore or worry about what would happen between them.

"I love that sound you make," Cole muttered, stopping long enough to look at her with eyes that had darkened with desire. "It drives me a little crazy every time I hear it. I know I should let you get up now. You must be hungry. You probably want to take a shower. Go home. Do something."

She put her hand on his neck and pulled his head down, touching his lips with hers, sliding her tongue between his lips in a kiss that made Cole sigh. "The only thing I want to do is make love to you again," she whispered against his mouth. "You know, the night isn't officially over until I get out of bed. That's a rule. And we promised each other a night."

"Really? Well, I wouldn't want to break any rules." He slid his hand across her breast, his fingers teasing her nipple into a tight point. He bent his head to suck the point between his lips, and she thought she might just die again. Her lower body pooled in delight and she kicked the covers off so she could rub her legs against his. Then she slipped her hands inside his boxers and pushed them down over his hips.

"I'm ready for you, Cole," she said softly, pulling him into the cradle of her thighs. "I'm always ready." She sighed again as he sank deep into her body. She wrapped her arms and legs around him. She might have to let him go later, but for now he was hers.

The persistent ringing of a doorbell finally brought Natalie back to awareness. Cole was sprawled on his back beside her, his eyes closed, but she could tell he was awake by the groan that followed and the way he squinted his eyes as he opened them. "Who the hell is that?"

"I have no idea," she said, a bit unsettled. "Whoever it is must have gotten past your doorman."

"It can't be a reporter then," Cole said, as he hopped out of bed and pulled on a pair of jeans. "It's probably Josh or Dylan."

As Cole left the bedroom, Natalie gathered her clothes off the floor by the bed. She intended to jump into the shower, but at the sound of loud voices, she paused and decided to put on her clothes instead. She could hear arguing, a man's voice, then a woman's. She didn't quite recognize them. Madison maybe? Dylan?"

"Where is she?" the man demanded. "Is she here? Is she with you?"

Natalie's heart sank. Now she recognized the voice. It belonged to Cole's father, Richard Parish, and he did not sound happy. She had a terrible feeling that the *she* he was referring to was her.

The bedroom door flew open and Natalie jumped. Her blouse was still open and she quickly pulled the edges around her body. Richard Parish stopped in midstride, a fiery figure of anger and pain. His hair, once a light brown, was completely gray now. His body, once muscular and strong, appeared thinner, softer. His eyes, Cole's eyes, were hard and unforgiving as they stared at her in disbelief. Then he looked back at Cole. "You slept with her? You slept with the girl who killed your sister?"

"She didn't kill anyone," Cole said, leaping to her defense, for which Natalie was intensely grateful.

"That's not what the book says."

Natalie drew in another sharp breath as Cole's mother entered the bedroom. She was an older version of Emily, dark chocolate brown hair, matching eyes, a small pert nose that set off her perfectly oval face. But Janet Parish had not aged as well as Natalie would have thought. There were lines around her eyes and mouth, and her skin was pale and filled with shadows.

"Natalie," she whispered, as if she couldn't believe her eyes. "It really is you."

"Yes," Natalie said. "It's me."

"Richard said he saw you on television last night. You and Cole were running down the street together. I didn't believe him, but here you are."

Damn. The reporters must have filmed their getaway. Natalie hadn't anticipated that. She felt guilty now for spending the last twelve hours wrapped in a cocoon of fantasy. Well, that fantasy was officially over now.

No one seemed to know what to say next. Natalie didn't like the silence, but she was afraid she would like conversation even less. She was right.

"You pushed Emily off the roof," Richard said, daring her to deny it. "I don't know why I didn't see it before."

"I didn't—"

He cut her off with a wave of his hand. "Everything in the book is true. You had a fight. You wanted Cole. You wanted Emily to get him for you. When she wouldn't call him, you pushed her off the roof."

"I didn't do that."

"But you don't remember, do you?" Janet asked her in a soft, sad voice. "Emily was so sweet, so kind. And she loved you like a sister. She told me so. You were her best friend."

Natalie's heart broke a little more. "I felt the same way about her. And I'm going to prove that Malone is lying."

"Mr. Malone had to get his information from somewhere," Richard continued. "The Santa Cruz Police will be calling you, Ms. Bishop."

"That's Dr. Bishop," she retorted, throwing her chin up. The Parishes might be hurting, but she didn't intend to be their whipping post any longer. "And I'll look forward to talking to them."

"So will I," Cole said. "There seem to be a lot of questions that need answers."

"No! I don't want you involved, Cole," Janet said sharply, with every last bit of energy in her body. "I can't bear the thought of something happening to you, too. You have to stay out of it. You're all I have left. I can't lose you, too. Promise me. Let your father handle it. Let the investigators do their job. I want you safe. You have to do this for me."

With Janet's words, Natalie could see Cole's shoulders sag under the burden of his mother's need. It was easy now to understand why Cole had never left his family or the paper. His mother was so fragile, like a China doll that might shatter into a thousand pieces at any moment. Emily had felt that burden, too, Natalie realized. Janet hadn't been quite this fragile back then, but she had needed her daughter's love and attention, and Emily had always felt trapped by that need.

"Nothing will happen to me, Mom. I can promise you that," Cole said.

"You can't promise me. Emily told me everything would be all right, too. She was wrong." Janet sent Natalie a troubled look, then glanced back at her son. "I don't think you two should be together."

"Natalie wants to clear her name, and I want to find out the truth."

"Those two may be in opposition," Richard said.

"They won't be. I'm confident of that," Cole replied.

"Because you're sleeping with her, blinded by sex and a beautiful woman. I thought I taught you better than that."

Cole stiffened at his father's harsh words. "Look, I know you're upset, but I can handle this. I know what I'm doing, and who I'm doing it with."

Natalie frowned, wishing Cole had presented a clearer defense of her character.

"You should have enough respect for your sister's memory to stay away from this woman," Richard said sharply.

"I did stay away from her—for ten years," Cole replied. "How many more do you want?"

"The rest of your life." He gave Natalie a hard, bitter look. "We took you into our lives, shared our holidays with you, treated you like a daughter, and what did you do—you got Emily drunk. You argued with her. You let her go out on a roof when she couldn't see straight enough to walk. And you either pushed her or you let her fall. Either way, you killed her."

Natalie couldn't breathe. She felt like he'd just stabbed her in the heart.

"You're going to have to choose, Cole." Richard tipped his head toward Natalie. "Between her or your family."

Cole's face turned white. "Don't give me an ultimatum," he said, but his words hit only air. His parents were gone, slamming the door on their way out of the apartment.

Natalie slowly finished buttoning up her blouse, realizing belatedly that she'd been talking to Cole's parents half-naked. Another mark against her. Cole finally moved toward his dresser, taking out a T-shirt and pulling it over his broad shoulders. They were dressed now; they had their armor back on.

"I guess the night is really over," she said, feeling a huge wave of regret despite her best intention to feel nothing.

"I guess it is."

She hated the way he wouldn't look at her and wondered if they were going to ignore what had just been said. Before she could ask, Cole walked out of the room. Apparently, they were going to ignore it. She followed him into the living room, where he was searching for his keys. "Are we still working together on this?" she asked. "You heard what your father said about me. And your mother—she begged you to leave me alone."

"I was here. I don't need a recap."

He sounded angry, and she wasn't sure who exactly he was angry at. "Are they always like that? So needy?"

"They lost a lot when they lost Emily," he said heavily. "They have a right to be needy. I just can't ever seem to give them what they want."

"Emily used to say that, too," Natalie murmured.

"We already discussed that. Emily was sick as a child. She had to be protected."

"But you weren't sick. You didn't need to be protected. You felt trapped, too. And you still do." She looked into his eyes and knew she was right. "Is that why you ran from me before, Cole? Is that the real reason you wanted to get out of our relationship as soon as I told you I loved you?"

Cole ran a hand through his hair. "I don't know, Natalie. I don't know anymore. Maybe."

In a strange way Natalie was glad Cole's parents had come by. She understood him better now. Cole was afraid of getting too much love. And she was afraid she would never get enough. How on earth could they ever be together?

"I'll take you home," he said. "I need to go to work."

*   *   *

Natalie spent most of the morning cleaning her apartment, catching up on laundry, bills, e-mail, all the while trying to ignore the memories clamoring in her head. She did not want to relive yesterday or last night. She did not want to think about how good it had been with Cole and how much harder it was to be alone again now that she'd spent the night with him. She had only herself to blame. She'd made love to him with her eyes open. She'd chosen not to think about tomorrow—so why was she surprised that tomorrow had come and bitten her on the ass? She'd known the time they had together was only a brief interlude. She just had to accept it and move on. Except she just didn't quite know how to move on.

There was still the problem of the book, the reporters, the fact that she couldn't go back to work. She felt trapped. And she needed a way out.

When the phone rang in the late afternoon, she let the answering machine pick up, expecting it to be yet another reporter asking her questions she couldn't answer. She was surprised to hear a familiar voice on the machine, another woman from her past.

"Natalie, this is Diane Thomas," the woman said. "I don't know if you remember me, but—"

"Diane," Natalie said, grabbing the phone. "Hi, I just got in and heard your voice on the machine."

"It took me a few days to track you down," Diane said. "I've been thinking about you ever since that book came out. I wanted to tell you I think it's appalling what's been written about you."

Natalie was touched by her words. Diane had

served as their sorority adviser and pledge confidante, and it was nice to know that she didn't believe the rumors in the book.

Natalie took a seat on the couch. "Thanks. You don't know how much it means to me to hear you say that."

"I know how close you were to Emily. This must be very painful for you."

"It is."

Diane paused for a moment. "Jessica Holbrook works here in my office now. She's the new adviser to the Gamma Delts. She has a different opinion than I do. I felt I should warn you, Natalie, that some of the girls think you did have something to do with Emily's fall."

Natalie sighed. Even though she'd already known that, it was tough to hear again. "I understand, but I'm not guilty."

"I know that. Emily was such a sweet girl, and you were best friends. I was talking to Connie Richmond yesterday," Diane added, referring to Natalie's sorority housemother, "and she and I would love to help you if we can. Is there anything we can do?"

"Not at the moment. Unless you know who the author of the book is."

"What do you mean?"

"I don't think Garrett Malone is the author's real name. I think he's using a pen name."

"Really? Why would he do that?"

"He must be protecting something. I don't know." Natalie started as her doorbell rang. She hoped it wasn't the press. "Can you hold on a minute?" She looked through the peephole and saw

Madison. Opening the door, she motioned to the phone and waved her hand to Madison to enter. "Sorry about that. There is one thing I did want to ask you, Diane. Did Emily confide in you about a guy she was seeing? I know she used to hold your opinion in high regard. She always said you gave great advice."

"I don't know about that, but I tried," Diane said with a laugh. "As for a guy, I don't recall anyone in particular. We talked more about sorority relationships, girlfriends, that sort of thing."

Which meant they'd probably spoken about her and Cole. "Did she say anything about wishing I wasn't involved with her brother?" Natalie asked.

There was a slight pause, then Diane said, "She mentioned things weren't going well between the three of you. I'm sure it wasn't as bad as that book made it out to be, was it?"

"No, of course not."

"Well, I have to go. Please feel free to call me or Connie if there's anything we can do. Emily's death was a tragic accident, but it was an accident."

"Yes, it was, and thank you. That's very generous. I appreciate the support." Natalie set down the phone and responded to Madison's raised eyebrow with, "That was Diane Thomas."

"Really? Another voice from the past."

"She doesn't believe the book, and she offered to help. She said she and Mrs. Richmond were talking about it the other day, and they both think I'm innocent."

"Good. I'm surprised Mrs. Richmond's still the housemother. Wasn't she like eighty when we were there?"

"More like fifty, Madison."

"She sure looked old."

"That's because we were young." Natalie perched on the arm of the couch. "What's up with you?"

"I saw Dylan last night." Madison sat down in a chair and crossed her legs. "He has a shrine to Emily in his apartment, hundreds of photos of her on every available piece of wall space in a locked closet."

Natalie was shocked. "Really? How do you know that?"

"I kind of let myself in. It's a long story. The gist of it is that Dylan was madly in love with Emily. He heard you arguing with Emily in her room the night of the party."

"So he was at the house that night. I thought so."

"He said he left because he didn't want to get into the middle of what was going on with you and Em. He wishes he'd stayed because if he had . . ."

"Emily might still be alive," Natalie finished. "He thinks I did it then, doesn't he?"

"Yes, mostly. We did discuss another possibility, but I'll get into that in a minute." Madison paused. "I think Dylan might be Malone."

Natalie nodded. "I'm thinking that, too."

Madison frowned. "Well, I thought I was going to be delivering a bombshell, but obviously not. Why do *you* think Dylan is Malone?"

"Because Cole and I tracked Malone to L.A. and found a disguise in his room—wig, makeup, the whole bit."

"Dylan was in L.A.," Madison said excitedly. "Josh told me that."

"And who better to have a disguise than a magician?" Natalie thought for a moment. "You said there was a lot of Emily memorabilia in Dylan's closet? I wonder if he has her journal in there. Cole and I think that a lot of the information from the book may have come from Emily's journal."

"Damn, I should have thought of that."

Natalie stood up. "We've got to get over there."

"I'll drive. What about Cole?"

She hesitated. "He's at work, and frankly, I don't want to call him right now. We had a bit of a scene this morning." Natalie was sorry she'd volunteered that much information when she saw the inquisitive gleam in Madison's eyes. "Don't ask."

"Oh, no, you don't get to say that. What happened?"

Natalie hesitated. Did she really want to confide in Madison? Madison was probably the only person who wouldn't judge her for what she'd done. She took a deep breath and said, "Cole and I slept together last night, and his parents walked in this morning and caught us practically naked."

"Holy shit!"

"You can say that again. They were furious and hurt. They said terrible things to Cole and basically told him to choose between me and the family."

"I hate morning-after conversations with the folks," Madison said lightly.

Natalie smiled. "This was a doozy."

"What did Cole say?"

"He was defending his position and saying we weren't on opposite sides, but he didn't exactly come right out and say he . . ." She shrugged, unable to finish the sentence much less the thought. "I know it was stupid to make love with him. I don't know what I was thinking. Where Cole is concerned, my brain takes a vacation. Anyway, it's never going to happen again, so that's that."

Madison laughed. "Nice try, Natalie, but you and I both know that is not going to be that. You and Cole aren't finished yet. You're not even close."

Cole left work just after four o'clock, knowing he'd accomplished absolutely nothing during the day. He hadn't been able to concentrate. His brain kept wandering back to the passionate night with Natalie, followed by the stormy confrontation with his parents. He needed to talk to someone. Josh hadn't answered his phone, so he decided to try Dylan.

The hostess at Club V said Dylan hadn't yet come in, so Cole went through the side door and up the stairs that led to Dylan's apartment.

His knock on the door was answered a moment later—by Josh. Josh wore a pair of faded blue jeans and a white T-shirt. He had a beer in his hand and the television remote in the other. "Cole, what are you doing here?"

"I was going to ask you the same question. Aren't you supposed to be at work?"

"I'm covering a game tonight, so I was taking a break."

"Don't you have your own place?"

"I was out of beer and Dylan has a bigger television."

Cole nodded, wondering why it felt like a lifetime ago when his needs had been as simple as a cold beer and a big-screen TV.

"Where's Dylan?"

"Gone."

A chill ran through him at the answer. "What do you mean—gone?"

"He left me a message this morning saying he'll be back in a few days."

"Where did he go?"

Josh shrugged. "I didn't ask. He didn't say. You know he never says." His eyes narrowed thoughtfully. "What's the problem? Dylan is always taking off. Why are you so concerned?"

"It's this damn book. I think Dylan knows something about it."

"You better come in," Josh said, closing the door behind Cole. "Want a beer?"

"No, thanks. Do you think there was something going on between Dylan and Emily in Santa Cruz?" Cole couldn't believe he was asking the question, but it had been rambling around in his head for a few days.

"It's an interesting question," Josh said after a moment. "Madison asked me the same thing the other night. I told her they were like brother and sister. Weren't they?"

"I thought so." He felt better having his opinion confirmed. Josh was Dylan's twin brother. Wouldn't he have known if there was something going on? "Of course they were just friends," he added. "I'm going crazy trying to figure out who wrote this book. Malone has gone underground. My best investigator is coming up with nothing. It's as if the man dropped off the face of the earth. And now my parents are back and going ballistic."

"Is there anything I can do?"

"You can help me find your brother." As Cole

finished speaking, a knock came at the door. "I'll get it." To say he was shocked to see Madison and Natalie at the door was an understatement. Apparently, they felt the same way about seeing him.

"What are you doing here, Cole? I thought you were at work," Natalie said.

"I wanted to talk to Dylan."

"So do we," Madison replied, looking around. "Where is he?"

"He's not here," Cole replied. "And no one knows where he is." He saw the disappointment flash across Natalie's face, but she quickly averted her gaze. How had they gone so fast from intimate back to strangers? He knew the answer to that. His parents had reminded them both that Emily was still between them.

"That's fine," Madison said decisively. "It might be a good thing that Dylan isn't here. He won't be able to stop us."

"Stop us from what?" Josh asked curiously.

"Going through his closet."

"Now hang on, Madison," Josh said. "I can't let you go through Dylan's closet."

"Try and stop me." She pointed to a closed door on the far side of the room. "Have you ever been in there?"

Cole followed her gaze, wondering what she knew that he didn't. It didn't take long to find out.

"Dylan has set up a shrine to Emily," Madison continued. "I saw it yesterday. We just need the key." She glanced at Josh. "Do you have it?"

"I might," Josh said slowly. "But I also respect my brother's privacy. Borrowing his television and mooching a beer is one thing; looking through his closets is another."

"We have to look," Cole said. "Give me the keys."

Josh hesitated, then walked over to the table and picked up the keys. He tossed them to Cole. "It must be one of those."

Cole had been in this loft dozens of times and never even noticed the closet. Now it looked somewhat ominous. He had the terrible feeling he didn't want to open the door. But something drove him across the room. After fumbling with each key, he found the right one. It slid in easily. He turned the knob.

Natalie, Madison, and Josh came up behind him as the door swung open. "There's a light," Madison said, reaching past him to pull a long, dangling chain.

The light came on, and Cole's jaw dropped as Emily's face stared out at him in a hundred different ways. Photos of her were plastered all over the small room.

"Shit!" Josh said. "What the hell is this?"

"A nightmare," Cole murmured, turning away. He thought he was going to be sick.

Natalie put a hand on his arm. "Are you all right?"

"No."

"Where are you going? We need to look for Emily's journal."

Cole shook his head. "I can't. I've got to get out of here."

Laura felt self-conscious and nervous as she walked toward Drew's office, located at the far end of a floor filled with cubicles. His secretary, Pamela Fryer, sat at her post outside his door, her gaze focused on the computer, her fingers flying across the keyboard. Like most of the women in the law firm that had been founded by Laura's father, Pamela was young, attractive, and well dressed. She'd been Drew's secretary for the past six months and Laura had barely exchanged more than a few words with her. That was about to change.

"Mrs. McKinney," Pamela said in surprise, as she approached. "Can I help you? Drew's not here."

"I know that," ·Laura said, trying to remember the story she'd concocted. After her unsatisfying conversation with Drew the night before, it had become clear to her that if she wanted answers, she'd have to get them herself. If Drew was up to something, he wouldn't leave evidence of it at home. He'd keep it at work, because she never came to work—until today. "Drew accidentally brought my daughter's permission slip to work, and she needs it. He said it's in his desk. It got mixed up in his papers last week. I'm just going to get it."

"Do you want me to help you look for it?" Pamela asked, as she stood up.

"No, I can do it."

"Mr. McKinney really doesn't like anyone to go through his desk," Pamela said hesitantly.

"Believe me, I know exactly what Mr. McKinney does and doesn't like," Laura replied, deciding it was time to show a little backbone. "I *am* his wife."

"Of course you are. I didn't mean . . ."

The phone on Pamela's desk rang as if by divine intervention. Laura escaped into Drew's office while Pamela took the call. Knowing she had only a few minutes, she riffled through his desk drawers as quickly as she could. Nothing, nothing, nothing. She took a quick look through the blinds in Drew's office and saw that Pamela was still on the phone. She had a few more minutes, so she turned to his filing cabinets. As she did so, Drew's computer caught her eye. He loved to do everything online.

Turning on the computer, she tapped her fingers impatiently on the desk as it booted up, keeping one eye on Pamela, the other on the screen. It would be hard to explain why she needed to look at Drew's computer when she'd come for a simple permission slip.

Finally, it was up. She glanced through his personal document files and her pulse quickened when she saw one labeled Malone. She opened it and skimmed the contents. It was another travel itinerary. Was this a copy of the one she'd found at the house? No, it couldn't be, because it showed travel to New York. Hadn't Drew gone to New York last month? The dates seemed to coincide with her memory. She scrolled down, hoping to find something more, but there was nothing. Closing out that file, she went back to the main document list. She ran her finger down the list of files. Most of the names meant nothing to her. Until she came to SC. Wondering if SC meant Santa Cruz, she opened it. A list of names and phone numbers jumped out at her. She recognized every single one.

Jessica Holbrook, Emily's big sister.

Connie Richmond, their sorority housemother.

Diane Thomas, the pledge adviser.

The list went on and on with names of girls who had lived in the sorority house at the time of Emily's death. Laura stared at it for several long minutes. Why did Drew have this list? And what had he been researching?

Did he want to find out who had written the book?

Or had he used these people to get information to write the book?

She shook her head, trying to rein in her imagination. Drew was an attorney, not a novelist. He had not written that book. He had no motive—except money. But he made plenty of money at the firm, obviously more than enough to move large amounts in and out of their bank account. Unless that money hadn't come from the firm.

Laura turned off the computer and stood up as Pamela appeared in the doorway, an inquisitive expression on her face.

"Did you find what you were looking for?" Pamela asked.

"I did. Thanks."

"Laura?"

She heard his booming voice even before he entered the office. Her father, Thomas Hart, was a big man, six feet three inches tall with a large, square face and an intimidating manner. He'd always scared the hell out of her, and now was no exception. She might be almost thirty years old, married, and the mother of two children, but when it came to her dad she felt like an uncertain little girl. "Hi, Dad," she said, forcing a smile on her face.

"Pamela said you were here, but she didn't say why."

So Drew's secretary had already reported her

presence to her father? She sent the woman a pointed look, and Pamela backed out of the office with a muttered, "Excuse me."

"One of Jennifer's permission slips got mixed up in Drew's papers. I came to retrieve it."

Her father moved into the office, shutting the door behind him. "Is that really why you came?"

"What else could it be?" she asked nervously.

His dark eyes bored into her and she had the terrible feeling he could see right through her.

"Drew has been out of the office a lot lately," her father said. "Is there a problem at home, a reason why he needs to be out of town so frequently?"

She looked at him in surprise. "He's out of town on business. I'm sure you know better than I do what that business is."

"I'm afraid I don't. Drew has been taking a tremendous amount of personal leave. He said he was having personal problems. I've tried not to interfere, Laura, but this is becoming a noticeable problem to the other partners. I can't cover for Drew forever."

Drew was taking personal leave? Was he lying to both of them?

"Look, Laura, I don't give you much advice, but I'll tell you this. If you want to keep your husband home, make sure he has something to come home to."

"What is that supposed to mean?"

"You know what it means. Men who are happy at home don't look elsewhere."

Her father left the office, and she was tempted to run after him and ask him if he'd used that same excuse to cheat on her mother. She'd always sus-pected he'd had more than a few affairs over the years. But no one ever said the words out loud.

Was she behaving just like her mother—looking the other way, pretending things were all right when they were all wrong? Was Drew having an affair? Was that why he was taking so much time off? She needed to talk to him. She needed to ask those questions straight out. No more beating around the bush. No more hoping the problems would all go away. Now she just had to find Drew.

Chapter 17

Natalie spent most of Friday morning looking for Cole. She'd been to his apartment, his office; she'd even driven by his parents' house to see if his car was there. It wasn't. She was getting more worried by the moment. Since Cole had stormed out of Dylan's apartment the day before, he had been completely unreachable. She'd decided to give him a little time to come to terms with Dylan's feelings for Emily, but that time was up. She wanted—make that needed—to talk to him, to make sure he was all right.

Taking a chance, she drove down to the marina and walked out to the base of the Golden Gate Bridge. Sure enough, he was there, leaning against a brick wall, looking out at the water. She pulled her sweater tightly around her body as a cool breeze made her shiver, then walked up to him.

"How did you know I was here?" Cole asked without turning his head.

She leaned against the wall, resting her arms on top of it, as she nudged his shoulder with her own. "Lucky guess. Aren't you cold?" He had on a dress shirt and slacks but no coat.

"I don't know. I haven't thought about it." He paused for a moment. "Did you find Em's journal?"

"No, it wasn't in Dylan's closet." She saw his pulse jump and knew he was still having a hard time thinking about that closet. "It wasn't as bad as it looked, Cole."

"How can you say that?" He turned to gaze at her, and she saw pain and anger in his dark eyes. "Dylan was obsessed with my sister in some weird, sick way. And I never knew. I thought he was my friend. I trusted him. We all did. My parents were happy when Emily went to Santa Cruz so Dylan could look after her. My God, we encouraged him to see her." He shook his head in self-loathing. "I can't believe I trusted him."

"Dylan did look after Emily. According to Madison, he was in love with Emily, but he never told her. And she never acted like they were anything but friends. I don't think he crossed the line, Cole, except in his own imagination." Natalie didn't know why she felt so determined to convince him, but she did. Maybe because Cole had already lost his sister; she couldn't let him lose one of his best friends, too. "There have been so many misunderstandings. Don't let this be another one. Talk to Dylan before you judge him."

"What don't I understand, Natalie?" he asked with a frustrated wave of his hand. "My best friend lied to me. Even if it was a lie of omission, it's still a lie. And why are you defending him? He hates you."

"Thanks for reminding me," she said dryly. "I know he's not my biggest fan, but we looked through the closet, Cole. Yes, there are tons of photos of Emily, but it's not like they're nude photos. We also found drawings that must have been done when Emily was young. It looked like she and Dylan tried to make their own magic tricks. And they wrote stories together about magical places. I guess Dylan based his virtual-reality games on some of those stories. From what I read, they were pretty good. The closet was like a big scrapbook. You should go back and look inside. You'll see there aren't any monsters in there."

Cole stared at her as if she'd grown two heads. "I don't get you, Natalie. You sound forgiving. Haven't you figured out yet that there's a good chance Dylan either is Garrett Malone or fed Malone the story because he wanted to punish you for Emily's death?"

That thought had definitely occurred to her. "Of course I get that, Cole. If Dylan believes that I hurt Emily, then he's wrong, and I will make sure he understands that at some point. Especially if he's the one who wrote the book that is destroying my reputation." She paused, wishing she could make him understand that she'd been touched emotionally by some of what she'd seen in that closet. "I have to tell you that I'm a little in awe of the love that Dylan had for Emily. He adored her. That's clearly evident. Whatever he did, he did out of love."

"A sick kind of love obviously."

"Why was it sick? Because he was your friend?"

"And she was my sister," Cole said with a disgusted edge to his voice. "And he took advantage of her."

"No, he didn't, and I'm beginning to see why he never told you about his feelings."

"He didn't tell me because he knew I wouldn't like it."

Natalie sighed, feeling like she was ramming her head against a brick wall.

"Only the newspaper is that black and white, Cole. The rest of life is more complicated, especially relationships. Dylan had every right to love Emily. And I'm sure she cared about him too. They were best friends. You have to talk to Dylan."

Cole didn't answer. It was clear he was still angry.

Natalie looked out at the water, watching a sailboat cross under the bridge. It was attempting to sail back into the bay, away from the open sea, directly into the wind and the swirling currents. But the sailors weren't giving up, turning left, then right, as they attempted to catch a cross breeze. She felt like she was engaged in much the same battle, but she wouldn't give up. She wouldn't lose, not when she was so close to having everything she wanted.

She couldn't let Cole give up, either. "You need to stay focused," she told him. "You're letting yourself get sidetracked. We still have to find Malone, the journal, and the truth. At least we're getting closer."

He shot her a skeptical look. "How on earth could you think that? Every time I turn around I find out something new about my sister. Emily is a stranger now. Was she the girl I remember in my head and my heart? Or was she someone completely different?"

"Maybe she was a little of both. We don't always show family our true faces, especially when we're teenagers, and Emily was nineteen years old when she died. She wasn't fully grown. She hadn't become all she could be. And she wasn't perfect."

"I thought she was perfect," Cole said heavily. "Every time I think about her now, I see her laughing brown eyes and her beautiful smile, and it pisses me off that she's gone. She had so much to live for. She could have been anyone."

Natalie slid her hand down his arm and over his clenched fist in a gesture of comfort. "I feel the same way, Cole. Emily is frozen in time for all of us. That's why we can't let go of her. We can't get past the fact that we had a chance to move on, and she didn't. Maybe that's why Dylan had to keep his memories alive in photos. Maybe we shouldn't judge him so harshly for that."

"I want her back," Cole said tightly. "I want five more minutes with Emily."

His words made her eyes tear up, and she bit down on her lip to stop the emotion. Where had all her defenses gone? And why couldn't she get those damn walls up again?

"Just five more minutes," he continued, gazing into her eyes. "I want to tell Em that I'm proud of her, that I love her, and that I'd sell my soul to relive that night again, to bring her back. Is that so much to ask?"

Natalie shook her head, unable to speak. She wanted five more minutes with Emily, too—time to say she was sorry for putting Emily in the middle, for not paying more attention to what was going on in her life, and for being selfish. But they weren't going to get five more seconds, let alone five more minutes.

When Cole put his arms around her, Natalie went willingly. She rested her cheek against the pounding beat of his heart and wrapped her arms around his waist. They stayed that way for several long minutes. She wanted it to last forever. She realized now she hadn't come back to San Francisco because of the beauty of the city or the memories; she'd come back for this. This was the only home she'd ever really wanted, here in Cole's arms.

Like all of her homes, she knew it would be temporary. There were no second chances. Not for any of them.

Cole's cell phone rang a moment later, and she pulled away so he could answer it. He checked the number and shook his head. "Josh again."

"He's worried about you. Aren't you going to answer it?"

"I'll talk to him later. I need time to think. Do you suppose he knew—"

"No. Dylan's relationship with Emily—whatever it was—was kept just between the two of them."

He frowned. "You don't think she was afraid of Dylan, do you?"

Natalie shook her head. "Absolutely not. I saw them together in Santa Cruz. There was no fear in their relationship. Not a speck of it. Emily made Dylan smile. And he made her laugh. And she loved to talk to him. It wasn't weird at all."

"I want to believe that."

"Then believe it. We have other things to worry about."

"Like what?"

"Madison and I sat down and compared notes. This is what we know. Emily had a crush on someone right before she died, someone she thought was unattainable. The only person we can think of that Emily might have put in that category is Drew, because of his relationship with Laura."

"Drew?" Cole echoed. "You think Emily and Drew had something going on? Are you serious?"

"I don't think we can rule it out. We know that Drew was in L.A. at the same time as Malone." She paused. "Isn't it interesting that as of today both Drew and Dylan are nowhere to be found?"

"It's not interesting. It's damned frustrating."

"Could Drew and Dylan be working together?" Natalie asked. "Dylan likes to write. Drew is conniving enough to keep this book just out of lawsuit reach. And they both share a passionate dislike of me."

Cole didn't reply. He just stared at her for a long moment, and she could see the wheels turning in his brain. "It's possible, I suppose."

His cell phone rang again. "This is my investigator. I better take it."

Natalie watched his face change during the course of the short conversation. He went from angry, tense, and sad to excited and eager.

"We've got a break," he said, as he ended the call. "My investigator found Malone. He traced his corporation back to someone named Jerry Williams."

The name didn't ring a bell. "I don't understand. Who is Jerry Williams?"

"I have no idea, but he has a Santa Cruz address. I think we should check it out."

"I don't know," Natalie said, hesitating. Did she

really want to go back to the place where Emily had died? Where she'd spent the worst night of her life?

"What don't you know?" Cole asked forcefully. "This is our first real lead. We have to follow it up." His eyes softened as he gazed at her. "I know it will be difficult, but I don't think we have a choice, not if we want the truth."

"Are you sure you want me to come with you? After what your parents said yesterday? The last thing I want to do is come between you and your family, Cole."

Some emotion flashed through his eyes, but it came and went so quickly she couldn't read it. "We're in this together until we get our answers. That's all I can think about right now."

Until we get our answers. At least he was offering a time frame this go-around.

"All right," she said, making a quick decision. "I'll come. Santa Cruz is where it began. With any luck, that is where it will end."

Madison tapped her fingernails impatiently on the top of her desk. She really needed to work, but she was having trouble concentrating. She couldn't get her mind off the past, and especially off Dylan. He would be furious when he found out that everyone now knew about his infatuation with Emily. He'd probably never speak to her again, especially since she'd been the one to blow his cover. For some reason, the thought made her feel more sad than angry. She'd begun to see a different side to Dylan in the last few days, and what she'd seen had impressed her. There was more to the man than the bad-boy image, a lot more. She just wished he'd open up to her. There was probably no chance of that happening now.

Shaking her head, she tried to focus on the details of the masquerade party that thankfully her staff was handling quite capably. But even as she read, her mind drifted and the words blurred in front of her eyes. She was grateful when her office door opened and her secretary, Theresa Myers, entered, several message slips in hand.

"You had some calls while you were in your meeting earlier. The first was from a Detective Robert Boland with the Santa Cruz Police Department. He asked that you call him back as soon as possible," Theresa said.

Madison felt her stomach muscles clench. Damn. That was not what she wanted to hear.

"Is everything all right?" Theresa asked curiously.

"Fine. Anything else?"

"There was also a message from a Natalie Bishop. She said she's on her way to Santa Cruz, and if you need to reach her, call her on her cell phone. Do you need anything else? I was going to run down to the printer to pick up the seating cards for the masquerade party."

"That's all." Madison waved the woman out of her office. She needed to think. Getting up, she paced around her desk. The police wanted to talk to her. That wasn't good. And Natalie was on her way to Santa Cruz. Had she also gotten a call from the detective? It sounded like the answers were in Santa Cruz. Maybe it was time she went back, too.

Taking her purse out of her drawer, she opened her wallet and pulled out the piece of paper upon which Laura had written her phone number. She dialed her home number, hoping she was there.

Laura answered on the second ring. "Hello?" she said, somewhat warily.

"It's Maddie."

"Thank God. I just got a call from a police detective. He wants to interview me again about Emily's death."

"I know. I got the same call. Listen, Natalie is on her way to Santa Cruz. I think we should go, too."

"Santa Cruz? I don't know. I'm afraid to go back there. I don't have a good feeling about this."

"Neither do I, but I'm going."

Laura hesitated, then said, "I'll get my mother to pick up the kids after school."

"Good. What will you tell Drew?"

"Nothing. He's still out of town, and I have no idea what he's doing. But that's another story."

"You can tell me on the way down. I'll pick you up in an hour. Give me your address." Madison jotted down Laura's address, then hung up the phone with a satisfied smile. She was happy to be taking some action. And this move felt right.

"Santa Cruz, here we come," she murmured as she headed toward the door.

When Natalie saw the Giant Dipper, a vintage wooden roller coaster at the Santa Cruz Boardwalk, she felt like she was home. This beautiful, lazy city by the sea had hosted some of the best days of her life, and even though she'd lived in the town for only sixteen short months, there were familiar scenes everywhere she looked. "Do you remember when we rode the coaster?" she asked

Cole, who hadn't said much on the two-hour drive from San Francisco.

"How could I forget? I think that's where I lost the hearing in my right ear."

Natalie was pleased by the teasing note in his voice. She'd been worried about him, but she sensed that he was bouncing back. "I didn't scream that loud," she said. "Anyway, everyone screams on a roller coaster. It's expected. The girl screams, and the guy holds on tighter."

"Ah, so that's the plan. You women are just too damn smart."

"It's about time you figured that out," she said with a smile. She hated to break the mood, but she saw him glance at the street sign and wondered if he knew where they were going. "Do you want me to check the map?"

"I think we're heading in the right direction. Haller Avenue should be coming up in about a mile." He paused. "Is that your cell phone?"

"Oh," Natalie said, realizing the ringing sound was coming from her purse. She flipped open her phone. "Hello?"

"Hi, Natalie," Madison said. "Are you in Santa Cruz yet?"

"Just passing the boardwalk." She relaxed at the sound of Madison's voice. "I guess you got my message."

"I did, and I'm on my way, too."

"You're coming down here?" Natalie asked in surprise. "Don't you have to work?"

"It's difficult to concentrate in between dodging calls from the police. Did you hear from Detective Boland?"

"No," Natalie said with a sinking feeling in the pit of her stomach. "What did he want?"

"To reinterview me. I haven't spoken to him yet. If you have a lead on Malone, I want in on it. So does Laura. She's with me."

"Hi, Natalie," Laura said in the background.

"So what have you got?" Madison asked.

"Maybe an address for Malone. Apparently, he set up his corporation in the name of Jerry Williams. Does that ring a bell?"

"I can't say that it does, but we'll be in Santa Cruz within the hour. Shall we meet at the sorority house?"

Natalie hesitated. She'd been thinking about the sorority house since Cole had asked her to go to Santa Cruz, but some part of her did not want to make that stop. Still, how could she come all this way and not go there? It was the center of the entire situation. "All right. Hopefully, we'll find Malone before then. I'll ring you if we do." She ended the call and slipped her phone back into her purse. "Madison and Laura are on their way down here."

"I figured that." Cole peered at a nearby street sign. "Is that Haller?"

"Yes, and we want 2302." Natalie noted the numbers as they drove down the street. "It should be in the next block. There it is." Cole pulled over in front of a large two-story building with a sign in front that read SUNRISE LIVING CENTER. "It's a retirement home," she said in surprise. "Garrett Malone isn't old. Even with a disguise, he couldn't be older than fifty. This can't be right, but it's the address your investigator gave you."

Cole shut off the engine. "We've come this far. Let's check it out."

They got out of the car and walked through the front door. A woman dressed in casual clothes sat behind a desk in what was obviously a lobby area, with comfortable couches and chairs set around coffee tables. There was a television on in one corner, an elderly woman knitting in front of it.

"Can I help you?" the receptionist asked.

"We're here to visit Jerry Williams," Cole said.

"Mr. Williams?" The woman appeared surprised. "Are you relatives?"

"No, we're friends," Cole replied. "Is that a problem?"

"Oh, of course not. He just doesn't get many visitors. He's on the second floor, Room 210. Some days are better than others, you know. It's just the nature of it. You need to sign in before you go up." She pushed a clipboard across the counter. Cole signed it, then said, "Thank you," and they headed up to the second floor.

When they walked into Room 210 Natalie saw an elderly man sitting in a wheelchair. He was all skin and bones, very thin and fragile looking with eyes that appeared vacant and distant.

"Mr. Williams?" Cole said. The man didn't even blink. "We want to talk to you," Cole said, trying again. No answer. Cole shot Natalie a questioning look. "What's wrong with him?"

"I'm guessing Alzheimer's or some other type of dementia. I know one thing; he's not Garrett Malone. Maybe we have the wrong Jerry Williams. It's a common name."

"I don't think so. The fact that Williams lives

here in Santa Cruz is too big a coincidence. Malone must have used Mr. Williams's social security number. That's the only explanation."

"Why would he go to so much trouble?"

"Because he was writing about a real event and trying to sell it as fiction. He didn't want anyone to know who he is, not his agent, not his publisher, maybe not even his friends."

"He wanted to protect himself. Keep his distance from the event while throwing the rest of us into the fire," Natalie finished. "I guess that makes sense. But how would Malone get this man's social security number?"

"He has to be connected to him in some way."

While Cole tried to get the old man's attention, Natalie moved across the room and opened the drawer by the bed. There were some blank notepads and pencils inside, a Bible, a box of chocolates, a CD player, and a book of poetry. Natalie opened up the book and caught her breath at the stamp. "Look at this," she said, holding it out to Cole. "Greg Martin, Ph.D., Professor of English Literature, Santa Cruz University. I know that name. He taught when I was there. I'm almost positive either Emily or Laura took a class from him. I remember, because he was considered pretty cute by professor standards."

"If he's still at the university, we can find him. Maybe we just found Malone. The initials are the same—Greg Martin, Garrett Malone."

"Maybe." Natalie still couldn't see how an English professor at the University would come to write a book about Emily, or about herself for that matter. "It's hard to believe he could have known so much about us, though."

"Not if he had Emily's journal."

"How would he have gotten her journal?"

"I don't know, but let's take this one step at a time. And think about this—an English professor would certainly know how to write a book."

"I guess."

"You don't sound convinced," Cole said, his eyes narrowing. "What's wrong?"

"I was just so sure it was Dylan or Drew or someone we knew more intimately. But Professor Martin—why would he take the trouble to disguise himself? What would his connection be to this man?" She waved her hand toward Mr. Williams, who had yet to acknowledge their presence in the room. "They don't have the same name, but he obviously came here to visit him."

"They're probably family of some sort. Let's go to the university and see if we can find this professor. He has a better shot at answering your questions than I do."

She nodded in agreement. "Let's pick up Laura and Madison on the way. Maybe one of them knows more about him. They're at the sorority house."

Cole's face paled. "That's the last place I want to go."

"I feel the same way, but I don't think this will be over until we do."

While Madison parked the car in the lot, Laura walked along the sidewalk in front of the two-story sorority house that had been her home for three years. She put one hand up to shade her eyes from the sun as she stared at the building. She'd had so many moments in this house, both good and bad. Coming back here wouldn't mean as much to Natalie and Madison as it did to her. After they'd left, the sorority had become her haven, her family of friends. While she'd never felt as close to anyone as she'd felt to Natalie, Madison, and Emily, she had managed to fit in and find a group of women with whom she could laugh and study, dance and party, and eventually share a graduation ceremony.

She hadn't been back to the house since that graduation, but it looked the same, maybe a new coat of off-white paint on the outside. White columns provided a covered walkway from the parking lot to the house. A border of flowers ran along that walk and a short patch of lawn led down to the sidewalk. The downstairs housed the library, living room, dining room, and kitchen, as well as the housemother's quarters in the back. The second story was all windows as bedrooms ran around the front, sides, and back, with communal bathrooms in the middle of the floor.

The very first day of rush, Laura had stood on this sidewalk with her friends, waiting to be invited in. It was the first house they had visited, and they had had no idea what rush meant. They had been shocked when the front door and second-story windows had flown open with dozens of girls in colorful costumes singing a sorority song and inviting them to come inside. It had seemed corny and silly and they'd laughed a lot, but they'd gone inside. A whole new world had opened up to them.

It had been Emily's idea to rush. They'd met

some sorority girls their freshman year in the dorms and had envied their parties and closeness. Sorority life had looked like a lot of fun. They'd decided as sophomores to give it a try. And they'd made a pact; they'd join together or not at all. Fortunately, the Gamma Delta house had invited all four of them to join.

The front door opened now and a young woman walked out, headphones in her ears, a book bag over one shoulder. She couldn't have been more than nineteen. To Laura she looked like a baby. Had they really been that young, that carefree? The girl didn't pause or acknowledge Laura as she made her way to a bike parked at the side of the house. She hopped on and rode off, perhaps to her next class.

"It looks the same," Madison said, coming up beside Laura.

Dressed in a black miniskirt, black knee-high boots, and a silk sweater, Madison looked sophisticated and successful. Laura felt like a frumpy housewife in her Dockers pants and cream-colored sweater.

"Frowns will make you wrinkle," Madison told her with a smile.

Laura's frown disappeared at that familiar comment. "I think that's one of the first things you ever said to me. We were in our dorm room, and I was thinking how small it was, and how narrow the beds were, and wondering what I'd gotten myself into. Then you came in, a blond bombshell with a sassy smile, who told me frowns would make me wrinkle."

"Oh, please, I was hardly a bombshell at eighteen."

"You were then and you are now. Don't even try to pretend you don't know that."

"Okay, I won't. It must have been strange to live here after Emily died and we left." Madison gave her a curious look. "Especially that first week."

"It was really difficult for a long time. Emily and Natalie's room was empty the rest of that year. The following summer they painted it. Some new transfer students moved in, girls that hadn't been here that night. They'd heard the stories, but after they put their stuff in the room, it looked different. I didn't go in there much; I couldn't. I couldn't go by the side yard or out on the roof either. Actually, they nailed the windows shut until they could put up a guardrail. By the time I was a senior, everyone was back out there again, as if it had never happened."

"Except for you."

"Except for me. No amount of time could ever make me forget that Emily fell off that roof." Madison didn't comment on that, and Laura couldn't help wondering what was going through her mind. Madison seemed so casual, unconcerned, yet she was here. She'd taken off work to come to Santa Cruz, so she must be worried about something. "I know you didn't come down here because the police called you, Madison. Or even because Natalie had a lead on Malone. What is it you're looking for? And don't give me some flippant reply. I want the truth."

Madison didn't answer for a moment, then said, "I want to know if Dylan is involved in the book."

"Dylan?" Laura echoed, sensing there was more behind her words. "You like him, don't you?"

"He intrigues me. That's all. I'm curious. Don't make more of it than that."

"I think there is more, but I'll leave it be for now."

"Thank God! Speaking of men, I have a question for you. I know Emily had a crush on someone right before she died. Did she ever tell you who it was?"

Laura was surprised by the question. "I—I don't know. Why?"

"Maybe that man is the key to all this."

Laura shook her head as she tried to remember. "We were always talking about guys. I can't remember one in particular."

"Do you think Drew might know?"

"I don't know why Emily would have confided in Drew and not us," she said slowly, not really liking the tone of Madison's question.

"They were pretty close, weren't they?"

"I guess. You're not suggesting that . . ." She could tell by Madison's expression that's exactly what she was suggesting. "You think Emily was interested in Drew? Are you serious?"

"He did go to her room that night."

"Yes, but he and I were planning to be together that night. If he was interested in Emily, he wouldn't have made such a point of wanting to be with me—would he?" She hated the insecurity in her voice. Drew had married her. He'd loved her. He still loved her. "And Emily, she wouldn't have gone for Drew. She knew I was interested in him."

"Which is why I asked. Emily used the word *unattainable* when she told me there was someone she wanted. And I was just trying to think who was unattainable, that's all."

"Unattainable? So you think it was Drew she wanted?"

"It was just a thought."

"You're wrong. They were friends, that's it. Maybe it was one of the Somerville twins, Dylan or Josh. Emily used to say that being Cole's little sister cut her off from a lot of potential dates, because everyone thought of her as the little sister."

"It wasn't Dylan," Madison said. "He had a huge crush on her, and he said it wasn't reciprocated. Although I never considered Josh. He wasn't around that much. He just came down with Cole sometimes."

"When they came down, Josh hung out with Emily, while Natalie and Cole took off together."

"That is interesting," Madison said. "Josh . . . I'll have to think about that." She glanced around. "I wonder what's taking Natalie and Cole so long. I really hate to wait."

A couple of girls turned the corner and came down the sidewalk toward them. They were completely dressed in red—sweaters, T-shirts, scarves, hats, all with university logos. As they passed by, Laura heard them laughing and talking. "Do you think he really likes me . . . I know he does, but he doesn't think you like him . . . Oh, my God, how could he not know that I like him . . ."

Laura looked at Madison, and they both laughed. "That was us," Laura said.

"We were never that stupid, were we?"

"I was."

"Yeah, you were," Madison agreed with a soft smile. "That was a million years ago."

"At least," Laura agreed, feeling old. What she wouldn't give to be that young and carefree again.

The front door to the sorority house opened and another group of girls came out wearing similar shades of red. They paused, catching sight of Madison and Laura. One of them came forward. "Hi, are you alumni here for the homecoming game?"

"Uh—yes," Laura said, grabbing at an answer. "As a matter of fact we are. We used to live here."

"Cool. Everyone has gone to the game, though. We're having the alumni open house starting at seven tonight, if you want to come back then."

"Thanks." Laura turned to Madison as they left. "I forgot it was homecoming weekend."

"That explains the clothes. I was beginning to think these girls had no fashion sense. Actually, this might work out to our advantage. I'd rather take a stroll through the house while it's relatively empty."

"I think we should wait for Natalie," Laura said. "This is something we need to do together."

Natalie's body tensed as they drove down the street toward the sorority house. Each roll of the wheels brought her closer to her past, a past she still wasn't sure she knew how to face.

"There they are," she said, spying Madison and Laura standing on the corner. "They look like they're waiting to rush. We stood in exactly that spot the first day we came to the house, waiting for the girls to invite us in."

"I wish they never had," Cole said.

"I know you do." She realized this trip might be even more difficult for Cole than for her. His only visits to the house had been to see Emily. And if Emily had never moved into the house, she might still be alive.

Cole pulled up in front of Madison and Laura. Natalie rolled down the window. "Get in," she said. "We found Malone. I'll explain on the way."

Madison opened the door to the backseat, and they climbed in. "What's going on?" she asked.

Natalie turned in her seat as Cole made a U-turn and headed toward the campus. "Cole's investigator tracked Malone's corporation to a man named Jerry Williams. It turns out Mr. Williams is an old man suffering from Alzheimer's and living in a retirement home. It quickly became clear he could not be the author of the book. However, in his drawer I found a book of poetry with a name stamped in it—Greg Martin, professor, Santa Cruz University."

"Professor Martin?" Laura echoed. "Emily and I took a class from him fall semester of our sophomore year."

Natalie felt a rush of excitement at that information. "I thought I remembered Emily mentioning his name. Was it a small class?"

"No, it was in a lecture hall. There had to be a hundred students or more," Laura replied. "Do you really think Professor Martin is Garrett Malone? How would he have been able to write a book about us?"

"That's what we need to ask him," Natalie said. "At the very least, the professor should be able to give us more information on this Jerry Williams and if he's tied in any way to someone else who might have written the book."

After parking the car in a nearby lot, they walked into the building housing the English department. Professor Martin's office was on the third floor. Bypassing the elevator, they took the stairs.

"It's so deserted," Natalie commented. "I wonder where everyone is."

"At the football game," Laura replied. "It's homecoming weekend. Kind of ironic, isn't it?"

Natalie didn't bother to answer that as they paused in front of a door marked with the professor's name. Cole knocked, then tried the door. No one answered, and the door was locked. "Damn." He hit the door with his fist. "I should have known he wouldn't be here. He's never where he's supposed to be."

Natalie sighed, feeling as discouraged as Cole. Before they could decide what to do next, Cole's cell phone rang.

"Parish," he snapped. "What? Are you kidding me? As a matter of fact, I'm in Santa Cruz. All right. I'll be right there."

"Be right where?" Natalie asked when he ended the call.

"The Santa Cruz Police Department. Apparently, they're questioning Dylan about something."

"Dylan? About what?" Natalie asked. "He can't be Malone if Malone is Professor Martin."

"We still don't know that he is. I'd better get over there."

"I'll come with you."

"No. The last place you should be is the Santa

Cruz Police Department," Cole replied. "It will just complicate matters."

"He's right, Natalie," Madison added. "You don't need to put yourself in front of a police detective right now. We have to find out what happened first."

"All right," Natalie replied. As Cole sprinted down the stairs, Natalie turned to Madison and Laura. "What should we do now? Any ideas?"

"Maybe we can find out where Professor Martin lives," Laura suggested. "I bet someone around here knows."

"Maybe Diane knows," Natalie said. "She did tell me she'd like to help if she could. Hey, wasn't she married to a professor?"

Laura's face suddenly paled. "Oh, my God, Natalie. You're right. In fact, I think Diane was married to Greg Martin."

Chapter 18

Cole couldn't believe Dylan was in Santa Cruz and at the police department. They had to be questioning him about Emily's death. But what did Dylan know that he didn't? Cole couldn't even guess. After seeing the shrine to Emily in Dylan's closet, he wasn't sure what to think of the man he'd grown up with. At one time, he would have said they had no secrets from each other. Now it was clear they had many. Well, Dylan had been playing the mystery man for too long. The secrets were coming out today.

As Cole entered the police department, he saw Dylan sitting in a chair next to a desk, talking to a detective. Dylan was wearing blue jeans, a T-shirt, and his usual black leather jacket, and the somber expression on his face made Cole feel even more uneasy. The men stood up when they saw him. The detective extended his hand. "Cole Parish, right? I'm Robert Boland. You might remember me. I'm the detective who was in charge of the investigation into your sister's death ten years ago."

Cole nodded, having a vague recollection of the man. He looked over at Dylan, his eyes narrowing as he noted Dylan's unshaved appearance, the dark shadows under his eyes. "You look like shit. What did you do?"

"He broke into an office at the university," the detective answered for Dylan. "The office belonging to Professor Greg Martin."

"He's Malone," Dylan said shortly, meeting Cole's questioning gaze. "Martin is Malone. I know he is."

"How do you know? Did you talk to him?"

"He wasn't in his office. And the door wasn't locked," he added, shooting the detective a pointed look. "I just walked in. Martin is the one you should be talking to, not me."

"He's right," Cole interjected. "I believe Professor Martin is Garrett Malone, the man who wrote the book about Emily's death. I can't prove it yet, but I have a private investigator working on it. I can give you his name and number. He can show you the paper trail we're following."

"All right," the detective replied. "As I'm sure you know, Mr. Parish, your father has put a tremendous amount of pressure on my chief to take another look at the case. I've made calls to the three women who were your sister's closest friends. I'd like to interview them again. I have to tell you that we still have no concrete proof that this was anything but an accident. That said, I'm very interested in speaking to Mr. Malone to discuss where he got his information." The detective looked at Dylan. "As for you, you can go. But don't go far. I've got your number, and if your phone rings, I expect you to answer it. Mr. Parish, I've already sent someone out to Professor Martin's house. Let us take care of this."

Cole didn't bother to reply. He didn't intend to make any promises he couldn't keep, and he'd do whatever it took to find Malone. But first . . .

Cole waited until they were out of the police station and halfway down the block before he swung around and punched Dylan in the face.

Dylan staggered backwards. "What the fuck is wrong with you?" he yelled, putting one hand over his eye.

"I was going to ask you the same question," Cole said, shaking out his right hand, which was stinging from the force of his blow. "I saw the closet, Dylan. I saw the photos of Emily. I know you were obsessed with her. Don't even try to deny it."

"You broke into my apartment?"

"That's beside the point. Now, are you going to tell me, or do I have to beat it out of you?" Cole's hand clenched once more into a fist.

Dylan took a step back. "It's not what you think."

"You don't know what I think. *I* don't even know what I think." Cole shook his head. "You look like the guy I grew up with, but I don't know you at all, do I? Did you and Emily . . ." He couldn't bring himself to say it. "God! I trusted you with her. I told you to take care of her. Watch out for her. Make sure she was safe. And all the time, you were—"

"I did take care of her, and we didn't do anything wrong," Dylan said. "We were friends. That's it. She never knew I loved her. Okay? She never knew."

Cole heard the raw pain in Dylan's voice, saw the agony in his old friend's eyes, and felt his anger begin to seep away. For a long moment, they simply stared at each other. Finally, he asked, "Why didn't you tell me how you felt?"

Dylan shrugged. "It wasn't your business."

"She was my sister."

"That still didn't make it your business. Emily had a right to her privacy. Your family watched over her like a hawk. When she got here, she was finally free. I couldn't take that away from her by reporting back to you. And I didn't want to take it away from her. She was happier than I'd ever seen her."

It hurt Cole to know that Emily had been happier here in Santa Cruz than she'd been at home with the family, but in the last week he'd come to a better understanding of why she might have felt that way. He just wished she'd trusted him enough to confide in him. "I might have been able to help," he said aloud. "With my parents. I might have been able to talk them into giving Em more freedom at home if I'd known she was feeling so trapped. She should have told me. You should have told me." He paused. "Why didn't you ever tell her how you felt about her?"

Dylan dug his hands into his pockets and shrugged. "I never thought it was the right time. And I didn't want things to change between us. I didn't want it to get awkward and uncomfortable. Then it was too late."

"Then it was too late," Cole echoed, as he let out a long, weary sigh.

"We can talk about this later," Dylan said.

"Right now I need a ride back to the university. Can you take me?"

"On one condition. You tell me why you think Greg Martin is Garrett Malone."

"Are you sure Diane Thomas is married to Professor Martin?" Natalie asked, still pondering Laura's latest bombshell as they walked across campus toward the Panhellenic Offices where Diane worked. "The last names aren't the same. And I don't remember her mentioning her husband."

"She told me once that she'd kept her maiden name when she got married," Laura replied. "At the time I thought that was so sophisticated." She paused. "I could be wrong though. Maybe it was some other professor. She was very closemouthed about her private life. What are we going to do? We can't just walk into her office and ask her if her husband wrote a best-selling novel about us."

"I think we should do exactly that," Madison said. "It's a little late to beat around the bush."

"Madison is right," Natalie agreed as they entered the building. "We can't afford to waste any more time. We need answers now." She paused for a moment outside Diane's door. "Before we go in, I just want to say I'm glad we're doing this together. It feels right, you know?"

"I know," Laura said softly, a smile on her face.

"Yeah, yeah, yeah," Madison said with a wave of her hand. "We'll do the mushy stuff later." And with that she knocked on the door.

Natalie felt a rush of adrenaline course through her as Diane's voice called them in. They were getting close to the truth. She could smell it.

Diane got up from her desk the moment she saw them. She was ten years older but still an attractive blonde. She was dressed in black slacks, a turquoise blouse, and a black jacket and looked every inch the sophisticated woman Natalie remembered. She'd been in her late twenties when they'd been in college and had been the perfect adviser, young enough to understand them, old enough to give advice.

"Natalie," she said. "This is a surprise. You didn't mention you were coming down here when we spoke yesterday. Madison, Laura," she added.

"I didn't know I was coming at the time. But things have changed."

"What things?" Diane asked quickly. "Do you have new information?"

"I do," Natalie said. She paused as Madison picked up a picture frame on the bookshelf behind Diane's desk and turned it toward them.

"Is this your husband, Diane?" Madison asked.

"Yes," Diane said warily.

"That's Professor Martin," Laura said.

"Is there a problem?" Diane's gaze darted about the room as if she were looking for a way out.

"Is that why you called me, Diane?" Natalie asked. "Were you trying to find out what I knew? So you could report back to your husband?"

Diane couldn't hide the fear that leaped into her eyes. "What are you talking about?"

"We know, Diane. We traced Malone to Jerry Williams to your husband, Professor Greg Martin. It's only a matter of time before we find the actual connection between Mr. Williams and your husband. If you want to wait for the police to question you, that's fine with me. I'm sure they'll be along shortly. Or you can talk to me."

"All right, fine." Diane walked over and shut the door. "Greg did write that book, but I had no idea until a few months ago that he'd done it."

"Oh, please," Madison said in disbelief. "How could you not know?"

"I knew he was working on a novel. He's been working on novels for years. He's an English professor, for God's sake. He loves books. I didn't think anything about it. He certainly never told me what he was doing."

"Where did he get the information about us?" Natalie asked. "Did he have Emily's journal?"

"What?" Diane asked in confusion. "No, I don't think he had a journal. He told me he made up the story based on things he heard from other students after Emily died." She offered Natalie an apologetic smile. "I realize you're not painted particularly well."

"That's an understatement. Your husband called me a murderer. He said I pushed Emily off the roof and killed her."

"He told me that no one was supposed to know it was you or that the story was based on anything real."

"I don't believe that for a second. I think he wanted everyone to know," Natalie said. "That's why he wrote the book, to tell Emily's story. Only he got it wrong."

"Did he?" Diane asked, her voice turning hard. "Is this about protecting Emily or protecting yourself? It was no secret that you were drunk that night, Natalie, and that you didn't remember anything. It was also known that you and Emily had a fight. If you'd stuck around, you would have heard all those rumors and more. Ask Laura, she'll tell you."

Natalie didn't bother to look at Laura, keeping her attention fixed on Diane, who was obviously trying to get herself off the hook. "I want to talk to your husband. Where is he?"

"I don't know."

"I think you do. He's in a lot of trouble, you know. I can sue him for libel."

"You won't win."

"I don't have to win to make your life miserable," Natalie said pointedly. "Don't make the mistake of thinking I'm scared, Diane, because I'm not. I'm furious. And if you think I'm going to sit by and let your husband's book ruin my career and the lives of my friends and most especially Emily's memory, think again."

Diane put up a hand in surrender. "Look, I honestly don't know where he is right now. And you have to understand that I had nothing to do with this. If I had known Greg was writing about Emily, I would have put a stop to it, but I didn't know until the book was published. You have to believe me."

Natalie didn't know whether she believed Diane or not, but it was a moot point. "The question is not what you knew when but what are you going to do about it now?"

Before Diane could answer, someone knocked on her door. Diane moved quickly to answer it. A woman waited in the hall, an expectant look on her face. "Ready for the game?" she asked. "I'm sorry. I didn't realize you had people in your office."

"I'm ready," Diane said quickly. "Would you give me one second?" Shutting the door once more, she turned back to Natalie. "I'll try to find Greg and have him get in touch with you. Are you staying overnight in Santa Cruz, or are you going home?"

"That depends on your husband," Natalie said. She leaned over and wrote her cell phone number on a piece of paper on Diane's desk.

Diane picked up the paper and put it in her purse, grabbing her coat off the back of her chair. "Are you going by the sorority house?"

"We're headed there now."

"You may not be warmly received, Natalie. A lot of the girls have read the book."

"I'm not scared of them, either."

Diane opened the door and motioned them into the hall. She locked her office and then walked off with the friend who was waiting for her.

Natalie blew out a breath, then glanced at Madison and Laura, realizing the two hadn't said a word in a long time. They were staring at her with varying degrees of astonishment. "What?" she asked. "Did I say something wrong?"

"You were amazing," Laura said. "You were so tough with Diane."

"You grew up good," Madison continued with an approving smile. "You kicked her butt."

"Thanks, but the butt I really need to kick belongs to her husband."

"Let's go," Madison said, taking off at a brisk pace.

"What's the hurry?" Natalie asked as she and Laura jogged to keep up with Madison's long strides.

"I think we should follow Diane. Actually, I'll follow her. My guess is that she'll run straight to her husband. You two go back to the sorority house. Maybe being there will jog your memory, Natalie."

"We'll go with you," Natalie said, realizing Madison was right. Diane would probably head straight for her husband.

"It will be easier for me to do it on my own," Madison replied. "I'll be able to fade into the crowd, and I walk faster than both of you. If she sees the three of us, she may not go to him. I'll catch up with you later," she added, as they walked outside. She broke into a jog as Diane and her friend turned the corner, disappearing from view.

"I guess that's that," Natalie said to Laura. "Shall we go to the house?"

"We can take that path through the trees," Laura said, as they changed course. "It's a shortcut."

"I remember. It feels strange to be back here. So much time has passed and yet it feels like yesterday. It's probably worse for you, Laura. You spent four years here."

"It's easier for me. I have good memories as well as bad ones." Laura sighed as they walked through a thick grove of trees. "The last time I came down this path was after graduation. Drew and I were walking back to the house, still wearing our gowns and holding our diplomas. And he . . ." She stopped and pointed to a nearby tree. "He kissed me right there. He said he loved me, and he couldn't wait to get started on the rest of our life together." A tear spilled from the corner of her eye, and she wiped it away. "Those really were the good old days."

"I'm sorry." Natalie wasn't sure how to respond. She was hardly the expert on relationships or marriage. "Maybe you can get the good old days back."

"I don't think that's possible. I can't even find Drew. I've left him a dozen messages, and he hasn't returned one of them. The last time I called I told him I was coming down here to Santa Cruz to figure out who wrote the book. I thought that would get his attention, since he wanted me to stay out of it. Oh, who am I kidding? He probably doesn't give a damn what I'm doing."

"I'm sure that's not true."

"At least I know he's not Malone. I have to admit I almost started thinking he was."

Natalie saw the guilty look in Laura's eyes and knew she'd played a part in putting it there. "I'm sorry if I implied that when I asked you to look for the journal. It's just that Drew was in L.A. and he knew so much about us . . ."

"I know. I also started thinking about what Madison said, that Drew had gone to Emily's room that night, and I wondered if he'd gone out on that roof with her." Laura clapped a hand over her mouth. "I can't believe I just said that out loud."

"I can't, either." Natalie wondered if Laura's instincts were correct.

"It's just that things aren't adding up right—the bank statements, the business trips," Laura said, drawing from some inner well of courage Natalie didn't even know she had. "Yesterday I went by Drew's office, and dad told me that Drew isn't in L.A. on business; he's taking personal leave. Why is he taking personal leave? What's he doing? Is he having an affair? Or does it have something to do with the book, with Malone? He had Malone's travel itinerary in his pocket. But that doesn't explain the money, does it?" Laura sent Natalie an imploring look. "What am I missing? You were always the smart one. You could always add things up. Add them up for me."

Natalie shook her head, her brain whirling with the information Laura had just given her. If Drew had been in Emily's room that night, what had he seen? What had he heard? Had he gone out on the roof with Emily? Had they had some fight? Was he behind the book? Would that explain the money? Before she could ask, Laura started talking again.

"I need to speak to Drew," Laura continued. "I need to confront him, ask him outright what he's doing and who he's doing it with. I've been afraid to ask those questions, because I'm not sure I want to know the answers."

"Knowing is always better than not knowing," Natalie said, remembering how frustrated she'd felt with Cole all those years ago when he hadn't been up-front with her. "Then you can deal with what is instead of what might be."

"You're right. It's just that I've been trying to hang on to Drew since the day I met him, and I don't know how to let go. I married him because he was the cutest, sexiest, smartest guy I'd ever gone out with and because my parents thought he was perfect. I had kids right away so he'd find it hard to leave. I even encouraged him to buy the big house, because deep down I figured that the mortgage would be one more tie that he wouldn't be able to cut. Despite the many ropes I've thrown around the man, he seems to be slipping away from me."

Natalie stared at Laura in amazement. "Wow, that's quite a bit of psychoanalysis."

"I watch a lot of daytime talk shows," Laura admitted with a guilty smile.

"Maybe you should turn off the television."

"You think that will help?"

"It can't hurt. If you really want to change the pattern of your life and your relationship, it seems to me you have to make some changes. Maybe you have to be willing to risk losing Drew in order to keep him. And if you want to keep him, you have to fight for him with everything you've got."

Laura nodded. "You really are smart, Natalie."

Natalie uttered a little laugh. "It's easy to tell other people what to do. I don't have to live with the consequences. It's much harder to make decisions about my own life."

"Speaking of which . . ."

Natalie let out a small groan. "Don't go there."

Laura ignored her. "What are you going to do about Cole?"

"I have no idea."

"You must have some idea of what you want."

"What I want and what's going to happen are two different things. I understand Cole better now, Laura. I know why he ran from me before. Maybe those reasons aren't there anymore, but we have new, insurmountable problems between us."

"Like what?"

"Like his parents. Richard and Janet hate me. They can't look at me without thinking about the loss of their daughter. His father already told Cole that he would have to choose between me and his family. He can't make that choice. I wouldn't want him to. They're a family, and I know better than anyone how important and precious a family is." She sighed. "As soon as this is done, I'm going to say good-bye, and that's going to be it—forever. I'll leave San Francisco. I'll start over somewhere else. That's the way it has to be. We can both get on with our lives."

"I don't want you to do that," Laura said in dismay. "We've just found each other again—you, me, and Madison. I don't want to lose you, Natalie."

"You won't. We'll stay in touch this time. But I don't want to talk about this right now. We have enough things to worry about in the present. Let's leave the future to another day."

"I'm still waiting for you to tell me how you figured out Malone was Martin," Cole said, as he pulled up next to Dylan's motorcycle, parked in a lot near the professor's office building.

"I was talking to Madison the other day, and she mentioned that Emily was interested in someone before she died. I started remembering things Emily had said to me, and I knew Madison was right. There was another man in Em's life. When I went back to my apartment, I looked through the closet, where I'd stored some of Emily's things—"

"When you helped me clean out her room in

Santa Cruz, you kept some of her stuff, didn't you?" Cole interrupted.

"Only things we worked on together. Emily was helping me plan my club back then. We'd drawn up ideas for games, magic acts, shows, virtual-reality stories. I knew she kept them in a drawer in her desk, so I dumped that drawer in a box and kept it for myself. I really didn't think it would matter to anyone but me. When I went through the box the other night, I found a film strip from the board-walk, one of those places you go to take pictures of yourself and a friend. When I saw the guy in the pictures, I recognized him as the professor Emily met with for supposed tutoring. All the puzzle pieces fell into place. Emily told Madison the guy she wanted was unattainable, and the professor was married. I figured he was the guy Emily was— was in love with."

Judging by the bitterness in Dylan's voice, Cole had a feeling that sentence had cost him dearly. He wasn't ready to forgive Dylan for his lies and secrets, but one thing was clear—Dylan had loved Emily. "So you came down here to confront the professor. Why didn't you come to me and tell me your suspicions?"

"I didn't know what the professor knew about Emily and me. I wanted to find that out first."

"Because you didn't want me to know."

"Yeah, I was trying to avoid a black eye," Dylan said.

Cole didn't feel a speck of remorse about the fact that Dylan's right eye was turning purple and swelling shut. He'd deserved the punch for keeping so many secrets. "I have another question for you.

What about your trip to L.A.? You said you just figured out Malone was Martin, so why were you in L.A. at the same time?"

"I went to L.A. to see a magician friend of mine. It didn't have anything to do with Malone or the book." Dylan paused. "We can do this later. I have something to show you. Follow me."

"You were just caught breaking into the professor's office. Now you want to do it again?"

"We're not going in." Dylan led him around to the back of the building. He walked over to some thick bushes. "When I heard someone coming, I tossed it out the window."

"Tossed what out the window?"

Dylan dug through the leaves of a bush and pulled out a purple notebook. "This. It's Emily's journal. I found it in the professor's office."

Cole felt chilled to the bone as Dylan handed the book to him. Emily's handwriting adorned the front cover along with doodles and girlish stickers she'd placed there more than ten years ago. He shook his head, feeling a rush of emotion that ranged from pain to anger to a deep, almost unbearable sadness. "Natalie was right. He had this journal all along. His words in the book were really Emily's words. At least some of them." He paused. "I've got to call Natalie. Tell her we found the journal and that Martin is really Malone. She's probably wondering where we are."

"You came here with Natalie?"

"Yes." Cole's eyes narrowed as he looked at Dylan. "I still don't understand why you don't like Natalie. Why you thought it was conceivable she had pushed Emily off the roof. What's that about?"

"I heard them fighting that night about you. I knew Natalie was drunk, and it was possible she and Emily continued their argument out on the roof. The fact that she claimed not to remember was always a little too convenient for me."

"That's it? That's all you have against her? That's weak."

Dylan tipped his head. "All right. Fine. Natalie didn't like me. Okay? She didn't want Emily to work the magic clubs with me. She didn't like my bike or my cigarettes. She thought I was leading Emily astray. I didn't like her. She obviously felt the same way."

"Good for her." Cole felt strangely pleased and proud of Natalie. She'd done what she'd promised his parents she would do—she'd tried to protect Emily.

"You're obviously back under her spell."

"Actually, I think I'm finally beginning to see Natalie for who she really is, not who I want her to be, or who other people think she should be. Natalie didn't owe any of us anything, Dylan. She didn't have to look out for Emily. She didn't have to protect her. She wasn't her mother. She was her roommate, her friend. I think she did her best to protect the friendship they had. What happened with me was never meant to get in the way of what Emily and Natalie had together. And I blame myself for that. I wasn't up-front with Natalie; that's why she went to Emily for answers. I'm the one who put Em in the middle."

"You're not the one who pushed her off the roof."

"Neither was Natalie. I'd stake my life on that."

Cole took a breath. "Are there any more secrets? Something else you know about Emily or Natalie or the rest of them? Were you the one who gave Emily the pills we found in her drawer?"

"Hell, no. That was McKinney."

"Drew McKinney?" Cole asked in surprise. Although was he really surprised? Drew had always been a little sleazy.

Dylan nodded. "I saw them in Emily's purse one night. I tried to take them away from her, but she told me to mind my own business and stop acting like her brother. Since I was trying to get out of the 'brother' category, I let it go. She told me Drew had gotten them for her. I guess she was feeling a lot of pressure about failing some of her classes. She didn't want to let the family down by flunking out of college or lose her chance at being free, living away from home." Dylan paused for a moment, his gaze turning reflective. "I thought for a while that McKinney might be Malone. He was around all the time. I figured he would have known a lot of what was in the book. And he was always out to make a buck. That's why he got Emily the pills in the first place. She had cash, and he needed the money."

Cole remembered what his investigator had told him—that Drew's roots went back to a trailer park in Modesto. "So now you're telling me Drew was selling the drugs to Emily, and you didn't think that was important enough to share with me? What the hell was wrong with you, Dylan?"

"It wasn't heroin, dude. Emily swore she wouldn't take them unless she talked to me about it first. I don't think she ever took one of those pills." He paused. "But I do realize that I made a few mistakes back then."

"You certainly did. Well, now I know why Drew was so nervous the other day when Natalie and I dropped by his house. He was probably wondering if we knew about the pills. If we were somehow going to pull him back into this scandal."

"It happened a long time ago. Do you really think McKinney is worried about getting in trouble for it now?"

"He might be. Laura said he has his eyes on a political career. I'm sure he wouldn't want any incident with illegal drugs to come out, especially if he was dealing. Maybe Emily wasn't his only customer."

Cole's phone rang. He saw Natalie's name on the screen. "Natalie?"

"Where are you?" she asked. "Did you find Dylan?"

"I'm with him right now."

"Good. Why don't you come to the sorority house? It's totally empty right now. Everyone is at the football game. The housemother, Mrs. Richmond, let me and Laura in. Laura is still chatting her up downstairs, keeping her busy so I can look around. I'm actually standing at the window of my old room, wondering if I have the guts to go out on the . . . Oh, my God!"

"What?" he asked when she didn't continue. "What's wrong?"

"You'll never guess who just pulled up outside. It's Drew."

Drew was in Santa Cruz? His stomach flipped over. "Natalie, you need to know something about Drew—"

"You can tell me when you get here. I want to go out on the roof before everyone comes upstairs. I think it will help me remember what happened that night."

Natalie hung up before he could tell her to stay away from Drew and, most important, to stay off the damn roof. He tried calling her back, but she didn't answer. "We've got to get to the sorority house," he told Dylan.

"What's going on?"

"Natalie is about to step onto the roof. And Drew just pulled up outside." Cole strode toward his car, wanting to get to the sorority house as quickly as possible.

"Whoa, slow down. He's not going to hurt Natalie."

"Are you sure about that? McKinney has a lot to protect: a wife, a family, a business, a reputation."

"If Natalie knew McKinney gave Emily the drugs, she could have revealed that years ago. Drew wouldn't be afraid of her," Dylan argued.

"Or he might think that piece of information is locked up in Natalie's head along with what happened that night. If she remembers one thing, she could remember something else. Or maybe it's not that at all." Cole shook his head as they got into his car, a sudden thought occurring to him. "Damn. Maybe Malone got it wrong. Natalie didn't kill Emily. Drew did."

Chapter 19

Natalie drew in a deep breath as she looked out the window that would take her onto the roof. She could see that at one time the window had been nailed shut, but at some point in the last ten years, the window had been opened, and it opened easily now. Could she do it? Could she climb out onto that roof where Emily had taken her last breath? Not yet.

Her stomach churning, Natalie looked away from the window, focusing instead on the room in which she was standing. Two sorority girls shared this room now. There were colorful bedspreads on the twin beds, stuffed animals and fluffy pillows, posters on the walls, and laptop computers on the desks. She wondered if these girls had any idea that one night a young woman, just like themselves, had gone out on the roof to gaze at the stars and had ended up dead.

Closing her eyes, she told herself to forget about the present and go back in time. She needed to see the room as it had once been, not as it was now. She needed to force herself to remember everything about that night.

There had been a quilt on Emily's bed, made by her great-grandmother. Her stuffed animals had included tigers in various shapes and sizes. Emily had placed a poster of the magician David Copperfield on the wall over her bed. She'd also had a picture of Cole and her parents on the desk and another one on her dresser. Natalie could see the photographs in her mind, the happy Parish family, not a care in the world.

How she'd loved them, not just Cole but all of them. They'd filled a need in her heart for family— for people to care about her. And Cole . . . he had completely swept her off her feet. He'd made her dream again. He'd made her want more from life than just basic survival. He'd shown her how to let loose, how to have fun, how to be herself. She'd loved him—passionately, with every fiber of her being. It was the first and only time she'd given her heart completely. And all she'd known how to do was hang on . . . That's why she'd begged Emily to get Cole to come to the party. But what had happened next?

She tried desperately to remember. The sights and sounds of that night trickled back into her mind.

She could hear the laughter, the music, the sounds of people talking. The downstairs was packed with kids. She could barely make it through the living room and up the stairs. But she had to go upstairs. She needed to find Emily.

Something wet splashed on her hand. She looked down at her soda can, realizing it was almost empty, and it wasn't soda she was drinking, it was vodka. They'd poured the soda out in the upstairs bath-

room. The vodka was supposed to make her feel happier. The other kids all got happy when they drank. Her mom certainly had a better time when she was drunk—so why didn't Natalie feel better? Why was she still so sad? Maybe she needed more to drink.

Upstairs. She'd just go upstairs, find Emily, get a refill, and when Cole came, she'd be the ultimate party girl. He'd forget she'd ever told him she loved him. It would be the way it used to be.

Her sense of desperation grew as she climbed the stairs. It was never going to be the way it used to be.

When she entered the room, she saw Emily sitting on the bed. She wore a short, black cocktail dress. Her legs were bare, her feet encased in high, strappy black sandals. And her toenails were a hot red, the same as her fingernails. They'd painted their nails red the night before at Madison's insistence that they shouldn't go into initiation without a little flash of color. Emily's head lifted as Natalie came into the room. Her long brown hair fell in waves against her face and down to her shoulders. There was guilt in her big brown eyes and sadness, too. In fact, she looked like she'd been crying. Before Natalie could ask her why, her gaze drifted to the pills in Emily's hand.

"What are you doing? Where did you get those?" Natalie asked.

"I need to take something to help me stay up tonight. After the party I have to study. I'm going to fail English. My tutor—I can't see him anymore. He can't help me. I'm in so much trouble, Natalie. I need these pills. Everyone takes them. They're safe."

"They're not good for you. They could hurt you. Who gave them to you? Was it Madison?"

"No, it was Drew. He said everyone takes them. He used to take them himself. They're safe."

"You don't know that," Natalie countered. *"It's different for everyone."* She tried to think of all the reasons why Emily shouldn't take the pills, but her mind was fuzzy, and her mouth wasn't working right.

"I don't care. I've made such a mess of things, Natalie. I'm in love. I did something stupid. I'm so embarrassed."

Natalie didn't know what Emily was talking about. *"What did you do?"*

"I fell in love with a married man. A professor."

"Oh, my God! Who? When?" Natalie stumbled as she moved toward Emily.

Emily's eyes narrowed in disappointment. *"You're drunk, aren't you?"*

"I just had a couple shots of vodka."

"Natalie, what are you doing to yourself? This isn't you."

"I'm fine. I'm just a little buzzed. I'm happy. Is Cole coming? Did you call him?"

"Yes, I called him. He's not coming to the party, Natalie. Or if he does, he might be really late. He doesn't want you to wait for him. I'm sorry."

"You don't want us together, do you?" Natalie accused. *"You're trying to break us up."*

"How can you say that? You're like my sister." Emily's eyes filled with hurt.

Natalie didn't care. She was hurt, too. *"But you won't help me get him back. And I have to get him back. I don't even know why I lost him. I love him, Emily. I need him."*

"*You have to let go, Natalie. Cole is . . . Cole is dating someone else in San Francisco.*"

"*What!*" She felt like she'd been stabbed in the heart, and she put a hand to her chest to see if she was bleeding.

"*Her name is Cynthia, and her parents are friends of my parents. That's why he didn't come down last weekend.*" Emily stretched out a hand to Natalie, but Natalie jumped back from her.

"*You're lying.*"

"*I'm not lying. I don't want you to get hurt, but I'm afraid Cole will hurt you. He doesn't stick to one person. He's not ready for commitment. You have to forget him.*"

"*I can't do that. I told him I loved him. And you want me to forget him? I can't forget him. I won't believe he's seeing someone else.*" She turned to the door. She had to get away from Emily. She needed another drink. Her glass was empty.

She ran out of the room, heading down the hall for Madison's room. Madison was talking to Drew. Natalie didn't want to see them. She slipped into Jody's room instead. The senior was known to have a stash of Johnnie Walker in her closet. And Natalie was in luck. The bottle was half full. She poured herself one shot, then another until she couldn't feel anything anymore.

Within a few minutes she was convinced that Emily had made the whole thing up. Cole wasn't cheating on her. He wouldn't do that. She got up and went down the hall, determined to talk to Emily again. As she neared the door, she heard a high-pitched scream. She wasn't sure where it had come *from, but it sounded awful, so awful she felt like she was going to be sick. She stumbled toward the bathroom, managing to get there just before she threw up.*

Natalie's eyes flew open as the truth hit her in the face. She'd heard Emily scream, but she didn't know what had happened. She'd run into the bathroom, where Madison had found her a short while later. Maybe if she'd run into this room instead of the bathroom, she would have known if Emily had been alone or with someone. It was frustrating to come this close and still not have the answers she wanted.

With a sigh, she knew there was only one thing left to do. She had to go out on the roof. She had to finish this. She had to stand where Emily had stood. At the very least, she could say good-bye.

She climbed out onto the flat roof, noting the guardrail that had been installed around the perimeter of the flat deck. She walked toward the edge, but stopping far enough away that she couldn't see over it—to the ground below. She wasn't ready to look there yet. Drawing in a deep breath, she wondered about Emily's reason for coming out here that night. She'd been upset obviously. And it was quiet out here. Even now there was a sense of isolation, a feeling that what went on here would never be known by anyone else.

Emily must have come out on the roof to be alone, to think, or maybe even to cry . . . about the man she'd fallen in love with. Who had it been? She thought for a moment and realized the answer was right in front of her.

"You know, don't you?"

The voice swung her head around, and she was shocked to find she wasn't the only one on the roof.

"You know I was out here with Emily that night. I knew that as soon as you came back here you'd remember."

"You?" Natalie questioned in shock. "You were with Emily?" Everything suddenly clicked into place.

Cole drove like a maniac to the sorority house. All he could think about was Drew . . . a man who would balk at nothing to get what he wanted. "If he hurts Natalie, I swear to God I'll kill him."

"I'll help you," Dylan said grimly. "If he had something to do with Emily's death, he will pay."

Cole hit the steering wheel with his fist as they were stopped by a red light. "Dammit all. I can't lose Natalie, too. There are things I need to tell her."

"Like the fact that you still love her."

"Something like that." He floored the gas pedal as the light turned green. A moment later he pulled up in front of the sorority house and jumped out of the car. The front door was open. Laura stood in the foyer talking to Drew. Cole came to an abrupt halt when he saw them. "Where's Natalie?"

"She's upstairs, I think," Laura replied. "Why? What's wrong?"

"You did it, didn't you?" Cole demanded, drilling Drew with a furious glare.

Drew took a step back, his eyes wary. "What are you talking about?"

"You pushed Emily off the roof. You were afraid she'd tell someone you sold her drugs."

"You sold Emily drugs?" Laura asked in amazement.

For a brief second Drew looked like a cornered dog. Then he threw back his shoulders. "You have no proof of that, Parish."

"I don't need proof to beat the crap out of you. Everyone knows you were here that night. You talked to Emily. Even your wife knows that much."

"I do know that," Laura said. "Why did you go into Emily's room, Drew?"

"I was looking for something."

"Maybe this?" Cole asked, holding up Emily's journal. "Did you think Emily wrote about your drug deals in her journal?"

"Where did you get that?" Drew made a grab for the book, but Cole held it out of reach.

"It doesn't matter where I got it," Cole said. "What did you do to Emily?"

"Nothing."

"Drew, you have to tell us," Laura pleaded. "Whatever happened, we have to know. Otherwise, this will never end."

"I didn't hurt Emily," Drew said sharply.

"Then why did you go to her room that night?"

"You want to know why? Fine. I went to Emily's room to look for the journal. I heard Madison joking with Emily one day that she could probably blackmail people with her journal, and I got to thinking that maybe she'd written something in there about me. I didn't get a chance to look for it, because Emily was in the room, talking on the phone to someone, so I left. I'm sure someone saw Emily after me. Maybe Madison."

"Madison?" Dylan asked. "Madison was with Emily that night?"

"I don't know for sure," Drew said, "but—"

"Shit!" Dylan swore.

Cole sent Dylan a curious look. "What's wrong?"

"Madison said she loved me when we were in college, that she was angry that I never paid any attention to her; I was always too busy with Emily."

Cole connected the dots and suddenly there was a new picture, one he hadn't considered. "Where's Madison now?"

"She left us a while ago to follow Diane, Professor Martin's wife," Laura explained, looking confused and troubled. "What's going on? You don't think Madison had anything to do with Emily's fall, do you?"

Cole took the stairs two at a time. He had to get to Natalie before Madison did.

"You pushed Emily off the roof," Natalie said, staring at the woman in front of her. Everything suddenly made so much sense.

"It was an accident. She slipped."

"That's what you wanted us to think."

"That's what everyone did think. You certainly couldn't remember anything. But your memory has come back, hasn't it? I knew it would. I knew you'd remember seeing me run out of Emily's room right after she screamed. I had an explanation all ready. I kept waiting for the questions to come. But they never did."

Natalie stared at the woman she'd thought she'd

known. Had she seen her run out of Emily's room? She blinked, remembering that dizzy, nauseous feeling as she turned toward the bathroom, her stomach churning. A flash of red had caught her eye, then disappeared. "I didn't remember until now," she said. "You shouldn't have told me."

Uncertainty flashed in the woman's eyes as she realized her mistake. "You won't tell anyone. I won't let you."

"How will you stop me? I'm not going to slip off this roof the way Emily did."

"No, she's not," Cole interrupted, as he came through the window.

Natalie was shocked by his appearance but relieved to see him, and was even happier when Dylan, Drew, and finally Laura followed him.

The woman between them suddenly realized she was cornered. "It was an accident," she said, putting up a hand. "A stupid accident. No one can prove otherwise."

"I can—Diane," Madison said, as she climbed out onto the roof. "And so can your husband. Come on out here, Professor Martin."

Natalie's jaw dropped as the man they'd spent the past week searching for came through the window. Professor Martin looked nothing like Garrett Malone. The beard was gone, as were the thick glasses and the long hair. He was pale with a crew cut and ordinary brown eyes.

"Tell them what you told me," Madison ordered, nudging the professor's arm.

Greg Martin was staring at his wife in disbelief. "Did they just say that you pushed Emily off the roof? How is that possible?"

"It was an accident. I came here that night to tell that little home wrecker to stay away from you," Diane replied. "I would have been justified in pushing her, but the truth is she slipped. It was an accident, and no one would have ever known if you hadn't written that damn book, Greg."

"I didn't know it was you. I thought it was Natalie. When I came to the house that night I saw two women on the roof. And I saw . . ." His voice broke, and he struggled for control. "I saw Emily fall. I heard her scream. I'll never forget the terror of that sound." He looked at Natalie. "I thought you did it."

"How could you think that?" Natalie asked.

"Because Emily had called me that night in tears. She said you'd had a terrible fight. That's why I came over. I knew she was upset, but I was too late." He shook his head with regret. "Later I found her journal. She'd left it in my office after one of our tutoring sessions. I read about her conflict with you over Cole. I put the two together."

"And came up with five," Natalie said harshly. "If you had suspicions about me, why didn't you just go to Cole or the Parishes? Why did you write a book?"

"I couldn't tell anyone about my involvement with Emily. I would have lost my job and Diane would have been humiliated. I knew I had already hurt her with the affair." He glanced at Diane, who quickly averted her gaze. "That's why I wrote the book under a pen name and took steps to make sure no one would know who I was. That's why I disguised myself for book tour appearances. I had no idea the novel would be such a hit. But I was

glad when people started to recognize the story. I
didn't even care that your true names came out. I
wanted you to pay for Emily's death, Natalie, because I loved her, and I thought you'd gotten away
with murder. Emily was beautiful and innocent, and
she didn't deserve to die," he said passionately.
"God, Diane, why did you do it? She was just a
kid, a sweet kid. She wasn't the guilty party, it was
me. Why did you go after her? I told you we'd
ended it. That it was over. You didn't have to come
here that night."

"Yes, I did. I had to tell that little bitch what I
thought of her," Diane said hotly. "She wasn't
sweet and innocent. She knew what she was doing,
and she wasn't sorry."

"She was sorry," Natalie interrupted. "She told
me so that night."

"It doesn't matter. None of you can prove anything," Diane said.

"We'll let the police decide that," Cole said
sharply. He moved to stand directly in front of
Diane. "I'll tell you this. If they don't make you
pay, I will."

"You can't threaten me." She looked around
wildly. "If something happens to me, everyone will
know you did it. I have witnesses. They all heard
you."

"If something happens to you, it might be me
who does it," Madison said.

"Or me," Dylan added.

"Or me," Natalie said.

"Greg—you have to help me." Diane turned to
her husband, her hand raised in a silent plea. "I

did it for you, for us. I just wanted her to leave us alone. I never meant for her to fall."

"But you didn't really care that Emily fell or that she died," he said flatly.

"And you didn't really care that you hurt me," she retorted. "If you hadn't written that damn book, this wouldn't be happening right now."

Which was truly the irony of it all, Natalie realized. Greg had wanted to expose the true killer, and he had—his wife.

"Let's go." Dylan grabbed Diane's arm. "It's time for you to have a little chat with the Santa Cruz Police."

With his grip on her arm, Diane had no choice but to go with him. Madison, Laura, and Drew followed, leaving Cole and Natalie alone with the professor.

"I'm sorry," Greg said to her. "Truly sorry. I honestly thought I was right about you."

"But you weren't right, and you will make a public statement as to just how wrong you were—about Emily's death and also about the pills that I did not supply to her," Natalie told him. "After that, I'll decide if I want to pursue legal action."

He nodded. "It doesn't matter. It will all come out now, anyway. I'm glad. Emily was too good a person to have been anyone's nasty little secret, including mine." He looked at Cole. "She was a wonderful girl. And she was crazy about her family. That's why we got together in the first place. She begged me to tutor her. She didn't want to let anyone down by failing my class."

"You seduced her," Cole said furiously. "You

made an innocent girl feel like she had no choice but to—"

"No, he didn't," Natalie interrupted. She saw anger flare in Cole's eyes, but there had been too many misunderstandings already. "Emily told me she loved him. She said it was all her idea. I remember that conversation now. I remember everything."

"Thank you for saying that," the professor said. He looked from one to the other. "I'd better go talk to the police."

Natalie watched him climb through the window, leaving her alone with Cole. They stared at each other for a long minute. Now that everyone was gone, she became acutely aware of where they were and what had happened here. Cole must have felt the same way, because he walked past her to gaze over the edge of the roof to the ground below. She wanted to tell him not to look, but she knew she couldn't. After a moment, he turned back around, his face pale, his jaw tight. She sensed he was battling for control, and she wanted to help. So she went to him.

She put her arms around his waist and held him close, burying her face in the curve of his shoulder. She could feel him shaking, but not a sound came through his tight lips. He wasn't a man to give in to emotion, but he needed to find a release. Natalie lifted her head and kissed him. The groan, which sounded more like a sob, burst through his mouth as he kissed her back with a passion and desperation that swept over her like a tidal wave. She wanted to give Cole comfort, but somewhere in the middle of the kiss, she found comfort, too. She was able to express all the words she couldn't speak and all the feelings she wasn't supposed to feel. It was both painful and liberating.

Tears began to spill out of her eyes and down her cheeks. Cole pulled away, his breath coming in deep, ragged gasps. He wiped away her tears with a gentle finger. "Don't cry, Natalie."

"I'm trying not to," she said with a sniff. She took a step back and drew in a long, deep breath of fresh air. "Everything just got to me."

"I know."

And he did know. She could see it in his eyes. "We should go down to the police department, finish this once and for all."

He nodded. "I have to call my parents, too. And then you and I—we need to talk."

"I remembered something else from that night, Cole. Emily told me that you were dating someone in San Francisco. Her name was Cynthia."

"I saw her a few times," Cole admitted. "She was a family friend, and I wanted to distract myself—from you."

"Did it work?"

His eyes were clear and honest when they met hers. "No. And it never went further than a few dinners. Does that really matter to you now?"

"No, but I can't help wondering if one of the reasons I couldn't remember all this time was because I didn't want to remember the pain of that knowledge. I know it hurt me at the time, because I didn't understand what was going on with you then. I didn't comprehend how I could tell you that I loved you and you would go out with someone else. Now I do. You saw my words of love like a steel trap closing around you, and you tried to escape."

"That's probably true."

"No probably about it. Anyway, it's all in the past."

"Is it?" Cole challenged. "What about now? How do you feel now?"

"Do you actually think I'm going to tell you how I feel—after what happened the last time? I'm not that stupid. Why don't you tell me how you feel?" she challenged.

He hesitated for one telling second too long. He obviously couldn't say the words she wanted to hear. "Natalie—"

"No, don't, Cole." She put up a hand to stop him, knowing that she couldn't take one more rejection from this man. "I'd rather not know." She took a deep breath. "There are no second chances, Cole. Not for Emily. Not for any of us. You need to move on with your life, and I need to do the same. This is over. It's all finally over. And we're done."

"It's over, Drew." Laura leaned against the door to Drew's car and folded her arms in front of her chest. She'd learned more about her husband in the last hour than she'd learned in the last ten years. "I can't believe you sold drugs to Emily. How could you have done such a thing?"

"They weren't dangerous. Everyone was taking them. And I needed the cash. Not all of us had parents with money, Laura."

"It was still wrong. Don't you get that, Drew?"

"It was a long time ago. We were kids."

"And that excuses it?"

"That incident has nothing to do with our lives now." Drew shrugged out of his sports coat, opening the back door of the car to toss it inside. "Can we do this at home? This isn't the best place to have a discussion."

"There's never a good time or a good place for you to talk. This suits me fine."

"We're in the parking lot of your old sorority house."

"Exactly. This is where it began, Drew. Where we really fell in love. Or was it just me who did the falling?" She searched his blue eyes for the truth, but as always Drew was very good at hiding his thoughts and feelings from her.

"I married you, didn't I?" he said wearily.

It wasn't exactly a declaration of love. "Why did you marry me? Was it because of my parents? My father's law school connections? My money?"

His gaze hardened. "Are you sure you want me to answer those questions?"

A shiver of fear ran down her spine. Was she being brave or stupid? Was she about to ruin her life and the lives of her children? She turned her head and gazed at the sorority house, drawing strength from the lessons she'd learned there and the people she'd known, especially Emily. Emily wouldn't have wanted her to waste her life, drifting, accepting instead of challenging and demanding. "Yes," she said. "I do want answers." *Please, God, let them be the right answers.*

"All of the above," Drew replied.

His words took the wind out of her sails. Well, now she knew, didn't she?

"And I—I loved you," Drew added. The words didn't flow smoothly from his mouth, but then, Drew had never felt comfortable talking about feelings.

"Do you still love me?"

"I'm here, aren't I?"

"Why are you here? And where have you been? I left a dozen messages that you didn't return. I know you were in L.A. on personal business. Dad told me." Laura drew in a deep breath and asked the question that had been rambling around in her mind for a long time. "Are you having an affair?"

"No," he said forcefully.

"Then why are you being so secretive? Where have you been the last week? And why couldn't you tell me?"

"Laura, I really don't want to do this here. Let's get in the car and drive home."

"No. It's here and now. Because later there will be another excuse why we can't continue this discussion. Answer the question, Drew."

"Or what?" he challenged her. "Because that sounds like an ultimatum."

She licked her lips, feeling nervous again. Did she really want to give him an ultimatum? What if he left? What if her marriage ended right here? What would she do then?

She'd survive. She'd go on with her life. She'd be all right.

The answers came from deep within her soul.

Squaring her shoulders, she straightened up and said, "Don't turn this around on me, Drew. I want to know what you were doing in L.A."

He studied her as if she were on the witness stand. "All right. I went to L.A. to talk to Garrett Malone. When I got there, I realized he was Professor Martin. I knew he and Emily had had an affair. I caught them one day. She made me promise not to tell," he said, putting up a hand when Laura started to interrupt. "And I agreed. We all had secrets. She deserved to have one, too."

"If Emily had a secret, you had something on her," Laura said, suddenly seeing the clear picture. "She couldn't tell anyone you gave her the drugs or you would reveal that she was having an affair. Is that what you went to tell her the night of the party?"

"I'd already told her that. I went there to see if she'd written anything in her journal about me."

"I wonder why she didn't write it down."

"She probably didn't want to incriminate herself."

Laura shook her head, not liking any of Drew's answers. But at least he was being honest. "All right. So you went to L.A. to talk to the professor. What happened?"

"I caught up with him before his book signing. I told him I knew who he was."

"How did you know? I saw him, and I didn't recognize him."

"His disguise was good," Drew admitted. "But I figured he was the one behind the book, so I just bluffed, and he admitted everything. I told him to get off the publicity circuit and make sure this book died a sudden death, or I'd expose everything."

"That's why he suddenly canceled all his engagements." She paused, still curious. "Why did you stay in L.A. after that? Because that sounds like one conversation."

"The rest has nothing to do with Emily or the book."

"I want to hear it anyway."

"Fine. I've been thinking about leaving your father's firm. I want more autonomy, more freedom, and more money. Your dad wants me to work my way up slowly. I've never been a patient man, Laura, you know that. I've been offered a job in L.A., and I was interviewing with several of the partners yesterday and today."

Laura felt her jaw drop. "Are you serious?"

"I didn't tell you, because I haven't decided what I want to do yet."

"You haven't decided? This isn't *your* decision. It's *our* decision. I'm supposed to be your wife, your partner."

"Calm down," Drew said, looking around.

"No, I'm done with calm. This is my life you're talking about. If you're not happy working for my father, then you should leave. But you need to talk to me before you make decisions about uprooting our family and moving to L.A. Or weren't you planning to take us with you?"

Drew ran a hand through his hair. "I don't know anymore, Laura. Can you honestly say you're happy?"

She stared at him in dismay. "I think I could be happy—if we made some changes."

"Like what?" he demanded.

Normally, his abrupt manner would have intimidated her, but she seemed to have grown a spine sometime in the last week. "Like you come home for dinner at least three times a week. We spend quality time alone together." She waved her hand in the air. "I want you to be part of the family. I want you to listen to me when I talk to you instead of brushing me off."

"Is that it?"

"No. I want to know where our money is going. I saw deposits and withdrawals in our accounts that I don't understand. Do you have some sort of side business?"

"I did a little moonlighting for cash. Some private consulting," Drew admitted. "I sent the money to my father to cover his gambling debts. Someone was threatening to break his legs. I probably should have let that happen, but he is my father."

The shame in his eyes touched her. Deep down, she'd known that Drew's ambition and drive for money and security, the perfect home, the perfect family were the result of his early unsettled upbringing, but that had never been clearer than it was at this moment. "You should have told me, Drew. I don't want there to be secrets between us. Whatever your parents need, I'm behind you." She took a breath, realizing she had to show him that she also understood that this couldn't be a one-sided endeavor. "I know it's not all your fault, Drew. I've been hanging on to you like a drowning swimmer clinging to a buoy. I've been pulling you down with me. I want to be more of my own person. I don't know exactly what that means, but I know it will include getting back to my music, playing the flute, having girlfriends who understand and inspire me. And I'm going to stop worrying about whether or not you or my parents approve of every move I make."

"Where is all this coming from?" he asked, clearly surprised by her outspokenness. "What happened to you, Laura?"

"Emily happened. The book happened. I ran into Natalie and Madison, and I was reminded of who I once wanted to be. I remembered how great you and I used to be, how we used to balance each other out. But somewhere along the way, we fell into these roles that exist on some parallel plane. I don't want you to have your life and me to have my life; I want our lives to be intertwined. Do you want that, too? Because if you don't, if you really don't, then you need to tell me."

Drew didn't answer for what was the longest moment of her life. "When I met you, I knew you'd make the perfect wife. You'd be the kind of woman who would want to stay home with the kids, want to make a home, a family. And I wanted that, something solid and permanent, not like the home I grew up in. My father was never around. When he was around he was drinking and gambling. He was a first-class loser. My mother worked a couple of jobs to keep a roof over our heads, so she was always too tired to care much about me. That's not what I want for my children." He took a breath, then continued. "I'd like to make things work with us, Laura, but you've got to open your eyes. I'm not your father, who's the perfect businessman, husband, and father. In fact, I've never been the guy you think I am. I've just pretended to be, so I wouldn't lose you. But I'm tired of pretending. I am who I am. I'm ambitious. Sometimes I cut corners. I don't always know which lines I shouldn't cross. I'm not sure how to be a good husband and father. I didn't have the best example myself. So maybe you should be asking yourself if you want to stay with me, instead of asking me if I want to stay with you."

She looked at him in surprise, unable to believe what she'd just heard. "I think that's the most honest thing you've ever said to me."

"Yeah, well, I guess it's that kind of day."

"Drew, I don't want you to be my father. I don't even like my father very much. He made my mother's life miserable. He was always working. He had affairs. His idea of family is nothing like my idea. I've been terrified the last few years that you were turning into him, and I was turning into my mother. That's the last thing I want, Drew. I want us to be us. I want you and me and the girls to make our own way. And I want you to share with me the way you just did—with honesty and candor." She paused. "I've been holding on to you for the last ten years, Drew. If you want me to stay—if you want me in your life—you're going to have to hold on to me. It's your turn."

Drew gazed into her eyes for a long moment, then reached out and took her hand in his. He gave it a squeeze and said, "Let's go home."

Her eyes blurred with tears. Home had never sounded so good.

Chapter 20

The drive home seemed to take forever. Natalie had chosen to go back to San Francisco with Madison, leaving Cole and Dylan to deal with the details of Greg, Diane, and the Santa Cruz Police Department. It was finally over. Her name would be cleared, her reputation repaired. She could go back to work, continue with her life. She should be feeling great.

"That's the third time you've sighed in the last five minutes," Madison said, darting a quick look at her. "Want to talk about it?"

"Not particularly."

"Does it have something to do with why you're driving home with me instead of with Cole?"

Natalie sighed again. "I really don't want to get into it."

"Are you having regrets about hooking up with Cole?"

"Yes. No. It doesn't matter." She tucked her hair behind her ear, realizing her answer had done little to satisfy Madison, who was casting her sideways glances every few seconds. "Look, Madison, Cole and I are over. We know everything there is to know. There's nothing left to find out. Cole will go back to his life, and I'll do the same. End of story."

"I don't think this is the end. You're in love with the guy, and I have a sneaking suspicion he's in love with you, too."

Natalie shook her head. "He isn't. I gave him a chance to tell me back at the house. He didn't. Cole knows as well as I do that we have nowhere to go with any kind of relationship."

"Why? The past is in the past. Why can't you have a future?"

"Because there's more between us now than there was before. His parents can't look at me without feeling the loss of Emily. Even if they're finally convinced that I didn't push her off the roof, they'll still blame me for not being there when she fell. I can't say that they're wrong. If I hadn't been drunk that night, if I hadn't been so self-absorbed, maybe I would have been there for Emily."

"Maybe, maybe, maybe. Life isn't about *maybe* or *what if*, or *should have*. We all make choices, some of them bad, some of them good. Emily made choices, too. She's the one who slept with a married man. She's the one who went out on that roof. She's the one who argued with Diane. You had nothing to do with any of that. Perfect Emily was not perfect. It's about time we all realized that and let her go."

"You're right," Natalie said. "I don't want to judge her."

"Then don't."

"But since I went out on that roof today, I can't stop thinking about that night. There must have been a moment when Emily saw the madness in

Diane's eyes, when she backed up, when she felt herself go over . . ." Natalie couldn't bring herself to finish the thought.

"Do you think Diane pushed her?"

"In a blind fit of passion, probably. Or else she just took a swing at Emily and Emily backed up and slipped off. I don't think we'll ever be able to prove it one way or the other. At least Diane's presence on the roof that night will prove that I didn't do it. Unfortunately, Emily's affair will probably come out, too. Unless the Parishes can bury it all. I wouldn't be surprised if they tried to do that. I wouldn't blame them, either. I don't think the world needs to know that Emily was in love with a married man. By the way, there's something I've been meaning to ask you. How did you find the professor and get him to come to the house?"

"That was easy. I followed Diane and her friend to the stadium. I was hanging around outside wondering what to do next when Diane came out again. She ran over to a car that had just pulled up in the parking lot. A man got out and she started yelling at him. I figured he was the professor. After their discussion, she took off, and I moved in."

"Just like that," Natalie said in amazement. "I've been chasing that man for days. And you walked over and said hello. Amazing."

"I got lucky. Not that we needed him in the end. Diane was the real villain in this. And it was her own husband's book that finally cleared the air. If he hadn't written *Fallen Angel*, we would have never known the truth."

"You're right."

"It's funny how we thought no one had spoken to Emily that night," Madison continued. "In actual fact, there was a damn parade going through her room. You were talking to her while Dylan was hovering in the hall; then Drew went in to see her. He said she was on the phone talking to someone— I guess it was the professor. No wonder she went out on the roof. She probably wanted to be alone."

"Instead, she was accosted by the wife of the man she was sleeping with."

"Hey, at least she had sex before she died."

"Madison!"

"Sorry, but you wouldn't have wanted her to die a virgin, would you? Isn't it better to know that she'd loved someone, had that experience?"

Natalie thought about that for a moment. "I guess it is better to know that. She always wanted to find love. And she did. I think Greg Martin truly loved her, even though he was married, and what they were doing was wrong."

"Love isn't always right." Madison paused. "Speaking of love, what's your prediction on Laura and Drew? Do you think they'll stay together?"

"I hope so. They have a lot of history together, not to mention children and a home." Natalie gave Madison a curious look. "What about you?"

"What about me?"

"Somewhere along the way I got the idea that you were interested in Dylan."

Madison uttered a harsh laugh. "Even if I were, so what? He's still in love with Emily. He probably always will be. You saw the closet shrine in his apartment. How could anyone compete with a goddess like Emily?"

"I think if anyone could, you could," Natalie said. "You're stunningly pretty."

"That's true," Madison said with a toss of her wavy blond hair.

"And you're smart, ambitious, competitive. Tell me something—do you really want Dylan, or is he just a challenge? The one who got away?"

"He is a challenge." Madison thought for a moment. "Sometimes I think he's a lunatic, but he's interesting. He's creative, different, bold, daring— not at all boring."

"Sounds like you're hooked."

"Not at all. I'm just intrigued. I'd like Dylan to see me for who I really am. He judged me early on, and he was wrong. I want him to know he was wrong. Then we'll see where we go from there—if we go anywhere. It's not like I need a man in my life. I'm doing fine on my own."

"So am I," Natalie said, but as she leaned back in her seat and gazed out the window, she knew she wasn't doing fine at all.

By Monday Cole was back at work. Garrett Malone, also known as Greg Martin, had held a press conference that morning from Santa Cruz stating that he'd made up the entire story, that he had no basis of proof for any of his allegations regarding Natalie or any other women named in his book. The Parish family had also offered a statement through their attorney that they were satisfied with the results of the police investigation and believed that Emily's death had in fact been an accident.

Cole had had a lengthy, emotional conversation with his parents, and they had agreed to ask the police to close the case. With no concrete evidence that Diane Thomas had pushed Emily off the roof, they didn't see the point of a long trial that would only damage Emily's reputation. However, in usual Parish fashion, his father had put pressure on the university to suggest that both Diane and her husband, Greg Martin, resign. While Cole hated the idea of Diane getting away with murder, he knew that his parents, especially his mother, could not handle the scandalous press that would go after a story about Emily's affair with the professor. He'd been raised to protect his little sister, and this was the last thing he could do to protect her.

Cole leaned back in his office chair, the panel of television screens on the opposite wall showing events happening around the world. Soon he would be one of those reporters. It was time—past time. Late last night he'd finally made the decision to change his life.

He looked up as Josh popped his head in the door. "Hey, how's it going?"

"That depends on whether the rumors are true." Josh sat down in the chair opposite Cole's desk and gave him a searching look. "Are you leaving the paper?"

"News travels fast around here. I'm not leaving the paper. I'm going on assignment to the Middle East."

"Why?"

"It's what I've always wanted. You know that."

"I know it's what you used to want. I thought that might have changed, especially in the last week."

Cole shook his head, unwilling to admit to Josh

that his passion for adventure didn't seem quite as strong as it had once been. "Did you talk to Dylan?"

"He filled me in on everything, except what's going on with you and Natalie."

"Nothing is going on. It's over."

Josh leaned forward, a knowing gleam in his eyes. "That's what you said the last time."

"This time it's true. I'm leaving. It's what I have to do."

"What you have to do? I thought you just said it was what you *wanted* to do."

"You know what I mean."

"I don't think you know what you mean. Do I need to throw a stapler at your head to get your attention? What you want—*who* you want—is right here in San Francisco, not the Middle East."

Cole stood up, not so happy to have Josh in his office anymore. "I need to brief Marty on some things. Why don't you buy me a drink later? I'm not leaving until tomorrow."

"When will you be back?" Josh asked, as he got to his feet.

"When I've had enough."

Josh walked with him to the office door. "Natalie is the one for you, Cole. No one else has ever come close. Don't you think it's about time you told her that?"

"It's too late for us. Natalie doesn't believe in second chances."

"But you do. You're getting a second chance at the career you always wanted. Why can't you have Natalie, too?"

"Because she doesn't want me."

"Are you sure about that?"

"Dr. Bishop? There's someone in the waiting room who'd like to speak to you."

"A patient?" Natalie asked, jotting down some notes on the chart of the last patient she had seen. It felt good to be back to work. The attending physician and significant others at the hospital had all apologized and welcomed her back. In fact, she'd been offered a full-time position at St. Timothy's if she wanted it. She was still considering that one. She wasn't sure how close she wanted to stay to Cole. San Francisco was his town. It always would be.

"She's not ill. She just wants to talk to you," the nurse answered. "She's sitting by the door, wearing an expensive black suit. You can't miss her."

"I'll be right there." Natalie finished her notes, then walked out to the waiting room. She didn't know who she'd been expecting, but it certainly wasn't Janet Parish. Swallowing hard, she stared at the older woman, seeing the lines around her eyes and the gray streaks in her hair. She'd aged in the last week. Yet there was something softer in her eyes that hadn't been there the last time they'd seen each other—which, of course, had been one of the more embarrassing moments of Natalie's life.

Janet stood up, clasping the strap of her purse tightly in her hands. "Natalie, I hope I'm not disturbing you, but I didn't know how else to find you without asking Cole or Richard, and I wanted to do this myself."

Natalie glanced around the room and waved Janet toward a quiet corner. "Do what?" she asked, as they sat down together.

"Thank you," Janet said.

"There's nothing to thank me for."

"Yes, there is. I went through Emily's journal last night. Did you read it?"

"No. It wasn't my place."

"It wasn't mine, either, but my curiosity got the better of me. I thought I knew my daughter, but there was so much I didn't know about her." Janet took a moment to gather her thoughts. "I didn't realize that I was holding her back. I didn't know that Emily resented our phone calls, that she felt we didn't trust her to take care of herself. I didn't understand until I read her journal that Emily went to school to get away from me." She bit down on her bottom lip, her eyes filling with tears. "I loved her so much, Natalie. She was my whole world. I wanted to know everything that she did, everything that she thought. I was so proud of her. I thought she was such a special person."

"Emily *was* special, and she went away to school to find herself," Natalie corrected, unwilling to let Janet live under any more misconceptions. "Like the rest of us, she wanted to experience life and independence. She was a typical college girl."

"That's nice of you to say." Janet drew in a deep breath, obviously fighting for control. "She loved you, Natalie. She thought of you as the sister she never had. I don't know if Emily told you, but I was pregnant twice after she was born. I miscarried both times. The second time I was seriously ill. They told me then that I couldn't have any more children. Maybe that's why I wanted to hang on so tightly to the two I had." She paused. "I'm sorry we blamed you for everything. I needed to blame someone. I couldn't get through it any other way. I was hurting so badly I felt someone else should suffer, too. And you were there."

"And I was there," Natalie echoed.

"You acted so guilty. You couldn't tell us what had happened. It was easy to think you were responsible in some way."

"I understand why you thought I might have been involved, and I deeply regret my behavior that night."

"Deep down, I knew the kind of person you were. You'd been in our home. You'd shared holidays with us. I knew you. I am very sorry, Natalie. I hope someday you can forgive me, and Richard, too. He just followed my lead."

"There's nothing to forgive. I mean that. We all made mistakes. But we all loved Emily. That's what matters. It's time we put the past to rest."

"Cole said you're an amazing woman, and he wasn't talking about the girl you used to be, but the woman you are now." Janet gave her a long, considering look. "I don't know what has happened between the two of you, but I wanted to tell you that Richard and I won't stand in the way of you and Cole being together, if that's what you both want."

Natalie immediately shook her head. "That isn't what Cole wants."

"I'm not sure my son knows what he wants. Apparently, he's leaving for the Middle East tomorow. He's going to be our foreign correspondent."

Natalie's heart skipped a beat. "Cole is leaving?"

"Yes. Tomorrow. Unless you can stop him."

Suddenly Natalie wondered if that wasn't really why Janet had come to see her. "Is that why you came here? Because I can't stop him. I won't even try. And neither should you."

"He's the only child I have left," she said with a helpless shrug.

"Cole is not a child. He's a man. And he needs to live his life. He's wanted this for so long. I'm glad he's going."

"I thought you loved him."

"Enough to want him to be happy." And she did want him to be happy. He'd given up a lot of years for Emily and his parents. He deserved his freedom.

Janet wiped a tear off her cheek. "I know you're right, but it's hard to let him go. Don't you feel the same way?"

"More than you know," Natalie replied. "I'll walk you out."

Cole's first story appeared in the *San Francisco Tribune* on Friday, when he reported on a terrorist attack in Turkey. His next story was published on Tuesday and discussed the plight of refugees along the Afghan border. In the Sunday edition, he wrote about the formation of new governments switching the balance of power in the fragile Middle East. The following Thursday his article focused on the changing value of the dollar in Asia. The next weekend he reported on an earthquake in China and four days later he wrote about the proliferation of journalists and media in every corner of the world, including war zones. That article was accompanied by a photo of Cole in a tank.

Natalie stared at the photo for a long minute, her finger tracing Cole's face with a loving sigh. She had learned a lot about world events in the past three weeks. Cole was certainly getting around, living the life he'd always wanted. And she was doing the same. She'd accepted the job at St. Timothy's. Since Cole wasn't in San Francisco, there was no reason for her to leave. And she was enjoying her renewed friendships with Madison and Laura.

Setting down the newspaper, she leaned over and slipped on her running shoes. It was Sunday, and she had nothing to do until the evening when she was going to attend the first concert of the Atherton Community Orchestra featuring their newest flute player, Laura McKinney. Just thinking about Laura's new independent venture made her smile. They were all moving on with their lives in good, positive ways. She knew Drew and Laura still had some marital problems to deal with, but Laura had said their relationship was much more honest now, and they were working hard to keep it that way. Drew had decided to turn down the job in L.A. but was interviewing with a new firm in San Francisco.

Natalie got up, stretched for a few minutes, then jogged down the stairs and out onto the sidewalk. It was a beautiful, crisp, and clear November day. There were a few wispy white clouds in the blue sky, but the storms of winter were still weeks away. As she turned down the street, she stopped dead in her tracks, unable to believe her own eyes. Cole was jogging toward her, dressed in navy blue sweat pants and a gray T-shirt. Even in the baggy clothes, he looked thinner than when she'd last seen him, and as he drew closer, she saw the shadows of fatigue under his eyes.

"What are you doing here?" she asked in amazement. "I thought you were on the other side of the world."

"I got back last night. You're getting a late start this morning. I thought I'd probably missed you."

"I was reading the newspaper. There's a foreign correspondent whose stories fascinate me."

"You've liked them?" he asked with a proud smile.

"Very much. They've been terrific. You're doing a great job, Cole. I feel like I'm right there with you."

"But you're not," he said, his smile fading. "You're not there with me, and . . ."

She waited for him to finish his sentence. Damn the man. He could write articulate stories about world events, but when it came to telling her how he felt he seemed to go completely speechless. "And . . ." she prodded.

"I miss you." His eyes darkened as he gave her a long, intense look.

A shiver shot down her spine. "I've missed you, too, but I'm glad you're doing what you always wanted to do. It's important not to give up on your dreams."

"It's not my dream anymore, Natalie."

"Are you sure? It hasn't been that long. Just a few weeks."

"I was there only two days when I knew that being a foreign correspondent wasn't what I wanted anymore. I stuck it out a few weeks, because I wanted to make sure this time."

"Sure of what?"

"How I feel."

She drew in a sharp breath at the desire that flashed in his eyes. She was afraid of what he would say and even more afraid of what he wouldn't say. "How do you feel?"

"Come with me, and I'll show you."

"With you where?" she asked in confusion. "Can't you just tell me?"

"Nope." He turned and started jogging back the way he'd come, pausing halfway down the street. "Are you coming?"

"I'm coming." She had no idea what he was up to, but she knew she had to find out.

"Are you ready?" Dylan asked.

Madison stared at the man who'd appeared on her doorstep. Her first thought was that he had to be an illusion, because it had been three weeks and she hadn't seen or heard from him. Now he was standing here, talking to her as if she should know what he was talking about. And she didn't know. In fact, she couldn't even concentrate on what he was saying. She was too caught up in how tight his blue jeans were and how good he looked in his black leather jacket and how much she'd like to run her fingers across his broad chest.

"Maddie?"

"What? What are you doing here?"

"I came to take you for a ride."

"Why would I want to go for a ride with you?"

"Because you do," he said simply.

She frowned at that, hating the fact that he was right. The man had completely blown her off. She should do the exact same thing to him. But she was curious . . . "Where are we going?"

"I'll show you." He handed her a helmet.

"I'm mad at you. You haven't called. You refused to work my party—which turned out to be a tremendous success, by the way. You would have gotten a lot of business. And now you just show up and expect me to hop on your bike and go God knows where. Do you think I'm completely crazy?"

"Yes. And so am I. Are you coming or not?"

She thought for ten long seconds. Dylan turned to go, calling her bluff. "I'm coming," she said. "This better be worth it."

Chapter 21

Cole hadn't said a word on their run, but it quickly became apparent to Natalie as they passed by the Marina Greens, the Palace of Fine Arts, and the St. Francis Yacht Club that they were heading for their usual spot at the base of the Golden Gate Bridge. When they reached the end of the path, they stopped and stretched, taking a few deep breaths of air as they looked at the bridge towering above them and the sparkling blue water flowing beneath it.

"I missed this, too," Cole said with a wave of his hand. "This is my city, Natalie."

She smiled. "I know."

"I didn't appreciate it until I left."

"Sometimes it helps to get perspective."

"Exactly. You know, I was sitting in a tank in the desert, and I started wondering what had happened to the parking meter increases in Union Square. I didn't even want to cover them in the newspaper and suddenly they wouldn't leave my head. I realized that what's important is relative to where you are, what you want, and what you need. I know now that I want to continue the tradition of the Parish family newspaper. I want it to be even bigger and better than it was before. I want the people of San Francisco to have all the information that they deserve to have, whether it's local news or world news."

"I'm sure your parents will be happy to hear that."

"I told them last night, and they *were* happy." He paused, smiling at her. "My mother is doing better than I thought after everything that's happened. She even started cleaning up Emily's room."

"That's a big step."

"She said she spoke to you before I left. She wanted you to persuade me to stay, but you refused to even try."

"She's right," Natalie admitted. "I wanted you to go. I wanted you to have a chance at your dream."

"Did you want me to come back?"

She could tell by the look in his eyes that he was asking her more than if she wanted him to return to San Francisco. How could she tell him that she wanted him back? She'd put her heart on the line before, and he'd stomped on it. "You always have more questions than answers, Cole."

"That's the reporter in me." He looked around, as if he were searching for something, then checked his watch.

"What's going on?" she asked suspiciously. "You said you were going to show me something. What is it?"

"You'll see."

"Will I see it anytime soon?"

"I certainly hope so."

"Am I going to like it?"

"I certainly hope so," he repeated with a grin.

* * *

Madison swung her leg off Dylan's motorcycle as he parked on the same rugged bluff he'd brought her to before. There were no city lights this time, but the San Francisco panorama of tall buildings, rolling hills, and colorful sailboats dotting the bay was as pretty as any postcard.

Dylan pulled a white plastic trash bag out of a compartment and walked toward the edge of the bluff. Madison followed him, wondering what the heck was going on.

"What's in the bag?" she asked.

He hesitated for a long moment. "Memories."

"Okay, this is starting to freak me out," she said, not sure what was in that bag, but she wouldn't put anything past Dylan.

"You're the one who told me to let go, aren't you? Didn't you stand here on this very bluff a few weeks ago and tell me it was time to move on?"

"Yes," she said guardedly. "But I'm surprised you'd listen to me. You never did before."

"You never made sense before."

"I don't think that's true. But—what exactly have you done?"

"I cleaned out the closet."

She nodded, trying not to show how shocked she was. "Go on."

"I burned everything, the photos, the stories, everything."

"Why?"

"Emily is gone."

"It was still a little drastic. You could have kept some mementos. You didn't have to burn everything. You're really an all or nothing kind of guy, aren't you?"

"That's the only way I know how to be. I don't need those things to remember Emily by. You might not believe this, but the truth is I hadn't looked in that closet in a long time—not until the book came out and you showed up. Then it all came back."

She was relieved to hear that he hadn't been visiting the Emily shrine every night for the past ten years.

"When I saw the closet through your eyes, I realized it looked kind of sick."

"Yeah," she said emphatically. "It did."

"So it's gone now." He held up the bag. "It's all in here."

"You could have just thrown that in the garbage. Why do you still have it? Because unless you have a good reason, I have to warn you that your behavior has not left the *sick* category yet."

"I like ceremonies—rites of passage. They're important. They help us move on." He paused. "It occurred to me that you didn't get to come to Emily's funeral so you never had a chance to say good-bye in any formal way."

"So this is like a funeral?"

His gaze met hers. "Yeah. What do you think?"

She thought for a long moment. "It really wasn't my choice to leave before Emily's funeral. My parents made me go. They didn't want me involved in any scandal. I did miss saying good-bye. Sometimes it was hard to believe she was really gone. It felt like a dream. I couldn't go back to the house and see that it wasn't a dream. It was weird, surreal. Maybe a funeral would have helped."

"Well, it's your choice now. Do you want to help me toss these ashes into the wind?"

"We'll probably get arrested for littering."

"Since when did you worry about breaking the law?"

"Since—never. All right. I'll do it."

Together, they walked to the edge of the bluff and turned the bag upside down. The breeze caught the charred ashes of the photos and papers and blew them down the hillside. "Good-bye," she whispered. "Rest in peace, Em."

They stared out at the view for several long minutes. Madison felt as if a heavy burden had slipped off her shoulders. The past was truly gone.

"No second thoughts?" she asked Dylan a moment later.

He shook his head. "Not one."

"What are you going to do now?"

"Get on with my life." He shot her a quick glance, then gazed back at the view. "I've been thinking about something else. Maybe you and I should go out sometime."

"You mean on a date?"

"If you want to call it that."

"Wow, that's the kind of invitation a girl finds hard to resist."

"Is that a yes?"

"I should have my head examined," she muttered. "Because I'm actually considering saying yes. But first I'd like to know why you want to go out with me. You don't even like me."

"You're growing on me," he said gruffly, as he turned back to look at her. "And you are hot, in case you hadn't noticed."

"Oh, I've noticed. I just didn't think you had."

"I'd have to be blind not to."

"So that's all you want—my hot body?"

"No, I want your annoying, outspoken mouth, and your really sexy lips, and—"

"Shut up and kiss me," Madison said.

Dylan caught her face with his hands and planted one long, thorough, passionate kiss on her mouth.

"Wow," she said. "Do it again."

"I intend to."

Before he could, a low-flying plane buzzed overhead, drawing their attention to the sky. "What's that guy doing?" Madison asked.

"Looks like some kind of a message," Dylan replied, as the letters began to take shape.

Madison gasped. "Does that say Natalie?"

"Watch," Cole said, pointing to the sky.

Natalie obediently followed his order, although in truth she was more interested in him than the plane flying over the bridge. That is, until the letters began to form . . .

"Natalie?" she read in amazement. "You did this?"

"Keep reading."

Her heart jumped in her chest as she read the message in the sky. *NATALIE, I LOVE YOU.*

"You're crazy," she said, as he took her into his arms. "Why did you do that?"

"Because I've never been able to say the words. I know you think it was just you I couldn't say them to but it was everyone."

"You haven't said them yet," she reminded him.

"I just wrote them across the sky."

"That's not the same thing."

"You're a tough woman. All right, listen up."

He leaned in, gazing straight into her eyes as he said, "I love you, Natalie. I've loved you since the first day we met and every day since then—even when I thought I hated you."

"That doesn't make any sense, Cole."

"Love doesn't make sense. We're connected, Natalie. We've tried to fight it. But the feelings are stronger now than they ever were. As Emily would have said, we're soul mates."

Emily *would* have said that, Natalie agreed.

"Now, don't you have something to say to me?" Cole asked.

Could she do it? Could she risk her heart again? But this time he'd said the words first.

"I love you, too, Cole, but I'm scared. You have so much power over me. It's terrifying."

"You have power over me, too, Natalie."

"That's just it. I don't want to be the person who makes you feel trapped. I saw how the love from your parents made you feel suffocated and smothered. I don't want to do the same thing."

"You're not trapping me. This is what I want. You're what I want."

"You have to be sure, Cole, absolutely sure. Because while you always had too much love, I never had enough. And I want it all now. I didn't think I did. I thought I could live without friends and family, with just my job to make me happy, but the last few weeks have shown me how wrong I was. So if you want to come back into my life, it has to be all the way, or not at all."

"I'm here, Natalie, and I'm not leaving."

"What about your family? I don't want to come between you. I couldn't live with that."

"They gave me their blessing last night."

"You told them?"

"I wanted them to know that I love you and that I wasn't willing to waste another day without you in my life. We've lost too much time as it is."

She touched his face in a tender gesture. "We weren't ready before, Cole, neither one of us."

"But we are now. Emily brought us back together."

"I think that was the professor," she said with a smile.

"No, it was Em. Somewhere up there, she's watching. I know it."

Natalie looked up at the sky where the lettering from Cole's declaration of love had turned into wisps of white. "I hope she approves."

"I know she does. She'd want us both to be happy, and frankly, I don't think we can be happy without each other." He dug into his pocket and pulled out a black velvet box.

Natalie's heart stopped. "You're not going to . . ." She couldn't even say the word much less believe what was happening. This was Cole, the man of her dreams, the man she'd loved forever, but she'd never really believed she could have him—until this moment.

"Propose?" he asked, as he opened the box and showed her a beautiful diamond ring. "That's exactly what I'm going to do. Will you marry me, Natalie? Will you make me the happiest man in the world?"

She stared at his face, at his strong, handsome face, and knew without a doubt that this was the one and only man she'd ever wanted to spend her life with. "This can't be happening."

"It's definitely happening. We just need an answer to make it really good."

"Yes," she said. "Yes."

Cole slipped the ring on her finger, then pulled her up against his chest and kissed her as if he never intended to stop. The sound of applause brought their kiss to an abrupt end, as they realized they'd become the center of attention.

"She finally said yes," Cole told the crowd.

"You finally asked," she retorted, and despite their audience, she couldn't stop herself from kissing him again. "I can't wait to spend the rest of my life with you, Cole."

"Let's start right now."

"Or maybe somewhere more private," she suggested.

He laughed. "I can't make any promises, unless you run really fast."

"I will," she promised, as they took off down the path.

They were breathless by the time they reached her apartment. Cole slammed the door shut and reached for her. "Someday we're going to do this slow."

"But not this day," she said, pulling his shirt up and over his head. "Because I've waited long enough to have you, and I don't intend to wait another second."

"I like the way you think." He stopped her as she reached for his pants. "One second."

"What now?" she asked with a groan.

"I want you to know, really know, that this is it for me. I'm not going to leave you, ever. You're my family now, Natalie. You and me, and whatever kids we decide to have. The past is gone. The future is ours."

Her eyes blurred with tears. "Boy, when you finally start talking, you do it right."

"Love me?"

"Forever," she said, sealing her promise with a long, passionate kiss.

Epilogue

Natalie and Cole snuck into the back of the Atherton Community Center just as the orchestra began to warm up at seven o'clock Sunday evening. Madison, who was sitting with Dylan, waved them over to two empty seats beside her.

"I didn't think you were going to make it, Natalie," Madison said with an arch to her eyebrow. "And look who you've brought. Isn't that interesting? I guess the skywriting worked."

"You saw that?" Natalie asked.

"I think all of San Francisco saw it. So are you happy?"

"Ecstatic. We're engaged," Natalie said, flashing her ring.

"Nice," Madison said to Natalie, then nodded approval at Cole. "You finally did the right thing."

"I finally did," Cole agreed. He sent Madison and Dylan a curious look. "I'm surprised to see you two together. What have I missed?"

"I was going to ask the same question," Natalie said. Not that she really needed an answer. She could see the happiness in Madison's eyes.

"We're on our first date," Madison said with a

grin. "He finally asked. It took him only ten years. The men in San Francisco are a little slow."

"But we're worth the wait," Dylan drawled.

"Damn right," Cole added, giving Natalie a delicious smile. "I can prove it later."

"I might take you up on that," she murmured. As she sat back in her chair, she felt ridiculously happy. She had a feeling Dylan and Madison were going to find their way to a good place—which only left Laura. Laura looked gorgeous in the front row of the orchestra, wearing a pretty black dress and holding her flute. She saw Natalie and waved, her smile proud and confident. Then she tipped her head toward the front row where Drew and two adorable little girls, who looked exactly like their mother, were sitting. Drew turned and nodded in their direction. His expression was cool but not filled with the animosity it had once held. He'd changed, too. They all had.

The lights dimmed, and the conductor motioned for the orchestra to begin.

The music was beautiful, emotional, haunting, and when the flutes played, Natalie thought she could hear the angels singing. Maybe they were.

Emily had always liked to sing. And all she had ever wanted was for her friends to be happy.

Natalie slipped her hand into Cole's and knew that the Fabulous Four had never been more fabulous.

Twenty-five Years Earlier . . .

She took her bow with the other dancers, tears pressing against her lids, but she couldn't let those tears slip down her cheeks. No one could know that this night was different from any other. Too many people were watching her.

As the curtain came down one last time, she ran off the stage into the arms of her husband, her lover, the man with whom she would take the greatest risk of her life.

He met the question in her eyes with a reassuring smile.

She wanted to ask if it was all arranged, if the plan was in motion, but she knew it would be unwise to speak. She would end this evening as she had ended all those before it. She went into her dressing room and changed out of her costume. When she was dressed, she said good night to some of the other dancers as she walked toward the exit, careful to keep her voice casual, as if she had not a care in the world. When she and her husband got to their automobile, they remained silent, knowing that the car might be bugged.

It was a short drive to their home. She would miss her house, the garden in the back, the bedroom where she'd made love to her husband, and the nursery, where she'd rocked—

No. She couldn't think of that. It was too painful. She had to concentrate on the future, when they could finally be free. Her house, her life, everything that she possessed came with strings that were tightening around her neck like a noose, suffocating her with each passing day. It wasn't herself she feared for the most, but her family, her husband, who even now was being forced to do unconscionable things. They could no longer live a life of secrets.

Her husband took her hand as they walked up to the front door. He slipped his key into the lock and the door swung open. She heard a small click, and horror registered in her mind. She saw the shocked recognition in her husband's eyes, but it was too late. They were about to die, and they both knew it. Someone had betrayed them.

She prayed for the safety of those she had left behind as an explosion of fire lit up the night, consuming all their dreams with one powerful roar.

Present Day

Julia DeMarco felt a shiver run down her spine as she stood high on a bluff overlooking the Golden Gate Bridge. With the Pacific Ocean on one side of the bridge and the San Francisco Bay on the other, the view was breathtaking. She felt like she was on the verge of something exciting and wonderful. Just the way every bride should feel. But as she took a deep breath of the fresh, somewhat salty air, her eyes began to water. She told herself the tears had more to do with the afternoon wind than the sadness she'd been wrestling with since her mother had passed away four months ago. This was supposed to be a happy day, a day for looking ahead, not behind. She just wished she felt confident instead of . . . uncertain.

A pair of arms came around her waist, and she leaned back against the solid chest of her fiancé, Michael Graffino. It seemed like she'd done nothing but lean on Michael the past year. Most men wouldn't have stuck around, but he had. Now it was time to give him what he wanted, a wedding date. It was the right thing to do. She didn't know why she was hesitating, except that so many things were changing in her life. Since Michael had proposed to her a year ago, her mother had died, her stepfather had put the family home up for sale, and her sister had moved in with her. A part of her just wanted to stop, take a few breaths, and think for a while instead of rushing headlong into another life-changing event. But Michael was pushing for a date, and she was grateful to him for sticking by her, so how could she say no? And why would she want to?

Michael was a good man. Everyone thought so. Her mother had adored him. Julia could still remember the night she'd told her mom about the engagement. Sarah DeMarco hadn't been out of bed in days, and she hadn't smiled for many weeks, but that night she'd beamed from ear to ear. She had been so happy to know that her oldest daughter was going to settle down with the son of one of her best friends. That knowledge had made her last days so much easier.

"We should go, Julia. It's time to meet the wedding coordinator."

She turned to face him, thinking again what a nice-looking man he was. He had light brown hair and eyes and a warm, ready smile. The olive skin of his Italian heritage and the fact that he spent most of his days out on the water, running a charter boat service off Fisherman's Wharf, kept his skin a dark, sunburned red.

"What's wrong?" he asked, a curious glint in his eye. "You're staring at me."

"Was I? I'm sorry."

"Don't be." He paused, then said, "It's been a while since you've really looked at me."

"I don't think that's true. I look at you all the time. So do half the women in San Francisco," she added lightly.

"Yeah, right," he muttered. "Let's go."

Julia cast one last look at the view, then followed Michael to the museum. The Legion of Honor had been built as a replica of the Palais de la Legion d'Honneur in Paris. In the front courtyard, known as the Court of Honor, was one of Rodin's most famous sculptures, *The Thinker*. Julia would have liked to stop and ponder the statue as well as the rest of her life, but Michael was a man on a mission, and he urged her toward the front doors.

As they entered the museum, her step faltered. In a few moments, they would sit down with Monica Harvey, the museum's event coordinator, and

Julia would have to pick her wedding date. Why was she so nervous? It wasn't as if she were a young girl—she was twenty-eight years old. It was time to get married, have a family, and Michael wanted lots of kids. He was one of six children, and two of his sisters already had three of their own, so he was eager to catch up.

"Liz was right. This place is cool," Michael said.

Julia nodded in agreement. Her younger sister, Liz, had been the one to suggest the museum. It was a pricey location, but Julia had inherited some money from her mother that would pay for most of the wedding.

"The offices are downstairs," Michael added. "Let's go."

Julia drew in a deep breath as the moment of truth came rushing toward her. "I need to stop in the restroom. Why don't you go ahead? I'll be right there."

When Michael left, Julia walked over to get a drink of water from a nearby fountain. She was sweating and her heart was practically jumping out of her chest. What on earth was the matter with her? She'd never felt so panicky in her life.

It was all the changes, she told herself again. Her emotions were too close to the surface. But she could do this. They were only picking a date—it wasn't like she was going to say "I do" this afternoon. That would be months from now, when she was ready, really ready.

Feeling better, she headed downstairs, passing several intriguing exhibits along the way. Maybe they could stop and take a peek on the way out.

"Mrs. Harvey is finishing up another appointment," Michael told her as she joined him. "She'll be about ten minutes. I need to make a call. Can you hold down the fort?"

"Sure," she agreed as he left the office. She smiled at a young woman sitting behind a desk, then took a seat on the couch. Barely a minute had passed before she jumped to her feet, too restless to sit and wait. "I think I'll take a quick look at the exhibit down the hall."

"I'll tell Mrs. Harvey where you are."

"Thanks." Julia walked down the hall and entered the exhibit, looking for some kind of distraction, anything that would take her mind off the wedding. It didn't take long to find it. The exhibit featured historic photographs from the past century. Within seconds she was caught up in a journey through time. The photographs were captivating. She couldn't look away. And she didn't want to look away—especially when she came to the picture of the little girl.

Captioned "The Coldest War of All—Orphans in the Soviet Union," the color photograph showed a girl of no more than three or four years old, standing behind the gate of a children's home. The photo had been taken by someone named Charles Manning, the same man who appeared to have taken most of these shots.

Taking a step closer, Julia studied the picture in detail. She wasn't as interested in the Moscow scene as she was in the girl. The child's heavy coat was black, her stockings a thick pale gray. She wore a black woolen cap on her head, highlighting the gold of her beautiful blond hair. Her eyes were a big, startling blue, and the expression in those eyes begged for someone—whoever was taking the picture perhaps—to let her out, to set her free, to help her.

Julia couldn't look away. The girl's features, the oval shape of her face, the tiny freckle at the corner of her eyebrow, the slope of her small, upturned nose seemed familiar. She noticed how the child's pudgy fingers clung to the bars of the gate. It was odd, but she could almost feel that cold steel beneath her own fingers. Her breath quickened. She'd seen this picture before, but where? A vague memory danced just out of reach.

Her gaze moved to the silver chain hanging around the girl's neck and the small charm dangling from it. It looked like a swan, a white swan, just like the one her mother had given to her when she was a little girl. Her heart thudded in her chest, and the panicky feeling she'd experienced earlier returned.

"Julia?"

She started at the sound of Michael's voice. She'd almost forgotten about him.

"Mrs. Harvey is waiting for us," he said. "What are you doing in here?"

"Looking at the photos. Doesn't the girl in the picture look familiar?"

Michael gave the photo a quick glance. "I don't know. Maybe. Does it matter?"

She could see it didn't matter to him. Michael wasn't much for history or anything academic. He was a working-class, hometown guy who liked living in the city where he'd been born. He wasn't interested in travel. He'd rather save his money for buying a house. "I have a necklace just like the one the little girl is wearing," she added. "Isn't that odd?"

"Why would it be odd? It doesn't look all that unusual to me."

Of course it didn't. There were probably a million girls who had that same necklace.

"Julia," Michael said again, more impatiently this time. "Are you stalling? Is something wrong? Do you not want to get married here?"

She looked into his earnest brown eyes and wondered how she could possibly tell him it wasn't the "here" part that was worrying her, it was the "married" part. He didn't deserve to get caught up in her jitters. He was right. She was stalling, looking for something else to think about. She needed to focus on the present and on the future—her future with Michael.

"I'm sorry," she said. "I'm ready to talk to the coordinator now." Hopefully, she'd be ready for the rest of it before the actual wedding.

As she turned to follow Michael out of the room, she couldn't help taking one last look at the picture. The child's eyes called out to her—eyes that looked so much like her own. But that little girl in the photograph didn't have anything to do with her, did she?

USA TODAY BESTSELLING AUTHOR
BARBARA FREETHY

"Freethy writes with bright assurance."
—Luanne Rice

"A fresh and exciting voice in women's fiction."
—Susan Elizabeth Phillips

Summer Secrets

0-451-41082-3

Eight years ago, the three McKenna sisters—Kate,
Ashley, and Caroline—had their fifteen minutes of
fame. Driven by their ambitious father, they won an
around-the-world sailing race as teenagers. But during
a fierce storm something happened out on the turbulent
sea, something that will haunt their past—and
could ruin their future.

Golden Lies

0-451-21126-X

This is the story of three remarkable families—the
fifty-year-old promise that once bound them together,
the fiery betrayal that tore them apart, and the ancient
bronze dragon that could finally destroy them.

Available wherever books are sold or at
www.penguin.com